The Midnight Tablet

CLARE C. MARSHALL

THE VIOLET FOX SERIES BOOK FOUR

Books by Clare C. Marshall:

The Violet Fox Series:
The Violet Fox
The Silver Spear
The Emerald Cloth
The Midnight Tablet

The Sparkstone Saga:
Stars In Her Eyes
Dreams In Her Head
Hunger In Her Bones
Darkness In Her Reach
Voices In Her Song

Other Titles:
Within
Gear and Sea

Marlenia

THE WEST

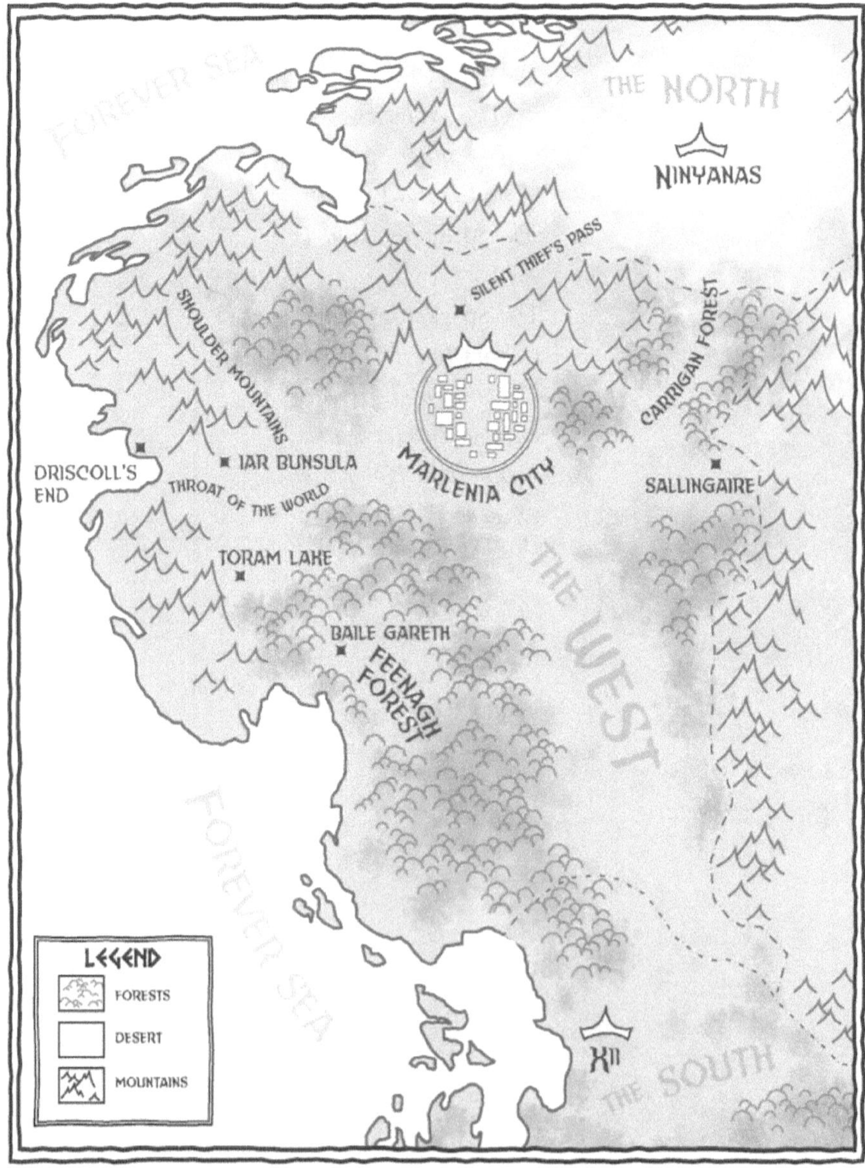

One

Run. That was what my people had done. Or what I hoped they'd done. For as my friends and I entered the capital in our rickety horse-driven wagon, we found Marlenia City ransacked and deserted.

Before I'd left, the market had been bustling. Our wagon should have been crawling at a snail's pace. What remained of the colourful white and blue canopies, patched from my occasional careless runs across them, flapped in the wind with no one to witness them. The vendors should have been bartering and watching for thieves—yet the streets were empty. The air was uncannily still.

Judging from the wreckage of the stalls and the abandonment of the permanent shops behind them, whatever had torn through the streets of our capital had been brutal. Wooden planks lay with exposed upright, threatening nails. Ripped fabric and signs blew carelessly through the narrow, dark alleyways threading the city, and toppled woven baskets held only seeds and chewed-through, browned fruit. No bodies—a small blessing. So far, the only living people we'd seen had been the guards patrolling the top of the wall surrounding the city. Once they recognized me and, more importantly, Keegan, it had taken them fifteen minutes to open the gate. Seemingly my people, surface-born and Freetor alike, had squirreled themselves away from some unseen threat. Assuming they were alive at all.

Or, this was a trap.

"We should have taken the tunnels," Laoise Mullen, my dearest friend, muttered over the crunch of the wagon wheels. She crouched behind me, tucking her short, dirty blonde hair behind her ears, hand ready to grab the knife from her boot at the first sign of trouble.

She was right. The Undercity tunnels may have been safer, but I was tired of sneaking around. I had been down this street thousands of times. Wearing a cloak and mask, I'd kicked up dust beneath my feet as I ran from the castle guards after stealing from the merchants and the rich, inspiring my people to continue believing that one day, they could be free. I had ridden in a carriage to retrieve a magical artefact while pretending to be Lady Dominique Castillo of the North. I had stood beside the love of my life, trying to embody good rulership, while I dreamt of adventure at the end of the world. I had snuck into the castle as a servant with Laoise when she'd disguised herself as Lady Linnaea Gareth. Now, I stood cautiously on top of a wobbly wagon with my closest, dearest friends—no longer hiding, no longer pretending.

We had accomplished our mission: save Prince Keegan Tramore from the clutches of our enemies and wake him from the magical sleep that continued to plague our world. Keegan Tramore—my love, my prince, and rightful heir to all of Marlenia, stood next to me as we rode through the eerily silent streets of Marlenia City. Even as the wagon rolled uncomfortably over the debris, I was relieved we had made it back home to the capital. I had to celebrate the victories, no matter how small, because the future seemed more uncertain than ever.

Ivor Ferguson, former Advisor to the Holy One, had escaped my grasp and had embarked on a maniacal quest to find the origin of all magic: the Midnight Tablet. He was already more powerful than any Elder or apprentice I had seen. If I failed to find it before him, he would use the Midnight Tablet for his own selfish ends instead of helping others in need.

He'd made his feelings clear when he'd used magic against me in the cathedral in Eastern-occupied Sallingaire. Oh, he'd wanted me to follow him on his quest. Deep inside, he knew we both relished the chase, because saving others from people like him was what I had always done. I was Kiera Driscoll, the Violet Fox, famed folk hero and protector of the Freetor people, secretly married to Prince Keegan Tramore, heir to the entirety of Marlenia, and wielder of the Silver Spear—the famed magical artefact that had started the war and the prejudice between the two distinct classes of my people over two hundred years ago.

He also told me I could control and wield Freetor magic, just as he could. Once I was more receptive to his worldview, he would mentor me.

Because that was what fathers were supposed to do.

The worst part was—I feared he was right.

I had channeled magic from the artefacts before, yet to call upon my people's greatest treasure was a singular gift only given to the now-dead Elders and their scattered, skittery apprentices. Magic had been tightly controlled in Freetor society. I'd always thought it was because the surface-born Marlenians equally feared and coveted it; now I knew it was because the desire for the dangerous lived within us all.

The four artefacts of Dashiell, the man-god, had an especially treacherous influence. They had been separated by four monks in order to keep any one person from becoming too powerful. The Orb of Dashiell could call lightning from the sky, even if you were underground. The Silver Spear had been cursed by the founder of the Freetors, Alastar the Hero, and would put any surface-born Marlenian into a frozen sleep that spread like a disease if another touched the befallen. The Emerald Cloth had soaked in the tears of the man-god, and had the power to heal—so long as you were willing to sacrifice your identity. The fourth and final artefact was the Midnight Tablet, which was still lost, for now.

We possessed two of the four: the Silver Spear and the Emerald Cloth. My father had the Orb of Dashiell. It took one artefact to correctly identify another: they glowed an intense, bright blue—the colour of Freetor magic—when other artefacts were near. As far as we knew, this glow could only be spotted by those with Freetor blood.

Because of the inherent danger the Silver Spear, we'd wrapped it in rags before our departure from Sallingaire. As we'd discovered with Keegan, the cure for the magical sleep-plague came with a terrible price. Pieced together and made whole again, the patchwork Emerald Cloth had managed to wake Keegan from his icy slumber. It had also taken all of his memories. Everything that made Keegan *himself* was gone. Including his knowledge of me and our marriage.

If I'd had my way, I may not have returned to Marlenia City. My father already had a head start chasing down the Midnight Tablet. He could've been anywhere in the world at this point. His mastery of magic had warped his mind, given him unnatural abilities, and had only deepened his thirst for power. If he reached the Midnight Tablet first, he would control the only known method to restore Keegan's memories.

It had taken us nearly five days to ride back to the capital. Far longer than I would've liked. A sudden array of frozen soldiers had appeared in and around the cathedral in Sallingaire—all thanks to my father and his careless use of the Spear. We applied the Cloth to those we found, yet the more we woke, the more questions they had: *Who am I? What place is this? Who are you?* As we couldn't give them a clear answer without alerting them to the fact they were our enemies, we had to make our escape from Sallingaire quickly. We slipped out of the Eastern-controlled city much the way we had come in, though the guards at the gate were far more concerned with putting out the fire Dominique Castillo had started in the cathedral and the confused soldiers to worry about a merchant wagon rolling past the checkpoint with inadequate identification.

Once on the road to the capital, we had to avoid the Eastern patrols and other curious merchants making their way between the two warring provinces. The open plains and lack of supplies made our stealthy journey difficult. More than once we had to ride the wagon off the road and hide in the tall grass to avoid being spotted. The Eastern patrols seemed uninterested in investigating our seemingly abandoned ride; they galloped by on their mounts, to and from the capital, often veering from the main road towards the mountains. They had a camp somewhere close, but we had neither the time nor the resources to infiltrate them. I hoped that Bidelia, with the Roamers' help, had some answers.

To pass the time and quell the gnawing hunger in our stomachs, Laoise, Monju, and I filled Keegan in on his previous life. We respectfully stuck to what we knew of Keegan's childhood, his relationship with his father, the now-deceased Holy One, our journey to retrieve the Silver Spear, and an overview of the world and the rulers who thirsted for his father's vacant throne. He absorbed the information gratefully and with appropriate scepticism. After all, who were we, a bunch of ruffians, to tell another equally scruffy young man that he was, in fact, the ruler of our world?

Now in Marlenia City, the mountain castle loomed ahead, its restoration incomplete, thanks to me and the rebellion carried out over a week and a half ago. I wondered if Bidelia and the Roamers had gathered everyone there for safety as they fought off the last of the oppressive Frostfire regime? Although in desperate need of repair, the castle's position on mountain high and its abundance of secret tunnels made it the obvious place to hide our vulnerable population.

"Is that it?" Keegan asked, pointing up at the imposing structure.

"Yeah," I replied. "It didn't always look like that. Parts of it were destroyed in a fire. The Frostfires were rebuilding it with slave labour. Which we stopped."

At least, I hoped we'd stopped it. When my father had delivered the Silver Spear in the cathedral in Sallingaire, he'd said Bidelia and the Roamers were successful at retaking the castle. What if he had been lying? What if everyone was dead?

This was looking more and more like a trap.

Monju Farin perched on the front of the wagon bed, deftly directing our one horse around the debris. We'd stolen fresh peasant clothes in Sallingaire, though his green trousers were already frayed at the ends and ripped at the knee.

"We should stop," I said to Monju.

He glanced over his shoulder with a grim expression. Monju, a travelling bard-assassin and once an agent of Dominique Castillo's was now one of my trusted friends, and Laoise's beau. "The Lady expected a more pleasant welcome?"

As he was originally from the South, Monju's speech rarely included informal pronouns like *you* or *I*, except in intimate or extremely informal conversation. Ever since I had saved his life, he considered himself in my service. If this madness ever ended and Keegan and I reclaimed the throne, we'd make him an official member of the guard.

In truth, I *had* expected a pleasant welcome. We'd returned Prince Keegan Tramore, the rightful monarch, to the capital. We'd driven out the Eastern invaders. Sure, we still had my father to deal with, and the East and the North were poised to strike again—but for now, we'd won. Or so I'd thought.

"Are we waiting for someone?" Keegan asked. "Or is it faster to go on foot from here?"

"Not once we reach the mountain," I said. He had a point, though. If there was a trap, I wasn't going to wait for it to trigger. The guards already knew we were here. Might as well get it over with.

Nodding to Monju, I called out, "Hello? Anyone?"

The wagon wheels turned slowly once more as we continued our punishing pace down the street, and as we passed by the dark alleyways, I could make out shapes peering out of the narrow strips of darkness. Laoise saw them too; she remained crouched and ready to defend us. I reached down and retrieved the Silver Spear. Only to be used as a last resort, I promised myself. If anything, the Freetors would see the blue glow of magic, and know that it was me, their hero, returning to save them and restore their lives in the sun.

"It's the Violet Fox!" someone said loudly from a nearby alley.

That proclamation unleashed my people into the streets. As our identities were traded among the populace, I heard hope course through the city once more. Men, women, and children poured out of the alleyways and surrounded the wagon, grasping for and then clinging to the rough, splintery sides of the bed. All of them with the same requests on their lips: *Help us.*

Until I'd become betrothed to Keegan, it was illegal for Freetors to *be* on the surface at all. The most notable physical difference between surface-born Marlenians and Freetors was the sun-starved skin. However, that wasn't the best differentiator, as Freetors snuck onto the surface all the time to steal or fight or both at the behest of the Elders—who were dead now. As most Freetors were living hand to mouth, despite our efforts to steal, collect, and distribute food fairly among the caves, the second, more obvious tell was our starved appearance. If you looked starved or even *seemed* impoverished, you were often branded a Freetor, even if you weren't. You were weighted with the consequences of the title: imprisonment. Slavery. Death.

Before Keegan, when I was just the Violet Fox, I had prided myself in seeing the differences. Now, everyone was equally poor, dirty, and desperate. These could have been people born in the caves or surface-born merchants who had lost everything. Between the fire at the castle, the Frostfires' invasion and terrible reign, and whatever had happened while we were gone, it was common folk who had suffered the most. More than ever, my people needed me.

They called to Keegan, too. He spun in place, taking them all in with surprise and wonder. Their questions tore through him like a blunt knife.

"Was the prince really imprisoned by the East?"

"How did the Violet Fox rescue her betrothed?"

"We aren't paying for your wedding with our taxes!"

"I wasn't sure I believed you when you said I was a prince," Keegan said to me, far louder than a whisper.

My Keegan had always been poised and confident in front of a crowd. He never faltered. He had grown up learning from a long line of rulers and advisors. All of that teaching had evaporated when he woke.

But no one knew that, except us.

As their questions and concerns grew louder and more insistent, Keegan leaned towards me, equally panicked. "Whose wedding are they talking about?"

I slid my free arm through his. The movement surprised him, and he stiffened. "Sorry," I said. "We have to show them a united front."

He frowned and gently, though not unkindly, removed himself from my grasp. "If you say so, but..."

I cursed internally. Of course he didn't want to touch me. He didn't *know.* This wasn't how I wanted to have this conversation. I'd hoped when we arrived at the castle and cleaned ourselves up, we could speak privately.

But I didn't have to tell him. My fears had drawn my face.

"We're...together?" he asked, incredulous.

There was no good answer. I lowered my voice and spoke into his shoulder. "We were married, in secret."

He began to protest.

"Not here," I warned him lowly. "They can't know that you *don't* know."

I hadn't found the courage to tell him about our romantic

history, and most importantly, that we had married. Yes, that marriage was just between the two of us, at the God Tears by the end of the world, with no witnesses. It was within Freetor tradition. This had proved inconvenient later. No one believed I, the Violet Fox, born from dirt, a liar and a thief, had married the heir of the world, despite our public betrothal. Princes changed their minds with the wind and the political climate, after all. That was why Sylvia Frostfire and her family had easily managed to capture and hold Marlenia City for so long, with Keegan as the convenient, sleeping hostage, none-the-wiser.

The wagon began to shake as our people shouted louder and louder for us to give them an explanation or excuse for *not* giving them what they wanted. One tried to grab on to Keegan's leg and pull him into the street. He recoiled, panicked, as others tried to climb aboard. I protected him with a decisive arm across his chest and warded the sides of the wagon with a wave of the Spear. My people, Freetor or not, watched the sharp, somewhat jagged tip of the legendary artefact warily.

"It has been a long journey," I told them carefully. "I know you have concerns, but so do we."

Monju couldn't move the wagon now, even if he wanted to. We were caged on all sides. The horse was getting antsy. Laoise stood, no weapon yet, trying to calm the crowd. Yet they didn't know her. They didn't want her words. They wanted Keegan's—and mine.

My mind leapt ahead with horror as I realized the terrible mistake I'd made. Laoise had been right. We should have taken the tunnels.

For if my people, surface and Undercity dwellers alike, realized that the knowledge of Keegan's past had been robbed...they'd revolt. The Freetors loved me, or, most of them did, at least. They'd support a Freetor High Queen. Yet, without Keegan, my presence on the throne would be seen as a hostile usurping of a kingdom held by a royal line. Dominique Castillo and the Frostfire family would use that against me and swoop into Marlenia City to pick up the pieces.

Keegan turned awkwardly, trying to avoid the reaching hands, and I caught his arm before he nearly stumbled over the side. His gaze wildly suggested I do *something*.

"What happened here?" I shouted, pointing at the debris with the Spear.

The people slammed me with their replies, each loud and demanding:

"The Frostfires took everything!"

"The Advisor is holed up in the castle, hoarding silver and food!"

"Armed mercenaries."

"Killers in the dark!"

I nearly asked them, "What Advisor?" for that had been my father's role, yet if I appeared incompetent, my lack of control over and knowledge of the situation would trump all else. Killers in the dark and armed mercenaries weren't surprising given the state of the city. All that mattered was the people were scared, and they were looking to Keegan and I for support and validation.

"We don't have any food," I told them.

Laoise began echoing my sentiment to the needy faces surrounding us. As this truth settled in, they relaxed. It was hard to lie about resources when the wagon hid nothing on its splintery, rotting bed. Most of the crowd detached and we could move again. As we cleared the market debris, Monju increased his speed. Some filtered off into the alleyways, but many stayed on the street, following us at a hurried pace as we made our way to the Grand Square.

The Grand Square was a wide stretch of stone-inlayed public space for gatherings and announcements. It was also the place where Marlenians would crowd around to watch the public executions of Freetors. I had to watch my brother Rordan burn, and

I did nothing, for I was on a mission. Now, I wondered if I had spoken up then and told Keegan the truth about my identity, what could have been different.

Built into the mountainside beside the Grand Square was the Cathedral of Dashiell, where Keegan had nearly married Sylvia Frostfire—where I had revealed my name to everyone. The holy site looked far worse than I had ever seen it. It, and the buildings surrounding the Grand Square, had been turned to rubble and partially destroyed. The work of explosives, perhaps? Only the Extremists employed that dangerous methodology, as they had little regard for the lives of the surface-born. The devastation extended out over several streets in a circular blast radius. Only a large explosive—or the work of magic—could have triggered it.

Ahead, a group of armed Roamers in a loose formation blocked the intersection between the Grand Square and the street. As we drew closer, Monju slowed the wagon. Behind us, our curious followers hesitated and kept a generous distance. They appeared to be no stranger to the armed Roamers.

I frowned. I counted less than fifteen people guarding the Grand Square. Someone must have run to tell them we were coming. We could spare no messenger from Sallingaire, so our arrival to Marlenia City, and by extension the castle, would be a surprise to Bidelia and the Roamers. Their armour, if it could be called that, was tattered and torn. Some had tried to patch it with official banners from the castle, or scraps of patchwork leather. None of their weapons were uniform either. While most had raised swords at our approach, a few wielded makeshift spiked clubs, and one carried a rusted halberd. I saw no Freetor apprentices among them, which was equally worrying.

By nature, the Roamers were a friendly lot, provided you left them alone and respected their traditions. I had trusted them to work with us to overthrow the Frostfires, and as far as I knew, they had. I expected them to be patrolling the streets, cleaning up the debris, and generally helping my people find their feet in the midst of this cruel war. Not blockading a public gathering place. Even more curious: the citizens, as frenzied as they seemed, outnumbered the Roamers. Sure, the Roamers were armed, but it wouldn't be difficult for an angry mob to overwhelm them if that was their desire.

I let out a slow breath as the unofficial leader of the Roamers, Pascal Antony, clapped one of his men on the shoulder and shuffled his way to the front of the formation. I raised the Silver Spear, proving that I had returned. He gave me a toothy grin.

"Do I know this man? I feel as if…" Keegan trailed off, and reached around to the scars on his back.

My heart sank once more. The body remembered, even if the mind did not. When Keegan, Monju, and I had passed through the Roamer camp at Toram Lake, the Roamers were attacked and a woman with a striking resemblance to me was murdered. Out in the wild, and with no real evidence as to whether it was the shadow killers who hunted us or an unrelated tragic act of violence, the Roamers dispensed their own justice upon those they believed to be guilty. As we had brought chaos to their camp, they judged we had to suffer punishment. Keegan insisted on enduring it himself. Twenty lashes on the back, in front of a maddened crowd, delivered by none other than Pascal Antony.

I searched for a hint of this memory within Keegan's gaze, but found only confusion there, and I felt relieved. I didn't want him to remember that. Why would his mind grasp futilely at a terrible event, instead of remembering me—his beloved?

"The Violet Fox returns," Antony said, standing awkwardly on his good leg. He nodded at me, and then stiffly to Keegan. "Your Grace."

Keegan pressed his lips in a firm line and returned the nod. Good. The fewer people that knew about Keegan's memory loss, the better.

"Monju," Antony said jovially, turning to the Southern

bard-assassin. "You're not dead yet, I see."

"Not yet, old friend," Monju replied good-naturedly. "Many adventures have been had."

"As always, I look forward to hearing them! Mostly the tale of how Kiera Driscoll bested Leszek Frostfire," Antony said with a sly grin. "Perhaps later, you'll regale me."

"Perhaps." News had spread fast. No doubt Dominique and Boris had fanned those flames. The Violet Fox killed the High King of the East with a magical Freetor weapon—juicy news that could be spun for good or ill on either side. I hadn't meant to *kill* the man. I'd stabbed him with the Spear while defending my father. I'd believed Leszek would freeze like the rest. He did freeze...and then fell upon the cathedral floor and burst into millions of shards. Dead. According to succession laws, that meant Boris Frostfire, Leszek's oldest son, was now High King, and Dominique, his new wife, was High Queen of the East.

Which was bad news for me and everyone else.

Antony still did not move from his spot, nor did those under his command. He glanced at the crowd gathered behind us. "Any trouble from the locals?"

This was not a good sign. I balled my hands into fists as my bitten fingernails dug into my palms. "N-no," I stammered. The city I had grown up in? In ruins. My people were terrified. Stunned. Leaderless. Governed by rebels. I saw it in their faces. They believed Keegan had abandoned them. They thought *I* had abandoned them. But we were back now. We'd lost the Orb of Dashiell to my father, but we had the Emerald Cloth, and that was what mattered. We'd be able to cure those affected by the curse of the Silver Spear. I'd explain everything to them, and after we'd dealt with my father and the Midnight Tablet, and the threat from Dominique and the East, then, then we could focus on reuniting our people, sharing the land, and distributing resources fairly to rebuild a stronger Western province.

First things first—returning my husband to his childhood home.

"Are you blocking our path?" I asked Antony.

His lips curled into a smile. My relationship with the Roamer was on uneasy ground. He had come to my aid, when the Frostfires and the Castillos had controlled the castle. Antony and one hundred of his people had agreed to help those loyal to me and the Tramores overthrow the oppressive regime—for a price. I had promised them land, silver, and whatever loot they found belonging to the Frostfires. Since I'd left in the chaos of the rebellion, I didn't know if they'd been paid at all. A former mercenary, Antony cared about such agreements, especially when his people's lives were on the line. It was only a matter of time before he would demand what he was owed, and I didn't know if I had the land or the silver to repay him for his generous service.

"Had we known you were coming, we'd have given you a more formal welcome," he replied. "We sent a runner to fetch a more royally appropriate carriage for your journey up the mountain. But no. That's not why we're here. We're still finishing up our end of the bargain, Violet Fox. Shadows and Frostfire soldiers lurk within the city. Not but a few hours ago there were reports of three hooded figures brandishing bloodied knives and swords. We're holding our position here in the open, waiting for two of our own kin to return with news. Hopefully of the invaders' deaths."

I glanced behind me. Some of Antony's men had corralled the growing crowd. They were out of earshot, or so I hoped. I counted at least twenty men, women, and children craning their necks, trying to get a better look at the Violet Fox and her prince.

I had left them. And for what? To chase magical artefacts. To rescue Keegan. That at least had been worth it. But my people had suffered—all because of this rebellion and my relationship with Keegan.

It was all my fault.

Laoise subtly nudged my shoulder. She could see my pain, even when others couldn't. "We will fix this," she whispered to me.

Keegan also seemed concerned about his citizens, though he said nothing, staring up again at the mountain castle he once called home.

A distant crunch of gravel became a covered carriage barrelling down the narrow, winding path—our ride away from the peasants and their pleas for help.

Antony seemed to be waiting for my instruction, or at least, an acknowledgement of his effort. "Thank you," I said.

Keegan jumped down from the wagon then, landing with a *clomp* on his worn boots. As he steadied himself, not an easy feat after our rocky ride, I leapt down and landed beside him. This only served to startle him: he spun like an alley cat, facing me with round eyes and raised, defensive hands.

"It's just me," I said. "Sorry." I was apologizing to him more today than I had in our entire relationship.

He blew out his fear in a prolonged sigh, but he did not relax. I couldn't blame him. Whatever curiosity Antony had provoked in him had passed. He was in strange territory with strange people once more.

Antony seemed to note our unusual exchange as the carriage came around and stopped behind his men's defensive line. He signalled, and two of his people parted for us as the carriage door opened.

Out stepped Bidelia Mullen, Laoise's mother, and long-time family friend. Stray hair blew from her otherwise neat bun. She sported a long blue coat, and although tattered at the hem it looked cleaner than anything I'd seen her in. I wouldn't have been surprised if she'd raided my father's wardrobe and then modified the coat for her use. He'd been partial to outlandish articles of clothing that announced his status from stone-throws away. To see her in it, as dignified as it was on her, marked the significant change that had occurred in the week and a half I had been absent from the capital. She had spent years on the surface, undercover as a leading servant known as Mother Margaret until her Freetor status was unearthed by the Frostfires. A royal purple scarf—fashioned from an old banner, trimmed and sewn in such a way that one would only notice its origins upon closer inspection—hid a ghastly rope scar around her neck, courtesy of Sylvia Frostfire.

Bidelia and Antony had a nearly wordless, grim exchange consisting of grunts and points, after which Bidelia's frown deepened. This didn't matter to Laoise. She raced for her mother and leapt into her arms abruptly. Momentarily startled, Bidelia realized her daughter was alive and present, and her steely mask of duty dropped long enough for her to enjoy their reunion.

"That's Laoise's mother," I explained to Keegan, who seemed touched by Bidelia and Laoise's display of affection amidst the armed guard and curious onlookers.

When Bidelia withdrew from her daughter's clawing embrace, I stepped forward to receive her. My older brother Rordan had raised me after our parents had left us, but Bidelia had looked out for me, too. She was my second mother. If something were to happen to her, I didn't know what I'd do.

Our gaze met, yet instead of embracing me as her own, she clasped Laoise's shoulder and whispered in her ear. Laoise nodded eagerly and headed for the open carriage.

"Bidelia," I said to her, desperate for acknowledgement and assurance.

"Kiera. Your Grace. You're all right." She blew out a sigh of relief, yet offered none of the affection she'd shown Laoise. Her mask of concern returned as she glanced back at the castle. "We should head up now. The days have been long and eventful. Antony, have you—?"

"No word from me and mine yet, but they'll come through."

Bidelia acknowledged his report with a curt nod and then headed for Monju, who was whispering promises of a long rest to the wagon horse. She whisked past me without further interaction. The days have been long and eventful. Something must have happened for the people to be *this* on-edge, and for her to treat me with such coldness just when I needed her the most.

Antony drew his barricade closer to the carriage. As soon as they realized we were leaving, the crowd, which had tripled in size, erupted into a torrent of rage and desperation. "Your Grace! Why are you leaving us?" and "We have been under attack for days!" were among the cries, and they bolted me in place. I reached for Keegan. The old Keegan would have grasped my hand and stood by me. He would have recognized that he needed to reassure his people.

But he wasn't there anymore. Not yet.

Just as Monju jumped up into the wagon, presumably to drive it up to the stables outside the mountain castle, I joined him, raising my hands and the Spear to catch the attention of the angry city folk I had promised to serve.

"Listen to me!" I shouted. "I, the Violet Fox, have returned with Keegan Tramore, the last of his line. I know things haven't been easy. I know you've lost and suffered. But I promise you that I'm going to fix this. If anyone in your family has been affected by the icy, sleeping plague, you probably know by now not to touch them. That, I can offer a solution for. Together, there isn't anything we can't face, especially if we have your patience and—"

And just like that, Bidelia was reaching up into the wagon, tugging at my trousers. "End this. Immediately." The worry on her face was palpable.

I swallowed the rest of my words, for now. "I'll return with a formal address as soon as I can. I promise."

"Stop making promises," Bidelia hissed. She nearly grabbed me out of frustration as I jumped down from the wagon. My cheeks reddened. The crowd yelled their replies, yet they seemed unconcerned that Bidelia had interrupted my impromptu speech. She lowered her voice and spoke calmly, yet firmly into my ear. "What did you tell them while you were parading down the streets with Keegan?"

That stung. I could see it in her intense, dark gaze: she was comparing me to Sylvia Frostfire, who had done the same thing when they'd taken the city over a month prior.

"I just…told them we were back. Showed them that Keegan was alive. Tried to give them some hope."

Antony's men struggled to keep the crowd at bay. Bidelia threw them all a suspicious glance. The people called out to her by name, her *real name.* "Advisor Mullen! Where is the food you promised? Are you hiding in your castle with those filthy—?"

The Roamers quieted the dissenter and my breath felt short.

"Say nothing else until we have spoken," Bidelia said decisively. "There is much you don't know."

"Apparently, Advisor Mullen," I replied.

She cast me a contemptuous look. I raised my hand to the maddened crowd and shouted, "I'll—*we'll*—be back down soon. I promise."

As I made my way toward the carriage, their outrage followed me, and I heard Antony rally his men to contain those desperate enough to approach us. Although it was against every instinct I possessed, I grabbed Laoise's hand as she helped me into the plush carriage. Keegan was already settled in. Bidelia climbed in and shut the doors on the cries of my people, which slammed into me:

"Your promises are nothing. Where were you?"

"We are starving, we are poor, the Frostfires took everything, and now you rebels hoard treasure and food up in your castle—"

"Why won't you help us?"

"Is that true?" Keegan asked. He sat to my right, hands folded on his lap to disguise his missing finger, and seemingly taking pains to not brush against my shoulder.

The carriage jolted into action, turning in the square. Seeing my forlorn look, Bidelia pulled the curtains over the window.

"Is it true that we live like kings in your broken castle?" Bidelia countered. "Of course not. We are barely keeping the city together, much less the province. Or the other provinces. Nice to see you have woken from your slumber, Your Grace."

Keegan quirked an eyebrow and remained steadfast. "Thank you, my lady."

Bidelia didn't miss a beat. "Have I earned a title in your absence, Your Grace?"

Laoise and I exchanged glances. We were fools if we thought we were going to hide the truth from Bidelia.

"Maybe we should start from the beginning," I said.

For as long as many could remember, Marlenia had been ruled by the Holy One, a High King of royal blood. For several generations, the throne of the Holy One sat in the West. Ever since Captain Killan Tramore took the sceptre from the Cathedral of Dashiell during the Marlenian-Freetor war and declared himself the first in a new line of royals, his descendants ruled not only the West, but the entire world.

Now, Eamon Tramore, the former Holy One, was dead. Keegan Tramore, his sole heir, stepped through the large wooden doorway of the castle into his ancestral home, and knew nothing of the blood, pain, and sacrifice that had reared and shaped him.

I stepped into the entrance hall in his wake. The first time I was here, I'd marvelled at the tapestries depicting and glorifying Marlenian conquest. A red carpet had punctuated the path down the cavernous corridor. Guards had scrutinized my appearance, my voice, my presence. None of that existed now. Returning to the castle was like stepping into a decrepit tomb. I had lived in the caves for most of my life, and never had I felt like I was crawling into bed with death. I lingered with my friends by the entrance, while Bidelia traversed the dark alone and with unyielding purpose.

"Close that. And follow me to the council room. Be quick about it," she instructed, her voice bouncing off the empty walls.

Monju pulled the heavy door closed, shutting out the sunlight. The lanterns lining the entrance flickered dimly. The lack of light was comforting, as Freetors had naturally good night vision from living in the caves for generations, and also an eerie reminder of the sacrifices I had made to stand within this castle. The silence and the chill of the stone triggered my deepest instincts: *It's not safe here. Run.*

"Does any of this look familiar to you?" I asked.

"No," he said shortly, gazing up at the ruined, blackened stone.

Laoise and I exchanged worried glances. How were we supposed to convince an entire city—and the world—that Keegan Tramore was the same as he always was? Could he still rule if he didn't remember his past?

As Bidelia continued down the yawning hallway, I pulled Monju and Laoise aside. I looked to Keegan and gestured for him to stop as well; to my surprise, he did, though he seemed concerned about letting Bidelia get too far ahead of us.

"We have to make a plan to go after the Tablet," I said in a low voice. Everything I said echoed throughout the corridor. "Keegan's memories, the plague—nothing will truly go back to how it was without it."

Keegan raised a suspicious eyebrow but made no comment.

"Could have skipped the capital and headed for Xii, to follow the Advisor," Monju said.

"Then my mother and the world wouldn't have known for sure that Kiera and Keegan were alive," Laoise countered.

"What are you chattering on about down there?" Bidelia called from further down the corridor. "There's no time to waste."

Resigned, we continued as a group after Bidelia, though we were certainly not in a hurry.

"How far is it to Xii?" I asked Monju.

"A week in a decent carriage," he replied. "Two in bad weather."

"Could we go by boat?"

"Unlikely, unless the Lady owns or has access to a trusty rig. Monju is not a particularly skilled rower or sailor. Waves make navigating difficult, especially at this time of year."

As we were nearing the cold seasons, the winds were notoriously harsh, and while deep waters were not to be trusted at any time of year, it was especially so now. "Fine. We'll take a carriage."

"And then what?" Laoise said. "Xii is huge, isn't it? How do we know what to look for? What if Conal lied to misdirect us?"

It was possible, though I felt he hadn't, not then. "He wanted me to join him. He knows so much more than we do, but I feel if I can track him, if we rely on the artefacts we have..."

"We'll figure it out," Laoise promised.

"The Lady need not fear," Monju added.

Keegan remained silent. We'd told him about the importance of the artefacts. Why we had to restore his memories and defeat my father before magic consumed him. I wondered if he cared about any of this.

Bidelia led us through a series of corridors and more than ever, I wanted to flee this elaborate prison of stone and grief. The many soldiers that had patrolled the castle and its grounds had been pared down to the remaining steadfast members of the castle guard and Antony's Roamers, who didn't look like they belonged next to the fully armoured castle guard. Many of the nobles and courtiers loyal to either the West or the East had fled the city, seeking favour elsewhere. We passed a few servants—possibly of Freetor origin, though I recognized some faces from my previous stay in the castle—and they stared, wide-eyed at Keegan's sudden return. I'd thought that the heart of traditional Marlenian politics and governance had begun to beat once more, but I had brought Keegan to a place that was not only unfamiliar to him, but also to me.

The council room was a closet compared to the rest of the castle. A thick velvet curtain separated it from the massive throne room and I noted the shadow of a guard posted on the other side. A blackened, sooty table and seven rickety chairs were the sole pieces of furniture. Bidelia stood at the head of the table impatiently as the four of us entered cautiously and closed the door.

"Pascal should be here soon," she told us. "Well?"

Laoise promptly took a seat. Monju settled in beside her. I stared at the empty chairs, remembering how Keegan had run these sessions, managed the complaints of men with power, and decided the future of thousands from this very room. Gripping the Spear tightly, I sat to Bidelia's left. If I were Keegan, I'd have a thousand questions. Yet his lips remained sealed as he sat next to me and regarded Bidelia, waiting for the meeting to begin.

Antony burst into the room without ceremony and slammed the door behind him. Remembering he was in the presence of a royal, he hastily bowed to Keegan and dipped his head to me, purely out of respect. I smiled grimly and Keegan acknowledged him with a curt nod. The Roamer pulled out a chair to Bidelia's right, acknowledging her and Monju with a sly grin.

"Did you settle the matter?" Bidelia asked him.

"As much as something can be settled right now," Antony replied grimly. "They followed a running, cloaked person for several blocks, but they disappeared. Must have escaped into the Undercity, or they duped us with multiple cloaked agents. Probably the former. Then, on their way back to the Square—" Antony slammed a fist into his empty palm. "Didn't even see it coming. My man woke up, and had this note pinned to his chest."

Antony reached into a pouch on his belt and retrieved a folded, dark red piece of parchment, and threw it on the table. Immediately, the scent of flowers invaded my nose. I leapt from my chair. No, it wasn't magic. The note was not glowing. Laoise shared my puzzled reaction, and even Bidelia looked perplexed.

Cautiously, I unfolded the dry parchment, and the scent intensified. It had been dipped in rose water and dried—recently.

Return Keegan to the rightful Frostfire Queen within five days. If this demand is not met, we will take him by force.

The overly floral note made sense. This was Sylvia Frostfire's doing. Was she trapped inside the city? I shook away the thought. She'd been with us in the cathedral in Sallingaire and then escaped. While she could have ridden by carriage faster than us back to Marlenia City, I couldn't see why she'd want to, especially given the grimy, depressing state of the capital. No, Sylvia wouldn't get her hands dirty. She'd get one of her trusted men to deliver this. I tossed the note back onto the table for the rest of my companions to read as I paced the room, stifling a laugh.

"What force would Sylvia possibly have?" I said, scoffing. She'd cooperated with us for a time—even if it was just to see Keegan again. The last time we'd seen Sylvia, she'd been distressed that Keegan didn't recognize her and alienated by the goals of her family. Her father had betrothed Sylvia against her will to Marin, Dominique Castillo's younger brother, but the boy was barely ten-years-old. Sylvia's eldest brother, Boris, was married to Dominique. She was trapped in an alliance and a future marriage she despised. Unless she was cooperating with Boris and Dominique once more for her own gain, I couldn't see how she could wrangle up enough loyalty on her own to carry out a legitimate threat.

"Could this be a trick, by Dominique?" Laoise asked.

"I doubt it," I replied. "Sylvia has always been desperate for Keegan's attention and affection. This is just her latest ploy. I don't see how she could take him or anything by force when all of her family's power rests with her older brother. I wouldn't be surprised if she arrives at the door and begs to see him."

Keegan took the note gingerly in his good hand and studied it closely. "I'm not sure I care to see the woman who cut off my finger."

"Wise decision," Bidelia said. "Right then. We'll keep an eye out for a young blonde woman in an inappropriately large dress wandering the streets. If she's here at all."

"Shouldn't we capture her?" Antony asked. "Allow her to join her brother in the dungeon?"

Now *that* interested me. "We have Leon Frostfire captive?"

"He's dead weight and holds no new information," Bidelia said, as if the topic bored her. "But we can't let him fall into enemy hands either. Who knows what he's overheard in the depths, from other prisoners or guards? Let him rot."

How many times had those very words condemned my fellow Freetors? But if there was anyone who deserved to be thrown down there, it was Leon Frostfire, the middle child of the reigning Frostfire family. A fanatic soldier who had travelled the West routing out Freetors turned drunk on power—and wine—in the Western castle, awaiting a marriage that would never happen and forgiveness he would never receive for his terrible crimes.

"As for Sylvia Frostfire," Bidelia said, touching her throat with a particular disgust, "she may be useful as a bargaining chit with the East, if she's in the city at all. If you see her, drag her up here and keep her under guard. More likely, we'll find and capture one of her agents. I don't like the idea of them discovering unprotected entrances to or wandering around in the Undercity."

It seemed unlikely that her influence stretched that far. The Frostfires had enslaved or killed many Freetors during their occupation of the city. The Freetors would steer clear of surface-born who had mercilessly and publicly executed them.

"We should search the tunnels, just in case," Antony suggested.

"I agree," Bidelia said, "but take an apprentice and one of the loyal Fighters with you. We don't want to cause more of a scene." The Fighters were the Freetor militia, as much as we had one. Some of our people had joined the effort to retake the castle in Keegan's name, solely because I was his betrothed.

Bidelia surveyed the rest of us grimly, took a deep breath, and released it in a huff. "I'm glad you're all safe. Truly. We are in the middle of a crisis that I can't fix alone. I'm not sure if all of us in this room, working together, have the resources and the expertise to fix it. But we have to try. Here is the situation.

"I am now known as Advisor Mullen, and Pascal Antony here is now acting captain of the guard. Or, general, I believe?" Antony nodded with a slight smile. It was difficult to say how official that title was, given his colourful career. He'd served the West, and then freelanced for the East during their trade war with the North. Bidelia continued, "We have no steward. I have been doing those duties as well. I realize that wasn't your particular instruction, Kiera, but as you left in such a rush, there was no time to assign commands. We took the castle and we've held it in Keegan's name."

Keegan's face paled. "Uh—thank you."

"Despite our titles, the people don't recognize me as their leader, nor do I want them to," Bidelia continued. "That is why you both must make a strong showing. Together. We are managing a particularly sensitive crisis: our food shortage. We no longer have trade with the other cities in the province, and we are rapidly eating through our stores. Marlenia City is starving to death.

"Our second problem is the lingering Eastern and Northern forces, which skulk in our alleyways, but more worryingly, in the mountains and forests surrounding the city. They have a camp that we're monitoring, but their activity is strangely stagnant. We don't know what their strategy is, as they seem to be regrouping, yet troops are leaving the area as well. It is a mystery."

"Don't forget our third problem—the icy, magical plague. For which we now have a working cure. Sort of," I said.

Laoise obliged me and removed the Emerald Cloth from her trouser pocket. She'd wrapped it in another piece of dirty, torn fabric to avoid contact with her skin. It glowed fiercely in the presence of the Silver Spear. Antony and Bidelia was visibly taken aback by its presence.

"The Emerald Cloth will unfreeze the plague victims, but it will also remove their memories," I explained. "The Midnight Tablet will reverse its effects. Which is why we need to find it before my father does, so we can restore the affected families." And Keegan, though I was unsure whether to say that out loud. Unless Bidelia had informed him before we entered the room, Antony was the only person who didn't know about Keegan's state of mind. Best we kept it that way. I was grateful to the Roamer for his service, but as he was for hire, his loyalty could be bought by anyone with more coin. Right now, every other ruler or lord fit that bill. "He's gone to Xii. If my father retrieves the Midnight Tablet first, the reported origin of magic, he will be far too powerful to defeat. If we can find it first and use it for its intended purpose—we will destroy it, along with the other artefacts. You were right about him, Bidelia. I should have listened to you."

"The Tablet has that power?" Bidelia asked.

"Well...yes. I think so."

"You think so?"

"The Advisor...Conal...he said as much."

"You wish to chase him down to Xii, based on something he said. Something that may or may not be true, as no one has held the Tablet for centuries."

"I know how it sounds. But it's our only chance to save everyone."

"It's not a practical response, Kiera. Every time your father has suggested that a magical artefact can solve your problem, you fight him until he gives you no choice but to retrieve it. Don't give in to him now."

"I'm not giving in. The whole reason we went to Sallingaire was to retrieve the Cloth. Now we have it. Now we can stop the plague!" I slammed the Spear into the floor. I heard a crack, and fearing I'd damaged the staff, I quickly inspected it. The floor was damaged, but the magical artefact was untouched.

I didn't know if Antony knew that Advisor Ferguson and Conal Driscoll were one and the same, but he certainly did now, and regarded me with renewed interest. Sylvia, and no doubt

Dominique, knew by now as well—there was no point in keeping his identity a secret any longer.

Bidelia pressed her fingertips lightly against the table. "The plague is difficult to contain—but as the Cloth doesn't cure it without adverse effects, then it may not be worth administering yet. And an expedition to Xii requires resources we can't afford right now. I know you don't agree," she said quickly, stopping my protest on the tip of my tongue, "but just listen to what I have to say, and then you can judge what is dire and what is doable."

I let out a slow breath. Problems with magic were always dire. "Fine. Sorry. Tell me everything that's happened since we left."

In my passionate outburst, I had forgotten Keegan next to me. He had done well so far, listening for clues about his former identity, chiming in with the appropriate words and phrases to allay suspicion. Now, the calm mask fell away to reveal the consternation there. He was afraid of the Spear. Perhaps he was even a little terrified of me. I leaned the Spear against the table. I didn't want him to be afraid. I wanted him to remember me, as we were.

Bidelia cleared her throat. "After Leszek Frostfire's impromptu wedding ceremony for Boris and Dominique, we were successful at driving out the Frostfires and the Castillos from the castle. Yet we didn't—and still don't—have the manpower to keep them from skulking into and around the city. At first, we put resources towards driving them out, but once the East ambushed our imports and blockaded the major routes into the capital, well, anyone in the city, regardless of whose side their on, is likely feeling hungry. The Frostfires didn't leave us much, given the amount of people they had to support during their occupation, and with the immanent cold weather leaving no time to grow another season of crops, we have a serious crisis."

"No blockade on the road coming from Sallingaire. Only soldiers on horseback, racing for the mountains," Monju said.

Antony nodded. "With Sallingaire in Eastern hands now, they

probably don't see the need for an extensive show of force, just patrols. Sent someone up to the mountains three days ago to investigate rumours of Eastern forces making camp outside of the capital, by the former Silent Thief Pass. They never returned and that's confirmation enough. They're trying to starve us out. We've got how many days of food left?"

"Seven, if we tighten the ration once more," Bidelia said.

"Seven," Antony echoed, in sad distaste. "A day or two more, if we ask the kind-hearted to forgo their rations for the soldiers and other fighters among us. After that, we're in trouble. While we have a suitably defensive position, they're hoping for us to venture out so they can pick us off one by one. Or, if we're smart, we'd mount a surprise offensive on their mountain camp and take out a few before perishing ourselves. Either way, the situation is dire, Your Highness."

"What about a stealthy raid? Surely they must have supplies?" I asked.

Bidelia smiled grimly. "Some enterprising Freetors tried that several days ago and supposedly made off with some food, weapons, and armor. But who do you believe they shared it with?"

Right. Other Freetors.

"We have collected everything edible from the castle stores and used treasury funds to purchase all available merchant goods, including food. We paid surrounding towns for their stores too—as much as they were willing to give up to the capital, which was very little. Even the glow moss in the Undercity has been picked clean," Bidelia continued. "We asked people to donate their raw crops and cooking ingredients to a communal collection so that we would cook here in the castle, and ration meals to them each day at sundown."

"And the citizens did that?" Monju asked, surprised.

"Some. It wasn't mandatory. Many protested, no doubt egged on by the lurking Frostfire supporters and soldiers." It was a

Freetor custom to pool any resources stolen or grown, so they could be redistributed fairly. Or, as fairly as one could in an unfair world.

No wonder my people were furious and desperate. Those in power held the key to their survival. "Is that what caused the destruction in the market? Protests?" I asked.

Antony sighed. "Protests and fighting in the streets, yes. Some of it was the Frostfires and the Northern shadows, going at it with the city guard, and some of my men, too. People tried to maintain their daily lives, but once the food shortage became public knowledge and Bidelia had the bright idea of hoarding it up here—"

"I did what I could," she interrupted.

"Not judging, just stating a fact. To the people out there, we are gorging on the hoarded food, even if we're not," Antony said, shrugging. "The market thievery became looting after we went around, buying what we could shake loose. It wasn't just the Freetors stealing—it was everyone. So we started doling out rations at sundown every day in the Grand Square, as Bidelia said. Tensions were high at first, but once we delivered on our promise consistently for several days, and people calmed down some, we thought we were in the clear.

"But all it takes is for one greedy family to cut in line and take more than their share. Then, the rioting started. Surprising that a city that's known poverty and hunger in and below its streets loses compassion once imminent starvation becomes the norm.

"One of the apprentices became involved. Chased the family down the street, away from the Square. Tried to retrieve the stolen rations and remedy the situation using a show of force. Well. It got out of control. Rarely have I seen destruction like that. The blast of his explosion...immense. Poor lad didn't even know what had happened. He passed out in the middle of it. That was unfortunate. Lot of casualties. A few deaths. We nearly lost our grip on the city that day."

The extreme destruction of the buildings surrounding the Grand Square suddenly made sense. The remaining apprentices' magic was unstable and untrustworthy, which made them all the more dangerous. If the East attacked and the apprentices defended us, casualties would be high on both sides.

"We moved the operation from the Grand Square into the Cathedral of Dashiell, hoping the old faith would lend some credence to our charitable act," Antony continued. "But it was the introduction of extreme force on our part—getting the apprentices involved—that really frightened people. They've all heard stories of Freetor magic. Having a few apprentices on hand put the old fear back in them. We haven't had troubles since."

Besides myself and my father, the apprentices were the only ones left who could wield magic. Before they were killed, the Elders would choose young Freetors who showed promise and just like that, they became Elder apprentices. Their training was mysterious and secretive, though it involved several years of silence. The three powerful apprentices I'd gone up against in the past told strange tales of perilous trials and grave mistreatment from the Elders. Magic had warped them all.

"I want to know who the apprentices are and how many are living in the castle," I said. I wasn't sure yet what I'd do with them. Some had scattered deep into the Undercity. But if others were cooperating with Bidelia and the Roamers, they'd likely have an opinion about my goal to destroy the artefacts. Perhaps they could teach me to control my own supposed magic to prevent me from accidently exploding any buildings.

"There are sixteen with us. Half are mute, or have chosen to be silent, we can't be sure." Bidelia seemed annoyed by this. "The other half, well, if they have magic, they haven't shown it, besides the one in the Square. The apprentices are a useful, ornamental force. For now. I will give you a full list of their names later."

The apprentices were probably afraid of themselves. At least they weren't power hungry. If they were scared, perhaps they could be trusted. "I'll do what I can to assure them. We'll need their help to start curing the plague."

Bidelia's discomfort increased as Antony leaned back, frustrated, in the creaky chair.

"What now?" I asked.

"I don't think that should be our priority," Bidelia said firmly.

My eyes widened. "You are letting our people suffer and spread—"

"Listen to me, Kiera," Bidelia said sharply. "Right now, the plague is working in our favour. You're not hungry while you're asleep. Some brave souls voluntarily submitted to the frozen plague and that suits everyone, as it's one less mouth to worry about. From last count, there are over five hundred confirmed cases. Possibly more hiding in the Undercity or in abandoned buildings."

That was far too many, more than I'd ever suspected. It also didn't count those in Sallingaire, those we couldn't get to—who knew how many my father had cursed? "We can help those people."

"We may not want to," Bidelia said, "until we have our food situation under control."

Her words were so sterile. *Food situation.* "The Freetors have always had a food situation. I'm sure we can manage this. The real issue is the plague, and how we are going to contain its spread if people keep submitting to it, and how are we going to explain the price of the cure?"

"Kiera, the Freetor way of life was always a burden on the food stores. The crown paid mounds of silver to farmers to produce extra crops and imported additional food from the South and the East. Conal Driscoll and his hunt for the Tablet is a concern, I hear you. But starvation will kill us all if we do not take action."

My people were voluntarily succumbing to a magical plague, just to avoid a potentially worse fate. A noble sacrifice just so others could have more until the city was ready to sustain them all again. Yet it was a terrible plan if we *didn't* have the Midnight Tablet to restore people's minds alongside their bodies.

"I see your point," I said finally. "But I can't have an entire city of people waking up and not knowing who they are. I understand we need to feed our people somehow. But we also need to protect them and our future."

Laoise shifted in her chair and cleared her throat, squaring me with a permissive look. "Monju and I could go to Xii."

"Just...the two of you?" I gripped the Spear and my fingers tingled with its power. *They don't want to include me. They want to go on their own adventure.* These thoughts slithered between and around my other fears, loud and envious. I dug my fingernails into my palm and they quieted.

Laoise leaned forward on the table. "Like you said. Your father will expect you to go, Kiera. He wants to lead you away from what's really important. He won't expect to see us."

"The Lady's father won't see anything," Monju added. "Will keep appropriate disguises. He has the disadvantage. Xii is Monju's territory."

"Let us do this. For you," Laoise finished.

My gaze slid to Bidelia. She didn't like this proposal either, yet she didn't oppose it. I was arrested by her silence as I remembered that Bidelia wasn't really in charge here. Keegan and I were. Antony aside, she had the most experience taking charge in difficult or desperate situations. I could leave the castle and gallivant with my friends to Xii and, regardless of whatever title she gave herself, she wouldn't be able to stop me. But if any of us left without her blessing, it would destroy a lifetime of trust.

My grip on the Spear loosened as I closed my eyes and made a decision I regretted. "All right. I acquiesce. Go to Xii and find the Tablet before my father can. I'll stay here with Keegan and manage our food crisis."

Bidelia looked relieved. "Good. That's settled."

Laoise and Monju joined hands and smiled. I looked away. I knew they were doing this for me, yet I couldn't help what I felt. Finding a new source of food for thousands of people was nowhere near as exciting as searching the world for an artefact. All I'd done was serve and inspire and lead my people against the injustices of the world, yet the task before me felt impossibly large. Finding an artefact? I'd done that. Even if it caused its own problems, it felt doable. And with the Spear in my hands, it felt *right*.

Keegan stared at my friends curiously. Did he want to go with them? I wished he'd tell me what he wanted. His silence and non-committal answers added to my cloying pit of uncertainty.

Feeling my gaze, his cheeks reddened, and he finally spoke. "Other than rationing the food, how are we supposed to grow or provide enough for everyone we have left when our enemies could invade at any moment? Do we have any allies we trust who might trade with us—someone who can get through the blockades?"

"If the North and the East haven't stopped potential aid, the fear of catching the magical plague has," Antony said sadly. "The surrounding bailes and their lords are scared. They've barely enough to feed their own. What little we coaxed from them was barely worth the effort. Others have ignored the capital's call for help. Especially Baile Gareth. They've hidden away in their forest. The man I sent there didn't return either. Not even the other Roamer bands want to risk coming near here. I don't blame them. Although...do we have any word on...?" He exchanged an uncomfortable glance with Bidelia. "Because they were supposed to be here two days ago. Did the blockade prevent them from passing?"

"Our eyes can't get confirmation on that," Bidelia said gravely. Seeing our confusion, she sighed reluctantly. "All right. Your Grace, we do have one potential ally. One that has some pull, who could grant us the supplies and military force we need to repel the North and the East. Though it is not guaranteed.

"Once we retook the castle, we knew we wouldn't be able to

hold it for long, especially in your absence. We took some…precautions. I wrote to High King Kamal Zaman of the South to request aid and that a delegation come to discuss the possibility of an alliance. One where he would provide military assistance against the blockade and imminent retaliation." Her gaze slid to Keegan, and explained for his benefit, "Just because you are the Holy One of all Marlenia, doesn't mean the other provinces automatically bend to your will. Charm and tact are required."

I frowned. "Keegan met with a group of Southern nobles just before the fire. They weren't interested in providing us support in any kind of war against the East."

"I was vaguely aware of that. I wrote them anyway, almost a fortnight ago. Not two days later did I receive a reply."

"How is that possible? Was there a royal seal?" I asked. Monju had said it would take a week, possibly two, just to get to Xii from here. A runner would know how to shave time off the journey, but a two-day response time?

"Nearby Roamers reported Southern colours travelling near our border carrying the Zaman family banner," Antony said. "A few went and boldly shared a campfire, I'm told. They were young nobles around your age out on an adventure with their servants. One noble identified himself as a close relative of the High King, and offered to pass along our message and pay Marlenia City a visit."

"Not uncommon for Southern noble families to allow their heirs to travel, so long as they remain within the province and announce their presence. Allows for the wealthy to know the plight of the poor. And experience the Race without watchful parental gaze," Monju added.

Race was an illicit drug commonly found in the Southern province. Highly addictive, it ate your body from the inside out—a slow, painful death. My stomach sank. "So you're saying the South is coming here, to the castle?"

"A delegation, representing their crown, yes," Bidelia replied.

"If they can skirt the blockades and make it to the city, we might have a chance. They will expect to be entertained, but more importantly, Keegan must decide what he is willing to part with in exchange for their aid. We need food and men to defend ourselves."

Keegan pressed his lips firmly together, showing off his scars. "I'm open to suggestions."

"I'm sure. I will discuss that further with you later, if you'd like. The time is short. Monju, if you wouldn't mind shedding some light on Southern customs for us, any information would be helpful."

"At the new Advisor's service," Monju said, with the dip of his head.

"I will take a horse and ride out. Or run out, if we can't spare any horses. See if I can spot any trace of a Southern party," I said, hoping to be helpful. "Just tell me where the East have set up their blockade."

"I can send a crew out to do just that, if you'd like," Bidelia said gently. "It's best you remain here. We can't have you getting into any skirmishes."

The words were on the tip of my tongue: skirmishes were my speciality. The Violet Fox could get out of any scrape, if she was given the chance. Anger swelled within me, even though I knew Bidelia was trying to protect me. What she was really saying was she didn't want me to be captured by the East and held for ransom. Once again, I silently nodded, and the gentle tingling of the Spear's magic returned. It was itching to be used, and sitting here in this council room did no good for neither it nor me.

Bidelia and Antony proceeded to lay out our current resources, in terms of supplies and people. The tunnels leading in and out of the castle had been collapsed, in case our enemies had obtained knowledge of them and to prevent thieves from raiding the food. They told us of the other, non-noble prisoners they'd captured and held in the dungeons. Worthless as bargaining chits, and a burden on our rations. I reluctantly agreed to freeze them with the Spear if our situation didn't improve in the next few days.

Eventually, Antony stood and headed for the door. "Thanks for hearing us out, but I should get an update from my people." Then, to Bidelia: "Sundown, in the bailey?"

"As per usual. Though perhaps Arnau would be a better choice as a driver tonight. Yesterday, Celso drove right over a rock and spilled a dozen apples. They fell right down the mountain. I was afraid they'd hit someone," Bidelia replied.

Antony took this under consideration with a thoughtful grunt. I stood and nudged Keegan to follow my lead, but he recoiled from my touch once more. Antony bowed to the two of us briefly as he exited the council room.

"Before you can ask," Bidelia said squarely to me, "yes, Pascal can be trusted. For now. I had the same concerns, the same reluctance. But he has made no mention of his payment—yet. I suspect it is coming. He may be waiting for the South to arrive. He knows that we, and namely the Violet Fox, are a better bet than skulking off to any other master. Trust in that."

"He seems competent," Keegan said, unconsciously rubbing at his back.

Monju and I exchanged glances. "Can be trusted," Monju confirmed. "Lady Kiera and her prince need every ally."

Keegan wasn't just a prince anymore. Even though he hadn't been sworn in as the new High King or Holy One, he was still our rightful ruler—and that weighed on me. How could I help him reign, when I barely knew how myself?

We filtered out of the room and the five of us lingered in the corridor. For the first time in a while, I felt aimless. I had gotten into the pattern of riding in the wagon, foraging for food, and hiding from the East. Before that, we were always moving or hiding, or pretending to be other people. It was exhausting. Now we had bigger problems, but we also had the castle, and that was reassuring.

"Are you tired?" I asked Keegan.

"Yes." He looked past me to Bidelia. "Advisor Mullen, I assume I have sleeping chambers, somewhere. If you would show me to them, that would be...appreciated."

She raised an eyebrow at the request and gestured for her daughter instead. "Laoise. Show His Grace to his chamber, if you would. I may have to ask you to take on managing what servants we have left until you leave for Xii."

"Of course, Mother," Laoise said. She gave me an apologetic look as she led Keegan down the corridor, towards his royal chambers. Monju followed jovially, with a slight skip in his step.

I went to follow—after all, this was supposed to be my home too, and Keegan hadn't said he *didn't* want me along—when Bidelia's voice stayed my step. "Kiera, with me, if you don't mind." Her tone suggested this was more than a mere request.

With one last look over my shoulder at Keegan, I followed Bidelia down the hallway.

For a while she didn't speak. We walked quickly through the stone corridors, the smell of dust and soot heavy in the air as I realized we neared the west wing, where my old chamber was. Every time the butt of the Spear touched the floor, Bidelia flinched, almost unperceptively. The presence of the artefact intimidated her. Once, it had done the same for me. I had sacrificed almost everything to obtain it. Walking with it now was like holding hands with an old friend; it warmed my palms and the blood in my veins.

Once we reached my chamber, Bidelia took a key from one of her many pockets, slid it into the lock, and twisted it. Wordlessly, we let the door creak open.

The room was pristine—as pristine as it could be, given the state of the castle. Bed made, looking glass clean in the vanity, floor swept. There were even a few dresses hanging in the open wardrobe. This was where I'd stayed as Dominique Castillo, and it was where I'd settled as Kiera Driscoll, future High Queen of the West. Despite how I'd slept on hard surfaces and in caves my entire life, I never thought I'd be grateful to see the made bed again. Evidently, Bidelia had prepared the room, hopeful that I would return.

She shut the door behind us and crossed her arms furiously. "Your behaviour in that meeting was appalling. You can behave however you'd like with me—I know you, and I am used to your temper and insolence. Yet in front of Pascal, and dare I say it, in front of Keegan, I expect better, considering his condition."

The words stung because she was right. "I'm just trying to think of the bigger picture. If we don't—"

"You've made your argument clear," Bidelia interrupted, holding up a hand. "And I understand it and we have a plan now, although I don't like it. Seeing Laoise run off to Xii with Monju. Well, he's fit enough, I suppose..." She trailed off, clearly thinking of something else entirely, and then said, "I won't tell you how to rule, Kiera. But if you will heed an inexperienced Advisor? Delegate your tasks. Even the Violet Fox can't be everywhere at once. Right now, we need you here. *I* need you here."

I looked up at that. "I'm sorry."

"You're only trying to think of what's best, I know," she said, accepting the apology with a grateful nod. "Laoise is right, though. I suspect Conal will be thrown off when you don't chase him down. I fear what he may do, just as you do."

"I know. He was just so...strong. And dangerous. He restrained me like it was nothing. Like *I* was nothing."

"How did you escape?" she asked.

I paled and leaned the Spear against my body. It was a comfort. "Keegan freed me. But...before Conal left...he said I could use magic, like he could."

"As in, channel the magic of the artefacts?" she asked inquisitively. I had done it before, with the Orb of Dashiell.

I shook my head. "No, like the Elders and the apprentices. I think maybe all the Freetors have the capacity, but the Elders were careful about the knowledge."

Bidelia wrung her hands and approached the bed. "I had similar suspicions, when I discovered Conal's fascination for magic and his subsequent rejections from apprenticeship. Perhaps your prolonged contact with the artefacts awakened the tendency in you."

"I haven't done anything yet," I said. But Bidelia's words rang true. The heat of the Silver Spear against my chest coursed through my body. Every time I'd used the artefacts, it was to create destruction, usually to thwart an enemy. Part of me didn't want to consider what I could do—I didn't have that luxury, not when I had people to save and protect.

All I had to do was reach out, and *release...*

"We need to destroy them," I said, finding my feet. "Once they're all located. We can't let one person have this much power. Especially him."

"How do you propose we do that?" Bidelia asked.

"Break them into pieces, smaller than before, and scatter them. Be smarter about hiding them. Leave no records or rumours. Conal said they can't be destroyed by mortal means. We have to be as thorough as possible."

Bidelia looked hesitant. "It is impossible to leave no trace. There will always be a Conal Driscoll, searching for that which will make him stronger. But if you can devise a way to make it difficult, once we have settled our more pressing crisis, I will help you carry out your plan. Laoise and Monju will bring the Tablet back safely and keep it from your father. I trust that you can control your magic, should it surface?"

I didn't even know how to answer that question. How could I control something that I didn't know how to wield in the first place? "All I want is to restore Keegan's memories using the Tablet. And everyone else's. I'm not my father."

"I know," she said. After a pause, she gestured to the Silver Spear. "I can do away with that if you'd like."

I wanted to say *yes, please take this terrible weapon that has caused hundreds of years of strife and suffering for everyone in this city. Please hide it so it doesn't accidently put my husband in a deep, frozen slumber.* And yet, after all I had been through, even after committing to destroy it later...I couldn't bring myself to hand it over. The faces of my people had been burned into my memory. The gleam in their eyes when they'd seen me raise the Spear—it had been a brief glimmer of hope, a sign that as long as I served them, they would recover. *We* would recover.

"I will wield it, for now," I said evenly, spinning it between my fingers. Even wrapped in fabric, the glow was magnificent, and in a pinch, its frozen power would be useful against my enemies.

Bidelia frowned. "I agree it's a useful display of power. It may ease the Freetors and keep the more rebellious commoners from attacking you directly. I don't have to tell you the risks. Just tell me when you want it hidden or destroyed, and I will do it. This time, I'll make sure no one can find it."

I nodded, unconfident in this promise. My father had stolen the Spear from her before being "captured" by the Frostfires. While he was at large, I could trust no one to conceal magic from one who had studied it intimately.

She shifted her weight, preparing to leave, and then thought better of it. "I've spent my life in service," she said, more softly now. "I am used to obeying and giving orders, especially to you. I also recognize, however, that you will be—*are*—my queen now. With the Freetor leadership essentially dissolved and the Marlenian royalty in disarray, whether anyone likes it or not, you and Keegan are the logical, best choice for Freetor and Marlenian alike, at least in the capital. I gave myself the Advisor mantle as a formality, to maintain order. But if you wish me to serve in some other capacity, or if you think someone else is more suited to the job—"

"There's no one I want to advise me more than you," I said firmly. "You have the most experience navigating castle politics, you know how the Freetors think, and you know my father, too. Maybe even better than I do."

But not really, said a small voice of doubt. *You have known magic as he has—something Bidelia will never experience.*

Bidelia looked relieved at my endorsement. "Good. Though I don't know if I will ever get used to calling you 'Your Highness' or 'my lady.'"

"It's pretty strange," I admitted. "Just call me Kiera."

"Very well. Kiera. High Queen Kiera Driscoll. Why the Marlenians had to describe every title so blatantly? Queen would suffice, wouldn't it? No, everything must be *high* or *low* or *holy* or small or *grand...*" She sighed. "You've had a long journey, but there isn't much time to rest. Help me dole out the rations this evening—if you please," she added, as a stiff formality. "Should I suggest to Keegan that he make an appearance as well?"

"Sure. I mean, I can do it." Any excuse to speak with him.

"If you wish." She looked uncertain. "We can bring Keegan up to speed on current affairs, but if he falters, you will be the South's main contact when they arrive, and we need their support. If our people discover what Freetor magic did to Keegan..." Bidelia sighed and edged towards the door, and then dipped in a quick bow. She smiled, shaking her head. "I'll have one of the girls bring you clean clothes. And, although this is now far outside my jurisdiction...may I suggest, after we finish dividing the rations...a bath?"

I smirked. "That bad?"

"Well," she replied. "You have been busy. I've smelled worse. But we must—"

"All right, I get it. Maintain appearances and standards of cleanliness. I'm not shaving anything this time." Marlenian noblewoman wanted nothing to do with their body hair, and often removed every trace of it below the neck; it was a custom I found strange and pointless.

"You are the High Queen," Bidelia replied, resigned, and with another exaggerated bow, left me alone.

As her footfalls disappeared down the corridor, I let out a slow, controlled breath and looked out the window. Dividing rations—just like we used to do in the underground. Begging the South for help—so we could be at their mercy. Keegan—once again, a ruler upon the throne, who knew nothing about the true needs of his people. Laoise and Monju—my trusted friends, leaving. Advisor Bidelia Mullen—her title might have changed, but she was still ordering me around. General Pascal Antony—another military man I couldn't trust, because he had wronged me in the past. The world was changing, and yet it remained the same.

Well. Not if I had anything to do with it.

There was one other important reason I needed to keep the Spear.

The best way to identify an artefact in the wild? Bring your own artefact.

Yes, I had to save my people from the variety of non-magical enemies plaguing the city. And yes, Laoise and Monju were capable of venturing into the world and hunting the Tablet down with the Emerald Cloth. Yet I was stuck here, just to be the face of the monarchy? *Keegan* was the face and the voice. Even if he didn't remember it, diplomacy and decorum was his strength. He didn't need me. He didn't *want* me. With Bidelia's help, he would have the South's support by the end of their visit. My father was the biggest threat, and if he found the Midnight Tablet before I did, he would uncover its magical secrets and use them against us. The plague would fester, and we would very well end up under his tyrannical thumb.

I knew him best. I was responsible for this mess. I had to stop him the only way I knew how: sneaking out of the castle, and undertaking a secret mission—alone.

As we divided the rations in the Cathedral of Dashiell, the mood was tense. Thousands of people funnelled into the cathedral via a more-or-less orderly line, maintained by Antony and his band of loyal Roamers. Keegan stood by the entrance, dressed in white ceremonial robes embroidered with the old Tramore crest: the sceptre, held up high. The older folks touched his hand as they passed; a simple reassurance that the new Holy One had returned to his proper place and respected the old ways. Covering his hands were a pair of white silk gloves, likely to hide his missing forefinger.

One by one, each person received their daily ration from Bidelia and I at the altar: two slices of thinly buttered and salted bread, a handful of uncooked beans, and an apple slice. Laoise and I had spent hours in the kitchen with the servants, slicing and dividing the food into equal portions, as they baked with what little ingredients we had left. We had enough to make loaves for another two days at most, perhaps three if we reduced the ration from two slices to one. The beans, we had plenty of, and served only for variety's sake. It wouldn't be long before that was the only item on the menu. Tomorrow the meal would be mainly fruit, as it was starting to go off. Once they received their rations, my worried people filled the pews. Eating, praying, and hushed conversations about the war gathered together in a sombre din.

I'd convinced Bidelia of the need to say a few words. I had promised my people an explanation. Yet after the meeting in the council room, I had spent my limit on listening and speaking. Bidelia, Laoise, and Monju helped Keegan prepare a short speech about how he'd been captured and imprisoned by the Frostfire family to validate their claim on the province, and his subsequent rescue by me, the Violet Fox. Although I had not helped with the speech—Keegan would barely look at me, much less speak to me—I uttered a few words on our rescue mission in Sallingaire. I left out my father's involvement, as my relationship with him and his obsession with the artefacts was not common knowledge, and avoided mention of the Emerald Cloth. No one could know Keegan had been cured of but altered by the sleeping plague. We neither confirmed or denied it, and no one dared to ask. There were few questions when we concluded our speech; the frenzied mob that had met us in the streets had been subdued by food and fear of retaliation from the Roamers and the apprentices.

I hated lying to them. To administer the Emerald Cloth to everyone in the city would be difficult, but doable—once I retrieved the Midnight Tablet. Then, I'd explain. Maybe they'd condemn me for omitting the truth and call for my death for deceiving them in their time of need. But at least I would have solved their problems. At least they'd have Keegan, a good and honourable man, to guide them into the future.

After our speech, Keegan remained by the altar at the front of the cathedral and greeted every approaching, concerned person, be they noble or merchant or Freetor, navigating pleasantries deftly and convincingly. He was learning what it was like to be me. Thinking on my feet in an unfamiliar, uncertain situation. My father had said this was the greatest gift I could give Keegan, because otherwise, how could he truly understand me, especially now that he had forgotten our love.

I'd lied to him—by omission, but still, a lie—about our relationship. He needed his space. How could he become the person he had been with me floating around, constantly putting him in danger? There was only one way my Keegan would return to me: by finding the Midnight Tablet.

I leaned against the westernmost wall, spinning the Spear between my forefingers as I surveyed each person entering and leaving the cathedral. It had been some time since I'd been here; the last time, I'd thwarted Keegan's wedding to Sylvia Frostfire. Lot of good it did us now. Everyone was trying not to stare at me, but I wanted them to see that I hadn't—wouldn't—abandon them. Not in my thoughts, at least.

Laoise appeared at my side and handed me a sliver of remaining apple slice. "Eat."

I shook my head. "If they see me eating, then the rumour that we've been stealing food will become true. You go ahead."

She sighed through her nose and gave the piece to one of the children sitting in a nearby pew. They gobbled it up gratefully, without a smile. "If you don't eat, they'll assume you ate earlier and that's why they're receiving less than yesterday. Besides, it's going to go off."

There was no way to win. In truth, I barely felt the gnawing hunger. My fingertips worked at the already fraying fabric wrapping the Spear. The warmth of it was like a salve, rejuvenating and subduing my senses. I could have eaten and felt fine, and yet, I couldn't bring myself to take away someone else's rations.

"Has everyone else gotten something?" I asked her.

She smiled. "Keegan ate. Mother shares your feelings. Monju seems to have had his fill."

Monju assisted Antony and the Roamers with keeping order in the line and then settled in one of the pews with a borrowed guitar, taking requests and singing plaintive tunes to ease and unburden the weary. Hearing music was a rare delight, and I too shared in my people's lifted spirits, though his music alone wasn't enough to quell the dark fears of *not good enough* and *hurry—leave*.

Among many of Monju's new admirers was the much afeared

apprentice, who had created the destruction by the Grand Square. He was tall for a Freetor, thin as a post, with pitted, shiny skin, red and inflamed. Like me, he had settled against the wall, his hands hidden behind his back as he stared intently at Monju's fingers tickling the strings. His hair was long, pulled back into a tight ponytail, though the sides had been burned away. His eyebrows seemed to have suffered the same fate. I suspected he was younger than me, though I wasn't certain. He wore tattered blue robes, worn and blackened at the hems.

This young man had let magic control him and exploded in rage, taking out buildings and injuring others. Yet here he was, enjoying music just a few stone-throws away from me.

There is magic within you too, Kiera, my father had said.

I stared at the Spear, glowing dimly blue.

"Is that the apprentice who instigated the riot?" I asked, gesturing across the cathedral.

Laoise followed my gaze. "Apparently."

"I think his name is Gobany. Do you recognize him?"

She shook her head, and then looked suspicious. "Why?"

I shrugged. I hadn't told her what my father had said to me about my own magic, even though it coiled around my brain like a poisonous snake. "Just curious if you had heard anything."

"I've been in the castle as long as you have." She picked at her fingernails. "I know you want to come with us—"

"It's fine."

"No, it's not," she hissed. "You're mad at me for suggesting that you remain here."

I avoided her penetrative gaze. "Maybe."

"But you know I'm right."

"Yes."

A pregnant pause. "And you *are* going to stay here. With Keegan. To sort out…all this. And protect them. In case your father returns here."

My breath caught. I hadn't considered he'd come here. He probably wouldn't, unless the trail brought him back to Marlenia City. He'd been here for decades already, I told myself. He'd have found the Tablet if it was here—right?

Laoise noted my hesitation. "Whatever it is you're planning— we've decided. You're not coming with us. I'm not telling you what day or what time we're leaving. We're just going to be gone. All... all right?"

All of my emotions shot up my throat in that one instant. The thought of her leaving me was so unbearable that I released the Spear and grabbed my best friend around the middle, pulling her into a tight embrace. The Spear slid down the wall and clattered to the cathedral floor, startling the nearby folk in the pews. My fingernails dug into Laoise's back. I couldn't let her go.

What if she didn't come back?

What if I was destined to face everything...alone?

Her arms slid around my back in understanding. "I can do this. You know that, right?"

I nodded against her shoulder. "I'm...afraid."

"Me, too," she said, pulling back. Her eyes were red and watery, like mine. She steeled herself. "This is a mission. Like all the other missions to the surface. My mother would be gone for so long, sometimes I wondered if..." She glanced over her shoulder to Bidelia, who was sauntering the perimeter with her hands behind her back, surveying the crowd with practiced detachment. "I don't have to tell you. You already know. But I'm asking you to believe that we can do this and return, either with the Tablet or with important leads."

It was difficult to lie and she knew it. I bent to retrieve the Spear, seeking time to form the right words. "I want to make it right."

"*We* will," she said firmly.

It was nearly midnight before Monju stopped playing; it was his captive audience that stayed to the last. He looked tired and his fingers had reddened from the performance, but he was all smiles in front of the delighted folk who appreciated his gifts. They tossed him a few silver coins, now worth less to them than the food in their bellies. He sighed as he and Laoise trudged out of the cathedral and jumped on the first carriage up to their cozy beds in the castle. They had to rest up for the long journey ahead of them—whenever they decided to embark.

The entertainment concluded for the evening, Gobany lingered in the pews, staring at the altar. He must have felt me watching him, for he looked toward the exit, but I slid into the seat beside him.

"I'm told you're Gobany," I said to him. "Do you speak, or are you in your years of silence?"

He quirked an eyebrow. "I don't do that anymore." He had a leisurely way of speaking. He knew I was the High Queen of Marlenia, a hero of the people, yet my titles didn't seem to impress him. What did concern him was the Spear, which loomed beside me, blocking his only escape. It was a symbol of hope and freedom to my people, ever since it had slain the favoured son of the tyrant who had pushed us down, hundreds of years ago. I saw no such hope in his gaze now.

"I would appreciate your council, Apprentice," I said formally, in a low voice. I glanced around me. Bidelia and Keegan had busied themselves with showing the rest of the people out. "What can you—or any of your fellow apprentices in the castle—tell me about the Midnight Tablet?"

Gobany stared at me, blank-faced, as if I had not spoken. Some apprentices could communicate without speaking, though it took considerable practice. I had been told that most of our apprentices had barely mastered the basics—whatever that meant.

"That is a dangerous question, Violet Fox," Gobany replied, tapping his fingers on the pew in time with a tune in his head. "Though I'm not surprised you're seeking the seat of power. As a matter of fact, I *do* know...something."

I nodded, bristling at his arrogance. "Anything you could share would be—"

"Not here." He stood suddenly. I did as well, in attempt to match his height. "Meet me tomorrow morning, when the sun rises, in the center of the hedge maze."

"Of course." I moved out of his way and cursed inwardly. If Laoise and Monju left tomorrow morning, I'd miss my chance to sneak out with them—even though Laoise had forbade me to do so. But I couldn't leave for Xii without knowing something about the Tablet; what I'd be up against.

"Don't bring the Spear," he said as he slid out of the pew and down the aisle.

"Why not?" I asked after him.

He didn't glance over his shoulder and shoved his hands into hidden pockets within his robes. "Just don't."

I grimaced at his insolence, but I couldn't blame him. It was familiar, because it was also mine.

Bidelia shot me a look as Gobany breezed by her and I shook my head. When the time came, I'd deal with him. The apprentices had no leadership, and if he was their strongest offering, then I had to keep him from exploding another street or starting a riot.

Like it or not, if I was to get what I wanted, I had to work with unpredictable apprentices once again.

* * *

I woke with the dawn, and threw off the covers. I was already dressed. My dreams had been light, consisting mainly of me running after Laoise and watching her and Monju leave the city without me. Then, I was running in the hedge maze, yet the way to the centre changed each time I made a choice.

Leaving the Spear resting in my chamber, I left the castle through the postern and headed for the maze. The last time I'd ventured through here, it had been with my father. I'd thought the Frostfires had hidden a frozen Keegan at the centre—yet by the time I'd gotten there, they'd moved him. Sylvia had followed us, and that had been the beginning of our uneasy allyship. Conal Driscoll had been apprehended that day. He'd sacrificed himself so that we could get away.

I'd really thought he was dead. He *let* me believe it.

The centre of the maze was a square, enclosed dome. The rectangular bier remained, though the drape covering it was gone now. Gobany and three other apprentices were waiting for my arrival. Gobany leaned against the bier, while the other three paced vigilantly. When I entered, they stopped abruptly, and I was reminded of the three apprentices who had tried to kill me months ago. My heart raced, and I grasped at nothing, remembering that I'd left my prized weapon in my chamber.

"Violet Fox," said Gobany in greeting, nodding.

"Good morning, Apprentices," I said.

The three apprentices I didn't know dipped in a quick bow. One was a young blonde girl; she couldn't be more than ten. Another was tall and lanky, and he smiled at me; he reminded me of Rordan, when we were younger. The third was older than me. She was missing an eye, though the wound had been stitched and healed some time ago. All of them wore the same blue robes in varying degrees of newness and quality.

"Thank you for agreeing to meet with me," I began.

"You're the Violet Fox," was all Gobany replied.

"And do you have names?" I asked the three silent apprentices.

"They are Katell, Ruchaan, and Binna. I speak for them," he said, gesturing to each one in turn. He said this as if it needed no other explanation.

I cocked an eyebrow at them. Steadily, they confirmed this with a nod. Either they had chosen a vow of silence, or some terrible trauma had stolen their will or desire to speak.

"They wanted to be here to observe. And because they helped

me compile the information you...requested." He looked uneasy. "So ask your questions. We're supposed to be helping the Roamers observe the comings and goings up in the Eastern camp today."

"I look forward to hearing about that," I said politely. "My first question is, why didn't you want me to bring the Spear to this...meeting?"

"You attract too much attention with it," Gobany spat.

Even here, in the maze, away from a crowd? From someone who had blown up a street—I could see his point. Magic was unpredictable. Though unlike him, I could control the Spear's magic. At least his fiery, riot-inspiring rage seemed to be in check today.

"That's not the artefact you want to talk about," Gobany continued, prompting me to get on with it.

"Correct. I want to know about the Midnight Tablet. Or the creation of magic."

Even the name conjured worried expressions from the three silent apprentices.

"The creation of magic is a...broad subject," Gobany said slowly. "And a dangerous one to discuss with a non-apprentice or non-Elder."

"But you do know about it."

"Sure."

I waited for him to elaborate, but when he didn't, I sighed. "Fine. We'll start with this. If the Midnight Tablet is supposed to be the origin of magic, or *contain* the origin of magic...why don't the Freetors have absolute knowledge, or possession of it? Why is something of this magnitude not a Freetor artefact?"

The four apprentices exchanged long, silent glances for so long I wasn't sure they were going to answer my question. When Elder Erskina had first sent me to the castle with Lady Dominique's identity, my mission had been to find Alastar's Tome, his life's work detailing the secrets of Freetor magic. As it turned out, such an artefact didn't exist. It had been a ruse to get me off the streets and into the castle to do Elder Erskina's bidding so she could take over everything.

"Sorry, I know that's a complicated one to start—"

"It's not," Gobany interrupted. "There is a difference, you see, between a Freetor artefact and the four artefacts of Dashiell. Freetor artefacts are magical items created by powerful Elders. Some were created by apprentices to practice imbuing an object with magic. The Temple of the Elders had many wonderous artefacts. Curio imbued with magic. Some Elders worshipped them. That was…before." The four of them bowed their heads and observed a moment of silence for their fallen brethren. I wasn't clear on the details, as the apprentices wouldn't speak on it, but Elder Erskina had been determined to be the most powerful magic user, period. She'd eliminated any perceived threat.

"The four artefacts of Dashiell—those are old," Gobany continued. "Older than the war, older than written history. They were supposedly created by Dashiell, or by whatever powers gifted him his man-god status. Alastar the Hero didn't invent magic, so, that's why the Tablet isn't a Freetor artefact. Magic existed long before the Freetor movement, and if we win the war against the East, it'll continue to exist after us, too."

According to the story my father had told about the Emerald Cloth, the four artefacts had been created at Dashiell's deathbed, by a force Pure and Good—but that was just his version of the story. And my father was a known embellisher and liar.

"The Silver Spear is both kinds of artefact, right?" I said. Alastar the Hero had found it encased in ice at the end of the world, as I had, and released it from its prison—and used it against the Holy One's favoured son. This started the Marlenian-Freetor war two hundred years ago.

"Yes," Gobany said slowly, somewhat uncomfortably. "That is generally agreed. In the Marlenians' minds, Alastar warped the artefact. In the cathedral at the bottom of the mountain, you'll see the Spear depicted as a staff. A walking stick. Appropriately down-played because of Alastar's use, or misuse, of the great weapon.

"What I'm trying to tell you, Violet Fox, is while Freetor arte-facts are generally known, and their origins committed to memory by the apprentices and the Elders before us...we can only take stabs at a guess about Dashiell's artefacts and their powers."

I nodded. "Stories can change with the retelling."

"Exactly."

My father had dedicated his life to picking apart fact from fic-tion when it came to magical artefacts. I was confident that he had told me the truth as he knew it about each one. "I know that the Midnight Tablet was last seen four hundred years ago in Xii. It's supposedly the source of all magic. You can know any secret and return what has been lost."

Gobany and his apprentice friends exchanged worried glances. "Might be true," he said finally.

"Tell me what you know," I said with a sigh. I was desperate for anything. Conal Driscoll had had decades to learn. I had a lot of catching up to do, and fewer resources.

"The Midnight Tablet doesn't have a creation story—no reason for existing. One day it wasn't. The next day, Dashiell and his fol-lowers brought it to the people, and it *was*. Long before Alastar the Hero, magic was common. It was for everyone. One simply read or touched the Tablet, and the impossible became possible. Whatever could be imagined, could be conjured. Imperfections, made whole. Enemies could become friends. The old could become young—you get the idea."

"That's a lot of different...powers," I said slowly.

Gobany looked grave. "No. It has one power: the Tablet trades in secrets and knowledge. It is the seat from which power springs. According to the stories, it gives the bearer what it wants—but exacts something in return from you."

"The Cloth does that, too," I replied, unimpressed.

"Does it? I'm not aware. While the Cloth is supposed to heal or treat any ailment or disease, the Tablet could teach the body how to live forever. It could ward the body from particular harm—in exchange for a weaker constitution. The trade is only limited by the imagination of the bearer."

"So I can ask it to...restore memories that have been lost? In exchange for what?" I asked.

The apprentices exchanged glances silently. Eventually Gobany said, "Your guess is as good as mine."

"So...what happened to it, according to the stories?"

"There are three main versions of the myth. The first: Dashiell saw the corruption and chaos the Tablet caused, saw that it was used for selfish rather than selfless means, and used it a final time to erase all knowledge of its power in everyone, except for himself. The second: one peculiar story tells of a man trying to bring back his wife from the dead, and succeeds in conjuring a passable image. A shadow. Dashiell saw the horror the man had created, and forbade further usage. Eventually, it became a legend, and knowledge of it fell from existence. The third..." He looked uncomfortable. "Dashiell was a man, perhaps with magical talent. Some say he didn't die, but used the Tablet to change form, and has done so for countless years, and still walks among us today. Some say he *was* Alastar. I've heard some foolish Marlenians say he's *you*."

I scoffed. "No."

"Exactly." Gobany threw up his hands. "You can't trust any of these stories. They're all preposterous. If you weren't the Violet Fox, I wouldn't tell you them. If the wrong story is told to the wrong person, well, they might get funny ideas."

Funny ideas...like going to Xii to find the Midnight Tablet? I kept my face a neutral mask. "Speaking of Alastar...do we know why *he* had magic? Could it have been because of the Tablet? Because magic wasn't commonplace, or known before him, was it?"

"That is one story," Gobany confirmed. "Most popular one,

anyway. It makes the most sense. It's hard to tell apart what came before the war and what came after. Stories get rewritten and retold through the viewpoint of the present teller. What we apprentices know, with relative certainty, is that those with Freetor blood can see and wield it, whereas those born on the surface cannot. Alastar may have bound fantastical abilities to himself and his offspring, though we were always taught he shared his talents with his friends and followers as well. If he had the Tablet, that would be one way of ensuring continued practice."

"So what happened after he died?"

"The Council of Elders was created. They were selected from Alastar's closest confidants, the strongest users among them. They polished and extended the Central Cavern and created the Temple of the Elders to ensure their continued reverence. Other than that…we don't know. The Elders had so much, but everything was forbidden until you showed some arbitrary sign or exhibited lack of control. Only then was knowledge imparted. We were at their mercy."

He leaned against the bier again and was silent.

"Do you know why it might be in Xii?" I asked.

"Who told you that?" he countered.

I hesitated. "Someone very knowledgeable about all artefacts."

"Who?" His expression was dead serious. I imagined he could extract the information from me if he wanted—or blow up the entire maze if I didn't answer truthfully.

"Former Advisor Ivor Ferguson," I replied.

Gobany sneered. "Is it true he's a Freetor?"

So word had gotten out about his heritage. I wondered who had done the damage: Dominique had been present during my father's exchange with High King Leszek, and I myself had told Sylvia that Conal Driscoll was my father.

"Yes," I said finally. "He's my—"

Gobany didn't care about my connection to him. "He sat in this castle and did nothing. He deserves whatever comes to him."

I gritted my teeth. I couldn't argue. He did deserve a painful fate. And I felt terrible for it. "He's an expert. He hasn't been wrong yet. If he thinks it's in Xii, there's a reason. Do you know?"

The apprentice paced the clearing and mulled on his information. "Freetor tunnels run extensively, not just beneath this city, but throughout the provinces. To varying degrees of stability. In my grandfather's time, you could move from here to the South easily without going above ground. It was a long journey and not many would choose it. Why travel via the Undercity, when you could walk beneath the sun?

"As the South was historically more lenient on the Freetors, or so they say, many escaped and made lives for themselves in Xii and the other Southern cities. Some even worked their way into the Southern court. Established noble bloodlines. Though, that may be a child's tale, meant to inspire hope.

"Xii has the best library of all the provinces. Perhaps it is so now that the Western castle has burnt and crumbled. The Zaman family has historically collected manuscripts, buying them from other royal and noble families to place in their collection."

That was probably where my father would head first. He might already be there, rifling through old parchment, breaking into archives, and plying his silver tongue in service of Southern nobility. I imagined a large slab, glowing blue with magic and runes, just sitting amongst dusty tomes, waiting to be read, overlooked by the surface-born Marlenians.

I couldn't let my father touch it. Somehow, I had to figure out a way to get in there.

"Alastar sought magic, as you do, and as others before you did," Gobany said carefully, seeing the faraway look in my eyes. "If we don't do something to protect magic, we'll have another Elder Erskina on our hands."

"I know." I couldn't let that happen. The Midnight Tablet was clearly the most powerful and most dangerous of the artefacts. The more I learned, the more dangerous it seemed. If my father got his hands on it, he could remake the world.

And so could I. To erase all knowledge of the artefacts, forever? My father had said the artefacts couldn't be destroyed by mortal means. If the Tablet was truly that powerful…that was the answer.

But what would be the price of erasing magic?

What if it asked for my life? I pursed my lips. Would even that offering be enough?

I glanced at each of the apprentices. If I told them my true plan, they would turn from me and I needed them on my side if we had any hope of repelling the East, however unpredictable their powers. It was likely they wouldn't let me destroy the artefacts—any arte-facts. Magic had shaped their lives especially. I braced myself with the knowledge that once I found the Midnight Tablet, and gath-ered the artefacts together, I'd have to deal with the apprentices separately. Magic corrupted, and Gobany was right—we couldn't have another Elder Erskina, or Conal Driscoll, ever again.

"Thank you, Apprentices," I said, inclining my head. "You've been incredibly helpful."

"What do you intend to do when you find the Midnight Tablet? I'm assuming that's why you're asking us these questions." Gobany gave me a scrutinous look.

I had to tread carefully here. "If Ivor Ferguson finds the Tablet first, he'll use it for selfish means. He's a tyrant and only I can stop him."

"Why only you, Violet Fox?"

I parted my lips to answer, and the words fell short. It was like I was back in the council room with my friends, Bidelia, and Antony. *Why* only me? I was the High Queen now. I had other responsibil-ities. Let some other adventurous spirit take up the mantle.

And yet there was no way I would stand for that. It was me against my father. That was how it would end. I was certain of it.

"I don't know," I said honestly. "I'm afraid of what will happen if I don't."

This answer, although vague, seemed to satisfy the four apprentices. Gobany launched himself from the bier and dusted off his robe.

"We should go," he said unceremoniously as he headed for the exit. The three apprentices followed his lead, stealing curious glances at me as they left. There were no pleasantries exchanged. They were apprentices, and they did as they pleased.

I wondered how much they could see inside my mind—if they knew what I planned. If they did, I suspected Gobany would have said something.

I left the epicentre of the hedge maze, my mind swirling with plans and regrets. I followed the apprentices at a respectable distance as we made our way out. I had to reach Xii. It was at least a week's journey with a carriage or horse. I'd need supplies—

I'd no sooner emerged from the entrance when Bidelia's voice called to me. "There you are!" She stood next to the postern, and eyed the four apprentices warily as two entered the castle, and the other two headed for the stables. "Is something wrong?"

"No. Why?"

"You came from the maze with them?" She gestured over my shoulder. "I'm surprised you agreed to be alone with them, given your history."

That was true. "I just wanted to familiarize myself with their faces, names, and backgrounds. Especially Gobany."

"Yes. Well." She crossed her arms. "A prudent move, I suppose, though I wouldn't go to him for advice on...*your* magic. If that was your plan."

I pursed my lips. I didn't want to think about that. "Did you want me for something?"

"Yes. Good news. We've heard from our scouts outside the city." She grinned slyly. "We've spotted Southern banners on a small caravan. They've made contact and they say they'll be visiting the castle tomorrow. And Kiera—there's a Zaman family crest on one of the banners."

The royal family of the South had come to Marlenia City?

The promise of help had finally arrived.

***

The castle erupted into a flurry of activity for the remainder of the day. I barely had time to ask after Laoise and Monju as Bidelia insisted the servants take my measurements so an appropriate wardrobe could be constructed. Not actually made, of course—there was no time or appropriate materials for a custom dress. When the Frostfires fled, their courtiers, nobles, and most notably Sylvia had left behind closets and wardrobes filled with fashionable attire, waiting to be modified to suit my pole-like frame.

Despite my intense dislike for standing still and being dressed like a doll, I endured Bidelia and her gaggle of servants as they remade my appearance from dirty Violet Fox to High Queen of Marlenia. They plucked my eyebrows, slathered cream on my face, and combed my hair so much the brush had to be sheered. When I asked if Keegan was going through a similar treatment in his chamber, Bidelia told me she hoped so. As the Holy One, he represented everyone and the precious man-god, so he had better be resplendent. I responded just enough to the servants' inquiries and Bidelia's chatter to appear present, yet the entire time, I was working on my plan.

That evening, after we had distributed the rations, I stayed in the cathedral with Bidelia and Keegan. I allowed Bidelia to direct me as I wrestled with my doubts. Sweep the floors. Pile the empty baskets and containers. Load the wagon. Search for stragglers. Check for crumbs or food remnants (there were none; there never were, Bidelia said, but just in case). I completed these tasks with no objection, for nothing could seem out of place if my plan was to work. Antony and the Roamers had already left on their nightly patrol of the city. It would have been too suspicious to ask for their routes. I'd just have to hope they wouldn't spot me.

Keegan scoured the cathedral with a dust cloth, cleaning the pews and the stained glass, but I suspected he also took in the history of the religion, too. He had questions that neither Bidelia nor I could answer about the lapsed theocracy cradling his upbringing: *Why are the rulers called Holy One? If Dashiell was a man-god, why did he die? Was I a religious prince?*

"No," I answered to the last question, despite my better judgement.

He fixed me with a curious look, the first since the council meeting. "How do you know for certain? This place feels…familiar."

I picked up the empty bread baskets and hauled them out to the carriage. "If it's familiar and you're certain, then don't ask me."

Keegan's face soured at that, though he questioned me no further. It was better that way. The cathedral was familiar and even Antony elicited a vague memory, but I did not? I had no place here.

Like a good High Queen, I returned to the castle with Bidelia and Keegan, saying little and feigning fatigue from the eventful day. Keegan stared out the carriage windows thoughtfully, casting curious glances my way that coloured my cheeks and splintered my resolve. Bidelia looked as though she'd aged since our arrival, but offered to escort Keegan to his chamber, as he had once again forgotten the way. Otherwise, the two of them bid me a hasty goodnight upon our return to the mountain castle.

I too found my way back to my chamber, but only to change from the respectable violet dress I'd worn to the cathedral, pack my things, and prepare for the long night ahead.

It wasn't uncommon to feel watched within the castle, at least in my case. I was always on my guard, because usually I was trying to get somewhere I wasn't supposed to be, like a rat pitter-pattering into a kitchen. Perhaps even more so under the East's rule, the castle had been bustling with life. Now the Frostfires were gone, the Holy One had perished, and only those loyal to Keegan and I had remained to pick up the pieces.

They would manage, I thought, as I slipped from my room. My few precious possessions weighed down the pack slung over my shoulder: a change of clothes, a few slices of stale bread I'd taken from the kitchen earlier, and two small, browned apples. The darkness was a comfort during my midnight stroll through the corridors. I'd considered climbing out the window, but I'd had a close call during my previous stay at the castle that made me think twice on this occasion. With the Spear, climbing would be a nuisance anyway. No, the best way was through the back of the castle. Once I nabbed a horse from the stables, I'd navigate down the slopes, into the outskirts of Feenagh Forest. Wildlife, blockades, and other encounters that would undoubtedly plague my journey to Xii. Nothing the Violet Fox couldn't handle.

I'd moved throughout the west wing of the castle undetected and was nearing the east wing. The uncanny warmth of the air filled me with determination. I heard the far-off sounds of snoring and rustling. Perhaps this was where the Roamers had decided to rest their weary heads. I lifted the Spear gently off the floor, so as to not make a sound as I slipped through the castle like a silent intruder, pushing my guilt down deep. It wasn't just about Keegan, or the others affected by the price of the cure exacted by the Emerald Cloth. This was about stopping my father, too. I had to keep telling myself that as the arguments made circles around my mind, dizzying and consuming. Once, just once, to silence the deafening sound of my doubts, I dug the butt of the Spear hard into the floor, and lingered, twisting the shaft and tightening my grip.

"I've made up my mind," I whispered to no one as I continued on. "I have to go where I'm useful."

The telltale signs dawned on me then: the coordinated crunch attempting to hide beneath the surrounding nightly sounds, the shallow breath and frustrated sigh, and the unmistakable, familiar gait.

Someone was following me.

"If you're trying to make yourself known, you've succeeded," I said, stopping in the middle of the hallway.

The footfalls ceased immediately. I turned, already knowing who it was. I regretted facing him.

"How is it you walk so silently?" Keegan asked, striding towards me.

"Practice," I replied. "Though I wasn't that silent, if you followed me this far. What are you doing up?"

Keegan hadn't changed from his ceremonial white robes, though he'd discarded the gloves. In the middle of the dark corridor, he stood out like a fresh disciple daisy. He ignored my question with a scolding look. "If the people living in this city are as important to you as you claim, you won't go off on this foolish errand."

"Don't condescend to me," I replied. "How do you know where I'm going?"

He pointed to my bag, overstuffed and rustling every time I moved. "I listened to your stories about sneaking around the city and tracking down artefacts. I also noticed you conveniently left *me* out of those adventures. Or lessened my role in them. I could only conclude that I wasn't around during your more prominent thieving days or, later, I went along reluctantly, which is what got me into this memory-loss mess in the first place. Which is why you're leaving me here to go off to find this Tablet of yours. In Xii, wasn't it you said? I have studied the maps. That's quite the journey to make, and as you are sneaking away now, I suspect Laoise, Monju, and the others don't know you're taking off without them."

My old Freetor training returned in moments such as these: say nothing.

Unfortunately, my silence was just as incriminating. Keegan

looked chuffed, and so continued, "I don't know much about myself, but I have discovered I dislike dishonesty, especially among those who promised to tell me the truth. So I'll ask you now, plainly, while we're putting the truth out there: why didn't you tell me we were married?"

"Would you have told me, if our situations were reversed?" I demanded. "I'd be no better than Sylvia Frostfire, the woman who cut off your finger because she couldn't stand that you had chosen me over her."

He regarded the stump of his forefinger. Ever since he'd arrived at the castle, he'd deliberately kept it hidden in polite conversation. It was a ghastly wound, done to him while he was in his icy slumber. Freshly wrapped now, no doubted tended to by the servants, it was a terrible reminder of how I'd failed to help him when he was most vulnerable. "When I freed you, I was afraid. I asked you to tell me the truth."

"I *did*. Everything else was true. As I'm sure you've discovered." I gestured to the dark castle walls surrounding us, absorbing our argument. "I didn't want to overwhelm you with our history. I wanted… I'd hoped you'd…" Frustrated, I grumbled. I hated talking about my feelings. "I'd *hoped* the feelings you had towards me would return. And I didn't want you to feel…trapped…by any obligations you didn't remember making. So I apologize for *lying*, but I'm not really sorry. You deserve to find out who you really are, and you can't do that if I keep dragging you into danger."

"Do you still have feelings for me?"

"How could you even ask me that?"

"With the way you're acting, I think it's easy to understand why."

I gripped the Spear tightly, wrapping it with both hands for strength and stability, and then met his steely, inquisitive gaze. "Yes." Then, while I still had the courage: "How do you feel about me?"

His eyebrows knitted in a pensive expression, but it was a ruse, to cover a deep feeling of regret and confusion. I nodded. I could expect nothing more. I was, and would remain, a stranger.

"I'll leave you alone then."

I turned and continued down the hallway, but Keegan ran beside me and kept pace. "No. Kiera. You cannot leave."

"Cannot? *You* don't order *me* around."

"Clearly. Fine. I would like it if you didn't sneak out of the castle on a suicidal quest against forces we don't understand."

"I understand them. Or...I sort of do." I could understand them, if I wanted, and I wasn't even sure of that. "These artefacts are dangerous in the wrong hands. My father's, most of all. Once we have the Midnight Tablet, and use it to..." I trailed off as the mention of the legendary origin of all magic created visible tension on his face. Retrieving the Midnight Tablet was important to restore Keegan's memory, and he knew it. It was one of the many tales we'd told him on our journey from Sallingaire to Marlenia City. "Are you afraid I'll succeed?"

"Afraid? No. You've done this before. I'm very confident you'll succeed."

"Well, then? If you have no feelings for me, why are you here? What *do* you feel?"

He blinked, surprised. "I'm not...afraid...of something intrusively magical restoring my memories," he replied, raising his eyebrows. "Well, perhaps I am. Wouldn't you? How am I supposed to know what is right and true when something can rip all knowledge from me, at any time?"

"I'm sorry this happened," I said. "You're not the only one affected. But this is my fault, like I told you. That's why *I* have to fix it. If I don't go, my father will beat me to it."

"So you'll leave me here. Alone. To rule in this...ruined fortress."

Alone. The word resonated through my skull, and I felt like

reaching out to him, because alone was what *I* was. "This is your home. This is where you belong. You never should have left."

"With all due respect, I'll be the judge of what is my home and what isn't. I may not remember anything about my life, but I know this isn't my home now. It was, perhaps, but no longer. I refuse to be abandoned here with strangers while you gallivant across the world on what I can only imagine is a quest of folly."

He didn't consider me a stranger. "For a person who remembers nothing, you sure know how to deliver a speech."

"Yes. It seems it's a strength of mine," he conceded, looking pleased and flattered that I'd noticed. "But the people here listen to you, too. I am not blind to the fact that you are the true power that binds this place together. In the cathedral, the people were grateful you took the time to notice them. If you leave, this city will crumble."

I hadn't noticed. My mind had been elsewhere. "They don't want me here. They appreciated and noticed *you*. They want you, your blood, your name."

"Within the past two days, you have brought more stability to this city than the people have seen in weeks. Yes, my face helped. But it was your words that greeted them on the streets, your guiding presence. Not mine. If I didn't have you here...I'd..." He composed himself. "I don't think I have the power or the authority over you to stop whatever it is you're planning. But I ask of you, kindly. Don't leave me here alone."

His gaze felt hot on my face as my hope and confidence dissipated. He thought I was going to abandon him. And I almost had—for what?

To find the Midnight Tablet. A task I didn't even trust my closest friends to carry out...because I, the Violet Fox, *had* to do it alone. Or so I'd thought.

To stop my father from controlling yet another artefact. What was it Bidelia had said? Delegate. I didn't want to send Laoise and

Monju to their deaths against my father. I didn't want my people to suffer needlessly under the spell of powerful, dangerous magic.

The one thing that would bring him back to me. Magic I feared to possess.

"All right," I said reluctantly, balling my hands into fists. "I won't leave."

This seemed to quell his fear, though he still looked uncertain. "You promise?"

I pressed my lips together and nodded. "On our marriage, I promise I won't abandon you. I'll...trust in Laoise and Monju to get their hands on the Tablet. For now."

Keegan smiled, though it didn't reach his eyes. "Thank you. I... appreciate this. In the long run, I think this is the best decision."

I nodded and averted my gaze. I wasn't sure if I agreed, but this was my sacrifice for him.

"I should get some sleep," I muttered. "And so should you."

"Good night, Kiera," he said plainly. "See you tomorrow."

No ensuring I made it back to my chamber. No wondering if he could trust me. He headed back the way he'd come, with renewed purpose.

Slowly, I sauntered down the corridor after him. Perhaps it was a blessing Keegan didn't remember our similar conversation, months ago, about me going after the Silver Spear. I'd asked for his blessing to mount an expedition. He'd refused—he wanted his soon-to-be queen ruling at his side. Only the near-destruction of the castle had forced us out onto the roads in search of the magical artefact. I wasn't about to resort to drastic measures just to make my quest easier. I had promised Keegan I wouldn't leave. I had to prove to him that I was a woman of my word—the kind of woman he'd someday, hopefully remember he had married.

EARLY THE NEXT morning, Bidelia shook me awake. The South would arrive at the castle just before noon, and I had better be ready to receive them.

Sleep had been fitful after my encounter with Keegan in the corridor. I'd nearly left him—and everyone—to deal with the starvation of my people. The shame of it permeated my thoughts. I'd been so sure it was the right thing to do. Part of me still believed it was. If I'd left, I wouldn't have to play dress-up in front of some Southern nobles just to convince them to give us aid.

I knew little about the South itself. It was it was ruled by the Zaman family. By its stereotype, the Southern people were good-natured, celebratory, indulgent, and often preferred to stay out of the affairs of other provinces. Monju had told us of Race, an addictive drug rampant in Xii and the surrounding Southern towns. He had left the South initially to sell his services as an assassin and bard to raise funds for a cure to counter the effects, only to realize that it was unlikely such a cure existed.

Although Bidelia had assigned a handful of servants to tend to my personal needs, Bidelia herself helped select my attire to greet the Southern delegation. I suspected she had other, more important items to take care of as the Advisor, yet I doubt she trusted my sense of style when it came to royal presentation. I was grateful for her help. Without it, I would have been content to wear ripped brown trousers and whatever blouse looked the cleanest. Instead,

I donned a royal purple, velvet dress. It had belonged to one of the courtiers who had fled, and one of the servants had stayed up through the night to embellish the hems and the neckline with dark lace. She'd also taken it in at the bosom and under the arms. Now, it fit me, for the most part, and according to Bidelia, it was appropriate for a High Queen.

It took most of the morning for the servants to ensure I was presentable, and the sun was rising quickly, but there was one task I had to see to before I greeted the South with Bidelia and Keegan.

Donned in my finery, including a simple silver circlet threaded into my lavender-oil scented hair, I threw open the door to my chamber...and ran straight into Bidelia.

"The delegation has reached the city limits," she remarked. She wore a similar style coat as the previous days, except today's was faded emerald. Seeing my eagerness to leave, she immediately looked suspicious. "Where are you headed?"

"I was hoping to catch Monju and Laoise," I admitted. "Weren't you assisting Keegan with his outfit?"

"I've checked in on him. He needs no assistance. He's surrounded himself with scribes and intellectuals. An attempt to soak up what he can, I imagine." She looked concerned by this, but continued. "And *I* thought Laoise wasn't telling you their departure plans."

"She didn't," I said hopefully. "You're telling me they haven't left yet?"

"No. They overslept. Sleeping in a bed for the first time in weeks can do that." She gestured for me to walk with her through the corridors, towards the back half of the castle. "They should have been gone hours ago. If you're going to see them off, don't be long. And you'd better not—"

"I'm not going anywhere," I promised reluctantly.

Occasionally, servants flitted up to Bidelia and asked for her opinion on the food storage, the Roamer patrols, and when she thought Keegan might oversee some minor judicial matters. Each gave me a nervous glance, wondering if Bidelia had the authority. With every response she gave, I nodded in agreement. At this point, she knew more than me and Keegan about the goings-on. Though if Keegan was being proactive—collecting scribes and delicately pressing them for political information and advice—I was really going to be out of the loop, wasn't I?

"I have to admit I was surprised to see you in bed this morning," she said.

I wondered if Keegan had said anything about my runaway attempt. "Me, too." I let out a slow breath. "Bidelia. Does the crown have silver to spare?"

"We need every piece we have to bargain with the South," she replied.

Right. I blew out a sigh. "Well, I've been thinking. Laoise was right. My father's expecting me to show up in Xii, Spear blazing. But what he's not expecting is tens, possibly hundreds, of treasure hunters descending upon Xii and the surrounding area to search for a mystical artefact."

She looked wary as she followed my plan to its natural conclusion. "I don't know, Kiera..."

"Make an announcement, spread a bulletin, whatever you have to do. One thousand silver quid for the safe return of the Midnight Tablet to the castle in Marlenia City. I will double any counter-offer in play."

"Kiera! That could bankrupt the crown! Think of all the charlatans and thieves that will descend upon us with their shiny rocks and magical baubles..."

"We're not rewarding just anyone. Only the real thing." If Laoise and Monju failed to find something, perhaps someone else would. Even if they didn't bring anything back, once we solved our food and magical artefact problems, I'd gift Laoise and Monju land and silver for their trouble. They deserved it. I continued,

"Wouldn't it be a good thing if suddenly a hundred people, of their own free will, decided to uproot and leave Marlenia City for a while?"

"I don't like this line of thinking," she warned, but her distracted air meant she had no time to argue. I wondered if she had had the opportunity to say goodbye to Laoise, or if it had been sacrificed to duty. She sighed and at the next junction, we parted ways.

I headed out the postern and around the hedge maze towards the stables. Perhaps pledging one thousand silver quid to a stranger who brought me the real Midnight Tablet was excessive. The odds of that happening were slim. As an artefact could only be easily spotted by a Freetor *with* another artefact, Laoise and Monju did have an advantage. But I would leave nothing to chance, not when it came to my father.

The fresh scent within my hair promptly faded as I neared the muck of the stables. I noted the near-empty stalls and wondered how long Bidelia and the Roamers had waited before ordering the slaughter of the horses. With Laoise and Monju taking two, we were down to just three, which were needed for carriage rides up and down the mountain. Otherwise, it was a long walk—or run— down to the city itself.

The horses Laoise and Monju were taking had already been saddled. Laoise was checking and double checking their supplies, not that they had many. We'd gifted them a sack of silver and two days worth of food, but they'd have to hunt and scavenge their way down to Xii. Monju was checking his curved sword and securing his new guitar. They had donned fresh clothing: a washed, hooded cloak each, which hid Laoise's long, green belted tunic and black trousers and Monju's white tunic, black vest, and green trousers. Both of my friends looked less like Undercity residents and thieves, and more like respectable travellers. They'd still have to deal with Eastern blockades and who knew what else—yet I had faith in them both to navigate and endure anything.

I lifted my dress, careful not to dirty the hem as I walked across the patchy grass towards them. When she saw me, Laoise dropped her brown knapsack and we enveloped each other in a long, clinging hug.

"I wish I was coming," I whispered.

"I know," she said, pulling away. I could tell from her furtive gaze at Monju that some part of her was glad I wasn't.

Monju approached us eagerly and bowed deeply. "The Lady looks exceptionally presentable."

"Thank you," I replied.

I was desperate to break the awkwardness of the goodbye, yet I couldn't bear to see them leave. "All ready?"

"Almost," Laoise said, just as Monju replied, "Yes."

I pursed my lips. "Send me a message as soon as you reach Xii. Via the underground. If you find the Tablet, hire someone trustworthy to bring me a message. I want to know as soon as you lay eyes on it."

"*If* I lay eyes on it," Laoise replied. "Xii is still a stretch. It may not be there."

"No, but if you see Conal—"

"We'll follow him," she promised. Awkwardly, Laoise used a step-stool to mount her horse while Monju spotted her. She smiled tentatively at him and watched as he expertly mounted his ride and gathered the reins.

"It may be some time before the Lady sees her friends," Monju said.

I didn't want to think about it. Seeing them up on their horses, freshly enthusiastic and trepidatious about their journey, it made me miss them already. "Just...promise me you'll stay safe. My father is clever. If you think he knows you're following, it's best just to step back and regroup or he'll lead you into a trap."

Monju nodded. "Will keep an eye out."

"Good luck," I said. "Be safe. Come back alive. And if my father sees you..."

When Laoise realized I couldn't finish the thought, she prompted, "Would you like me to give him a message?"

I steeled myself. "Tell him I'm not like him and I never will be."

"No, that's right," she said confidently.

Bidelia's warning of the similarities I shared with him echoed in my ears, inescapable as the wind. I nodded and backed away, but Laoise's voice caught me before I could escape.

"Hey. Remember he was in a position of power for a long time. He said he wanted to help, but he ultimately did more harm than good. But he had the choice. He made the wrong one. You'll do better than him. I know it." She smiled. "And if you don't know it, my mother will. So, listen to her sometimes, all right?"

I wished I had her confidence. "I'll try."

* * *

I made it across the castle just as Bidelia said to the two burly servants manning the entrance to the castle, "We'll just have to start without her."

"Here!" I called, slightly out of breath. If I didn't have to lug this dress while I ran, I'd be fine.

The entrance hall had filled me with awe and terror when I'd first stepped foot into the castle, months ago. Large, intricate tapestries spinning the history of Marlenia used to line the corridor, informing all visitors of the glory of the West. Many of them were surface-born propaganda, depicting cruel scenes of the Tramore family casting the Freetor threat down into the depths of the caves. The Frostfires even had time to commission a victory scene of their own to display during their reign. Sometime during my departure, Bidelia had ordered it taken down. There had even been busts and statues of previous Holy Ones, and a carpet to cushion royal and noble feet alike. All of that was gone. Now, the walls were bare, save the impossibly high lanterns that gave the hall its dim lighting, and the floors, while recently swept, still appeared grimy and gritty.

"Sorry," I muttered as I took my place between Keegan and Bidelia.

Keegan looked magnificent. He had chosen a silver stiff jacket with violet accents that nearly reached his knees, accompanied by matching trousers. His blouse and vest were shades of purple. The silver circlet cradling his tamed curls was far more intricate than mine, different than I'd seen him or any Holy One don: upon closer inspection, I noted the faded violet gems embedded in the band.

"We're a matching pair," I said to him, immediately regretting it.

He rewarded me with a shy smile.

At least he didn't hate me anymore. That was something.

He didn't let you leave. He made you stay, said the nagging voice within.

My grip on the Silver Spear tightened. Being without the Spear had been like going for a walk without my left hand. I couldn't greet the Southern delegation without it. The Spear had a troubled history with royalty and nobility, especially recently, but I needed to show the South that we were strong. That *I* was strong.

Bidelia curled her lip at the Spear. She knew I'd had to run to my chamber to retrieve it, and then ventured to the entrance hall after saying goodbye to Laoise and Monju, which meant delaying the ceremonial greeting even further. Since our encounter less than half an hour before, her tightly pulled back hair had frizzled. My tardiness probably didn't help. She fixed me with a scrutinizing look and then sighed. "We're ready to receive."

"Should Antony be here?" I asked her.

"He's on the streets, doing crowd control," she replied.

Right. I wondered how our people would react to seeing Southern banners floating through the streets. I hoped the South had a far tamer welcome than we'd had. Best we didn't appear too desperate to our sole lifeline.

The two servants pulled open the large wooden doors and blasted my eyes with the force of the sun. From Antony's description at the council meeting, I was expecting young, proud nobles to stride into the castle and either charm us with their good manners or stonewall us with royal decorum and tradition. Instead, the shadow of one visitor stepped from the sunny exterior into the dim light, each step punctuated with the unmistakable sound of a heavy staff.

One of the servants stuttered in surprise as she looked between us and the visitor. "Presenting High King Kamal Zaman of the South, Your Grace."

Bidelia shared my shock as the lithe man strode deeper into the castle. He was tall, perhaps the tallest man I'd ever seen. If he had not been announced as the High King, I wouldn't have believed it. I'd known him to have had a long reign, yet to look at him, he seemed younger than my father. Only a shock of white above his ears—and his reliance on a tall metallic staff—portrayed his true age. He had intelligent dark eyes, a trim black beard streaked with white, and a dark mole, which decorated his right cheek. Possibly just a beauty mark, though it looked real enough. His silky, golden robe-coat trailed on the floor behind him. Although he wasn't limping or favouring one side, he moved deliberately and gracefully towards us as if he had all the time in the world. The cane dug into the divots and minor cracks in the stone floor.

He surveyed the three of us, and then the two servants manning the doors behind him, and appeared confused. Likely, he expected more fanfare.

"An honour to see Prince Keegan once more," Kamal Zaman said, bowing as far as he could while leaning on the staff for support. "Or Holy One, as is the young High King's title now? I look forward to the official coronation."

"The honour is mine, Your Highness," Keegan replied, inclining his head without missing a beat.

Yet that wasn't the entirety of the visiting party. The High King of the South wouldn't deign to travel alone. Two men and a woman entered after him, dressed in their finest. The young nobles squinted in the dim light of the entrance hall.

The servant who had announced the High King faltered. She no more knew who these nobles were than I did. She looked apologetically to me and pursed her lips.

As I hadn't been introduced yet, it was impolite for me to speak—yet the faster we got this over with, the sooner we could know if the delegation had brought good or bad tidings. "Your Highness. Welcome to Marlenia City. We weren't expecting the High King to travel all this way, but we are…honoured, nevertheless. I don't believe I've had the honour of meeting your travelling companions."

Kamal Zaman fixed me—and the Spear—with unexpected amusement. "Hmm. Very well, the High King of the South shall do the introductions." The annoyance in his voice was not lost on me, however, he set upon his task with grace in his rich baritone and melodic Southern accent. "His Highness is accompanied by Lord Hon'niz Zaman, grand-nephew to His Highness, the esteemed and distinguished Lady Danyal Nimra, and their compatriot Lord Omju Slaaz. Respected nobles of the South, all."

Hon'niz stepped forward and bowed deeply. Of all of them, Hon'niz had dressed the least practically for travel, and looked far from pleased at the state of our castle. The white frills of his long sleeves bloomed from his bright pink coat. A gold belt, worn high around his waist, accented his dark trousers. He held his hands in front of his chest, pretending to pick at his fingernails, though he was probably trying to hide the grass stains streaking across his white blouse. This must have been the relative of the High King Antony had spoken of during the council meeting—though if the High King of the South was travelling with the three young nobles this entire time, how had the Roamers not noticed his presence?

Immediately assessing us with a cool gaze, Danyal Nimra seemed to be at ease among the multitude of strangers. Her long dark hair had been braided with intertwined fuchsia and bright blue beads. She inclined her head politely and kept a close proximity to the High King. Although she was trying to hide it, she'd adopted a protective stance, her right shoulder just barely angled in front of him. The other nobles had respectfully kept their distance and stood behind the High King. She wore no weapons that I could see, but that didn't mean she had none beneath her blue, long-sleeved, belted dress and shining tall boots.

The Northern province employed and taught an elite few the art of shadow killing. While I couldn't be sure that Danyal Nimra had received such training in the North or elsewhere, I recognized a certain air of contempt and comfort that came with extreme mastery and control over one's body. Monju was a practitioner, and in one deep, intense moment, I missed him and Laoise.

Omju, the shortest and scrawniest of the three, glanced over his shoulder at the closed doors. His overcoat was pastel yellow, freshly made, though perhaps not for him specifically. He brushed his hands down his chest, running his fingers over the many silver and gold buttons of his coat. I noted the crusted mud on his boots, something the other nobles didn't share. Only someone new to the noble lifestyle would dare to show up in a royal castle with dirty footwear.

Or, a clumsy spy.

Keegan fidgeted beside me. No doubt he felt he should know these nobles, as any good ruler would. Aside from the Zaman family, I certainly couldn't begin to guess who the other two were in relation to the High King, why they were privileged enough to travel with him, or their family status within the South.

The servant, relieved that the South's introductions had been completed, cleared her throat and took three paces towards us. After a dramatic heel-turn, gesturing to Keegan and I, she said grandly, "May I present Keegan Tramore, High King of the West, Holy One of Marlenia, and Kiera Driscoll, High Queen of the West, the Violet Fox, hero of the Freetor people, his wife and consort.

Also, I present the esteemed Advisor Bidelia Mullen, lead liberator of the Eastern occupation."

Lead liberator. I smiled at Bidelia. She paled at the moniker. Only months ago, she'd been known as the head servant. This was a big step up.

Kamal Zaman's eyes narrowed at my introduction. He raised a feeble hand to point in my direction. "Wife? Since when? The Holy One did not mark his most auspicious of occasions?"

"Things have been complicated, as you've seen, Your Highness," Keegan said cautiously.

Kamal took a careful step forward. The staff dragged and I noted the slight tremor in his hand as he worked to steady himself. I frowned. The three nobles with him looked uncomfortable, especially Danyal Nimra, who stepped in time to accommodate him.

"We appreciate your hasty response to our letter," Bidelia began.

Omju's expression caved. Hon'niz looked unsettled. Only Danyal knew how to hide her emotions, it seemed. Kamal inclined his head to Bidelia in acknowledgement.

Something wasn't right here. "How did you get past the blockades?"

Kamal's expression flickered with amusement. "The Violet Fox means, how did an old king manage the journey so quickly and secretly, and arrive in a timely fashion?"

"Yes," I said firmly. Although I didn't mind the High King referring to me under my folk name, it belied his feeling of superiority towards Keegan's choice in me as a wife. Nevertheless, I relished the feeling of being in control of the conversation. I didn't even need the Violet Fox mask or a disguise to feel bold in front of this powerful king. A rush of warmth filled me, and whether it was from the wrapped Spear or the rush of being defiant, it felt *good*. I felt more like myself than I had in a long time. "Especially with your banners. Surely the East wouldn't let anyone flying Zaman colours anywhere near us."

"Kiera," Bidelia hissed.

"Hmm. Well." Kamal smiled smugly. "Physical might is not the only way to take down a barrier. When the High King of the South knows what another, lesser person wants, getting what the High King wants is relatively simple."

Oh. The rush of power I felt dissipated. I flushed red. "Bribery."

The other Southern nobles stifled their laughter.

"One calls it bribery, and another would say, generous gifts. A mighty army falls in the face of the many delights and offerings of the South. So it was in the past, so it will always be with the Southern province."

I wasn't sure what he was talking about, and Keegan likely didn't either, but it was clear I'd had my moment, and screwed it up.

"As for why the High King travels abroad, that is royal business to speak about, once agreements have been reached," Kamal added.

I raised an eyebrow at that. Why was the High King of the South skulking around the border with Southern nobles who were not his immediate relatives? He had brought the appropriate attire to see the Holy One of Marlenia. Surely there were easier ways to fish for an invitation. Instinct told me to hush up, so I pursed my lips and nodded slightly to Bidelia, urging her to lead the charge.

"As I was going to say, we appreciate your delegation and official visit," she continued, with far less confidence. "We hope that you bring a favourable response to our request for aid."

He barely acknowledged Bidelia. Instead, he fixed his intensity on Keegan. "If the South may speak informally, Your Grace?"

"We would be honoured," Keegan replied. Monju had told us it was common for nobility to ask before introducing first-person pronouns into a conversation with outsiders. Regardless of how awkward the speech, it was considered rude otherwise—a remnant of an older language still spoken deep in the Southern province.

"I realize my presence is sudden and unusual," Kamal began.

"Forgive me for the intrusion. I simply felt it best to see the West for myself. It has been some years. My grandniece, Lady Na'ima, was here for your Gathering celebration months ago. I admit I was intrigued by the happenings."

"I remember Lady Na'ima," I said politely. "I trust she is well?"

"She is," he said, brightening, "thank you for remembering."

"Please send her our best," Keegan added diplomatically.

The High King inclined his head once more, yet he peered at Keegan with deep suspicion. He was waiting for Keegan to do or say something. The pit of unease grew within me, yet I stood within it. My fingers reached slowly for Keegan, wishing that he would take my hand. If only I knew how to control the magic within me...

"I am surprised Your Grace does not ask after Lady Jameela," Kamal said finally, after the longest, most awkward pause.

My face turned a deep red. The name conjured a long-ago conversation I'd had with Sylvia, when I was pretending to be Dominique. Sylvia and her flock of friends—including Lady Na'ima—had gossiped about Lady Jameela and Keegan, and how they had engaged in a long-distance courtship via letters. I had assumed there was a grain of truth in the gossip. After all, what kind of prince and future ruler of the Marlenia would Keegan be if he didn't return a letter written by a lady? Whether or not it was a true courtship, I never bothered to find out, as Keegan and I had fallen in love and that was all that mattered. That, and, the South never contested my betrothal to him.

"I suspect that Keegan slipped on his correspondence with her shortly after we met," I said, giving Keegan a small smile.

Keegan quickly noted the change in my complexion. "I apologize, Your Highness. With everything that has happened, it's foolish that she slipped from my thoughts. How is Lady Ja...Jameela?"

My stomach tightened as Keegan faltered on her name. Kamal Zaman blinked. "She is well, Your Grace," he said slowly. "Your invitation to her betrothal celebration must have burned in the devastating fire."

"Yes, that must be what happened," I said dryly, and with relief.

"No matter," Kamal said, just as quickly. "The betrothal was called off when her intended was found with an unfortunate amount of Race in his possession."

"A distasteful turn of events. Perhaps a better match is on the horizon," I said.

"Perhaps," Kamal agreed, with a smile.

As this round of pleasantries had naturally reached a lull, Bidelia took a limping step forward and bowed. "If you would follow me, Your Highness, I will personally show you to your quarters. Is this the entirety of your delegation?"

"It is, aside from the servants," Kamal said, gesturing dismissively towards the exterior of the castle. I wondered how many more mouths we'd have to feed. "Unfortunate that more of my blood could not join me. Not that they would enjoy travelling with an old man as much as they would with say, two lively Westerners with a taste for adventure. You will tell us your story over dinner, I hope." He eyed the Silver Spear with great interest.

Just how much of our adventure had reached his ears? Surely he knew that I had killed Leszek, even if it was just an accident. Was he afraid of suffering the same fate?

"That can be arranged," Bidelia said carefully. "Once you've had adequate time to rest, Your Highness, we hope you will join us. We have prepared a full itinerary to keep you entertained during your stay."

Kamal leaned on his staff as his condescending amusement grew. He regarded Bidelia as if she was a child. "Hmm. Much appreciated. However, as I requested, let us be informal. I realize that your situation is...dire. It took only a ride down your main streets to see that. Therefore, I will dispense with the usual ceremonies and get right to the point. You require supplies and military aid because of your…skirmish…with the East? And the North." He smiled wryly at me. "In short, we are prepared to help you. Providing you agree to help us."

"And how might we do that?" Keegan asked.

"Hmm. Well. There is no delicate way to put this, so you must excuse my lack of decorum. We had tentative betrothals with the East for many of my progeny, but as High King Leszek is dead, and their caravans have stopped being pleasingly full, I am forced to look elsewhere.

"In response to the West's desperate request for aid, the South humbly asks for the hand of Keegan Tramore in marriage."

"He is already married. To me," I said, gripping the Spear tighter.

Kamal's smug smile twisted into a grin. "That remains to be seen, doesn't it? Literally, as some bards told it, Prince Keegan Tramore and the Violet Fox were married in the mountains, with only Dashiell or whatever Freetor gods you have as witness. Surely you know, that means nothing to the South."

"Well, it means something *here*, in this province," I retorted.

"Hmm," Kamal said noncommittedly. "What do you say, Your Grace? You let your non-royal consort-wife speak for you?"

Enraged, I pressed the butt of the Spear into the stone. How dare he speak to me that way? Bidelia subtly gripped the underside of my arm, warning me to control my anger.

Keegan retained his cool. He even smiled. "She isn't wrong, Your Highness. You are asking me to break a contract. Some consider marriage the most important commitment in life."

The High King bowed his head in respect. "I am glad you appreciate the weight of the arrangement, Your Grace. If you are worried about the perception of such a…breach of contract…we can ensure that any records of your agreement with the Violet Fox are expunged. Or officially annulled, if that is your wish. It is not uncommon in the South for lords and ladies to make mistakes in their youth."

"I am not a *mistake*," I spat.

"The South is speaking with the Holy One, now," Kamal said, in a tone laced with warning.

Hon'niz sniffed and guffawed, and I fixed him with a spiteful glare that made him think twice. He covered his mouth lightly in an attempt to regain his composure. Omju looked embarrassed and Danyal smiled. Her fingers twitched; I recognized the itch to fight, as I felt it, too.

Desperate to keep the peace, Bidelia said, "Who is it that His Highness has in mind as an appropriate match?"

"Ah. Hmm. With that, we are flexible. Lady Na'ima, you are already acquainted with, and she is quite fond of His Holiness. My youngest son, Lord Jorju'dun is also unmarried. They are both close to Your Grace's age. And as I mentioned, my granddaughter, Lady Jameela, is now available to be wed. Whatever pleases the Tramore line the most. Any details about lineage and inheritance of land can be discussed in a more formal setting. What matters is the immediate request, does it not?"

He knew we were desperate. He could ask for whatever he wanted, and unless we gave it to him, our people would starve and the North and the East would gobble us up. But if we gave him Keegan…even if he still ruled here in the West, as the Holy One, no doubt the South would have one hand deep in Keegan's pockets and the other resting on his rightful throne.

Kamal surveyed our silence with another smug look. "Hmm. I can see you have a great deal to consider," he said. He tapped his staff-cane lightly into the stone once more. "Perhaps, Advisor Mullen, I will see my rooms now. I will give you until the day after next to make a decision. Dinner and entertainment will not be expected until then. You deserve time to make a good showing. The South ends their informality."

"Not a word," Bidelia whispered as she released me.

I levelled the High King with an unrelenting glare that he ignored. As he brushed past me, his silky train and his staff became caught with the Spear, and instead of wrenching it away, he stopped. Without a word, Danyal bent down and freed the fabric from our crossed staffs.

As Kamal began to move again, his large golden sleeves angled in such a way that I caught the flash of a bright blue glow on his wrist. I breathed sharply inward. Only Freetor magic glowed in such a way. It appeared to be emanating from a beaded bracelet. It was faint, so I had not noticed it beneath the fabric, but at this proximity, it was all I could see. Whatever magical properties it possessed, it was probably harmless, yet my palms felt warmer all the same just thinking about the possibilities.

The Southern delegation continued down the corridor after Bidelia, and as I watched and listened to their echoing conversation, my rage grew. Hon'niz requested loudly that a fire be crafted at once in his room, for the "northern" climate was already "getting to him." Bidelia was trying to explain how they were welcome to what we had, though we were trying to be frugal, given the circumstances. Hon'niz and Omju began to complain and Kamal, once again, made a loud dismissive sound.

What arrogant, selfish…!

I slammed the Spear into the stone, which sent a shock of lightning up my arm. I recoiled from the artefact, yet managed to save it from clattering to the floor at the last moment. The lightning momentarily numbed my senses, yet I felt no pain or adverse affects. On the contrary, I felt more clear-headed than ever.

Keegan was too busy watching the High King and his delegation to notice the bit of stray magic. It was best to keep it that way for now, until I figured out how to control it. Or eventually—rid myself of it.

As Bidelia lead the way around a corner, the three young Southern nobles diligently in tow, Kamal dared to turn his head towards me. Though I couldn't make out his expression, I felt like he was goading me. Danyal looked inquisitively to him. He shook his head, and together they strode deeper into the castle.

My gaze narrowed.

Had he seen the lightning crawl up my arm?

The servants who had opened the doors had disappeared. I jerked the heavy handles and the castle door creaked free. Squinting against the cold and the sunlight once more, my eyes adjusted just as two carriages drove out of sight around the castle, presumably towards the stables. I spotted two servants accounting for the luggage atop the carriage, one footman on the lead carriage, and another servant driving the second. Luggage and supplies had been expertly strapped to the top of both, and through the pulled curtains of the second I spotted unmistakable, boxy shadows. Not another soul scurried in the cool exterior. Only a single Roamer, standing guard beside the door, dared to look my way and nod in greeting. I listened carefully. Only the sound of the Southern carriages rolling over gravel reached me; there were no other carts or traffic coming up the mountain. Given what I knew about the South, two carriages seemed light for three nobles, the High King, and their servants—especially when one carriage was filled to the brim with supplies.

"The Southern delegation, was that all they had?" I asked the Roamer, pointing after the carriages.

"Yes, Fox," the Roamer replied, and then noted my circlet and noble attire, and seemed to think better of her answer. "Your Highness? Yes, Your Highness."

The corners of my lips twitched upward as I shut the heavy door, though just staring down the dreary hallway, and Keegan's helpless expression as he gazed upon me, weighted my spirits once more. The South could not be trusted.

"Well," Keegan said, trying to appear light. "How often do I get a marriage proposal as part of a negotiation?"

"Never," I replied sourly, and started down the corridor. "I'm getting out of here."

"Hey. Wait!" Keegan called, and followed me.

I sighed. I didn't mean I was leaving the castle, but I was too angry to form a cohesive explanation. I headed for my chamber.

It was the only place I trusted to be myself, and not some pleasing version of a royal or the Violet Fox.

I threw open the chamber door so hard it banged against the wall. I threw the Spear on the bed and, noticing one of the servants had changed the sheets and fluffed the pillows, I grabbed one and threw it to the ground. It was not as satisfying as throwing something hard and heavy. I picked it up and threw it again, this time across the chamber, towards the vanity. It landed on the wood and tumbled to the floor.

My hands tingled warmly. I made them into fists. There was power in there, something primal that wanted to be released, if I'd just *let* it.

Keegan shut the door carefully and remained at the entrance to the room, giving me a wide berth. In fact, I was surprised he was still here.

"Do you want me to give you a moment?" he asked.

I stared at my palms. I'd always had trouble containing and expressing my anger. My father had tried to help me. Maybe that's why he taught me to journal, all those years ago, to put my feelings on magical paper instead of out in the world. Now that journal was at the bottom of the God Tears. A worthy offering to a man-god that no longer listened or cared or appreciated that he'd witnessed our marriage.

"Kamal is an arrogant bastard, isn't he?" I muttered under my breath. "He thinks he can come in here and demand whatever he likes, just because he's High King of the South. Obviously he's been ruling for a long time. And…he's soft, and…his stupid nobles make stupid demands…" I was running out of awful things I felt comfortable saying out loud in front of Keegan, and he knew it. The tingling in my hands dissipated. "I don't know how you're so…calm! How are you not fuming right now?"

"You think I'm not angry, just because I don't threaten or interrupt or throw things?" Keegan replied. "I am not calm. I am…

frightened. Confused. *Worried.* Angry, yes. Of course. Feelings aside, we need to come up with an appropriate counter-offer."

I scoffed. The counter-offer should have been, goodbye High King Kamal, go find yourself another groom for your calculated grab at power. Who knew what he was doing, skulking around the border? He was up to something. I'd felt it the moment he walked in the door, hadn't I?

"So," Keegan prompted. "I have some ideas, but if you have any...?"

"Everything is a transaction to him," I said. "He bought the East and the North at the blockade, and he's trying to buy us now. If we could just fool him into..."

The scene played out in my mind. Keegan in the Cathedral of Dashiell, with a faceless Southern woman. Then, I run in. I stop the wedding.

But I'd done that already. Maybe if we did it again, it would trigger Keegan's memory...but no. I put myself back in that moment, when I'd exposed my identity to him for the first time. What if I'd said nothing? What if he had married Sylvia? He'd still be safe. Yes, Dominique would be a problem, but I would have handled her privately. We wouldn't be in this war, I would have gone back to being the Violet Fox or dead from my impersonation, and Keegan would still be himself.

Now, Keegan had a second chance at a regular, royal life. Keegan could have a better marriage with another, here in the castle, or in the South, if that was the arrangement. He would gain the South's support and perhaps the West could finally beat the North and the East back to their rightful cardinal directions. I could remain as part of the council...but of course, I wouldn't. I wouldn't be able to stand seeing him with another, even if he would be happier with someone else.

"I don't know," I said finally.

"You can't be considering this," Keegan said. "I've just learned you are married to me, now you want to marry me to someone else!"

"Of course I'm not considering it." And yet, I couldn't shove it from my mind. "Our marriage is real! I will not barter my husband to a stranger in exchange for…" The words died on my lips. *For peace.* It would keep my people safe.

All I'd have to give up is my love.

The love who no longer knew my name.

He sensed my hesitation. "They don't know our province like we do. Like…you do. We can't let them in, no matter how noble their intentions. And besides…I don't want to marry someone I don't love."

I pursed my lips. He'd loved me once. How could he love me now? He was staring at me again and I averted my gaze, my cheeks flaming.

"There has to be another option. Something we can offer them. Bidelia must have an idea or two," I muttered. I started towards the door. I couldn't be alone with him anymore, especially not in my chamber, where he had kissed me before he knew my real name. Not when he wasn't *my* Keegan, and may never be again.

"Kiera." The way he called me, so soft and deliberate. My feet slid and scuffed on the floor, unable to move further. Suppressing a sigh, I wiped at my eyelashes and balled my hands into fists just to steel myself to face him.

But he wasn't staring at me anymore. He was tracing his good forefinger along the vanity, pacing thoughtfully around the room. "I've been reading up on Marlenian law from what tomes survived in the library, and from what has been recently restored. Also I may have had some discreet conversations with the few scholars and scribes that have remained inside the castle walls. There's the Firstchild Custom, in which a ruling couple promise their first-born, even an unborn eldest child, to another kingdom to secure a future alliance."

My cheeks felt hot once more. "We haven't even been…" Nope.

I wouldn't go there. His gaze snapped to mine in surprise. "We've been very busy. Our marriage ceremony was... There were no witnesses. But you already knew that. Anyway." Why couldn't I just shut up? "I won't discuss future, unborn children when we don't even know how we're going to survive the next few days, much less months or years. What if you have no children? Or what if you don't want them? Are you obligated to, because of a promise you made under duress?"

"Why are you saying *you* and not *we?*" he asked.

My shoulders sank. I had promised him I'd be honest. "What if you never get your memories back? What if you choose not to be with me?"

"Kiera." He drew nearer to me, and took my hands in his. My knees shook. This was the first time since he'd woken that he'd deliberately reached for me. "I won't know what to choose if we don't try to get to know each other. Again."

It wasn't really him. My Keegan was gone. He wasn't coming back. This was someone new, with my Keegan's voice and his face and his dreams and morals.

How could I allow myself to be vulnerable to a stranger?

"All right," was all I could say. I took a deep breath. "I...suppose promising firstborns and the like to the South when we can't even feed our own people is foolhardy."

"Agreed," he said. "So that's out. What else do we have that they could possibly want?"

Difficult to think when his touch consumed much of my thoughts. I closed my eyes. "Leon. Leon Frostfire. Sylvia's brother, the one we have in the dungeons."

"Is he valuable?" He released my hands and looked pensive.

I took a deep breath as the warmth of his hands faded from mine. "Not really." I wasn't entirely comfortable with letting him out of the deep, dark dungeons, regardless of how the South felt about the Frostfire family. Leon Frostfire had a reputation for being quick to anger, anti-Freetor, and also, someone who was overly fond of drink and didn't know the meaning of the word *no*. He and I had had multiple run-ins while I was pretending to be a servant just weeks ago. He deserved to rot in the dungeon for a while longer.

Keegan had already moved on. "Do we have any silver? Bidelia had mentioned a treasury."

"I'm not sure what we have, though with the number of times the castle has been attacked and looted the past month, I doubt we have much." Some of it I'd have to set aside for the Roamers—yet another loose end to tie up. Once Bidelia sent out a bulletin about the Midnight Tablet reward, well, that was another expense as well, if it came to it. "The South might take our silver or other equivalent valuables, but if they wanted that, they would deal with the East. They are far richer than the West, always have been. Or at least, that's the perception." More than one person had let on to me that the Frostfire family may not be as wealthy as everyone had been led to believe.

"There is someone else we could offer," I continued quietly. "Myself."

Keegan raised an eyebrow. "You? But you are not of royal blood. I mean, not that that matters to *me*." He cleared his throat awkwardly. "I mean, despite the name you've made for yourself and the loyalty you inspire here, not to offend you, but why would the South take you over Leon, for example?"

"Like you said. I have loyalty. People do follow me. It would free you. If that's what you wanted."

"You do seem to be under the impression that that's what I want," he said, concerned.

"I'm just trying to give you options." I shook my head. This was going all wrong. I'd barely slept and now Keegan and I were alone, finally...and yet he still didn't know me. He may never know me again.

I wrapped my fingers around the door handle, and just before I could yank it open, I felt him behind me. I gripped it tighter, yet I didn't move.

"I don't want options," Keegan said quietly. "Do you?"

As I shook my head, my curls brushed against my bare neck. "I just want things to be like they were. Before magic. But...different, too." Too many people were dead that could have been alive, if only I'd ignored my father and resisted the urge to go after the Silver Spear.

"I don't know how to change the past. I don't know how things were before. I only know about now. Do you accept me now, as I am?"

I shifted and glanced over my shoulder. Keegan, with his dark curls, bright and distinct yellow-green eyes, and the scar on his lips. I reached for it, and this time, he didn't recoil. Gently, I ran a finger over his lips and the scar I'd created during our first meeting, and I scolded my past self for believing he could ever be ugly or undesirable to me.

Was he still my Keegan, even if he didn't remember his past? *Our* past? His life had been more than just me. Could we really be together again, and have it be as before, after all we have been through?

"I don't know," I said, allowing my hand to fall away.

He breathed a deep sigh. "At least it's an honest answer."

I nodded, feeling my throat tighten. "I've always done what is best for my people. You were the only part of my life that I chose for myself. And when you woke up, not knowing me... it was like you had died. It's like I'm standing here, waiting for you to come back to me...when I know that there's a good chance you never will."

The tears loosed from me then, and I silently crumbled into him, but he was there, ready to take me in his arms. He held me when he didn't have to, whispering silently into my hair as I mourned the

Keegan I had lost, and pressed against the Keegan I had with me, here and now.

** * **

The rest of the day passed in a flurry of incidents that, fortunately, I didn't have to manage. Bidelia had her hands full with the three Southern nobles and keeping track of their flock of servants. She couldn't peg down the exact number in the caravan—three? Seven? Some of them expected to sleep in the stables, which I didn't understand. Others were directed to the appropriate servants' quarters by the kitchen and were promptly assigned tasks, such as cleaning, cooking, and sorting that evening's rations.

After our conversation, Keegan had kissed my hand chastely and left my chamber. I had closed the door and lay against it for what felt like hours, silently sobbing and giggling. I must have crawled into bed at some point, for I woke to a servant shaking my shoulders gently to offer me some tea.

As High Queen, I wasn't expected to manage my guests' stays on a personal level, though I did make a point to sleuth around the entirety of the west wing, where guests traditionally stayed. No part of the castle was restricted for me now. The servants scurrying around to serve our guests and the one Roamer guard patrolling the area questioned my activities with their gaze, but said nothing. I could no longer sneak around like I used to. I was High Queen. My business was my own. That didn't mean they wouldn't gossip about it in the evening. I tried kept my pace to a leisurely stroll. None of our guests were out in the corridor, and as all their rooms were closed, I assumed they were resting or had taken Bidelia's offer of a tour. When I was alone in the corridor, I listened at Kamal's door.

The urge to search his room overwhelmed me. Between his magic-imbued bracelet and the Zaman family's predilection for collecting priceless artefacts and manuscripts, I wondered what else Kamal Zaman had brought with him from Xii. Checking the corridor once more, I tried the door. Locked. I stared at the keyhole, wondering if I had it in me to blacken it, to use magic the supposed magic within…

No. I backed away, into the wall. Magic was not for petty thievery.

And yet, I felt something within reply: *It could be.*

The servants returned to the hallway, and once I saw they were still cleaning Kamal's room, I hurried away. I had missed my chance on that one—today.

Although invited to the cathedral during the evening ration distribution (which I heard some folk call "the rationing" and "the birdfeed" but also "the ration ceremony" among the pious), High King Kamal sent word via Danyal that he would not be attending. To Bidelia and me, this was a relief. I suspected the journey had tired him, for other than a brief tour of the castle, he too had rarely left his quarters. Both Danyal and Omju had opted to go as representatives, and while Keegan and I shared a carriage ride down the mountain with them, Omju opened up about their journey north to the capital.

"His Highness is young in spirit," Omju explained as we traversed the bumpy dirt road. "Enjoys the adventure on the road. Was invited to guide the esteemed families through the…less travelled…regions of the South to make the journey smoother. An honour for Omju to be included. Then—" Danyal fixed him with a glare that halted his story. He cleared his throat. "Then, received an invitation to Marlenia City. Another honour."

My gaze narrowed at Danyal. Why had she silenced her fellow noble?

"Strange," I said to both of them, "that when the Roamers first approached your caravan about the passing on our aid request, that they didn't mention that the High King was travelling with you. Only Lord Hon'niz identified himself as a Zaman to them."

"That is not strange," Danyal replied icily. "Would His Grace not disguise his presence when travelling across the land?" She gestured to Keegan, sitting quietly beside me. "The Violet Fox sees only deceit, because she knows it well."

Omju looked more uncomfortable. I tried to keep control of my anger. "And why, Lady Danyal, were you invited on this exciting road adventure?"

Her fingertips grazed the curtain hiding the evening view of the capital. "Is not uncommon for His Highness to require aid from the Nimra family, Violet Fox. Adventure can lead to trouble." Her voice was gravelly and barely louder than a whisper.

"We know that firsthand," I replied, just as coolly. "How long were you planning on...adventuring...before you received our invitation?"

Danyal shrugged nonchalantly. "One does not question the whims of the High King. One only ensures he is kept safe." Her dark gaze met mine then. There was a warning there: *your questions will bring trouble.*

I continued anyway. "I couldn't help but notice you brought two carriages. Seems light for a potentially long journey. Seems like the High King and his esteemed nobles would travel the provinces with somewhat more supplies, no?"

Omju pursed his lips. He knew something, yet in Danyal's presence, he was unlikely to speak up. I stole a glance at his boots; they were even dirtier than this morning. He had explored the grounds, no doubt, but Danyal had also been out and about, and her footwear was pristine.

"A rude assumption, Violet Fox." She spat my street name with all the filth she could muster. "Perhaps the rat should keep her prying eyes inside the castle, instead of—"

"You will not address the High Queen of Marlenia in that manner," Keegan said forcefully.

He had inadvertently held out his hand, and their attention had been captured—by his missing finger. He wasn't wearing his gloves. Quickly, Keegan retracted it and continued, "Apologize."

"Apologies," Danyal said coolly, unable to remove her gaze from his hands. "Though if His Grace wishes his people to have full bellies and peaceful homes here in the capital, *she* will not be High Queen for long."

My gaze narrowed at her. "We'll see about that."

"Yes, the Lady will," she replied rancorously.

During the rationing, our relations did not improve. Omju nervously paced by the entrance, frequently opening and closing the cathedral doors, as if afraid our carriage and horse would be stolen. Like an alley cat, Danyal skulked the perimeter of the pews, and the citizens of Marlenia City gave her a wide, fearful berth. She watched my people with interest, unabashedly eavesdropping on the Roamers' conversations near the front of the cathedral, perking up with curiosity whenever Keegan addressed a stranger, and scowling in disgust when filthy commoners blocked her patrol. Bidelia worked hard to keep our people in an orderly line, directing them to Keegan and I as we dished out today's rations, and ensuring they proceeded to a pew far away from Danyal.

I didn't like this one bit. And neither did my people. I saw it in their faces, as Keegan and I served them, and as Bidelia tried to pretend nothing was out of the ordinary, I wanted to confess everything. Some proud Westerners didn't want to accept the help of the South. They loudly protested the Southern woman's presence—why wouldn't we throw her out? Why was she there? Was she supposed to be someone important? Why is the South eating our food and enjoying the luxuries of the capital while they had to live in squalor?

Then they'd look to me. And again, I had to bite my tongue.

"The South will only be here for another few days," I told a woman and her young son as I handed out the stale bread, browned fruit, and an empty mug for the meager soup—today's portioned meal.

"They shouldn't be here at all," she replied. "You of all people should know how to fix this."

I took it to heart—because she was right. I did know how to fix it. I could use the Spear to freeze them all and flee on my own adventure to find the Tablet. But I'd made a promise, to Keegan and my friends. I would remain and try to solve this the old-fashioned way. Because magic only made everything worse.

Yet nothing we were doing seemed to be making anything better.

"No. She's right," Keegan muttered beside me. He was in charge of the soup, which was mostly broth. "Lady Danyal."

My eyes widened as his voice rang across the din of the cathedral. "Keegan. What are...?"

Danyal, hearing the authority in his voice, reluctantly turned to face the young Holy One and regarded him indignantly. "Yes, His Grace?"

He lifted the ladle from the massive pot of soup, inadvertently flicking droplets onto the altar, and held it out to the Southern noblewoman. "It's your turn."

She parted her lips to protest in jest—because I was suppressing a laugh—and then she realized Keegan was serious. Those before her parted a path towards Keegan and the serving station. The woman I'd just served, her face lit up in delight. Her son mirrored her expression, and all the children around him shared in the satisfaction of the illicit payback. A few started cheering and broken applause broke out throughout the cathedral. Danyal, seeing her choice was to disobey an order from the Holy One—in a cathedral, no less—or suffer embarrassment, chose the latter. She fixed me especially with a fuming look as she gingerly wrenched the ladle from an amused Keegan. I gave the noblewoman space as she, to her credit, scooped the broth deftly into the remaining bowls and mugs for the waiting commoners.

Keegan had always been a popular prince, but this kind of mischievous justice had tickled the masses on this night, and for a moment, I forgot our troubles—and the people did, too.

THE FOLLOWING MORNING, Bidelia sent word that she'd like to meet me in the council room. After the servants shoved me into a tight-fitting blue dress, I arrived to find Keegan and Bidelia deep in conversation around the table.

They both stood. "Good morning, Kiera," Bidelia said with a small smile.

"Morning," I replied. I glanced behind me, expecting others to join us. But Laoise and Monju were long gone. They wouldn't have reached Xii yet, but likely they'd be traversing the coastline. Assuming nothing had happened to them.

Keegan inclined his head in greeting. His forehead bore the gem-inlaid circlet, as it had the previous day, though his attire was simpler: a white flowing tunic, tight trousers, and a button-up blue vest. Once again, we matched. I tried to hide a smile.

Bidelia narrowed her gaze suspiciously. "You look unrested, Kiera."

My cheeks heated and I stared awkwardly at the floor, attempting to hide my embarrassment. I'd spent part of the night wandering the castle, trying to walk myself into a sleeping stupor. I'd passed by Keegan's chamber six times, hoping he'd hear me. He was probably asleep. I'd tried to sneak into Kamal Zaman's chamber once more as well—until I spotted Danyal patrolling that stretch of corridor. I wasn't sure if she'd seen me. I'd thought it best to return to my quarters at that point. Her behaviour the previous night at the cathedral had left a sour taste in my mouth and I'd been unable to corner Omju to get answers about their unusual caravan—mostly because, *his* room seemed strangely unoccupied.

"Antony isn't joining us?" I asked as I took a seat across from Keegan.

"No," she replied. "I've asked him to entertain the High King this morning. Kamal Zaman expressed an interest in Feenagh Forest and so Pascal took him and two of the nobles to the outskirts to see if they can catch any game for tonight's dinner."

Her tone suggested it was a longshot, but tonight was the South's final night with us. Kamal wanted an answer to his proposal by tomorrow, soon after which, they would depart. Presumably. I didn't know how long our supplies would hold out if he had to entertain them longer than that. There was probably some game left in Feenagh Forest at this time of year, though much of it had probably been hunted by the lords of the surrounding bailes in preparation for winter.

"Only two of the nobles went? What about the third?" Keegan asked.

I smiled at his cleverness. "Lady Danyal is the one to watch. I could barely follow her yesterday. Do we know what she's been up to?"

"The apprentices say she left the castle at one point and walked down the mountain, into the city. She returned some hours later, with nothing. There are some enterprising merchants selling their wares, just to put on a good show for the South, but in general, it's a hungry mob down there and it's only going to get worse if we don't resolve this quickly." Bidelia leaned back in her chair. "Otherwise, this is standard noble conduct. I'm not unaccustomed to demanding, selfish behaviour. They can do what they like, as far as I'm concerned, so long as they don't put either of you in direct danger."

"If they pose a threat, I'll handle them," I said. "But um,

speaking of danger—did you put out word?"

"Word? Oh. The Midnight Tablet." Bidelia waved a dismissive hand. "I haven't had a moment yet, but I will, once the South is dealt with."

My gaze narrowed. I'd asked her, what, two days ago? "It has to be found. We need every advantage."

"I'm sorry, what is this?" Keegan asked.

"I asked Bidelia to have word spread and official announcements drawn up about...possibly...offering a reward for the return of the Midnight Tablet." Explaining it made me feel naïve.

"What kind of reward?" Keegan asked suspiciously.

"It's just silver. Some silver." I curled my hands into fists. I shouldn't have brought it up. I knew they wouldn't understand. I'd agreed to stay here and aid my people from the castle, without resorting to magic, and now I was making myself the fool. "Fine. We can talk about it after the South have gone."

Keegan and Bidelia exchanged glances. I knew their looks well. They thought I was overreacting. Using the crown's silver for my own ends—was it really *her* silver? Keegan was probably thinking. He was right. And yet, I would give all of it to retrieve the one thing that could restore him to his former self.

Bidelia decided not to pursue the matter further. "So. Thoughts on the South's offer?"

"The marriage is not reasonable," Keegan said firmly, looking me at me squarely. "We've discussed other options. Trading the prisoner, Leon? Might be our most sailable offer."

I hadn't seen Leon since our return. I felt strange trading his life and freedom—but it was him or Keegan. The way I saw it, Leon didn't deserve his freedom. He had to earn it back to pay for the terrible things he'd done.

Bidelia looked uncertain. "I suppose we could. It's not as if the East will be any more furious with us. I'm not sure it equates to a marriage to the Holy One."

"Yet it could be a door into East for the South," I pointed out. "Boris is their High King. Or emperor. Or whatever he wishes to call himself, but in our eyes, he is High King. If Boris dies without an heir, Leon is his successor."

"All the more reason to keep him," Bidelia replied sternly. "Despite him being an annoying bastard."

She had a point. Boris had no children that I was aware of. He'd only been married to Dominique for, what, a fortnight? If he fell in the coming days or months, Leon would be his successor to the Eastern throne, and in that scenario, we could trade Leon's freedom for peace.

I shook my head. "I don't know if we can deal with maybes and what-ifs. Besides, if the South does install Leon as High King of the East in any circumstance, I doubt he'd inspire his people to fight for him or prove a challenge for us. He's our most valuable asset right now, despite the risk, whether we like it or not."

Our most valuable asset, besides me, I wanted to say. Or, for that matter, the apprentices. I shivered, unwilling to think about Kamal kidnapping them for his own personal use.

Keegan looked thoughtful. "We have until tomorrow to finalize the deal?"

"Yes, but the sooner we tell them our decision, the sooner our people can be fed and our fears about the East allayed, somewhat. So if you have something concrete, propose it tonight." Bidelia smoothened her long coat and looked to me. "A meager but entertaining dinner this evening should help charm them, so long as we present something favourable. I suspect they are hoping for a reply then, so they have a reason to celebrate or lick their wounds."

"Can we spare the supplies?" I asked.

"If we don't, we might not secure the alliance," Keegan said.

"That's right," Bidelia said. She stood. "That's all I wanted to know, really, if you'd come to any conclusions or needed my perspective. Be prepared to offer Leon in addition to the promise of valuables or silver. We don't have much, but regular payments could be arranged with interest. Your father was a shrewd man, Your Grace. I feel he respected High King Kamal, though I cannot say how the South felt about him. Use that to your advantage. Even though I know your memory is not what it was"—Keegan fidgeted—"do not hesitate to massage the truth in this area. Tell him about your father, Eamon Tramore. Ask the High King for stories. They may have a history you don't know about. He has visited this city multiple times throughout his long reign. Use that to your advantage. I imagine the South will do what it can to preserve its alliance with the West, if it knows what's best."

"Thank you. I appreciate your advice," Keegan said kindly, standing to face her. "Yet you're assuming that I will be the only one communicating the offer to him. Is that the case?"

"He doesn't see me as an equal. You must have noticed," I said. "We can present the offer together, but he'll likely want to discuss details with you." This was fine with me. I preferred to observe the High King from afar and gauge his movements than have to speak with His Imperious Majesty again.

Keegan let out a slow sigh. "I'll do my best."

"That's all we can do." Bidelia started for the door. "Don't go too far today, whatever it is you're planning. We're doing rations earlier than sunset to free up the evening, and then you'll need time in your respective chamber to don respectable outfits. And no, Kiera, what you're wearing is not good enough, and I don't want to hear further complaints about it."

I supressed a grin. "Bidelia," I said, before she could escape us. "Are there still some bluesberry wine stores left? Or any kind of drink?"

"I believe the Frostfires brought some, and yes, there's a few bottles left of the Tramore family wine." She narrowed her gaze as her hand rested on the doorknob. "Why?"

"Let it flow freely at the dinner tonight."

Bidelia didn't inquire further, but nodded, intuiting correctly that I was working on a plan that I wasn't yet prepared to share.

As she hurried out of the room, a flock of servants descended upon her. She towed them down the hallway with loud requests and hurried orders. I realized once again she had directed us. She had arranged the dinner. She knew more about the Southern delegation's movements within the castle—because she was the Advisor, and that was her duty.

I was supposed to be High Queen. Keegan held the title of ruler of the land, but I was an equal in the eyes of most of our subjects. Yet what had I done these past few days, besides assuage the fear of starvation for *some*? Meanwhile, Laoise and Monju and others had ventured into the unknown to retrieve the one artefact that could save us all...

Keegan interrupted my thoughts. "Were you going to mention to me the reward for the Midnight Tablet...or...?"

I sighed. "It was just an idea. I hoped that if more people went looking for it, the faster it could be found."

"You can...tell me when you have *ideas*," Keegan said gently. "Not that you need my permission, I just want to know what you're thinking. What you're planning. I don't want to be caught unaware. Especially in front of Bidelia."

I looked away. Although I could sympathize with his position, he was just afraid I'd run away and leave him here to govern this skeleton of a castle himself. "Sorry. Next time I have an...idea... I'll make sure you know about it."

"Good. Thank you. On that note...if you're planning to ply the South with wine, does that mean we should keep our minds clear?"

"It might not be a bad idea," I replied with the barest of smiles. We strode together out of the council room and down the hallway with no particular destination. "If we propose an unfavourable deal, I'd rather have them celebrating or drowning their sorrows properly, and carry them to bed, rather them…well, awake during the night to kidnap you."

"I thought that was Sylvia Frostfire's plan," Keegan replied wryly.

"Yes, it was, wasn't it?" I laughed and rolled my eyes. I'd nearly forgotten about her floral note. As if she could successfully pull off such a heist, even with the help of her loyal bodyguard. "It's within the South's power to whisk you away in the night. We can't be too careful."

"If any mysterious shadows grab me from my blankets, I'll put up a fight," he said, smiling.

I mirrored his grin. "Good to know."

* * *

Bidelia arranged our post-negotiation dinner on the balcony that evening. While smaller than the throne room or any other hall within the castle, I hoped the chilly evening air and the view of the gardens below would distract from our meager offerings. We hadn't yet thrown a dinner or a gathering for our Southern guests, which was highly unusual as far as royal etiquette was concerned.

The last dinner party I'd attended on the balcony, I was playing the part of Rorda Cloth, servant to Linnaea Gareth, played expertly by Laoise. I'd nearly died at Dominique's hand because of my clumsiness and indiscretion. I hoped this event would go more smoothly. At least I was only attended as myself as High Queen of Marlenia tonight.

My personal maidservants had worked tirelessly to conform yet another outfit for the occasion, as it was unfitting for the High Queen to wear the same design twice in one visit, even if I wasn't the one doing the visiting. This dress fell off the shoulders, which meant I couldn't lift my arms higher than my chin. Lace formed a loose sleeve, which fell gracefully around my elbows. The dark, vertically striped bodice dug into my ribs and forced curves into my otherwise pole-like figure. I shone with the moonlight in the pale violet, shimmering fabric that trailed behind me as I strolled onto the balcony. I used the Spear, my trusted walking staff and constant companion, to nudge the fabric out of the doorway. The Roamer guarding the entrance bowed in greeting and closed the door behind me.

I wanted to arrive first. I watched the servants haul and dress the tables and chairs—and they in turn watched me, warily. They probably thought I suspected them of some treachery. They had a Western look to them—darker hair, sun-kissed, freckled, and chattier than the Eastern servants I'd worked with. The Eastern servants I'd met while pretending to be one had scattered to the wind. If the servants traversing the balcony now were Eastern spies...arrogantly, I thought I would *know* if they were. Which, as I watched them set the table, made me more deeply suspicious of them.

What if the girls who dressed me each morning were reporting to someone other than Bidelia?

The warm tingle of the Spear's magic ran up my arm and swam through my body. There were enemies nearby. I felt them, yet I couldn't see their true form.

Stop. I slammed the Spear into the stone, startling the servants. Their innocent chatter halted. I had to get a hold of myself. My skin was ripe with gooseflesh. The castle was safe. My enemies wanted me and Keegan dead, it was true, but they had far better methods than to use servants to feed them information.

I was shaking my head of these dark thoughts as the balcony doors creaked open. Keegan appeared in the threshold. My mouth fell open. My servants weren't the only ones who had outdone themselves. His white sleeves billowed in the slight wind, tastefully contrasting with his textured black vest. His curls had been pulled away from his face and tied in a tight band. Dainty, white lined gloves covered his hands. From the stiffness in his right hand, I realized that the missing finger in the glove had been filled. A dark violet cape had been fastened with a silver chain, matching the gems in his circlet.

His gaze settled on me first and his step faltered. He drew his hands closer to his chest, covering one with the other. My face heated, though I approached him, and guided him further from the door, deeper onto the balcony. He didn't take his eyes from me, nor did he shy from my touch.

"You look very distinguished," I said.

"So do you," he replied. He pulled at his vest uncomfortably. "The servants pulled this from my wardrobe, though it feels like someone else's."

"It could be. Frostfire nobles left a lot of clothing behind when we rebelled. Almost everything I've been wearing used to be someone else's." I suspected the vest and much of his wardrobe was originally Keegan's—yet between his journey to the end of the world and his time as a frozen corpse, he had become slimmer. Even his face appeared gaunt. None of us were eating enough.

In a few minutes, that would all change.

"So. Leon. That's our offer," Keegan said, staring out at the empty balcony.

"Yeah." Trading Leon to the South was a gamble; it took the heat off the West, especially if we made it clear to the East that the South had Leon, and not us. Kamal would have to bargain with the East or keep Leon for their own purposes. Although Leon had been a burden to Boris, no doubt he wouldn't allow Leon to remain with the South for long.

"Do you think this will work? I don't feel...prepared. They may use Leon to trade with the East in exchange for a non-aggression agreement," Keegan pointed out. "Which would make their military aid pointless."

He really had been doing his research. "They could. But at least our people will be fed."

"Agreed," he said with a sigh. "Are you ready?"

I nodded. I had to make a good show for the South, yet the feeling of unease had returned. If they didn't accept our terms, not only would the East have succeeded in starving us out, but we'd be vulnerable to the South as well. They'd seen the state of our skeleton castle. They could easily team up with the North and the East and take us out before we'd have time to create an adequate defense. Magic would only get us so far, given the apprentices' cagey attitude and the Spear's limited range as a weapon.

You only need to kill one, said a deeper voice, somewhere within me.

Bidelia had arranged the finer details of the negotiation and dinner. Kamal would meet us on the balcony and we would propose our offer. Only when we completely agreed or disagreed on terms would the dinner be served and the rest of the castle residents be allowed to venture onto the balcony.

Staring out at the looming mountains beyond the capital, I couldn't help but feel watched.

Keegan didn't hate me. We were doing what we could to keep the city together.

And yet...

You aren't doing enough, said the voice within, and the Spear warmed and glowed brighter.

I quickly leaned over the railing and peered into the night. I saw a Roamer and a castle guard patrol together in the garden, resting for the winter ahead, beneath us. I listened for extra pairs of boots, or strange rustling, and squinted further into the darkness, hoping to see the glow of Freetor magic.

Nothing. Just a pleasant, albeit chilly evening in Marlenia City.

"Are you all right, Kiera?" Keegan asked, nearing me once more.

More servants arrived, this time carrying standing lanterns. They placed them around the balcony and the dinner table and lit them carefully. This simple act warmed me as the magic within had not, and some of the melancholy melted away.

"Yeah. Yes. I'm fine."

"You seem distracted. Are you sure? If you're not well, we can—"

"I'm all right," I said, too quickly. I pursed my lips and searched his caring face for understanding. "Just nerves."

"I also feel like I'm not going to be able to keep this dinner down," Keegan admitted, his gaze finding the balcony doors. "Let's just try to get through it. And then..." He cleared his throat, his cheeks filling with colour as he fixed me with his intense, yellow-green stare. "I was hoping you had time this evening to...talk."

My eyebrows lifted. "Talk?"

"Yes. Well. We're supposed to be married, and I feel like we haven't really spent any time together. I...went to your chamber again yesterday but you were gone. I know we both have duties, and I've been spending my time trying to learn as much as I can to appear half competent as the ruler of the entirety of the world...I just want to get to know you. Know you better, that is. In a respectable way." He shook his head. "I've gone on too much, haven't I?"

"No. And yes, I'd love to just talk. Spend time. Like before," I said, unable to supress a smile. "If the dinner doesn't run too late, or even if it does, that sounds...really lovely."

Keegan looked renewed. He glowed with confidence, and despite the chilly air and the sense of foreboding, I felt that perhaps I had the strength to see the night through.

The balcony doors opened and Bidelia emerged. She was wearing her blue coat again, buttoned up to her neck, accented with a silver scarf and broach. She quickly side-stepped to reveal High King Kamal Zaman.

The South was famous for its days-long festivals, its generosity, and its love of entertainment. As the embodiment of the South, Kamal took this seriously. I'd thought he was particularly well dressed when we'd met, but this was an official meeting of kings, where our people's fates would be sealed. He did not disappoint.

Similar to the golden silk he'd arrived in, he entered the balcony in a magnificent silver robe. Silver was the accepted colour of royalty, which Kamal was—though in the presence of the Holy One, the king of kings, it was far more acceptable for the High King to wear golden accents. This silver robe emulated the Holy One's ceremonial dress too well. It said, *I am chosen. My reign is ordained. You are not above me.* Each finger sported gold and silver rings with various gems, probably all real. Although he walked with the confidence of a man who ruled his own patch of dirt, he clutched his staff tightly, for he would fall without it.

He scrutinized the two of us and I touched my simple bodice, feeling extremely underdressed.

The three Southern nobles had also accompanied the king, shadowing him as he stepped luxuriously into the night. The tallest of them all, Hon'niz drew the eye with his pale-yellow blouse with an overly large collar, partially unbuttoned and half-tucked fashionably into his trousers. The trousers themselves cut off before the ankle, which may have been practical in the sunny South, but not here in the West, where our climate was not as friendly. A small gold and silver chain adorned his left ankle. I felt the chain was supposed to be ostentatious, yet I was reminded by the thousands of Freetors that had been enslaved and put in chains. His hair was once again pulled back into a respectable ponytail and although he looked like he had just rolled out of bed, he had the ease of someone who had been to a thousand diplomatic meetings and walked away with a desirable outcome.

Danyal wore a black, flowing one-piece, with translucent dark fabric flowing from the shoulder and the waist, creating the shadow of a fuller dress, yet allowing the wearer to retain full movement. I felt immediately jealous—given Danyal's attitude toward me, I accepted she would be unlikely to share her seamstress. She wore her hair high on her head in a loose bun, once again adorned with blue and dark pink beads.

Omju no longer looked like a stable boy in noble's clothing. He had saved his cleanest, pale pink shirt with gold button detailing and tight-fitting white trousers for the occasion. I even smelled a hint of floral perfume as he sauntered closer. His boots? Cleaner this evening—though traces of dirt remained. He deliberately avoided my gaze, seemingly under orders to remain silent, even now.

From what I'd been able to ply from the servants, Hon'niz rarely left his chamber. Reportedly he'd become enamoured with one of the Roamers. Omju spent time with the remaining horses in the stables and traversed the remnants of the hedge maze. And Danyal had been caught trying to explore the dungeons and had been promptly given a tour of something less exciting. I didn't like the idea of her conversing with our prisoners—especially Leon—or seeing the fate of the frozen. No doubt Kamal Zaman had encouraged them to roam free. Dinners and gatherings weren't the only place information and alliances were forged.

The nobles promptly surveyed the balcony, as if fearing an ambush. I swept the balcony with a discerning gaze once more. The servants who had dressed the table had disappeared, and not even a Roamer or castle guard stood over our proceedings. The negotiation would be witnessed by Bidelia, and the three Southern nobles, and no one else. My fingernails dug into my palms and I pressed the Spear into the stone. I wouldn't let them intimidate me. I had a right to be here. I was the Violet Fox. The High Queen of Marlenia. One by one, I greeted them with a determined stare.

"Good evening, Holy One," Kamal said, inclining his head to Keegan. The staff wobbled in his unsteady hand. He eyed me up and down and spared a glance at the Spear. "Violet Fox."

"Hello, Your Highness," I replied evenly. I wasn't about to let this old man treat me like I was beneath him. "I hope your visit has been pleasant."

"It has been," he replied, equally measured in his tone. "Have heard the Holy One has formulated an answer to the South's offer."

"We have, yes," Keegan replied, choosing his emphasis carefully. He inclined his head diplomatically. "I cannot in good conscience accept your offer of marriage. I apologize. This is not the answer you'd hoped to hear. You've travelled a great distance and we don't want to send you away empty-handed. Therefore, we have an alternate offer we'd like to discuss with you, if you'd be so gracious to hear it."

Kamal betrayed no hint of disappointment. "Unfortunate. The South will hear the West's counter-offer."

"Very well," Keegan replied. "For supplying the West with food, supplies, and military aid, the West offers our most valuable prisoner, Leon Frostfire. Second son to the now-deceased Leszek Frostfire, former High King of the East."

"Hmm. That is an offer the South did not expect." Hon'niz and Danyal also looked surprised, while Omju's eyebrows knitted in concern. Kamal regarded Keegan with renewed interest. "The West has Leon Frostfire secured in the depths of the dungeons? No doubt captured during the East's...*departure?*"

"No doubt," I replied dryly.

"Would have to see him. To ensure he is fit," Kamal said. *And legitimate*, was what was unsaid.

"That can be arranged," Keegan replied.

"Leon Frostfire is not Keegan Tramore," Kamal warned us, finally including me in the conversation with a leery stare.

"In addition, we are prepared to offer a smaller payment, to make up for the diminished value," I said.

"Hmm." Now he was intrigued. Kamal's gaze passed over me in an unsettling way as he angled his staff towards me. Once again, through his sleeves, I caught the unmistakeable glow of Freetor magic from a beaded bracelet. Did it serve some function? Or was it the afterglow of a previous owner, bought and worn without knowing the meaning?

I remembered the face cream my father had made to disguise

my features when we'd infiltrated the castle weeks ago. What if this bracelet had similar properties? He seemed like he was a king from the South, but what if he was an imposter?

I gripped the Spear tighter as he considered our request with due seriousness.

"The South tentatively accepts the West's offer. Happy to discuss the details of a smaller, *ongoing*, additional payment, so long as it's over dinner."

"Of course," Keegan replied. He gestured to Bidelia, who had lingered patiently at the doorway. "We can proceed. Initial terms have been accepted."

"Pleased to hear it, Your Grace," Bidelia replied, bowing. "I will inform the kitchen to begin bringing up the food immediately."

"Forgive the South, but these bones must rest," Kamal said, gesturing to the dressed table.

"Allow me to show you your seat, Your Highness," Keegan said politely.

As the High King trudged sluggishly toward the table, leaning more heavily now on his staff, Keegan leaned in and whispered to me, "That went better than I expected."

My eyebrows knitted, though I kept up a mask of extreme indifference. The High King appeared tired. Perhaps the long day in Feenagh Forest with Antony had been too much for the old man. "Too well. He must have known we'd say no."

"There is a lot at stake." He straightened his vest. "How do I look?"

"Princely," I replied.

He feigned disappointment. "Shouldn't I be kingly? Or perhaps...holy?"

"Don't push it. Good luck."

He grinned a reply as he hurried to the table and showed Kamal his place, just to the right of the head—Keegan's spot.

The three Southern nobles remained by me reluctantly, bound by decorum.

"I can escort you to your places, if you'd like?" I said to them.

"If Lady Kiera is offering, will tolerate her presence," Hon'niz replied.

"Good to know we're tolerating each other equally, then," I muttered into my arm as I gestured for him to lead the way.

Keegan and I sat on opposite ends of the table, to divide and conquer the task I least enjoyed: small talk with nobility. Hon'niz sat to my right. I had ensured that Omju sat to my left, to see what else I could learn about their mysterious journey. As Advisor to the Holy One, Bidelia enjoyed a spot to Keegan's left. Danyal settled in next to Kamal. There were four empty seats. One for Antony, who hadn't shown yet. Another I'd told Bidelia to save for Gobany. I'd sent a runner to invite him to dinner and received no reply. Third and fourth, empty seats and place settings in the middle of the table, because I had a fantasy of Laoise and Monju bursting through the balcony doors, holding up a large glowing granite tablet. Then the South would truly see what we were capable of.

The first course arrived without incident: rabbit and vegetable soup. Presumably made possible from their successful hunt today. The servants brought up the large pot and served it in shallow bowls from a side table. I hoped some of it had been made available during the rationing this evening. As I'd requested, the servants had also stacked a second side table with the rest of the wine from the cellars. Thirteen bottles of various vintages stared at us—likely enough to keep the South jolly throughout the evening and prevent any feelings of ill will. It was served in large goblets; embarrassingly deeper than the soup bowls.

Antony showed up halfway through the first course, dressed more spectacularly than I'd ever seen him. He sat next to Bidelia in the center of the table. He wore a dark shirt with cooper buttons and clean trousers. He made a show of removing his weapons at the table. When Kamal took interest, the Roamer showed off his swords and daggers to the High King, and regaled him with the stories of who he'd assassinated and traded with to acquire them. Bidelia was less than pleased to have such gruesome and inappropriate tales at the table, yet her disapproval of him turned to a small smile as he sat beside her.

All of us were hungry from the lack of proper meals; that didn't stop the nobles from consuming their food at a polite pace. The conversation occupied our minds and made us forget the lack of substantial vegetables and the sparse meat within the soup. At first, Antony took up the mantle, delighting the High King with some of the more humorous aspects of Roamer life: strange visitors who turned out to be castle guards poorly infiltrating their camp, uproar from Lord Paddon, who'd turned up naked at their makeshift camp in the middle of the night to drive the Roamers from his baile, and his time surviving in the Eastern deserts with no trousers and one satchel of wine.

While I tried to hide my amusement at his frighteningly large collection of stories involving him, his friends, and his enemies suddenly having no access to decent clothing, I waited for the inevitable moment when I'd be asked to share one of my own adventures as the Violet Fox. As Antony winded his stories to a close and Kamal began speaking with Keegan on more serious matters, the conversations became more scattered, and I couldn't help but feel a little relieved—and disappointed, admittedly. No one questioned me about my days as the Violet Fox. This was the perfect opportunity for Kamal to ask me how I'd killed Leszek with the Spear. Antony kept meeting my gaze. I knew he wanted the story to be performed so he could embellish his small role in the tale of retrieving the Spear, no matter how gruesome. No one brought up the current political situation. The North nor the East were barely mentioned, and if it weren't for the sparsity of the meal, I might have forgotten that without the South's help, we were on the brink of collapse.

I shivered at that. I'd leaned the wrapped Spear against the table while I ate. I grazed it with my pinky finger and it filled me with warmth.

Bidelia threw me a look: *Why do you have that at the table?*

I shrugged dramatically. *Why wouldn't I?*

As the servants wrapped up the first course and refreshed the wines, Roamers and the few castle guards under Keegan's command casually circled the balcony. I watched them with vigilance, keeping my hand near the Spear.

"Lord Omju," I said carefully, while the others were engaged in a lively conversation about Southern fashion. "In the carriage yesterday, you were going to tell me something. Weren't you?"

He shot a quick glance at Hon'niz, who was leaning toward the other end of the table, delivering a loud speech about the significance of pale pastels during the Festival of Lights. Omju slowly shook his head at me.

I tried a different track. "You didn't see anything strange during your travels in the South?"

"Always strangeness in the southwest forests," he replied slowly, and more to his soup than to me.

I subtly caught the eye of one of the servants, and she promptly topped off Omju's goblet.

"You know, His Grace and I once fought a beatag in Feenagh Forest," I said. "Have you seen one of those before?"

That got his attention and a sly smile crossed his face as he took a generous drink. "So that story is true."

"It is. And I'm happy to share how we bested it." I folded my hands neatly on my lap as the servants took away my empty soup bowl.

Concerned but intrigued, Omju considered my veiled request. My suspicion that he valued or had a strong interest in animals and the outdoors had proved correct. "The South is full of wonders, Violet Fox. Many stories about creatures. Treasure. The High King has a particular interest in items of note. Especially stories of certain items with the ability to create magic."

"Is that so," I said quietly. The other side of the table was still in debate about spring fashion, though I noted Danyal's sudden interest in my private conversation with Omju. I pretended to look disinterested in him and took a small sip of my bluesberry wine. "There are many items that could fit that description."

"Agreed. Not that Omju is an expert. Suspects that the Violet Fox knows more. Though His Highness pays serious mind to the rumours of a highly powerful slate in the—"

The conversation at the other end of the table died down and so Omju once again fell into silence. He took another long drag of his drink and fixed me with a heavy stare.

If Omju was to be believed, and I was interpreting him correctly, the rumour of the Midnight Tablet had captured the High King's attention.

Why else would he be wandering around our border, seemingly aimlessly, and in secret?

Did he know something about the Tablet's location that I didn't?

What did he know *about* the Tablet that I didn't?

As the servants replaced my utensils and prepared my place for the next course, I did my best to keep calm. My father had known so much about the other artefacts. The wife of Dashiell had wiped his tears with the fabric of her dress, and thus it had become the Emerald Cloth. The Silver Spear had its own mythology among the Freetors, and as it had been encased in ice at the end of the world, it was a dangerous weapon to be respected. Yet aside from the frustratingly little information I'd obtained from the apprentices, I struggled to piece together anything new about the Midnight Tablet, or the Granite Slab as it was sometimes called.

I stared at the empty chair. Gobany had not come, and as the second course arrived, I doubted he would. I wondered if he had made any observations about the South during the past few days— and if he would tell me them.

The smell of cooked rabbit, potatoes, and small carrots penetrated the air as dinner carried us deeper into the night. Wine goblets emptied and were refilled. I regaled Omju and Hon'niz with our journey through Feenagh Forest and our frightful battle with the beatag. By the middle of the story, the rest of the guests had tuned in to listen as well, especially Keegan. Keegan deftly avoided questions about the event, politely and smartly telling the High King that he preferred to hear the tale in my voice. He flushed when I mentioned that he had delivered the killing blow.

"Travelled with a Southern bard, yes?" Kamal asked, when I had finished the story.

A sense of dread filled me, but I saw no reason to lie or withhold information. "Yes. His name is Monju."

"Monju Farin?" Omju piped up.

"Yes," I said slowly. "You know him?"

"No, but have heard his ballad..." Once again, Omju quieted after noticing Danyal's death stare. As they had hoped Keegan would marry one of their own, I imagined Monju's ballad "The Violet Fox on Mountain High" was not in favour at present.

"Why is the famous bard not here, entertaining?" Kamal demanded, throwing up his hands in mock jest.

Keegan exchanged a questioning glance with me and chuckled politely. "Your Highness, Monju is taking a deserved rest outside the city to visit his family."

Of course. He didn't remember the ballad Monju had written for us. The very reason we'd agreed to employ him at the castle—other than the fact Monju had been stalking me in the alleyways at the time.

"Hmm," replied the High King, with a curious look at me. "So he has gone back to Xii?"

I gritted my teeth and held my breath. If Kamal was interested in the Tablet, and suspected it was in the South or near our border, of course he'd want to know if *we* suspected that as well.

"Honestly, Your Highness, I'm not sure where the bard's family resides," Keegan replied brightly. He pushed his rabbit meat around his plate nonchalantly.

"Hmm," Kamal said again, and exchanged a glance with Danyal. "Well, if the South can give the West some advice? Never let the talented go travelling on their own. Especially a Southern bard, as he is wont for the best, most dangerous adventures."

Hon'niz erupted into laughter so suddenly, he nearly fell backward in his chair. Omju joined in, and the rest of us indulged the High King with a polite chuckle.

While I traded conversational barbs with Hon'niz and listened to Kamal babble on about the booming trade in the South, my gaze kept finding Keegan's, and for a moment, everything felt right. We had found uneasy, but common ground with the South. I suspected within a few days, our people's bellies would be as full as ours, and then we could focus on the East.

But Omju's words spun circles in my mind. What use would the South have for the Midnight Tablet? How much did they know?

As we neared the end of desert—sweetened potatoes pulped to a mush—the wine had had its intended effect. Bidelia was on her third goblet; I was surprised she had indulged. She deserved it. Without her, the South wouldn't be here. Indeed, even Kamal Zaman seemed to be enjoying himself. He spoke animatedly with Keegan. I smiled. He must have worked out the additional terms of the trade for him to be so pleased. What a relief. Yes, the West would be poorer for a while, but the people would be fed, and once Laoise and Monju returned, my people would be saved as well.

After dinner, other residents of the castle emerged onto the balcony. Word must have spread that the West and the South have come to a favourable agreement. Roamers, castle guards, scribes, apprentices, and servants alike joined in, eating leftovers and partaking in the wine and the general spirit of celebration. Those of us who had feasted rose from the table to mingle informally as servants on duty cleared away our dirty dishes. I gripped the Spear tightly, relieved, with a wash of warmth from head to toe, that it was back in my hands once more. Keegan was deep in conversation with Kamal again, and I was about to join him when I noticed Gobany, the apprentice, on the other side of the balcony with the three other apprentices—his silent companions from our earlier encounter in the hedge maze.

They remained close to the entrance, as if to make a hasty escape at any moment. Gobany caught my movement and fixed the Spear with an intense stare. I gripped it tighter.

Did he want it?

The other apprentices, as if sensing my attention, also locked their inquisitive stares on me and the artefact.

I quickly surveyed the people enjoying themselves on the balcony. No one else was an apprentice that I could tell—just these four. Where were they hiding? My thoughts swam in dark waters. They had better control over magic than I did, but the Spear was safe in my hands. No one was going to take it from me.

But what if they knew I wanted to destroy it? Would they try to stop me?

Could I stop them, if they moved against me?

Gobany nodded and gestured for me to move closer.

He was summoning *me*?

Trying not to seem too desperate, I held myself gracefully and approached the infamous apprentice. The other three fanned out at my approach, greeting me with silent, respectful nods, yet they didn't stray far from Gobany.

"Apprentice Gobany. Didn't you receive my invitation to dinner?" I asked him, trying not to sound slighted.

Gobany narrowed his gaze at me and bowed deeply. "Violet Fox. Yeah. I received the invitation. I ate earlier, with the others."

That stung. I pressed my lips together, feeling guilty at my indulgences tonight with the nobility. I had to be up here, I told myself. I was representing my people. Yet it didn't make me feel any better.

Gobany continued, lowering his voice, "We have to talk about the South. You can't trust them."

Now he had my serious attention. I leaned in closer. "Kamal is after the Tablet too, isn't he?"

"Likely. The bracelet he's wearing. I recognize it," Gobany replied. "It was in the Temple of the Elders."

Was. "How did he get it? What kind of power does it have?" I whispered.

"Don't know how. An enterprising Freetor stole it and fenced it? The whole place is in ruins. It isn't that powerful, but—"

I saw it in the apprentices' faces first. All four, including Gobany, shot me a quick but polite bow and backed away. My stomach twisted into a knot. Startled, I let out a faint gasp as Kamal Zaman's hand rested just above my arm.

"Apologies. The Violet Fox has a moment?"

His closeness raised my guard, though I inclined my head and moved with him towards the balcony railing. Far enough to be out of earshot, but not so far from Antony and Bidelia, who were conversing near the table. They could rush to my aid if necessary, though it was far more likely I'd slay Kamal with the Silver Spear first.

Kamal peered over the edge of the balcony with interest into the darkness below, one hand behind his back, and the other on his staff. "In the South, the trees bloom at this time of year. Very beautiful gardens in the castle in Xii. The Zaman family has cultivated the fauna and flora for generations."

"Perhaps someday we'll see it," I replied politely. "I've never been to Xii."

"Hmm."

I suppressed an annoyed sigh. I was getting tired of that vocal tick of his. "I heard that Xii has a formidable library. That your family enjoys collecting old and rare manuscripts."

Although I stared down into the gardens below, I felt his gaze on me. "Who says this?"

I tried to brush it off. "Just something I heard once."

"Hmm."

If I pried about the Tablet too closely, my interest would be exposed. My interest in the artefact was likely assumed, given my possession of the Spear, yet I couldn't have Kamal hold it over me.

"May the South speak frankly with Lady Kiera?" he asked.

I was taken aback by his use of my assumed title. Maybe I was getting to him. "I'd be honoured."

"Thank you," he said. "Lady Kiera, I must confess my...disappointment with Your Grace's rejection. And you are the reason behind—"

So he didn't want to talk about artefacts and libraries after all. "We are married, Your Highness."

"As you say," he continued. "I only dropped formalities to give you some, how would you say it? Friendly advice. It is in your interest to discontinue this arrangement, regardless of how real it is. If you give him up, I can offer the full force of the South. He is worth that."

"I know he is, which is why we together, as a couple, have refused your offer of marriage," I said evenly. "Leon Frostfire is not worth nothing. If you'd like, tomorrow we can visit him in the dungeon." We hadn't discussed the offer with Leon, but just picturing his face when he found out how we were going to punish him was entertainment enough. "What else has been added to the deal, to make it more appealing to the South?"

"Silver. Though I am aware that your coffers are nearly empty, and will be for some time. Keegan is the valuable gem in your proverbial crown, and you have known it since we arrived. Your love for him blinds you. Prevents you from doing what is best for your people, who starve as we dine. You must think of your people, Violet Fox."

I gritted my teeth, biting down an angry reply. I could have said the same about him, a High King, gallivanting around the South solely based upon rumours of an ancient artefact. At least Keegan and I had had guidance and intelligence on the Silver Spear's location—even if Keegan hadn't believed it until he'd feasted his eyes upon the frozen block containing the weapon.

Keegan drifted through the crowd aimlessly. He caught my eye and must have seen me panicking, for he drifted closer, empty wine goblet in hand as he pretended to be engrossed in the nearby burning lanterns.

"His Holiness mentioned something else that would make the deal more...equitable," the king continued.

My heart leapt. "What?"

His gaze narrowed as he looked from the evening view to me. "I think you know."

He must have overheard me speaking with Omju. What precious little I knew about the Midnight Tablet I'd never give to him. I gripped the Spear tighter. "I don't know anything about...that."

"Hmm. I suspect you have misinterpreted me. Perhaps it is my poor grasp of your tongue. Allow me to try again, Lady Kiera." He shot me a dark look. "Your husband has made promises I don't believe he can keep. But he mentioned other tradeable commodities *you* possess, here and now."

I thought back to my conversation with Keegan in my chamber. I'd been so distraught. Angry. We'd discussed firstborns—no, those were future unknowns. I steeled myself. I didn't have to play his game. "Tell me."

Surprised and frustrated by my directness, Kamal glanced over his shoulder at the other guests on the balcony. "Not here, Violet Fox. If you're willing to discuss the terms further, *privately*, I could accommodate you."

The way Kamal looked at me then, and pronounced the melodic words with his rich voice, a deep, dark dread bubbled and rose from the depths of my stomach, all the way up my throat.

If he wasn't after the Midnight Tablet or magic itself, there was something else only I could provide. Keegan had mentioned something else during our private conversation—the only other thing of value that Kamal could use, barter, and trade.

Me. Keegan had offered *me* to the South.

No. That couldn't be. He'd wanted me to stay. He'd made me promise.

Then...Kamal wanted me to offer myself. Willingly.

I glanced over at Keegan. He had moved on to the other side of the dinner table, now deep in conversation with Omju. If he'd worried about me before, that concern was gone. If the South really wanted me, they could have kidnapped me—or any of us, for that matter. No, they wanted us to go willingly, and aid them in their quest for power. Keegan could provide a marriage and a path to ensuring the Zaman blood lived on in the holy royal line. But the Violet Fox, the embodiment of Freetor hope, could inspire loyalty from a whole group of disparate souls, ready to pledge their loyalty. To ask for my hand in marriage, or even asking me to serve a term at a Southern court would be scandalous. I was not of noble blood and I was a polarizing public figure, whose skills included stealing, lying, and starting fights. Yet I controlled the artefacts—I was the logical, most valuable here-and-now offer. Control the artefacts, become godly. Control the woman behind the artefacts—control the world.

That was worth food and military aid for centuries to come.

I should not have dismissed this before. Keegan had also downplayed me as an asset. He hadn't seen my value either. We were both fools.

"I think you know what I want," Kamal said, lowering his voice.

After everything we'd exchanged last night—could I really leave Keegan and sacrifice my freedom for the safety of the West?

If we didn't give Kamal what he wanted, my people would

suffer. Kamal Zaman seemed to be the kind of man who always got what he wanted.

I had to know for sure. "Fine. I will meet you by your chamber later this evening."

"Come alone," he said, and brushed past me without acknowledging me further. "The South ends their informality."

I held the Spear closer to my chest. People came and went and the balcony grew colder. Bidelia said something to me in passing, yet it was in one ear and out the other. The apprentices left one by one as the night grew longer, including Gobany, though his scrutiny of the Spear lingered as he opened and closed the balcony door. Every time I wanted to speak to Keegan, someone swooped in to steal him away, and I remembered this was how it was, before. He always had demands on his time. Sometimes, it was more important than the time we spent together. Because the good of the realm came first.

I headed for the doors. It was time I did some good for the realm, too.

The Roamer at the doors opened them swiftly. I nodded in thanks and stepped into the dim, quiet corridors of the castle. They were no warmer at this time of night, not with our scarcity of candles and firewood. As I gathered my dress train so the guard could properly close the door, a gloved hand stuck through the threshold and the doors swung open abruptly and fully.

"Keegan," I said, surprised.

"Allow me," Keegan said, and gently gathered my train and placed it delicately within the corridor. The Roamer inclined his head and promptly shut the doors, leaving us to our dim, shared solitude. "Leaving so soon?"

I had to surrender to the South. I couldn't get the thought out of my head. "I think that's best, don't you? Long day tomorrow."

"It will be, though I was hoping you'd help me draw up the agreement tonight. I know, we'd promised, no work, just talk." His face was hopeful.

Right. I had so desperately wanted to leave, to find the Tablet, to get the old Keegan back. Now, I had been offered the opportunity to run away to the South. I should have been grateful. Instead, I was just angry. Confused.

"I just have to take care of something first. Then we can talk. Meet me in the council room?" Once I dealt with Kamal, I'd tell Keegan about his offer. My mind could not rest until I figured out his connection with the Midnight Tablet, and what he truly wanted from me. If it was what I feared...

I smiled and inclined my head at Keegan, and started down the corridor.

"Kiera."

I stopped, one hand bunching the fabric of my dress.

"I know I said it already. But you look...very pretty."

I closed my eyes and turned my head sideways. To see him fully now—I'd lose my nerve. "Thank you."

I aggressively relied on the Spear as a walking staff as I traversed the castle, making my way to the west wing. Kamal's words raced through my mind. My hands ran hot, as they had before when I'd become angry at him. The Spear glowed.

He wanted me to surrender to him. Because the High King of the South always got what he wanted.

What about what I wanted?

You must think of your people, Violet Fox.

If I could save myself from sacrificing my freedom and secure the future for my people—maybe the consequences justified what I was about to do.

Kamal Zaman had tickled my instincts the moment he arrived. There was something...off about him, yet it had taken me this long to put a finger on it. Now, if I could just prove it, I would have something against him.

I met only a few servants carrying warm stones for our guest beds and full latrines. I climbed the stairs to the west wing and before I rounded the corner towards the High King's chamber, I heard movement. I quickly glanced down the corridor and pressed myself against the wall.

I swore under my breath. Lady Danyal paced before her liege's chamber. Waiting. She must have left the balcony before me. I'd been so caught up in my own fears, my vigilance had suffered. I waited behind the corner, yet after five minutes, it was clear she wasn't going anywhere. Perhaps I was supposed to interact with her—after all, Kamal had agreed to meet with me in his quarters.

Taking a deep breath, I rounded the corner, adjusting my large train so it followed me gracefully as I trudged down the dark corridor. "Lady Danyal. Good evening. Did you enjoy the dinner?"

Danyal turned to greet me, her hands behind her back. She nodded respectfully. "How long was the Violet Fox planning to hide in the shadows?"

"I thought it best to stop playing games," I replied coolly. "The High King requested to meet me in his chamber."

"Yes. Aware." She opened the door and gestured into the warmly lit room. "Wait inside. His Highness will be with the Violet Fox shortly."

I hesitated. If Danyal was standing guard, she could easily trap me in the room. I should have told Keegan or Bidelia where I was going. Yet if I backed down now, Danyal would see that as weakness. I couldn't afford to be powerless in front of her. I needed no one's permission to deal with the High King of the South.

After all—I had the power of the Silver Spear.

"Very well," I said, inclining my head. I strode into the room with more confidence than I felt, and once my long train was inside, Danyal carefully shut the door behind me. I heard no click of the lock, yet she was most certainly standing outside, ensuring I didn't leave.

This was one of the nicer chambers in the castle, fit for a High King. Danyal or someone had prepared for my arrival: a fire roared in the fireplace. A single window overlooked the capital city, its lantern lights far and few between compared to the twinkling evening sky. The bed had been made, the floors were somewhat dusty, and a giant wardrobe peeked open, stuffed to the brim. To my disappointment, nothing in sight glowed. No apparent Freetor magic on display.

No matter. That wasn't what I was looking for.

I didn't have long. I leaned the Spear against the wall next to the window to free up my hand and began my search. Cursing my awkward dress, I started with the wardrobe. I threw it open and rummaged through his clothing. All of it, soft to the touch. His coat pockets held crumbs and handkerchiefs—nothing of value. Wiping my hands on my dress, I closed the wardrobe and hurried to the bed. I carelessly rifled through the five fluffy pillows, shoving my hands through the cases and throwing them against the headboard in defeat. Nothing. Under the bed? Struggling with the tight bodice, I dropped to the floor and lifted the bed skirt. No unusual shadows in sight. I felt around as best I could. Again, nothing.

There were nightstands on either side of the bed. I checked the one nearest me first. I slid the drawer out. A book: *Freetor Magic Through The Ages: A Dissertation On The Underground Struggle.* Certainly supported Omju's story, but not suspicious or useful. I replaced it and felt in behind. Nothing but dust. I checked the headboard too, moving the bed as much as I could. I couldn't see anything.

I hurried around the bed, gathering my train up to enable quick movement, to the second nightstand. I opened the singled drawer—yes. This was it.

A velvet pouch with a silver drawstring, and nothing else, lay inside the drawer. Carefully, I picked it up and inspected the interior.

A crushed up, fine, sparkling powder, hidden away for safekeeping?

My suspicions had been correct. The smell was familiar: it was the stench he'd been carrying around for days. The tremor and the High King's sluggish movements had not gone unnoticed. Danyal and the other nobles must have known—they probably guarded this knowledge carefully.

My familiarity with Race stopped with the knowledge that it was derived from a flower that grew almost exclusively in the South. Highly addictive, it made you stronger—temporarily. Then, it slowed your body and deteriorated your organs until you expired. I wondered how long he had before his body gave out on him? How long had he been dependent on the illicit drug?

I shook my head. His reasons didn't matter. If it became public knowledge that High King Kamal Zaman was a user of Race, the most dangerous drug in Marlenia, his long reign would be finished.

Blackmailing a High King. Just add it to my list of crimes.

Lady Jameela's intended had been found with Race in his possession, which seemingly was enough to invalidate a betrothal in the High King of the South's eyes...freeing her up to marry Keegan, if that was his desire. If possession of the drug could disgrace Lady Jameela's intended, it would no doubt disgrace the Kamal. Unless he gave me the information I was looking for—and ensured the safety of my people.

I had to. It was the only way.

I drew the drawstring tight, tucked the bag in my bosom, and slid the drawer shut.

And then, the door also slammed shut.

"So, Violet Fox," Kamal said, brandishing his staff. "You have come to discuss terms."

My heart sunk into my stomach as I whirled around. Smoothening out my bodice, I carefully made my way around the bed. "There you are."

The High King regarded me with suspicion. He held his staff away from his body and used his free hand to grip the bedpost to stop his trembling hand. He noted the disorganized pillows. "The Violet Fox was…conducting an inspection?"

"Perhaps," I replied noncommittedly. "Wouldn't you?"

"Hmm. Unsurprising," His gaze slid to the Spear, leaning against the wall behind me.

Suddenly filled with fear, I acted on instinct. I grabbed it with both hands and pointed it at him.

He looked surprised—and concerned. "That would be unwise, Violet Fox. If the South can speak freely?"

"Yes," I said, nodding quickly, yet I kept the Spear squarely on him.

"Good," he said. "I am pleased you brought your staff. Was hoping for an opportunity to unwrap it, and view the artefact in its full glory. As in the stories and songs."

"That's not a good idea," I replied. "I'm done dancing around. I know why you came here. Why you were sneaking around at the border. You're looking for the same thing we're all after, and you're out of luck. The Tablet isn't here. Believe me, I'd know if it were."

"Ah…the Tablet," Kamal said evenly.

"Yes. Even if I had it, I'd never give it to you. It's too powerful." Who knew if he could handle it without suffering some adverse effect—not to mention, the sheer danger of a man in power holding the origin of all magic. "But I think you know where it is. Otherwise, you wouldn't have left your castle, taken a guide, and a potential shadow killer with you? Tell me where it is."

A low chuckle escaped him. "This was not how I expected to discuss terms with you. I know precious little about your illusive Midnight Tablet."

"You're lying. I know you have a fascination with Freetor magic." I gestured to the gentle glow beneath his sleeve.

He followed my gaze and nodded with amusement. "Hmm. Yes. A gift, from a fellow traveller. I was told it held Freetor magic within. Thank you for confirming this. It has been...helpful, in maintaining my health these past several days. Please, put down your weapon. You are embarrassing yourself."

I gritted my teeth. So, the bracelet did have magical properties, but it wasn't disguising his form, if he was to be believed. I couldn't afford to lower my defenses. He might be a slow, drug-addled older man, but his staff likely wasn't just for support. I had the upper hand. To ensure his cooperation, however, I did lower the Spear— but only a little.

"If you know precious little about the Midnight Tablet, tell me it. Consider it part of the terms we will discuss as part of the trade between our two provinces."

His amusement deepened. "As you wish. Here is what I know. It is an artefact of Dashiell. It is sought by many. Including myself." He admitted this with the gravitas of one speaking about the weather. "Could be very useful. As you so clumsily pointed out tonight, my family has collected artefacts and curio for generations. We're aware of the potential properties. The possibilities. Thought it best to collect the entirety of the Tablet myself, before my bones can move no more."

The drawstring in my bosom felt heavier then. I wonder how much longer he had before his body stopped working. The Tablet could relieve his symptoms. It could relieve the symptoms of every Race addict. Perhaps our motives weren't so dissimilar after all.

"Wait. The entirety of the Tablet?" Oh no. Just like the Emerald Cloth. "Someone broke it, separated the pieces, didn't they?"

"A long time ago. Likely to prevent it from working as it should. My substantial piece of it was in the Zaman family vault for years until a cunning young noble stumbled in—and brought its value to my attention." He smiled slyly. "I resolved to find its mate. So, I wrapped it up and set out along the border, following information gathered by my brightest."

"You have it." The relieved whisper escaped my lips. It was

real. Keegan would be saved. My people would live free once more. "Let me see it."

"*Had* it, Fox. Until Ivor Ferguson waltzed into my caravan and stole it."

My throat tightened. "Conal? How? Where is he now?"

"Conal. So that is his true name. A Freetor too, I suspect?"

"Suspect away. Tell me where he is."

"If I knew, I would send men to retrieve what he stole from me." He shook his head. "I believed his stories. I allowed him by our campfire, because he knew my face, and I knew his. I am clever and cunning, yet he predicted my every move. He knew I had the Tablet half. Before I knew it, *he* had it. He destroyed many of our carriages and horses when we tried to get it back."

No wonder their caravan seemed small and packed to the brim. My father had been with the High King. I wanted to know more, but Kamal continued his story.

"Then your Roamers came to our fire, with your letter. And I gave it great thought. I remembered the stories of the Silver Spear." He gazed at its sharp tip. "And the Orb, yet that is useless for my purposes. Thought perhaps I should pay the Violet Fox and her hovel of a city a visit." He inclined his head. "You did not disappoint. I thought, if the former Advisor is collecting artefact pieces that don't belong to him, it would only be a matter of time before he showed his face here."

"Listen to me carefully," I said. "If Conal finds the rest of the Midnight Tablet before me, he will become unstoppable. People will die. He'll try to take over not just the West, but the South, too."

"He is welcome to try. The South cannot be won. Once you and I have come to an agreement, I will deal with him."

"We can both deal with him. Together. Let this be part of our agreement." I lowered the Spear. "You can have Leon and whatever silver you want. And we will still take the aid you have offered.

But I suggest we pool our resources to find the Midnight Tablet—to solve our respective problems. We can rid our people of the ice plague. We can alleviate the addiction to Race."

Kamal blinked, and as I realized he didn't share my enthusiasm, I felt trapped. The apprentices' warning rang in my mind: *You can't trust them.*

"An interesting phrase, *alleviate the addiction*," he said. "Yet a foolish one. Race runs through Xii like a river. It dries up, and so does the silver it delivers. Imagine. The Race, available at selected shops, for a premium—and the antidote for its devastating effects, generously provided by the Tablet, for those who are willing to pay the price."

I stepped back, horrified. "You'd do that to your own people?"

"There is silver to be made, Violet Fox." Kamal took an awkward step towards me and released his hold on the bedpost. A sly smile crossed his face as he examined me from head to toe. "Now. Terms. No pooling of resources. You will give me what I want. Now."

"I'm not surrendering to you," I spat.

"The Violet Fox believes...?" He laughed and then sneered. "The South doesn't want *you*. *You* are a Freetor. No."

"I thought because I control the..." Oh no. Stupid, stupid Kiera.

Kamal gestured to the Silver Spear as the realization dawned upon me, and his smile became a grin.

"The Silver Spear? You want *this*? Something you can't even touch without cursing yourself?" His fascination and his lingering glances at me made a different kind of sense now. "You know I can't trade this. It's far too dangerous."

"I've seen the results. Confirmed the rumours. The ice sickness is unfortunate, but it is still a prize. If I cannot have the Tablet, then I can die knowing I added another piece of history to my vault." He held out his hand. "I assume it is wrapped for the non-Freetors' benefit? The South will relieve your burden."

"No." I held it closer to my chest. I remembered my father's obsession with it, how he had travelled to the ends of the world to find it, nearly dying. Him, standing in the cathedral in Sallingaire, after carelessly using it on Eastern soldiers. The Silver Spear must not fall into the hands of tyrants. Their desperation and lust for power obscured the strife it shaped.

Kamal shook his head, unrelenting. "You are blind, Violet Fox. The most valuable of collectible pieces, in your grasp. You realize once Ivor Ferguson has found the other piece of the Tablet, he will come for this." He stepped closer, thumping his staff into the floor confidently, and held out his hand. "Think of your people, Violet Fox, and give me the artefact."

"Don't you understand? No. You will have to *kill* me to get it. I won't let another fall under its spell."

"There is no spell," Kamal said forcefully. "There are only the powerful and those who let themselves be deceived. I will not let that happen again. The staff, Violet Fox."

Desperately, I pulled the drawstring pouch from my bosom and held it up like a talisman. "I know you're a Race addict. Maybe you should think of your reputation before you make impossible demands."

Concern marred his features. "Blackmail, Violet Fox?"

"I am just thinking of my people, High King."

He took another step closer and reached for me with his free hand. "Give them...to..."

"Back away!" I jabbed the Spear at him half-heartedly, deliberately missing. I didn't *want* to hurt him. Wrapped as it was, the Spear wouldn't freeze my opponent upon impact—I hoped. I couldn't have another dead king in my wake.

He smirked. "Has been some time since I've fought."

"I don't want to fight you. Just promise you'll—"

He gripped his staff with both hands. From his sluggish movements, I thought he was just going to adopt a defensive position.

Instead, he thrust his tall, blunt staff square into my stomach.

The bone bodice shielded me from some of the impact, yet the mind exaggerated the blow. I was at Driscoll's End once more, and Dominique was using the Spear against me, driving it into my midsection...

I recoiled against the wall. The pouch had fallen to the ground between us.

Kamal leaned to retrieve it slowly, but I kicked it from his grasp. I attacked with the Spear, this time in earnest, yet Kamal blocked readily.

Spears were not my medium. Close-quarters knife fights? That I knew well. Kamal knocked the Spear from my hands easily. It clattered to the floor.

"Hmm," he said, amused.

I leaned to get it, yet there was his blunt, metallic staff again, pushing into my stomach. My former wound there had been healed by magic and yet, in that moment especially, it was tender and raw. He put all his weight into his weapon and pinned me against the wall. Although slow, his body had been enhanced by Race for who knows how long. My bodice bent from the impact. I grasped his staff. There was no real pain, just the anticipation of pain, that sent me into panic. The pressure against my previous wound filled my mind with a familiar sense of doom. It was unlikely that the staff would penetrate my dress—yet it *could*.

I clawed at him, I kicked, refusing to scream—and he stepped closer, putting more of his weight on the staff. I almost always had a knife in my boots for an occasion such as this. Yet as I lifted my leg, my stomach muscles clenched, and he put more pressure on the staff. There was no way I could get at it—my dress had too many layers. He was sweating with effort. His gaze darted between me and the Spear. He couldn't hold me back and retrieve the artefact at the same time. He snarled at me, finally. No, he was going to kill me first.

But he couldn't, not like this, and he knew it. He relieved the pressure on the staff for just a moment, pulling it back sluggishly, preparing to swing it at my head as he angled for the Spear.

I gulped a deep, desperate breath.

The Spear—if I went for it, he would bludgeon me one way or another.

I dove for the floor, towards the wardrobe and away from the Spear as Kamal completed his swing, easily missing.

Groaning, I tried to shimmy backward from the enraged High King, yet the fabric of my train prevented my feet from finding purchase. I crawled on my elbows, trying to path a way back to the Spear—and got nowhere. Kamal stepped on my train, and then the dress itself, pinning me once more. He advanced slowly, his eyes round and empty, positioning his staff to bludgeon me down for good.

Panicking, I pulled hard on the fabric. It started to tear—but not fast enough. The staff was over my head. His lips twitching into a maddened grin, Kamal took a mighty swing at my face.

No one knew where I was—and now, I was going to die.

"Don't touch me!"

All of the anger, all of my fear coalesced into one spark of urgency. The lightning flew, not from the sky, but from the tips of my fingers, and struck Kamal Zaman between the eyes.

Stunned, he dropped his staff and collapsed next to me on the floor.

For several seconds, I lay beside him, unable to move. Our struggle had lasted less than a few minutes and the heavy silence that followed kept me pinned in place.

What was that?

My hands shook, numb and glowing from the magic. A wash of horror sent me into denial. It wasn't me who had struck the High King down. I was the Violet Fox, a thief and skilled impersonator, not an apprentice wielding the coveted secrets of Freetor magic.

The Spear remained next to the bed, out of my reach. It hadn't come from there.

I suppressed a sob as feeling returned to my fingers with a satisfying tingle. I tensed them, and for what felt like a long time, I just...stared, my mind reeling.

My father was right. I have magic. I used it against my enemy. My father is the enemy and he has magic and he was right.

What if I'm the enemy now?

How could I destroy magic with the Midnight Tablet—without destroying myself? I tried to subdue these thoughts, but I was suffocated by them, and the unconscious ruler beside me kept my mind in an endless loop.

I gathered the dress—torn and dirty—and climbed to my feet, panting furiously against the tight bodice, taking in with horror what I had done. A blackened spot, angry and rapidly bruising, sat squarely in the middle of his forehead. His chest slowly rose and fell—barely. His staff lay across his body.

I carefully stepped around him and grabbed the Spear. I had mortally wounded the High King of the South. If I hadn't, he would have killed me. I had killed before, and while it had taken a toll, it was nothing like this. I had used the unfamiliar, unpredictable magic within me, and now that it had awakened fully, I was aware of its presence—as if I had grown another stomach or lung. It had lingered just below the surface, waiting for me to call upon it in my time of need. Rordan and Conal and Bidelia and the Elders had always told me: *Control your anger. You're too immature. Too impulsive. You don't* think, *Kiera.*

Perhaps they feared what I would become, if I gave in to the anger and fear.

There was a knock at the door.

"His Highness?"

No. no. no. I'd forgotten about Danyal.

I set the Spear reluctantly on the floor. Brushing aside the many layers of my dress, I retrieved my knife. A difficult task, as my hands were full of static—the fabric stuck to me, annoyingly. I stuffed the sheath in my mouth, removed the knife, and cut the straps on the dress. The hard work of the seamstresses fell to the floor beside Kamal. Now, at least, my arms would have free range of movement. The bodice would hold snug around my torso as I was laced in. I started sawing at the remaining fabric of my train.

Things were only going to get worse from here.

"His Highness? Lady Kiera?" Danyal called again. She stopped knocking. Waiting for a response.

The tearing of the fabric cut through the silence. The window—open, but in this dress, climbing wasn't an option.

Hiding? Again, my *dress*. I sliced the fabric faster, but I was running out of time, and there were too many layers.

"We're fine," I responded, ripping away a large chunk of the front of the dress.

She wouldn't believe me. *I* wouldn't believe me. Especially with the mounting pile of fabric on the floor around his body. I resheathed the knife, stuffed it in my bodice, and retrieved the Spear. Quickly, I nudged the High King's head with my foot, turning it—

—and Danyal threw the door open.

Her eyes bulged. She looked to me, my knife hilt sticking comically out of my bosom, the torn fabric littering the room—and finally at Kamal, unconscious at my feet.

She rushed for Kamal and knelt by his side. "What happened here? What did you…?"

I backed away from Kamal, sidestepping carefully towards the door, holding the Spear with both hands. "I don't know, he just… collapsed."

As Danyal inspected his face, I darted out the room and down the corridor.

I didn't get far.

"The Fox defiled the High King!"

When I turned, she was already in the hallway, advancing towards me. From the folds and flowing fabric of her outfit, she drew two shortswords, curved at the end. Monju had a similar weapon. They were the traditional weapons of a shadow killer.

"I figured," I said, raising the Spear in defense.

She rushed for me, and once more, I surrendered myself to instinct. Her blades sliced, one, two at my torso—and I jumped back before they could rend me in half. She evaded the tip of the Spear deftly, yet she was not expecting the torrent of lightning from my left hand. Her blades conducted the magical energy up her arms and throughout her body, surrounding her like a beautiful halo as she collapsed to the floor.

My teeth chattered for no reason. My hand, numbed and glowing, recovered more quickly this time. *I have magic. I used it on my enemies.* And yet, I had defeated my enemies. I was stronger. I had the power to defeat anyone.

We didn't need the South. We didn't need *anyone* to help us solve our problems. Once I had the Midnight Tablet and fixed all the damage I'd caused...*then* I'd destroy magic. For good. Because we wouldn't need it anymore, once our bellies were full, my enemies vanquished, and Keegan was restored to his rightful state of mind.

Until then...

"Kiera? I've been looking everywhere for..."

The voice wasn't in my mind. I turned, and there was Keegan, as if I'd conjured him myself. I grinned. He was so handsome, so princely. A laugh escaped me and if it weren't for the Spear, I would have hugged him.

As he trudged closer, his expression melted my euphoria. "What...?" He took in my rugged, ruined appearance with concern...and to my despair, disgust.

The bodies. Our agreement with the South. Just a moment ago, a solution seemed within my grasp. Yet now, looking at downed

Danyal, I smelled her burnt flesh, how her hands had blackened and her unconscious fingers still clutched her weapons fiercely. What if they were fused, forever? Her face was severely red and her mouth open with shock.

I did that. With magic.

Magic was the enemy, and it had used me, and I had let it. It had been so easy.

Keegan was speaking. "What happened, Kiera?"

He hovered around me, afraid to touch me.

"We were going to meet in the council room," I said distantly. "Why…why did you come here?"

He held up a rolled piece of parchment, tied with a purple ribbon. "I started drawing up the agreement since you were… taking so long. A servant said you had gone this way. Did you…do this?" He pointed at Danyal.

"Before you judge me," I said, my voice wavering, "let me explain."

"I hope you will," he replied coldly. He leaned around me to inspect Danyal. "Is she dead?"

I couldn't say—and given Keegan's insistence on the truth, I pursed my lips.

"Talk," he said.

"Kamal wanted to discuss terms. I went to his room. Then he attacked me."

His eyes widened further as he noticed the ajar door to the guest chamber. "Kiera. Did you kill the High King?"

"No!" I held out my hands to stop him—and then thought better of it. I wished he wouldn't say my real name in such a disappointed, desperate way. Keegan breezed past me and Danyal. He lingered in the doorway, his hand resting on the jamb.

"He's alive," I said, leaning on the Spear for comfort. "If I didn't attack him, he would have killed me."

"Why?" Keegan demanded. "And why is your dress…?"

I swallowed. What he must've thought of me in that moment—torn dress, unconscious man, weapon stuffed in my bodice. An unconscious, charred body. My eyes narrowed. His voice, his stance—there was no sympathy or understanding there.

My Keegan would have understood.

"I had to be able to fight. I was defending myself. After I took him down, I modified the dress because I knew Danyal, with her shadow skills, would have a greater advantage."

"She looks like she was burnt." He looked up to the torches lining the hallway. They could only be reached with a stool-step, and since the fire, they'd been partially encased in metal. He blew out a deep breath. "Kiera...this...this is bad."

"Yeah. It is. Kamal tried to take the Spear from me. Because he seemed to believe that the terms you offered him *weren't enough.*"

"You mean the terms *we* offered. They were enough. He... agreed to a monthly sum of silver, to be delivered by cart to Xii, protected by our finest fighters."

"He wanted the Spear. And he was looking for the Tablet. He had a piece, before my father took it from him. Then when I refused to give him what he wanted, he attacked."

He glanced warily at the Spear. "Why didn't you give it to him?"

"What kind of question is that? It's a dangerous artefact. It turned your mind to—"

Keegan waved his arms, cutting through my desperate words. "Enough, Kiera."

"Keegan, I'm trying to explain..."

"I know. Just, from the beginning."

I slammed the butt of the Spear into the floor with a deafening crack. "Don't you believe me?"

"I do. But if another noble shows up here, and sees this, what are you going to do?" He gestured once more to Danyal. "Tell me everything so I can help you, before this turns into a diplomatic incident."

My heart was racing. So that's what he was most concerned about. Not my well-being. Not my rampant misuse of magic. But the safety of trade agreement we'd made. The worst of it was—I accepted that. I had always put the needs of my people first. The individual meant little in Freetor society. I'd only become well known because of the gossiping, angry surface-born Marlenians. *Think of your people, Violet Fox*, Kamal had said. Because my feelings were nothing. I had pushed them down, down, to do my duty.

But now...

My voice shook. "Kamal asked me to his room. He tried to take the Spear. He attacked me..." I clutched my stomach. Didn't Keegan know I'd nearly died at Dominique's hand, during a similar attack? He'd already been cursed when it happened, yet I thought I'd told him. "Kamal is a Race addict, too. I found his stash. Tried to use that against him, but—"

"So you blackmailed him, and he attacked you?"

My eyes narrowed. "You're taking his side."

"I'm trying to understand. Wait, how did you find his stash?"

"While I was waiting for him to arrive, I...inspected the room."

"You searched his room?"

I looked around the corridor dramatically. "I did tell you I'm the Violet Fox, right? That's what I do. I steal and occasionally perform espionage. All in the service of making our lives better!"

"Is that what you call it?" He gestured to the two unconscious bodies.

We were not on the same page at all. "I don't have to explain myself further. You're going to help me drag them both to the dungeons. When they wake up, we'll be in a better position to enforce the trade agreement. They'll have to help us."

"And what will we tell our people?"

I frowned, guilt surging through me. "They don't have to know everything about this. All they'll care about is the food we've secured."

"You want to lie about this? This is not just a lie. This is a cover-up. A coup."

"You want to tell the truth about the power-hungry king of the South to a bunch of starving commoners? You don't know what they'll do. I do. They won't care—they'll revolt and storm the castle and take everything we have left."

"They won't, if we explain. Do you really think that little of your own people?"

"I'm being practical," I spat. "You didn't grow up in the dirt. I did. I know what they're capable of." I examined Danyal, trying to figure out the best way to get her down to the dungeon without attracting attention, when I realized Keegan was still staring at me, unmoving.

"Well?" I asked him.

He parted his lips, his face pale. "We...we should fetch Bidelia."

"What? No." I blocked his path. "She'll just get angry. First we take them to the dungeons, before Hon'niz or Omju shows up, then we find Bidelia."

Keegan fixed me with a concerned look. "Kiera. Please do not put that"—he gestured warily at the Spear—"in my way."

My blood ran cold. I wasn't thinking. I held it with both hands in front of me defensively. I took a step back, yet I couldn't bring myself to let my guard down. The fear, as strong as glue, kept my hands wrapped in their positions, unyielding.

"Kiera," he said again. "I need you to listen to me. Put down the Spear."

"What? No." I shook my head repeatedly, unable to stop.

"Yes. Drop it on the ground."

"No!" I thrust it forward, careful not to point it at him, yet somehow doing so anyway. "Why would you ask that of me?"

"Because it is dangerous! Haven't you noticed?"

"It's only dangerous to the surface-born, if it touches their skin. And I didn't use it against them. They're not frozen."

"If you didn't use the Spear, how did you manage to knock *both* of them unconscious? And...burn Danyal?"

I wet my lips. My throat tightened. I'd promised to tell him the truth. "M-magic."

"Yes, clearly. So drop the Spear."

"No. It's different. It has nothing to do with that. It's...my... magic."

"Your magic? Like...the apprentices? You're an apprentice? When were you going to tell me about that?"

"I...I don't know..."

"You don't know. Just like me, it seems," Keegan said, quieter now, as he backed away. "I don't have to know about our marriage, until it's relevant. I don't have to know about the extent of your fighting and magical abilities, until it's relevant. It seems I don't really know my wife at all."

That stung. "I'm just trying to protect you." *Like I failed to before.*

"I don't need to be coddled." Keegan let out an impatient sigh. "The artefacts corrupt those in power. You told me that."

"But I'm...I'm fine. And I'm not...in power." I laughed at the thought. I was the High Queen, yes, but the Holy One ruled Marlenia. Everyone knew that. Except for Keegan. "If anything, I'm trying to prevent magic from falling into the wrong hands. The Spear is safe with me, the Cloth is safe with Laoise, and once I'm able, I'm going to get the Orb and the Tablet and hide them from my father. Then—"

"Then, then, then. I am talking about now. Giving him the Spear would have been preferable to blackmail and throwing people in the dungeon!" Keegan's expression hardened. "Your mind is not here, Kiera. I thought I knew you. Clearly you aren't *you* right now."

"You don't know me! You're the one who isn't *you!*" I exploded. Tears rolled down my face. "You refuse to let me help you remember..."

"If this is who my wife is," he said, turning away slowly, "then maybe I'm lucky I don't remember. I thought that we could…" He shook his head as he turned away. "I can't stand by and watch magic destroy you. Not now." He tossed the parchment agreement on the floor and it rolled towards me.

"Where are you going? What about—?"

"Don't. I don't want any part of this!" His shout echoed throughout the corridor. He wouldn't even dignify me with a look. He just kept walking, further rand further away. "You've made your choice."

My heart pounded in my ears. But I hadn't made any choices at all…had I? The magic, it was just there. And I'd used it to save myself. If only I could make him understand everything without saying a word. All I could do was stand there and watch the love of my life abandon me to clean up the mess I'd made.

Alone.

"THIS IS AN act of war," Bidelia said, surveying the bodies.

Keegan—even thinking his name hurt—had been right about one thing. I'd needed to fetch Bidelia.

Before another noble or servant could venture down the corridor and see Danyal's form, I'd dragged her carefully into Kamal's chamber. She groaned momentarily and remained unconscious. If she didn't receive treatment, it was possible she would suffer permanent burns—or worse. I considered trying to use magic on her, but the idea of tapping into it filled me with terror.

The night had grown long and most everyone had gone to bed. Evading servants and drunken nobles alike, I'd found Bidelia nursing the last of her bluesberry wine in the council room, going over other parchments Keegan must have been working on. One look at me was all it took to get her up to Kamal's chamber, and up to speed on everything I had done.

Unlike Keegan, she didn't interrupt my explanation to ask questions. She listened to my account. I left nothing out. I could not afford to keep anything secret, not now. Bidelia had spent most of her life working undercover at the castle, and while I didn't know specifics about what she'd handled over the years, I guessed that she'd never encountered anything like this.

Still—remaining calm in a life-or-death crisis was her job. When I finished, she let a long, slow breath through her nose. "First. No one can know about this. Agreed?"

"Agreed," I said eagerly. "Not even Antony?"

"Well, we…" She was trying to choose her words carefully. This had been a sobering experience, though I expected she hadn't gotten the bluesberry wine out of her system yet. "Antony will do as he's told, though this may stretch his conscience. The High King said they were to depart tomorrow at midday. Though kings and nobles change their minds about many things and no one bats an eyelash. Do you have the agreement?"

I nodded and handed her the rolled-up parchment Keegan had dropped. She untied the ribbon and unfurled it. "I see Keegan has signed. He should have waited for a witness, but he was likely as anxious as you to get this over with. Unfortunately, there's no signature from the South."

"So? Kamal told Keegan he conditionally agreed, and then they discussed the modifications, and—"

"This isn't an Elder decree, Kiera. Verbal agreements mean nothing. This is Marlenian politics, of the highest order. If it isn't in writing, it isn't real, and no one will have food."

I clenched my fists hard, my fingernails digging deep into my skin. "So we fake Kamal's signature."

"Do you know what it looks like, Your Highness?"

I glared at her. "Don't you, Advisor Mullen?"

"Many of the records were burnt in the fire. It would take days to sift through what survived to find something comparable."

Loud, drunken singing interrupted our heated discussion. Bidelia and I inclined our heads toward the door, listening. It sounded like Hon'niz had retired from the balcony celebrations. He passed by Kamal's chamber slowly, shuffling around—dancing, perhaps—and stopped at the adjacent chambers. He pounded on the door. "Danyal. Danyal! Awake?"

I stiffened. Bidelia shook her head, annoyed. "He was a bottomless pit, deeper than the dungeons. I'll be surprised if *he's* alive in the morning."

I sat on the bed, running my hands through my hair. "Could Lord Hon'niz sign the agreement?"

"In that state, he'd likely sign anything. But a signature from the grand-nephew of the High King would mean nothing. If anything, it may anger High King Kamal's closer blood relatives, which would only stir up other problems. We need High King Kamal's signature, or someone who can forge it. Good luck explaining that to a drunk man."

She was right. We had until tomorrow morning to sort this out. Whether that was detaining the remaining two nobles and forcing them to forge High King Kamal's signature—I highly doubted the High King himself would sign anything, even if he managed to find consciousness anytime soon—or somehow concocting a story and sending Hon'niz and Omju back to the South without the High King and his protective bodyguard of noble birth.

Hon'niz was still banging on Danyal's closed chamber door, asking her to come out and sing with him. At the rate he was going, the whole wing would be awake soon.

Bidelia let out a long breath through her nose as she searched my face. "You know we have to freeze them, don't you?"

I squeezed my eyes shut as my body wobbled with a sob and shook my head.

"Yes, Kiera." Her tone was sympathetic, but firm. "You know it's our only recourse here."

I'd known it since the moment Keegan left me. Admitting that I had to steal away the memories of yet another person I'd done wrong by…I didn't know how much more I could take. When I stopped shaking and opened my eyes, Bidelia was plying Danyal's fingers from her blades. They came off without incident and Bidelia carefully placed the blades by the door.

"We're going to need all the steel we can get if this comes to war," she muttered.

I stared at the Spear, propped against the wall by the window.

After inadvertently threatening Keegan with it, I didn't know what to do with the artefact. If I wasn't careful, I'd hurt everyone around me. "I shouldn't be High Queen."

"Now isn't the time for that kind of talk. You are what you are. We have a small window of opportunity to get this right." She sighed. "Think this through, Kiera. We could put the four nobles in the dungeon. We could also scour the castle and the stables for their servants and imprison them, too. No Southerner leaves the castle without our knowledge. We force the nobles to sign the agreement—but how do we return it? It will be another fortnight, perhaps more, before food and military aid arrives from Xii." I saw where she was going. By then, the South would be asking questions. Namely, what happened to their king? "Eventually, someone will arrive, asking questions about his absence. We will not be able to take on all three provinces at once. It will ruin us completely."

I felt the full weight of the world on my chest. "I know! I didn't...I didn't mean to..."

"Control yourself." Fearlessly, she gripped my wrists and bored her gaze into mine. "Hear me? Control. We can't have another accident."

I swallowed a sob and balled my hands. How was I supposed to control my magic if I barely knew how to control my anger? "It was just *one time*." Then, when Laoise and Monju returned, I could make everything right again, by curing everyone and destroying the temptation to ever do something like this again...

And yet, that was impossible now too. Unless there was another piece of the Tablet in Xii, Laoise and Monju's journey would be fruitless. If the High King's story was true, and Conal had a piece of the Tablet, he would never surrender it to me. We had nothing.

My people were going to starve. Keegan would never return to himself. Because of me.

Out in the hallway, Hon'niz had stopped his incessant knocking.

I wondered if he'd be suspicious that Danyal hadn't emerged from her chamber, what with all the noise. I heard him shuffle further down the corridor.

Bidelia sighed and released my wrists. "Grab the blankets off the bed. We'll wrap them first and take them to the dungeons."

Numbly, I stood, using the bedpost for assistance. As I stripped the bed, Hon'niz began his tirade again, this time on a different door further down the corridor. The noise grated my nerves. I gathered the sheets with Bidelia's help and covered the High King first, then Danyal. I considered grabbing the Spear and marching into the hallway to quiet Hon'niz myself when I heard the door creak hesitantly open.

"What... Lord Hon'niz." It was Omju. "Still celebrating?" He yawned loudly.

"Little...er, Lord Omju!" he said joyfully. "Look...just..."

"Go to bed, friend." Omju sounded amused, but sleepy. "Can discuss in the morning."

"No. Have been...rude, to Omju, in the past..."

"It has been forgotten. Please. Rest. Sleep off the terrible wine." Terrible! I scoffed.

"Focus," Bidelia said. She delicately covered Danyal's face with the white sheet and lifted the noblewoman's arms in a haphazard attempt to wrap the sheet all the way around.

"Just..." Hon'niz's boisterous voice trailed off. *Slide. Thump.* "Hon'niz!"

Bidelia and I exchanged looks. *Don't do it*, hers said.

Before Bidelia could stop me, I abandoned the blankets and the bodies and threw open the door.

Omju, wearing silk light blue pajamas, stood over Hon'niz's unconscious form slouched against the wall. Omju was startled by my sudden arrival from within Kamal's chamber. "Violet Fox."

"Lord Omju. Is...Lord Hon'niz all right?"

He narrowed his gaze suspiciously at me and he leaned over

Hon'niz to check his breathing and heartbeat. "Seems fine. Just… too much wine. Not unusual."

With Hon'niz down, there was no way he could plausibly sign the contract. Not without great effort tomorrow. "Right. I was just concerned. Have a good evening." I went to return to Kamal's chamber, realized how strange that looked, and then remembered the strangeness of my attire. Bidelia stood within the High King's room, horrified that I'd inserted myself into an awkward situation.

I inclined my head at Omju, and waded down the hallway in my tattered dress, away from him and Hon'niz.

"Wait, Violet Fox."

Hesitantly, I shuffled to a stop, and turned. "Yes?"

He cocked his head. "Have your celebrations…been satisfactory?"

That was an odd way to put it, though polite, given the circumstances. I clasped my hands in front of me. "No, Lord Omju. How about yours?"

The corners of his lips twitched upward. "Not what Omju was expecting."

I held his gaze for a long moment and made my hands into fists. I could make him sign. I could make him do whatever I wanted. The magic was within me. I had already bested the others.

But there was something about him that made me pause. He was not afraid or intimidated by me, certainly not now. His pajamas were the most noble part of him and even they seemed ill fitting. He scratched his arm absently, unused to the fabric against his skin. His boots were still caked in days-old mud—he was *still* wearing them.

Only a select few were so paranoid that their circumstances would change for the worse that they would wear their boots to bed.

"You're not a real Southern noble, are you," I said.

Bidelia, still in the room and out of sight, hissed at me and mouthed, *What are you doing?*

Omju raised an eyebrow at me defiantly. "Omju is of noble birth as much as the Violet Fox is the High Queen."

"You were born into nobility from parents of humble origins."

His smile grew wider. "The West makes these distinctions. The South…accepts more."

I stuck my hand through the doorway. Bidelia didn't have to ask. She retrieved the Silver Spear and placed it in my waiting hand. As I withdrew it from the room, Omju followed it with an unwavering gaze, containing more awe than fear.

"Could ask why the Violet Fox is in His Highness's quarters," he said.

Spear in hand, I sauntered towards him. The artefact kept time menacingly with each step. *Thunk. Thunk. Thunk.*

"The High King confirmed what you tried to tell me tonight. He also said offhand that some noble had recognized the value of his half of the Midnight Tablet, sitting in the Zaman family vault. I wonder how such a noble could recognize the value of a Freetor artefact…unless he himself was able to see or sense the magic?"

"What can Omju say, except that he also wants freedom under the sun?" He crossed his arms defensively. "Omju's parents fled the underground years ago and emerged in Xii. Omju was but a young boy…but remembers the taste of glow moss well." He wrinkled his nose. "Created a successful life, breeding horses and selling feed of the highest quality. Profitable. With enough silver, anyone can buy nobility."

I smiled. "The High King knew."

"Who else to buy nobility from? But the High King is also clever."

"And greedy."

He shrugged. "Yes. As are many Southern nobles."

"Did you know he was going to use the Tablet to make the Race trade in Xii even worse?"

Omju paled. "No, Violet Fox." His gaze slid behind me. "He said this?"

Bidelia had emerged from the room. She held the unfurled agreement tenderly.

"He did, before he attacked me," I said honestly. I held my breath. It was a risk to tell him the truth. I had done so much wrong tonight—I just wanted to make the right choice, for once. "Unfortunately, he didn't have time to sign the trade agreement my husband drew up."

"Walls thick, but Omju's hearing is...extraordinary."

I nodded. "You wouldn't happen to know how to forge a signature, would you, my lord?"

* * *

Once Omju signed the agreement on the High King's "behalf," I thought I'd feel better. I had fought my entire life for the equality of all my people, and maybe I was playing favourites with Omju, trusting him just because he was a Freetor. Foolhardy or not, I needed the distraction. My explosive argument with Keegan had shattered me. Just thinking about him tightened my throat and sent me into panic.

There was little time to dwell on my feelings; I only had space enough in my mind to deal with one problem at a time. Bidelia and I worked throughout the night. I changed into more suitable clothing—simple trousers and a long-sleeved blouse—and together we finished wrapping Kamal and Danyal in bedsheets. The tricky part was lugging them down into the dark, dank dungeons. One would think a Freetor would find comfort in the robust smell of soil, dust, and grime, yet I was reminded of my prolonged stay there, after I confessed my true identity to Keegan and stopped him from marrying Sylvia Frostfire. I hadn't toured the dungeons extensively, yet Bidelia was familiar with the winding, dirty staircase and narrow passages, leading to small, enclosed cells. Leon was down here somewhere, too, and dwelling on his villainy only deepened my own guilt. We placed Kamal in one cell and Danyal in another.

I loathed unwrapping the Spear...and yet, seeing it as it was, beautiful and raw and glowing in the dark dungeons...my throat tightened. It shouldn't have had to hide who it was. It had waited so long to be itself, and now, it could perform its dark curse—its secret yearning.

My hands trembled as I gently pressed the spearhead to exposed skin on Kamal's arm, and then Danyal's. The ice encased them, saving and damning them both.

I had used magic to protect my people. It seemed a good enough reason when it ran through my head a thousand times, over and over, and yet I knew it was desperately, horribly wrong—and simultaneously, perfectly natural. I was just doing what Alastar the Hero had done before me: keep the powers of the tyrant in check.

After much discussion, we decided to send Hon'niz back to Xii with Omju. As a favourite relative of the High King, he held some sway in the Southern court, and could attest to the verity of the trade agreement. Omju helped us settle his incoherent friend in bed with water. He likely wouldn't wake up fully until they were in the carriage—and hopefully, Omju would feed him a plausible story about Kamal and Danyal staying behind.

Although Omju asked after his liege lord's health, he didn't pry about what had happened, and what we planned to do with Kamal and Danyal. I refused to let him help. Deep down, he knew, and the less he was involved, the better. I hoped he trusted me enough to know that I would set them both free, once I had the Midnight Tablet in my grasp.

I kept telling myself I'd done the right thing. That I hadn't meant to hurt them. The fear I'd summoned and used against them hadn't dissipated. Without sleep, it intensified and begged to be released once more.

When the sun rose and the servants busied themselves once more with meal delivery, changing bedsheets, and preparing for the South's departure, I felt as if I was swimming through clouds.

I yearned for a bed—or a slab of stone, that would be more familiar—to curl up on, just to silence the intense anxiety wheeling me ever forward into the next second, and then the next.

Yet sleep was not in my immediate future. Protocol and ceremony had to be observed. Bidelia and I—and hopefully Keegan—had to pretend like nothing had happened last night, and more importantly, I had to ensure no one *believed* anything had happened.

I stood outside my body as we gathered in the entrance corridor, bidding Omju and a confused, hungover Hon'niz a protracted farewell. Words were exchanged, though I couldn't say what, and then the Roamers opened the large castle doors…and they walked through them, rolled-up scroll secured tightly in Omju's Freetor hands.

"Your *husband* isn't here," Bidelia whispered in my ear.

"It's probably for the best." He hadn't left his chamber yet, according to the servants' chatter. He was probably still sleeping, like I should've been.

Bidelia shot me a worried look. "Should I speak to him on your behalf?"

"What? No." My head pounded. I leaned on the Silver Spear. It was the one thing keeping me upright. I'd wrapped it again, much to my distaste—and to the disgust of the Spear. It was silly to think of it as having feelings. Lack of sleep played odd tricks on the mind. "He said he doesn't want to *do* this anymore. He needs space. Maybe I do, too."

Did that mean we were still married? I didn't know. Freetor separations were as casual as the marriages in comparison with surface traditions, and I couldn't bear to think about losing Keegan again. I squeezed my eyes shut and gritted my teeth. *Stay awake. I am strong.* Just thinking the words shot renewed energy through my veins. Magic. It could do anything.

No. I couldn't let it. I had to fight…

Bidelia was speaking again. "You'll both need to make an

address tonight, in the cathedral, about the agreement. Once I get confirmation from our scouts that Omju and the caravan have left the city limits—and the province—we can rest easier." She yawned. "We best sleep in shifts. Just in case."

"You can go," I said sleepily. "I can handle the city. The world."

Bidelia eyed me from head to toe. She looked wrecked—yet her gaze was as sharp as ever. "Are you all right, Kiera?"

No. I wasn't. "Fine," I said, mustering up a winning smile as I twirled the Spear between my thumb and forefinger. "Better than ever."

* * *

Keegan did not appear at the cathedral that evening. I stood in front of a thousand faces and promised them the South would send us food and other aid within a fortnight. Again, I felt as though it wasn't me speaking, but some other me—a confident, bold Violet Fox, that could enrapture a crowd and entrance them, if she so chose. I expected a lukewarm response from my people. When it came to promises, they'd heard them all over the years from the Holy One and my father. The awakened magic within lent a new gravitas to my words, for when I finished, I was greeted with uproarious applause.

I'd enjoyed the attention when I was the Violet Fox, but this was different. I was the High Queen of Marlenia. I wasn't just a woman standing next to the Holy One. I was in control. I held their fates in my hand. They depended on me to protect them.

We had forged the agreement with the South...and gotten away with it. For now.

I could take them on if need be, I thought absently as I greeted and received my people in line for their rations and afterward. Their chatter was jovial: apparently, a child had been saved by a young man in the streets today. She'd nearly been hit by a work cart, lugging away the debris in the market, when the dashing hero had leapt in, swept the girl away, and returned her to her mother. No one could point out which child it was in the cathedral, for some had already fallen asleep in the pews. It sounded like the kinds of stories they used to tell about me, and I felt a pang of jealousy—and excitement. Had someone taken up my mantle already? They needn't bother. I was still the Violet Fox, after all.

A darker thought: my father had saved a young Keegan from an out-of-control cart, earning him a position in the court. Had Conal Driscoll returned to Marlenia City?

No—no, I wouldn't let him ruin this moment. I pushed all thoughts of my father and Keegan from my mind as my people readily accepted their reduced rations. Within two weeks, our bellies would be full and everything would be as it was. We just had to survive until then.

From the other side of the cathedral, Gobany and his three apprentice friends kept their distance. I could almost hear their whispers. They were talking about me, I was sure. Their penetrative gaze was unnerving, but to be expected. I had performed a great feat. I thought about telling them—but it was too painful. They'd judge me. Think me unfit for the crown.

Magic corrupted, I had said once. Yet the people loved me. Things were looking up. I was *fixing* the corruption. My people needed me and all of my talents.

"Violet Fox," Gobany said, approaching me outside in the Square as the cathedral cleared out at midnight. I was heading for my carriage as Bidelia closed up for the evening. "Are you…feeling yourself?"

I couldn't feel myself, and that was the problem. I didn't know who I was anymore. "Better than ever," I replied. "Why?"

Gobany regarded me—and the Spear—with cautious respect. "The highs of magic can be…unlike anything. The lows, even more so." He ran a long finger over his facial scars. "Don't suffer the lows alone."

"Lows?" The night air shifted. I tasted the coldness of it in the back of my throat.

Keegan. He's rejected you. He didn't want to stay with you—because you have magic.

"Did you have any other questions about the seat of power?" Gobany asked.

"Why do you call the Tablet that?" I asked.

He raised his eyebrows. "Elder Raibeart would say it at times, since it contains the source of our magic."

Our magic. It had been some time since I'd thought of the Elders. Elder Erskina had been their leader and the others had suffered because of her grab for power.

I wet my lips, shaking my head as I quickened my pace. The Square at this time of night, even with the manned carriages, was frightfully open. Someone could see me. They would know I committed a terrible act...and attempt to hold me accountable. I had to get back to the castle.

"No thank you, Gobany. I'll let you know," I called out evenly behind my shoulder, as I left him in my wake.

I hopped in one of three readied carriages and slumped in the plush seats. Gobany stood in the middle of the Square, facing the destruction he had wrought in the surrounding streets...but he wasn't alone for long. His three fellow apprentices joined him, and after a brief discussion, they boarded the second carriage together.

My body shook with a sob. I missed Laoise. I missed Monju. I even missed Keegan, though he was just in the castle, avoiding me and everyone.

Because I had done a terrible wrong. I had used magic, the magic I had swore to destroy. I had done it for a good reason, and yet, I wasn't sure if it was *good enough*.

"I'm not like Conal," I said out loud, to the Spear. "I had to use it. You understand that, right?"

The Spear rested between my knees, facing me, unjudging. Its gentle plodding knocks against the side of the carriage were like little nods. It understood.

"Once we have the Midnight Tablet back, we can unfreeze them and...well, I'll figure it out. I always do. Now, the people won't starve, and we have a chance against the East. Just...no more magic unless absolutely necessary. Life or death. No...attacking anyone."

And yet, as I stared up at the castle, I feared the enemy lingering in the dark mountains. If I let my guard down even for a moment, I would be made.

* * *

I didn't wake until midday. I felt surprisingly even. No highs. No lows. I stared out the window and the curtains waved in greeting. The air filtering in was chilly, yet a servant had been in and left warmed stones under the blankets.

The Spear rested beside me. Wrapped, but safe. I was safe.

Leisurely, I dressed in clothes that had been laid out on the chair beside the vanity: a long, comfortable, muted purple dress and authoritative belt. High black boots that clomped satisfyingly against the floor. I stood in front of the looking glass, and crowned myself with the silver circlet.

I smiled at my reflection. The dress fit well, it wasn't too garish, and I could move around in it easily. I was adequately dressed to move bodies to the dungeon, should the occasion arise. No more ridiculous gowns. I was the High Queen of Marlenia, not a doll. I would decide how I was seen.

It was nearly imperceptible at first, catching the lantern light only as I tilted my head, yet there it was. Two single white strands sprouting from the center of my head.

I couldn't have that. I plucked them without wincing. There. Better.

An urgent knock cut through the silence.

"Come in," I said.

In the reflection, I saw Bidelia throw open the door and quickly shut it behind her. Her gaze darted about, as if she expected someone else to be present. I spun to face her. "What's wrong?"

"Keegan's not here with you," she said.

I frowned. "Why would he be here?" I had to respect his space. Keegan definitely didn't want to talk to me, not after what he'd witnessed. Not after what I'd *done.*

Bidelia lifted her brows. "He's your husband, isn't he?"

"That doesn't mean we're...sharing a room." Or on speaking terms. "He lost his memory. I wasn't going to..." I blushed, not wanting to say more. It wasn't her business anyway.

Bidelia moved on. "He's not here then. You're sure."

The hair on my arm rose. "Tell me what's wrong, Bidelia."

She took a deep breath and glanced over her shoulder. "You can enter, Pascal."

Antony gingerly opened the door to my chamber and stuck his head in. I frowned, but nodded in confirmation. The Roamer wore heavy shoulder pads and a chestplate, and as he secured the door and limped deeper into the room, I caught the distinctive whiff of the forest surrounding the city.

"Are we being attacked?" I asked.

He grunted. "Not yet, though that's another matter entirely. Violet Fox, your husband isn't in the castle."

"So...he went for a walk? In the city?"

Bidelia was trying hard to be patient with me. "Kiera...Keegan has disappeared. We don't know where he is. No one does. As far as we are concerned, he has evaporated."

"That can't be." I scoffed at the idea. At best, His Holiness was lost in his own castle. He'd said he wanted nothing to do with me. "He's still furious with me."

Antony looked uncomfortable. I wasn't sure how much Bidelia had told him about what had happened with the South. "But if this is a lover's quarrel, you best fix it quickly. I was supposed to meet with the young lad this morning and he didn't show. I'm wading around in various reports about the East's movements, trying to figure out what's accurate."

"What's happening?" I asked, suddenly alarmed.

"More strange activity. The East brought tunnelling equipment into their camp. A large drill, the largest ever seen. Requires three people to turn it. They've been creating holes in the rock. But more peculiar: well-known Eastern fighters have been moving out of their camp. They've finished packing most of their tents and they're loading caravans."

That didn't sound terribly exciting. "What are they trying to do? Tunnel through the mountains into the castle?" It would take years to make an effective path with a man-sized hand drill. "And why would they be leaving?"

"Can't say for certain. They likely know we're watching. They're sending caravans and armed mounts in all cardinal directions." He huffed a large sigh. "Though you may find it interesting that Lady Dominique Castillo was spotted in the camp. She's one of the few staying behind. She's got a personal attaché of Northern shadows. Never seems to leave her side."

That *did* interest me. If Dominique was in the Eastern camp, she was likely up to something. From the way she had ordered around the soldiers under the Frostfire family's command during our last encounter, she seemed to have just as much sway as her new husband, Boris Frostfire. She was cunning, intimidating, and not to be underestimated. "And the new High King of the East?"

"He's there too, we think. Spends most of his time holed up in the largest tent on sight. Torn down by now." He shook his head. "We couldn't get any closer. Something's odd about the whole situation. Were he his father, he would have attacked us now. Why bother creating new tunnels? They lived here. They know where the collapsed ones are, though if they tried to enter the castle that way, they'd receive a nasty surprise from an apprentice. Either Boris is a cautious coward, or he's a regular coward, or they're dealing with a succession crisis...or they're working on a larger plan."

Sobered by the thought of a secret Eastern attack, I nodded. "Keep me apprised. In the mean time, tell me about Keegan. When's the last time anyone saw him?"

"He wasn't at the cathedral last night," Bidelia said gravely. "That in and of itself was a bad sign that I should have...we *both* should have immediately checked on him. But I was exhausted. You were, too. According to the servants, his bed hasn't been slept in for over a day. Even the apprentices can't...sense...him in the castle."

Sensing people—I hadn't thought of that. Could I...?

I gritted my teeth. No. Magic was for *desperate* situations. We weren't there yet.

Still, a dark dread filled me. "Sylvia's note. She threatened to kidnap him. It has been more than five days. Could she really have gone through with it?"

Bidelia paced the room. "Unfortunately, we don't think that's the case."

"I asked my men when they'd last seen the young prince. Holy One." Antony corrected himself hastily. "They said two evenings ago, he *walked out the front doors* of the castle."

Two evenings ago—the night he'd seen the darkness within me and the disastrous effects of my magic. "He just left? With no explanation? No one tried to *stop* him?"

"He's the Holy One, Kiera," Bidelia said. "He doesn't need to tell people why he does something. He can just do it."

I was High Queen and yet I didn't seem to have the same freedom. "Who knows he's missing?"

"Hard to say." Bidelia pursed her lips in a fine line. "If people realize he's left because of what you've done...if he *tells* people what you did..."

"No one will find out. We'll handle it," I said dutifully. Just as bad: his memory loss becoming public knowledge. He had done well until now, piecing together every scrap of history he could find. As the ruler, he could be detached and uninvolved to an extent. But on the street, wandering around, with such a recognizable face...

"If you're sure he's not in the castle, we have to search the city. And the underground." Though I doubted he knew how to enter the Undercity. If anyone still guarded the entrances, they probably wouldn't allow him to enter unaccompanied. Still, with Sylvia threatening to kidnap him, hidden shadows lurking in the alleys, and the risk of our secrets being exposed—I couldn't allow him to wander around the city alone.

Bidelia and Antony exchanged concerned looks. "Violet Fox," Antony began, "I get the urgency of both situations, but we don't have the resources to scour the city for the lost Holy One and continue surveilling the East. I can put all of my people up in the mountains. Maybe I can even send one into the camp in Eastern uniform. Or we can spend time searching for your husband."

Find Keegan. That was my heart's priority. "What do you suggest, General?"

"I serve *you*. Not the Tramore crown. I'll do as you say. But I can call upon my debt at any time."

"I'm more than aware of that." That's exactly what I didn't need—the Roamers asking for silver or land. I had no idea how to pay him. Of the three things he'd asked for, I only had apprentices and magic in abundance, and I would never give that up. At the same time, I couldn't afford to lose the Roamers, and Antony knew it.

"Also be aware that in Keegan's absence, be it from sickness or something more sinister, you are the regent," Bidelia added. "You have complete control, final say, and discretion over the realm. You will have to decide what we do next, for good or ill."

Bidelia's words hung heavily on my chest. Although Keegan had lost his formative years, he had still proved useful and competent as a Holy One. Together, along with Bidelia, who was indispensable, we had managed to keep Marlenia City and the entirety of the Western seat of power from falling apart. With Keegan gone—possibly missing—I was left to bear the burden of rulership. I didn't know anything about military strategy and my diplomacy was fueled by impatience. I was good at pretending and breezing my way through a conversation—less good at real governance.

And, I'd lost the one person binding me to the castle.

If I wanted, I could leave and conduct my own search for the missing Midnight Tablet…and no one, barring perhaps the apprentices, would be able stop me.

I balled my hands into fists. I wouldn't let the magic control me. Not this time. "Continue observing the East with the majority of your troops," I told Antony. "Bidelia, have the apprentices sweep the Undercity. Quietly. We'll keep the remainder of the castle guard here in on regular patrol. If he's not back by tomorrow… we'll make a different plan."

Bidelia and Antony nodded and I felt relieved. I was tired of fielding their questions when there was so much to do. After they left me alone in my chamber, I examined myself in the looking glass once more.

No, this outfit wouldn't do for today.

Rummaging through my wardrobe, I found a black robe with a large hood and dawned whatever peasant clothing I could find. Leaving the Silver Spear resting on the bed, and the silver circlet on the vanity, I set out for the streets of Marlenia City. I had to play into my strengths and do what I did best.

* * *

I had not been on the ground for an hour, combing streets and alleyways, searching for the best way into the Undercity, when the fight broke out.

The shouts emanated from a gathered crowd in the middle of Deacon Street. No wagon or carriage traffic plagued the streets much now, as many of the horses had been slaughtered for food or traded to farms outside the city for their winter stores. With the South gone, most shops had closed in fear of looting or for lack of merchandise to sell. It seemed many people were content to hide in their homes, or in the Undercity, biding their time for the next rationing. But when life was hard, and entertainment was sparse, a private argument escalating in public was as exciting as attending an execution in the Square, and so many had gathered to witness the show.

A middle-aged woman was accusing a man of being in league with the East. They were trading barbs, encouraged by some of the surrounding folks as everyone contributed stories or evidence of traitorous activity.

At first, I skirted the pack of people trying to get a better look. Keegan wasn't among them. He wouldn't stand for such a brutal display—he'd never cared for them, and only endured the spectacle to impress his father, who had acquired his cruel tastes from his father, and so on, back to the original Marlenian-Freetor war.

I thought about interfering. I was the High Queen and the Violet Fox—wasn't it my job to settle disputes, especially in Keegan's absence? I circled the crowd once more, keeping an eye on the adjacent alleyways. I hadn't seen in the sun in days. Despite the hurt burning within me, the lightness of being anonymous in the city, as dirty and destitute as it was, this felt right. I was the Violet Fox again, close to my roots: skulking around the city, pretending to be no one, as I spied on the enemy and retrieved what had been lost.

The woman lashed out at the man. It was becoming physical. No, I couldn't let this go on. This was a task for the Violet Fox.

Before I could rush in to save the day, another figure parted the crowd. Not with bravados or a weapon, but with his sheer presence, the people made room for him. His shimmering white tunic from the dinner days ago had been soiled by dirt and large splotches of dried blood. Not his: I saw no evidence of anything more than scrapes and bruises beneath the thin, stained fabric. His dark hair was messily knotted on top of his head, held in place with thick grey fabric that ran down his back. The top half of his face was obscured with trouser fabric, clearly ripped from his legs and fashioned into a mask.

"Crimson Prince," said the woman who had accused the man. She sounded like she had expected him.

He placed his hands on his hips—and then I noticed his three-fingered hand.

I knew those yellow-green eyes peering from beneath the mask. Those scarred lips, demanding silence and understanding from the crowd.

Keegan.

And yet…my Keegan would never do something like this.

Right?

"Stop this," he said, with booming authority. His voice carried over the abandoned streets. My brief admiration for his ingenuity turned sour. Who did he think he was? Just because he fashioned a mask from some old cloth, gave him the right to patrol in *my* domain? He clearly wasn't fooling anyone...right? He was the Holy One. Not some...folk hero.

That was...my identity.

"Why do you believe he's an Eastern spy?" he asked the woman.

"My lord, I saw him with a Northerner just now, in the alley." She pointed behind her, between the nearest two buildings.

My lord. They did know—or at least, they suspected. They wouldn't have called him *prince* otherwise, even though that wasn't his official title.

"That Northerner moved here long before the Violet Fox made a mess with the other provinces. She's innocent," the man protested. "Not a spy or a shadow or anything else. I was just helping her out because *someone* seems to think she's a spy, too."

The woman paled and tried to garner support from the crowd. "How are we supposed to know anything anymore, if Miss High and Mighty Fox sits on her throne all day? At least our decent and good lord has the decency to—"

To my surprise, the crowd hushed her. "He's the Crimson Prince, nothing more," they said.

My blood ran cold. They were protecting him. Someone had mentioned the story of a dashing young man, saving a child. He had won their favour and gained a new identity. He had shown them he was willing to get his hands—and his clothing—filthy for them. He would not sit in the castle like his High and Mighty Fox wife, who cut down kings and shadows alike.

Keegan—as the Crimson Prince—held up his hands to quiet our people. "Where is the Northerner now?"

"He helped her escape the city. Showed her the tunnels," the woman said accusingly. "My lord, that is unforgiveable. I wouldn't show any Marlenian the way, not even you."

"Is this true?" the Crimson Prince asked.

The man crossed his arms and said nothing.

"You see, he's a liar and a traitor as well!" the woman continued. "He's reporting our movements to the East and helping the North. He must be punished. There must be justice, Crimson Prince!"

"Just-ice! Just-ice!" The crowd began chanting. Even the two who had started the argument mouthed the words angrily at Keegan. Some among the crowd drew rusty swords and handmade clubs spiked with nails—where had those come from?

Bidelia hadn't held court since they'd taken the castle, and neither had we since our return. Usually disputes such as these would be logged by the Advisor and brought before the Holy One, so he could dispense final judgement. In the space of two days, Keegan had found himself with a new name, a new identity—and the same responsibility. As loud and as furious as my people were in that moment, they respected him. He walked among their suffering.

Last night, they'd loved *me*. They'd clapped and cheered at *my* speech. Keegan had walked away from them when he'd thrown that agreement with the South on the floor. I'd sacrificed my sanity and my judgement.

What had he sacrificed?

The tingling in my hands intensified all in one moment and I barely suppressed the urge to lash out. I turned away and kept walking further down the street, counting my steps. No, I couldn't let it control me. Not again. Keegan had lost plenty, just like all of us. It was not a competition.

"All right," he said, lifting his hands once more. The chanting ceased almost immediately. "I declare this man is an Eastern spy. Take him to a safe entrance and imprison him in one of the caves."

The man protested his innocence, but the Crimson Prince had spoken. Some large, armed men from the crowd forcefully led the alleged Eastern spy down a narrow alley. I pulled my hood around my face and scuttled behind a brick building. With most of the crowd gone, I was a lone woman, staring strangely at the people's new favourite. Others lingered around Keegan, congratulating and thanking him for keeping him safe. The older people among them touched him as if he were holy—because to some, he was. He tried to wade through their admiration and the street with a smile, but the crowd had attached themselves to their rightful ruler.

Did they know he couldn't remember his former life?

Maybe that was appealing to them. A prince who didn't remember he was a prince. The perfect blank slab on which to write their own ideas of the perfect monarch. One who lives among them, suffers with them, and dispenses justice in under a minute.

This wasn't his place. I couldn't allow him to stay here. They'd eat him alive.

The magic danced inside me, demanding to be released. I balled my hand into a fist against the wall. All it would take was one blast, I could knock him old cold, and drag him…

Our gazes met.

I parted my lips—and the cry died.

They knew who he was, though they may not know why he was gallivanting around the city, dispensing justice under a moniker. His face and name were protected for a reason. Likely because of Eastern and Northern spies—but also, because of *me*. If I called to him, everyone would know he'd run from me. They'd know he acted on his own, and they'd support him, not the Violet Fox, sitting on her throne in the castle with all the food and supplies. Only rioting and revolt would follow.

Some of his new comrades noticed his far-off stare and followed it. I quickly flattened against the wall and closed my eyes. The Violet Fox was no longer welcome on these streets.

Guilt surged through me. Whenever I thought of him, I saw his face, disapproving of me, unbelieving, uncaring. I balled my hands into fists. Once I had the Midnight Tablet and his memories were restored, he'd understand. He would love me as he did before.

When I dared to peek again, his followers had swallowed him whole, chattering loudly about the justice they had dispensed and waving their fashioned weapons like flags. They disappeared into an alley. Perhaps revolt was inevitable.

I wouldn't let them take him away from me.

I crept along the buildings, following the mob at a safe distance as it faded into the din of the city. His words lingered in my mind: *Clearly you aren't you right now.*

Well, clearly *he* wasn't *him* either—that's why he ran away. My Keegan wouldn't have done that. This wasn't his world. I had to find him before an Eastern soldier or Northern shadow stabbed him and left him for dead in an alley. He wore no weapon at his side, yet the people acted as one. A mob could take on an army—to an extent.

Maybe he would survive.

Leave him, said a voice, deep inside me. *Leave him to discover what true freedom tastes like. Or find him with your new power and show him what you have become.*

"No," I whispered. I could do neither. He had feared the Freetor magic. It had always made him uneasy to know that some uncontrollable, manipulative force ruled the lives of the obsessed and the elite. Now, he had run from me because of it. I couldn't let that happen again. I controlled the magic; it didn't control me.

Their trail had gone cold—they must have disappeared underground. Not Keegan, though, they wouldn't *let* him. At least they'd maintained that separation. That would make our search easier. I hurried down another alleyway. I was in the merchant district now. I just had to find where he'd made his lair. Then, I could confront him, and—

A flash of deep red fabric caught my eye, traversing down the adjoining street. *There you are.*

I stepped quietly to the edge of the alleyway and peeked around.

A few stalls had been haphazardly repaired and some fearless merchants sold faded scarves and other bric-a-brac. Fires burned high in large metal barrels, warming several people at various points throughout the street. I pulled part of my hood around the bottom half of my face. I felt the gazes of many—but they said nothing. I was too nondescript to be the Violet Fox, and without the Spear, I was not the High Queen.

At first, I thought I'd lost him. But that was because it wasn't Keegan I'd spotted. The flash of red was hidden beneath a layer of dull wool acting as a cloak, dirty from days of travel. The hem of an overly extravagant, red dress shined through, filthy, yes, but rich. Her blonde curls had been shoved beneath a hood. Her pouty face surveyed the poverty with disdain. She turned to the four large men surrounding her—all tall, confident, and blatantly armed— and barked a shrill order above the din, "Hurry *up!*"

Onlookers regarded her suspiciously, though they didn't dare follow or interfere. The large men escorted Sylvia Frostfire down the alleyway, and she went with them consensually. One of the men I recognized as Gabian, her loyal personal guard. He stood between her and the other men, who had the swagger of hired swords.

I pressed myself against the scratchy brick walls as they disappeared into the shadows. What was Sylvia Frostfire doing in Marlenia City with a band of ruffians? Yes, she had sent that note, threatening to kidnap Keegan *or else*, but to see her here personally was troubling. Keegan, my husband, the rightful heir to the throne—he was within reach, for both of us. What if Sylvia had gotten word of his *departure* from the castle? Suddenly her frilly threat was not so frivolous. The crowd could barely keep Keegan's identity hidden as they carried out their justice.

Unless Sylvia's prize was a different man. One whose whereabouts I *did* know. Her brother, Leon Frostfire.

Regardless of her intentions, I couldn't have the Daughter of the East roaming the city. Either my people would find her and dispense their own brutal form of justice, or she would find Keegan, and her men would take him from me. Neither I could abide.

I could take on the four men and capture Sylvia myself—remove her from the streets. Keegan would be safer.

One problem at a time. Easily solvable by me, alone.

I crossed the street hastily. Sylvia and her companions had moved through the streets and alleyways to enter the outer range of Gobany's destruction. I hadn't examined it this closely in daylight until now, and it was more extensive than I had initially seen. At least five streets had been levelled. Buildings—homes and shops—now wood and stone rubble. No one lingered here. There was nothing left but raw, damaged materials. A small wasteland within the seat of power.

I pursed my lips. I had come close to spinning out of control. Gobany had sensed it. Yet I hadn't. I would be smarter than he was.

A few caved-in structures remained within the outer radius of the blast. I weaved around them, attempting to keep some cover as I approached Sylvia and her four men. They were easy to spot as they argued by a half-collapsed two-storey home, her voice carrying through the abandoned rubble. "—know where he is, then why aren't you *getting him*?"

A deeper, rougher voice said something I couldn't quite catch. I snuck closer. I was running out of places to hide and the ground was not even.

"I did that!" Sylvia replied. "Just capture him. Then we can get out of this city."

"We've already killed two," said the same man, with the rough voice. He appeared to speak for the other two men in their group.

"I didn't ask you to kill those innocent people! I just wanted to send the castle a message! Now that we know he's on the streets—"

The men shrugged. "No one is innocent, my lady. If you want to order another death, you know the terms. Silver up front."

"I don't have any more silver!" Sylvia read the warning plainly on Gabian's face, and said no more. "Killing is cruel. You really shouldn't have done that."

The man shrugged. "You paid the silver for two deaths. Your brother paid us for the planting, and that's done. But if you say you have no more silver..."

The planting?

"I didn't mean for you to kill those Roamers. And of course I still have silver, I always do..." She trailed off nervously.

When we'd first entered the city, Antony had described three hooded figures with bloodied weapons. We'd suspected Eastern soldiers had murdered people in the streets, and I suppose they weren't wrong. The thought of it being a misunderstanding sent shivers throughout my body. Sylvia had to be removed from the streets before she got more innocent people killed. No doubt those intended hits were for me and well...possibly my father. We'd both played a part in getting Leszek Frostfire killed.

I stared at my hands. I didn't have the Spear. The urge to use magic wasn't immediately there—but I could force it. Somehow. Last time, I'd been afraid, angry, and desperate. I couldn't rely on that. Too risky.

It was too late to back out now. I moved around a rubble heap and into plain view. Gabian spotted me and drew a longsword at his waist. The other men turned, hands hovering over their hilts. Sylvia emerged from behind them and scowled. "You."

"Welcome to Marlenia City," I said dryly, kicking a path through the charred wood and rocks. "Though had I known you were coming, I would have given you a royal welcome."

My sarcasm gave her pause—but not for long. "Where is Keegan?"

"Around," I said casually.

"You've turned him into your sorry puppet," she said.

I said nothing. Best she thought that was true. Slowly, I made my way towards them. There wasn't going to be an easy exit from this encounter. No running. I had gone in without a plan, no aid, and only a knife tucked away in my boot. At least this time, I didn't have a dress in my way.

I stopped several stone-throws away from Sylvia and her men. Let them wade through the rubble to get to me. "Sylvia, why don't you come with me to the castle? Where we can discuss things more civilly."

"Absolutely not! You just want to stuff me in dungeon! Or worse, you'll stuff me in a cart and kidnap me again! I'd rather be out here in the filth, than underground, beneath your thumb!"

I hadn't kidnapped her—she had willingly cooperated with us! She was just being dramatic in front of her hired swords. "Are you sure about that? You're safer with me than with them. Especially when your brother attacks us."

Her eyes widened as she began wading a path through the rubble towards me. "How do you know about that?"

I hadn't meant anything by it. I was speaking generally, as we had all assumed it was a matter of time before Boris Frostfire descended upon us with the full force of the East—combined with whatever help Dominique commanded from the North. If Boris and Dominique were planning something specific, all the more reason to take Sylvia into my custody. I smiled and shrugged. "Well? If you're not coming with me willingly, I will fight your men for you."

"Romantic," she said chillingly. "Fight her. I'll pay you silver to kill her later. Gabian, stay by my side."

Her loyal guard obeyed without question. The three men, however, looked dubious as they evaluated their chances. One stepped forward, easily dodging the rubble, but he didn't draw his weapon. "Violet Fox?"

"Yes," I replied, spreading my arms in invitation. "Are you going to fight me?"

He sneered. "You're an unarmed woman. So no. It's an unfair match."

"That's what you think." I drew my boot knife. "How about now?"

The sellsword and his friends chuckled—and I joined in. Sylvia looked horrified. If they attacked me, I would fight for my life, and if a stray bolt of lightning hit them in the face...

"You're the High Queen. Supposedly. Whatever that means these days," the man continued. "But I suspect you have more silver than that one?" He jabbed his thumb over his shoulder at Sylvia.

Now his two friends were interested—and Gabian's expression darkened.

"I *have* silver. Just not on me. Obviously. I am not a walking vault," Sylvia said haughtily.

"Could have fooled us," said another one of the men, and they laughed again.

I betrayed nothing and acted casual. "As the High Queen, I have access to...discretionary funds." I wasn't sure what that meant exactly, but I had heard the previous steward say it at our council meetings from time to time. That seemed a long time ago now. "However, I'm not hiring swords at this time. If you fight for me, you're a Roamer or you're part of the castle guard, which requires some preliminary training."

"Hmm. We're not good enough for your castle guard, Violet Fox?" He shook his head. "So the West has no silver either."

"That's not what I said," I retorted. "Why would I hire three men who try to sell themselves to the newest threat? If you knew what was good for you, you'd stop fooling around with silver and start worrying about her brother. And certain other, more magical dangers. Which if you were on my side, you'd already know about."

The hired swords laughed again. "*Magical* dangers?" They

shook their heads. They didn't believe me.

Sylvia pursed her lips. A fire lit in her eyes. "She's telling the truth! She killed my father with her cursed Spear! She...she..." After several false starts, she scrunched up her face, trying not to cry. "I even tried to gather the pieces. But...I couldn't..."

Behind her, the three men began to snicker.

"What's so *funny*?" she screamed at them. "Have you ever picked up a dead man, piece by piece?" She returned her glower to me. "You are going to pay for what you've done."

I rarely took Sylvia seriously. She and I were night and day in nearly every way—but something in her tone struck a chord. She meant what she said. Although she and her father hadn't seen eye to eye—he'd arranged her betrothal to Dominique's nine-year-old brother without her consent—I imagined I'd feel similarly if she had managed to kill Laoise or even my father.

"Sylvia, I'm genuinely sorry. If I hadn't stepped in his way, your father would have killed mine."

"Better yours than mine! At least he wasn't an obsessed traitor wandering around with uncontrollable magic."

My breath caught. "Sylvia...have you seen him?"

She frowned. "Why would I tell you *anything*? Your whole family is a menace! Well, what are you standing there for? Knock her out. Anything so she shuts up."

Again, the three men didn't immediately jump into the fray. The man closest to me, the one with the rough voice, said to Sylvia, "Do you think you're worth your weight in silver?"

"I'm worth ten times my weight in silver," she said easily. Sylvia was heavyset, though her time in the wilderness had shaved off some of her curves.

"Even better." The three sellswords drew their weapons: they hadn't even cleaned their swords from the previous kills. "Come with us, princess. Time for your brother to pay up."

Gabian unsheathed his weapon and stepped between Sylvia and

the three advancing men. I too danced between the large stone rocks and piles of debris to enter the ensuing fray.

A loud, familiar voice cut through the destruction. "She's going nowhere."

Keegan. No.

He and twelve citizens, all armed and varying in age and size, fanned out of and between the neighbouring half-destroyed buildings surrounding the explosion radius. They forged towards Sylvia and the men, holding their weapons aloft. The Crimson Prince himself had no weapon, as before, and three of his followers flanked him, protecting their precious ruler.

I sighed. He was going to get himself killed. He was going to get our people killed.

Sylvia grinned excitedly at Keegan. "Oh, I knew it was you! And you've come to—"

"Now the Spoiled Daughter can be taught a lesson!" shouted the same woman who had enjoyed "justice" earlier.

The gathered mob prepared to strike.

"Wait!" Keegan and I cried.

They halted at his command, but barely. They glanced between me and their righteous ruler—many of them hadn't even registered me as present. No doubt they were wondering why the mighty Violet Fox had crawled off her throne. Let them wonder.

Keegan eyed me carefully. I inclined my head. I would follow his lead. For now.

The three hired swords used our hesitation as an opportunity. They unleashed their weapons as Gabian raised his sword protectively—but he was only one man. Two of the hired swords cut him down, while the rough-voiced man grabbed Sylvia under the arm, and pointed his weapon at the Crimson Prince.

"We'll be taking our leave now," he said to him, and then to me, he said, "Last chance to purchase the Daughter of the East."

I stepped closer, cautiously. I was perhaps two stone-throws away now. Sylvia screamed Keegan's name and then saw Gabian, bleeding out amongst the rocks, and screamed some more.

"Let the woman go, and I will consider a lighter sentence for the three of you," Keegan said, alarmed, holding out his hand to Sylvia.

His citizen protectors cast him suspicious looks and my stomach dropped. He didn't recognize Sylvia. He'd seen her once, when he woke in the coffin. She'd tried to convince him they were in love, and failed when he realized she was the one who had cut off his cloth-ringed finger. All he saw was a young noblewoman in distress—not a participant and former benefactor of a province-wide occupation.

I touched my own cloth ring. Although frayed and worn, I had never considered removing it, not even now. I wouldn't blow his cover. We had to be seen as a cohesive team. He had already worked his followers into a frenzy just by being among them, holding their hands and giving the mob exactly what they wanted: bloody, immediate justice.

The woman from earlier who had accused her neighbour said, "She doesn't deserve to be saved! Let them kill her!"

Keegan looked alarmed. "Wait, I—"

But the mob had spoken. They began their chant, *"Kill her! Kill her!"*

The small crowd's reaction surprised the hired swords. They started to move away from the half-collapsed home, nearly tripping over Gabian in the process. As much harm as Sylvia had caused, I couldn't let her leave the city like this. Yes, she was the enemy. And yes, she had betrayed me the last time we cooperated. But without her, I wouldn't have found Keegan in the first place. It was her obsession with him that had helped us in the end. I owed her.

And, as she herself suggested, she was worth ten times her weight in silver.

"I'll buy her freedom," I shouted.

The hired swords hesitated. The one holding Sylvia whirled around with her in tow. She struggled against him and he held up his filthy sword in a palatable threat. He chuckled humorlessly. "I don't think you can afford her, Violet Fox."

"Try me," I said. I took another few steps closer.

The crowd's chanting turned uproarious.

"Don't let her spend our taxes on the East! Just capture her, now!"

"Kill her! She deserves to die!"

Sylvia gasped at the mob. "How dare you!"

Her protest only egged them on further. I managed to edge closer. I was one stone-throw away.

"One thousand silver quid."

Now, the mob hushed. The Crimson Prince's nostrils flared. "One thousand...?"

"Hmph," said the swordsman holding Sylvia. "If you had that much in your coffers, Violet Fox, your people wouldn't be starving. Do you really want to pay a thousand quid for a noblewoman?"

"We'll pay you five quid to kill her!" said a man in the mob.

"No, she's only worth one!" shouted another.

A new fire lit among the mob, and even Keegan's booming voice couldn't quiet them this time. Justice had its own volume. I glared at the Crimson Prince now—he had no control over his newfound power. He had thought he could wield the people for his own purposes. They would never be able to bring him inner peace or provide him with answers about his identity. He was a ruler—but he lacked the knowledge he once had of his own people.

The Crimson Prince pointed a definitive finger at Sylvia and her captors. "Let her go. Let her—"

It didn't matter what he said. He could have said nothing. His pointing was a sign to begin the charge.

I couldn't let that happen. What if she knew something about my father? About the East's plans?

"No! No one is going to die!" I shouted.

A quiet moment bloomed within the noise, where my hands rose of their own volition, my fingers splayed. My heartbeat was the loudest sound, aside from the whispers—not from the mob, whose cries had muted—but whispers that echoed within my mind.

He will never act. He surrounds himself with human shields and doles out justice without evidence or feeling. Your Keegan killed. This Keegan bears his scars, but cannot truly know why or how, and can only wonder.

No magic, except when necessary.

The shouting mob ran through the rubble. Keegan ran after them, trying to stop the impending slaughter. Sylvia reached for him. The hired swordsman shifted Sylvia, throwing her behind him, and thrust his blade at Keegan.

In Marlenian society, nothing was more polarizing than magic. For over two centuries, the surface-born had coveted it. They feared it as well, and had banished my ancestors underground for the rebellion they'd instigated.

Now, I was a Freetor High Queen, endowed with magic, and I'd use it only as necessary. For good.

I raised my hands—and without further thought—I screamed.

There was a brief moment between the sound erupting from my lips and the splay of my fingers when nothing out of the ordinary happened. The swordsman's blade still moved toward Keegan at a frightening speed. A sob caught in my throat. Maybe I didn't have magic after all. Perhaps my attack on Kamal and Danyal had been the result of some build-up from the Spear within—

A bolt of lightning split the air three times. One. Two. Three. *Zap. Zap. Zap.*

The swordsmen's blades clanged on the rubble. Thin grey lines of smoke wavered where their bodies had been.

And then, I wasn't the only one screaming.

Chunks of human remains covered the side of the half-collapsed building, the surrounding debris, and everyone who had entered the fray. Sylvia bore the brunt of it. She was covered in pulverized guts. Her eyes bugged out of her skull in horror, and then rolled into the back of her head as she fell in a heap next to Gabian.

The Crimson Prince's followers paled and covered their faces as they scattered away from the smell of burnt flesh and bits of human being stuck on their clothing and the debris. Some slipped on it as they hurried away like mice from the alley cat.

Only the Crimson Prince remained standing. His stained blouse had attracted brain matter and soaked in new blood; he regarded it, mouth agape. This was this Keegan's first real battle, and his hands trembled. They went for his side, and when he grasped the emptiness, realizing he wasn't armed, hope rose within me.

What else did I have to sacrifice, just for him to glimpse his former self?

I moved towards him sympathetically as his attention turned to the now-unconscious Sylvia and Gabian.

"Keegan...I-I'm sorry, I didn't mean to—"

"That's what you said last time," he said absently. He picked a piece of red goo from his sleeve. He tried to flick it away, but it stuck between his fingers. Eventually, he just wiped it on his ripped trousers and scowled in disgust. "You...*slaughtered*...them."

"They were going to kill you."

"You don't know that!"

But I did, and he shook with the knowledge that I was right.

I gestured to Sylvia and swallowed over the lump in my throat. "I'm taking her into custody. Where she can await proper justice." Or potentially, I could exchange her for peace with the East—though that was hopefully implied. I crossed my arms. "What are you doing? What is...all of this?" I gestured to his outfit.

"You think that you're the only one who can wear a mask, run around the city, and save lives? I've heard the stories. You told them to me yourself." He glanced after his new band of friends and followers. "They need me. It is lawless down here."

"It is lawless because you are encouraging this individualized justice. It isn't a game or a story, Keegan! You are a ruler. Of the entire world. You can't just run away from the castle and decide people's fates on the street! You don't even have a weapon."

"I don't need one."

"You will," I said darkly. "The Keegan I knew didn't hesitate to shed blood when the situation called for it. I don't like that I had to do it." I pointed at the remaining bits of the three hired swords. "But if I didn't, you would have died. If only you could see yourself now, as you were before. If you knew what we had gone through and suffered..."

He looked away, closing his eyes, and his mind.

One of the Roamers must have noticed our unusual gathering in the rubble. A royal carriage wheeled its way around the mountain. I hoped they'd somehow recognized Keegan beneath his disguise and were coming to drag him back to his throne. I wasn't leaving until he was safe in his chamber—away from the Daughter of the East.

Keegan noted the carriage as well. "I can't go with you."

"Yes, you can."

"Are you going to force me?" He was staring at my hands. I hadn't even noticed; they were fists, warmed by the thought of impending battle.

I bunched my robes. Control. I was in control. "I would never do anything to hurt you, Keegan."

"Can you really make that promise?"

"Yes." I held out my hands to help. "Please, come back with me. I don't completely understand the magic I have, but I *feel* I am getting better—"

"You feel, but you don't know. That's why the High King is in the dungeon, isn't it?"

I turned away. Trading barbs would get us nowhere. "I did

what I had to in order to survive. You would have done the same."

He shook his head. "That's not how I want to rule. If you want to stay in the castle and murder royalty—"

"He's not *dead*—"

"—then go ahead. I literally can't stop you, Kiera. I'm not strong enough. Not yet."

"Keegan..."

He darted away through the debris. He was not practiced at making his way between the obstacles; he nearly tripped, and my heart leapt as I moved forward to help him. But his followers appeared out of the ruins to stabilize him. They cast me suspicious, envious looks that turned into victorious grins as they lead him from the explosion radius, deeper into the labyrinthian streets.

He wasn't strong enough to stop me, he'd said. We both knew he could waltz back into the throne room and resume his rulership at any time. I would welcome him back. I wanted him to rule at my side. But he would never accept me now that I had magic—and had used it twice to save our lives.

How long before the feelings he once had for me turned to hatred and loathing, because I was unafraid to do what must be done?

How many more followers must he earn to strike me down?

And how would I find the strength not to surrender to him, but to fight him to the bitter end, not out of bitterness, but out of love for the man he was—and the man he must now become?

* * *

Gabian was not dead, though he was not fairing well. I knelt by him and tore up his regal cape and part of Sylvia's hem to staunch some of the bleeding. I hoped he survived long enough to transport him up to the castle. Our herbal and medicine supplies were dangerously low, but perhaps some could be spared to help him—even though he was somewhat the enemy. The line had blurred.

I was the enemy now. I heard the commoners watching me at a safe distance, whispering about my misdeeds. They were afraid of me. Best they gossiped about me and not Keegan. Word would spread of my powers quickly. At least they didn't approach or attempt to stop Bidelia as she made her way awkwardly through the rubble.

"So," she said, "should we wrap and transport them to the dungeons, too?"

"No," I replied, standing. My knees were numb from kneeling in rubble and body muck. "We'll confine them to one of the spare guest chambers."

"As you wish," Bidelia said stiffly. She wasn't keen to help the young woman who had caused her so much suffering. Her gaze passed over the bits of brain matter, organs, and blood that stained the rocks and the half-collapsed ruins—and made no comment.

Two Roamers ventured towards us to help carry Sylvia and Gabian to the carriage. I crossed my arms and stared up at the castle on mountain high.

"Don't make me be the woman who drags the regent back up the mountain and forces the silver crown upon her head," she said bitterly, surveying the onlookers perched beyond the explosion radius.

"I don't deserve it," I muttered. I flexed my fingers as feeling returned to them. "To rule, I mean."

"No," Bidelia said. "You don't. You have to earn it. And more so now, by proving you can learn from your mistakes. But you can't do that down here, in front of them. You have to make the hard choices, even when they're not watching. Then, you have to live with those choices."

"Is this supporting me now the hardest choice you've had to make?"

She smiled, a little. "No. Not even close."

I sighed. "I just wanted to find him. And I did. He won't listen to me. So what am I supposed to do with a king who wants to run around in the filth?"

"Ask the queen," Bidelia replied. Her expression was grim. "His attire and actions were far from princely. No one will believe that he's out here for a *sane* reason—unless you concoct one."

This isn't what I wanted. Keegan was supposed to be a High King—the Holy One, the coveted title of the ruler of the entire world. It wasn't right that he was reduced to this. I had come from the dirt. I had grown in it. To have him running around, bloodied and scared...

No. I wouldn't allow it. The Keegan I knew wouldn't want this. Wouldn't he?

"I didn't come down here just to fetch you," Bidelia said, as the two Roamers quickly applied herbs to Gabian's wounds and prepared to move him to the carriage. "We've just received word from Laoise." She allowed joy to seep into her words. "It seems they've found the Tablet."

My heart leapt. "You mean, they've found the other piece? Where are they?"

"It just said they have it in their possession and they're on their way back. From where, I'm not certain. Nothing about halves or pieces, just that they had the Tablet. The message was written a few days ago and in Freetor code, not in her handwriting. Likely Monju's, given the brevity and shaky construction of the lettering." Laoise had only recently been learning to read and write and, as Monju wasn't a Freetor, his grasp of the code would be poor.

"Did they mention Conal?" I asked.

"Yes. They had an encounter. That's all it said."

That wasn't reassuring. I remained troubled. They were alive, at least. Though if Kamal encountered my father not far from our border and he managed to swindle a piece of the Tablet from the High King...had Laoise in turn stolen Kamal's half from Conal? Or had they found a different piece in Xii?

Kamal had said he'd been resolved to find his half's mate, meaning, he believed there were only two pieces. Maybe, Laoise and Monju had managed to snag both halves. Optimistic, yes, but I needed it to be true right now.

"When are we expecting them?" I asked.

"Tomorrow, or the next day. They still have their horses." She waved away my follow-up questions. "Not here. Let's get moving, before you cause more trouble."

The words were meant to be jovial, but they stung regardless. "You don't have to drag me back. I'll go of my own volition. Thanks."

"At least follow me to the carriage," she said. "You have a meeting with Pascal and his Roamers in an hour to discuss our next move, with regards to the East. It would be prudent for you to review the reconnaissance from the East and the South before that. We may have gotten *lucky* with the South, but we cannot expect that from the other two provinces. Once Boris finds out we have both of his siblings in our custody, he'll likely escalate matters. After you are appropriately dressed, should I meet you in your chamber or the council room?"

I resented Bidelia's tone. I didn't have time for meetings. I couldn't unsee the terrifying destruction I had caused. I had deeper issues to contend with. But she was right. Taking one last glance at the crumbling city, I followed Bidelia back to the Square to await our transport up the mountain. We had a day, perhaps two at most, before word reached Boris Frostfire about my new powers and his sister's capture. If Laoise and Monju really did have the Tablet, then we stood a fighting chance against his army. If they didn't...we needed another advantage that wasn't centered around unreliable, all-consuming magic. It would take time for Sylvia to come around, and even longer for her to be willing to talk and disclose potentially damning information about her brother and his plans.

So I had to visit the next-best thing.

***

The dungeons twisted deep within the mountain like an ant-hill. One could get lost or spend days wandering the dark, uneven corridors. A single torch flickered at the end of the hallway. The Spear glowed dimly and my Freetor eyes adjusted to the darkness in gratitude. Other than dragging our Southern guests to the safety of their cells, I'd spent little time down here. I had been a prisoner, briefly, after I'd admitted my true identity to Keegan and the entire world in the cathedral, during his almost-wedding to Sylvia. Now, Sylvia was imprisoned in the safety of her guest chamber, Gabian was receiving the care he (perhaps) didn't deserve, Keegan was running amuck with misguided ideas of making a difference—and I was still a prisoner of duty in this castle.

The walls between the cells in this block were rough, gritty stone, meant to discourage prisoners from forming relationships or passing objects. The front was made of solid metal bars, and the door, also barred. Each section of the prison was different, built by different rulers for various purposes. At least this configuration allowed me to speak with him without having to enter his cell.

I had changed for the occasion, back into the simple dress I'd dawned this morning. I had to show the prisoner how far I'd come. As I approached his cell, he stirred from his crouched position in the corner, and evaluated me bitterly.

"I heard Prince Keegan has slipped through your fingers," Leon Frostfire said smugly in greeting.

Did no one in this castle know how to keep a secret? It was a wonder I was able to last undercover for weeks while I was Lady Dominique.

"Your father is dead. In case no one told you," I said evenly.

His gaze narrowed and he rose to his full height. "Oh no. They told me. I heard you did the deed. Congratulations, you've triggered succession protocols for my family. I'm sure Boris is blandly pleased, as much as he can be."

I stiffened. He *really* wasn't going to help me now. "I didn't mean to kill him."

"Sure you didn't."

"No, I really didn't. He was awful, but—"

"There's no *but* in there. He was a ruthless ruler, a terrible father to me and Boris, and cruel to his enemies. Which was, chiefly, whoever threatened the great efficiency of our economy." He said the last part as if he'd heard it a thousand times at his father's knee. "The real question, Violet Fox, is if you're here to finish me off, too?"

The Spear warmed at the suggestion. I took a deep breath. Leon Frostfire had travelled the Western province during the occupation, paying families to rat out their Freetor neighbours and underground colonies. Then he and his men murdered them. Oh, he'd told me he'd had a moment of regret when he'd refused to kill a Freetor child, and not even all the bottles in the cellar could erase the feeling. But it was hard to feel sympathy for a man whose heart only stayed his hand when he had something to gain.

My silence intrigued him. "Well? If you're not going to kill me, then I'd hoped we could talk. With no false pretenses. Or masks."

Last time, he'd thought I was his intended, Linnaea Gareth, disguised as a servant. He was inappropriately aggressive—and I'd fought him off, each time. When Leszek Frostfire surprised us all by marrying his sons publicly, I had stood in Laoise's place—who had been pretending to be Linnaea. Then, it was chaos. "I haven't forgotten what you did to me. And to my people."

"I'm not surprised. I drank an entire vineyard and couldn't forget. But I've had a lot of time to think down here. And to sober up, as much as I hate feeling like this." He shrugged. "I can't change what I've done, Violet Fox. Are you going to torture me, in the name of the dead? Throw tactless barbs? Or do you actually want something, now that you are High Queen?"

I closed my eyes, unexpectedly moved. I also couldn't change the past. "I need information about your brother."

"What do you think I would tell you that I haven't already told your other rat associates?"

"You mean I'm not special enough to you, Leon, to warrant special treatment?" I said bitterly, feigning offense.

"Not unless you're willing to reciprocate," he replied, just as smoothly. I saw the menacing white of his teeth in his toothy grin. "You'll find I'm much better at conversing when I'm somewhere more pleasant. Or when I've had a drop of bluesberry. My favourite year is 27 HOET. Though I may have drank that already."

"You'll tell me what I want to know, and if it's useful, we can discuss other arrangements for you." Promising this weasel anything was out of the question. He would probably know I was lying anyway. He had no idea how close he became to being Kamal Zaman's indentured servant or political pawn. "Boris is in the mountains surrounding the city. He's gathered an army. Mostly Eastern soldiers, though Dominique is with him and commands some Northern shadows. They've been spotted trying to tunnel their way into the city. An effort that would likely take years. So. What do you think he's actually up to?"

Leon stared blankly at me. "That's what you came down here to ask me? What I think my idiot brother is thinking? He's likely thinking that tunneling is a *good* strategy. He is a patient bastard, you know."

I sighed. Maybe this wasn't such a bright idea after all. Here he was, sitting in his cell as arrogant as ever, eating into our precious rations. It would be a fitting punishment to put him to sleep with the Spear, and then use the Cloth to return his mind to a blank slate.

My stomach felt cold. The Spear sent power through my hand, and for a moment the euphoria of magic overwhelmed me. *Yes— kill him. The Freetors would love that. Kill him like you did the other Eastern mercenaries. Keegan will never love you now, so why stop doing what works? Because that's what you are—a ruthless, brutal murderer.*

Just like my father.

I drew a deep breath and shook the thoughts away. But I *wasn't* my father. I was the High Queen. I was in *control.*

My fingernails dug deep into my palms. "What do you know?" I spat at Leon. "Enjoy your stay in the dungeon. It will be years before your brother tunnels his way in to rescue you."

I turned and made my way down the corridor.

"Wait!" Leon stretched his hands through the bars. "Wait. Don't...don't go."

His desperation made me pause. "Yes?"

He huffed a low sigh. "Maybe he does believe tunnelling will work...because...that's how he would place the explosives."

I nearly bit the inside of my tongue. Antony hadn't mentioned anything about explosives. I made my way slowly back to his cell. "You have my attention."

I searched his face, but there was no trace of sarcasm or joviality. "Look. Sometimes, Boris would get into these long discussions with his loyal men. Dominique would join in too, when she could stomach his droning. They worried about not being able to hold the West. We had the forces, but it's hard to account for, well, Freetor magic. Once, Boris went on at length about...a contingency plan. If the Freetors or the Western Marlenians rebelled, they'd blow up the castle."

I scoffed. "That doesn't even make sense. Your father put a lot of effort and silver into trying to rebuild this castle."

"Sure. Because for generations, the West has been the seat of power for the world. But Boris isn't our father. This castle suited him fine, but why live here, when he could return to the East? Fewer Freetors, fewer Violet Foxes running around disrupting plans, and further away from the North and South's influence.

Why not make Cogold the capital of the world, a place our family has worked for generations to perfect? Leave Marlenia City to the rats. Level it to the ground."

"That...that is terrifying." I didn't know what else to say. Marlenia City was old. It had history. Religious significance, to those who cared about that. Not to mention the rich and developed Undercity. Even if they only planted explosives in the castle, the avalanche would cause irreparable damage to everything beneath it. It wasn't just the destruction of the castle and the surface—it was three separate ecosystems of people they sought to annihilate. "Why are you telling me this now. Why not tell Bidelia or anyone earlier?"

He shrugged. "You weren't here when they put me down here. I could barely speak for days. At least, I think it was days. It was a long time without wine, or food, or anything."

"So you were likely drunk when you heard this."

"Doesn't make it any less true."

But it did make it less reliable. Still—it was something. I knew the East's behaviour in the mountains was strange. Likely, they'd camped there to prepare and distribute the explosives.

If they hadn't done so already.

The three swordsmen I'd pulped. They'd talked about Boris paying them to *plant* something around the city. They had a secondary mission, other than doing Sylvia's futile bidding. If there were explosives sitting in abandoned homes and buildings, just waiting to be triggered...

Keegan. He was in grave danger.

And so was everyone else.

I pressed my forehead against the Spear to gather my resolve, and then turned to leave. I had to warn everyone.

"Hey, hey, wait a minute. I was useful, right?" Leon called after me. "Now for what I want."

"Shut up, Leon. Not now."

"No, I refuse! Put me on the throne, Violet Fox. Not the Western throne, you can have it, if you can save it. Just let me warm my family's royal seat. I'll make sure your precious Freetors are safe. Because, do you know what the first thing Boris will do, when he gets here? Besides killing you and Keegan and everyone else with a modicum of power? He and Dominique are going to kill *me*. Even if you trade me to them for a veil of peace, I'm a dead man. He will guarantee that he and his descendants are Emperors of Everything, and I'm a threat to that! So is Sylvia."

I hadn't thought of that. Although it didn't sound like something Boris would do, Dominique had a singular thirst for revenge and tasteless brutality. Leon's proposal wasn't to be taken lightly—not that he could be trusted.

"I can't just put you on a throne while Boris and Dominique are in power."

"Unless you let me *go*," Leon said with a sly grin. "Or, I'm sure you can think of something appropriate to take them out. But when I'm High King, your people *will* be safe. You'll have my word."

I couldn't stoop to condoning the assassination of kings. I'd come too close to skirting that line. I would kill when necessary, I'd use magic when *absolutely* necessary—but I wouldn't plan a cold-blooded murder. That was what Dominique would do. And I certainly wasn't pretending to be her anymore. But to defeat her... what if I had to adopt her tactics?

"Hard to be king from the dungeon. King of the rats, maybe," I said ruefully.

He chuckled. "I wouldn't mind that, for a time. But only if you were the queen."

I returned to his bars a final time and pressed the Spear against them threateningly. "Have you gotten desperate enough to eat a rat yet? They're tough to get through raw. But maybe you'll get used to it. Maybe. Until then, don't ever speak to me that way again. You'll get nothing."

"Whoa. Get that thing—" He backed away from the Spear. It was wrapped, but the head was still sharp. "What happened between you and Keegan? Is he even still—?"

"Be. Quiet." I was more than done with him. I stormed down the corridor, this time for good.

"Violet Fox. Wait...uh..."

"Goodbye, Leon."

"Turn around. Violet Fox, turn *around*!"

"You're such a—" I spun on my heels, the Spear glowed brightly, sudden as a sneeze, and none other than Conal Driscoll loomed before me.

"Hello, Kiera," he said. He grinned.

In his hand, was a glowing piece of a glowing, granite slab— one half of the Midnight Tablet.

Ten

CONAL REGARDED ME warmly, inclining his head. "You look elegant today."

"I'll show you elegant," I muttered, and jabbed the Spear at him.

He recoiled, his boots scuffing against the gritty dirt floor. I couldn't let him get away. He had a piece of my people's freedom in the palm of his hands. Had Laoise and Monju known? No time to think about it. As he had no visible weapon other than his magic—and perhaps the Tablet half—he could only dodge my attacks. I gripped the Spear with both hands.

He tucked the Tablet half under his arm. It was as large as a tome but far thinner. He'd partially wrapped it in fabric: when two artefacts were in close proximity, they ran hot. The Spear heated under my palm, but it wasn't uncomfortable. Perhaps the Tablet half wasn't strong enough on its own to illicit a full reaction. One edge appeared jagged and vastly uneven, as if a monster had taken a bite from the powerful artefact. Strange runes, similar in shape to Freetor code, pulsed a bright blue on both sides. If I could read them, I'd know the secrets of magic. It could all be mine.

And then, I would trade everything to return Keegan to me.

"I sense something different about you," he said slowly.

I took another swing and he dodged it readily, ducking under me with incredible speed. I turned to face him, our positions in the cramped corridor now reversed.

"You've had your first taste of magic. Your own."

"What are you doing here?" I demanded.

"Because I wanted to see you. Tell me. Is the High King of the South still paying you a visit? I have some unfinished business with him."

I jabbed at him again and he scooted backwards, narrowly missing the glowing spearhead. "Give me the Tablet piece. We both know it doesn't belong to you."

"Ownership is a rather loose concept. Where is the High King?"

"If you're so clever and powerful, why don't you find him yourself?"

His gaze narrowed as he examined me closely. "What happened, Kiera?"

"You have magic. You figure it out."

Leon gripped the bars of his cage, watching the two of us with interest. "She most certainly killed someone. Probably Keegan."

"I didn't!" I swung the Spear towards Leon to silence his flapping tongue. He jumped away from the bars.

Conal ducked into the cell across from Leon, attempting to bypass me—but I wasn't about to squander an opportunity. I slammed the door shut with a deafening bang. I didn't have the keys, so I held the bars together as tight as I could. Conal wrapped his free hand around mine, but not to pry me away from the bars.

I couldn't meet his gaze. "Does the Tablet half work by itself?"

"No," he replied softly. "We have to make it whole. Did you find the other half?"

I gritted my teeth. Wrenching away my hand, I shoved my friends from my mind, in case he could see my racing thoughts plainly.

"The High King believed it was underground, though he knows more than he lets on. He thinks he's very clever," Conal continued. "Where is he now?"

I squeezed my eyes shut. The magic swirled within like the urge to vomit.

You could take care of him now, it said. *Then you could take his half, and when your friends return, presumably with the other half...Keegan could finally be with you again.*

"I can't," I whispered.

The cage was unlocked. Conal could have escaped. Instead, he reached for me, through the bars. "I know what you're going through. I can help you control it."

"No. I can do it myself."

His fingers relaxed and curled as he retracted his arm, his gaze sympathetic. "Then you are stronger than I was."

"Kiera. Kiera Driscoll!"

Bidelia's shrill voice sent waves of regret down my spine—but also, relief. "Bidelia. Quick! He's here!"

I only looked away from my father for a moment. Bidelia appeared at the base of the narrow stairway, lifting her coat suspiciously as she ventured towards me. Her gaze rested on Leon, and then me. "There you—"

"I've trapped Conal. He's—"

I turned back to the unlocked cell—and he was gone.

I threw open the door so hard it banged against the bars. I even waved the Spear inside. It hit nothing invisible. The other cages, empty. Leon leaned against the bars of his own cell, alone. Conal couldn't have gone down the stairway, as Bidelia was right there, blocking the only exit. The Spear, once glowing with absolute brilliance, had dimmed in repose.

"I was waiting for you because the meeting has begun, and here you are, cavorting with the enemy!" Bidelia scolded as she advanced on me.

"Cavorting! He's a disgusting—" He wasn't even worth the words. "Tell her, Leon, who you saw just now."

Leon scoffed and rested his head comfortably against the dank walls. "I don't know what you're talking about."

"Don't play dumb. You saw him. You warned me he was there!"

Leon shrugged innocently. "Just me and the rats. King of the rats, that's me." A beat. "And you're one of the rats. Was that not clear?"

"Idiot." I looked up imploringly at Bidelia. "I swear, he was here, and he had part of the Tablet in his hands. He's probably still here, listening, unseen because of his…"

"Come," Bidelia said gravely.

There was no room to argue. I surveyed every small corner of the darkness as I followed Bidelia down the passageway to the stairs. My father had found me. He'd *seen* the terrible magic within.

He had come back for me. I shook my head. No, not for me… for the artefacts.

Did he know the city was rigged with explosives?

As we ascended the cramped, chilly stairs, Bidelia said, "I'm your Advisor, not your maidservant. It isn't my job to fetch you and ferry you to your appointments."

"Then don't," I replied flippantly, regretting my words immediately. I sighed. "I wasn't wasting time. I'm sorry I kept you waiting, but I got something out of Leon."

"Really," Bidelia said dryly. "We already pressed him for information. He gave us little."

"He and I have more of a rapport." A shiver went down my spine. "He says that—"

"Tell me when we're in the council room." She glanced over her shoulder, down into the darkness warily. I couldn't blame her. Revealing sensitive intelligence around my father was not a good idea.

Unless he could *help*.

No. I gritted my teeth. He couldn't help me—no one could.

We reached the top of the stairs and Bidelia knocked three times. A castle guard unlocked the door, cracked it open, and examined us both. Satisfied we weren't escaping prisoners, he allowed us through.

"Don't open that door for anyone else. Always get voice confirmation," I told him as we closed the door and he locked it once more with a giant metal key.

"Yes, my lady," he replied.

Would that be enough to keep my father in the dungeons? How had he gotten there in the first place? The breadth of his powers was unknowable. Could he walk through walls? Imitate voices? Appear completely as another, down to the clothing?

If he can do it, so can you.

The possibilities swirled in my mind. I followed Bidelia to the council room, my grip on the Spear tightening. It could light up at any moment, announcing his arrival.

"You believe me, right?" I asked Bidelia finally, as we walked. "My father is here, skulking around the castle. Any magical items we have should be secured. If there's some way to get word to Laoise and Monju, to warn them—"

"No." Bidelia stopped and swooped in front of me, pointing a menacing finger. "Everything has been taken care of, Kiera. They'll be here soon—we have to trust them to complete their mission. Laoise has been instructed to hide the Cloth in a different place on her person each day. You yourself flaunt the Spear in plain sight, a beacon for your father's greed."

"It's not my fault that he's—"

"I know, but it doesn't help." She heaved a weighted sigh. "Pascal and the others have gathered. I wanted you to be more up to speed on the reports his people have dictated, but perhaps I could just give you the details..."

Bidelia started rattling off various accounts of Eastern activity in the mountains and the surrounding forests as she led me through the corridors to the council room. I tried to absorb as much as I could, but my entire body felt numb. The city could explode at any second. Keegan had abandoned me. My father was here. How long had he been hiding in these walls? Wandering around in the dungeons, it wouldn't take him long to figure out what I'd done to Kamal and his shadowy bodyguard. As he didn't have the Cloth, there was nothing he could do to defrost the High King—but the thought of him knowing what I'd done made me sick.

He'd offered to teach me control. I should have, I *could* have—

I shook my head as Bidelia opened the council room door. The closet of a room was packed to the brim with people. My stomach dropped. I wasn't ready for this. I stepped backward into Bidelia's hand, which pushed me forward into the room.

Antony sat at the head of the square table, and around him, five other Roamers. As they weren't traditionally a military band, I couldn't tell if they were ranked soldiers, or if they were just Antony's friends. The six of them stood and bowed to me, though they looked worried. I tried to embody the emotions of a person who didn't just murder three people.

To my surprise, Gobany stood in a corner, along with his three apprentice friends, Binna, Katell, and Ruchaan. Katell's presence surprised me especially, given her age—though I too had stayed up far later than Rordan had liked when I was ten. Gobany's posture strengthened when he saw me, and I felt exposed. I held the Spear closer to my body. Had he heard or *seen* what I had done? Of all of them, he would understand the most how I felt. His eyebrows lifted in question and I nodded. Perhaps he would allow me to discuss it with him later. If there was time.

Keegan would be the one to run these meetings. He should have been here. But it was up to me now. I had to keep going. I had a city to save.

"This is a full room," I muttered to Bidelia.

"It's important," she replied, shutting the door behind us. "Thank you for waiting. We can begin now."

My cheeks coloured. They'd held the meeting for *me*. "Yes. Sorry, General. I want to hear your report."

"Eastern activity has escalated," Antony said, without preamble.

"Eastern soldiers have been spotted in Feenagh Forest. They're looking for Undercity entrances. Managed to stop them, though it cost us a man. Another, larger troop of Northern shadows was seen coming up from their southern blockade. They were carrying supplies toward the city. We were hoping the nearby bandits or some enterprising citizens would take care of them, but they're shadows walking the road in broad daylight, so no one wants to engage. There's also been an avalanche in the mountains. Not a large one. Caused by their strange drilling, it seems."

"I think I know what's going on," I said. I explained his story about Boris's dream of moving the seat of power to the East—by destroying Marlenia City.

Antony looked sceptical. "Our scouts saw no evidence of explosives." He glanced at the Roamers for confirmation. "Though they were unloading large metal barrels, filled with some kind of sloshing liquid. We assumed it was beer, though the East doesn't usually condone their men partaking in the drink while in the field. One day, they unloaded them. The next, empty barrels were left in the camp. They're still there, along with the skeleton crew guarding the area."

I wasn't certain what went into the creation of explosives. That was the realm of the Extremists. The Freetor Extremists used explosives and extreme tactics to protest their right to live on the surface. They didn't care who they killed—children or soldier, as long as they were born on the surface, they were a target. If my brother were here, he'd know. He had been one of them, and had died publicly for it. I hoped he was someplace better now.

"I heard Lady Sylvia's mercenaries talking about planting *something* within the city," I continued. "If they manage to plant some in the castle, or in the underground..."

"Too bad those men aren't around for us to question," Antony said dryly. He held up a hand in forgiveness—he sensed it would be unwise to discuss the pulverised remains among the ruins. "We'll perform a sweep of the city and attempt to locate them. Though placing individual explosives seems a waste of time for the East—they'd need individual triggers."

"The East is innovative. They may have discovered some way to trigger them remotely," Bidelia pointed out.

"Or with magic," Gobany said quietly. Gobany had done enough damage himself, and had paid dearly for it.

Boris and Dominique would never resort to magic to do their dirty work—but I refused to venture near the thought of magic and explosives.

"Can always count on Eastern efficiency," Antony said. "If they want to blow us to the sky, they'd have to do it all at once, to catch us off-guard. That means planting explosives in the city and in the castle, and potentially in the mountains, to trigger a large avalanche. That would guarantee complete annihilation."

"So there's no chance of attacking the camp? Is there anyone left? Any useful supplies?"

"We were there a few hours ago," Gobany spoke up, gesturing to his apprentice friends. "There are thirty armed soldiers and at least five Northern shadows. They've also put up more tents. The cold winds in the mountains have slowed them down. The cold will make its way here, just wait." He pulled his robe closer around his body. "And High King Boris and High Queen Dominique are there as well. They met with another soldier, possibly a mercenary. Mostly, they are still packing."

I wondered if the mercenary also worked for Sylvia—and was relaying his fellow's fate to Dominique. "Unusual for Boris and Dominique to be doing manual labour."

Antony grunted in agreement. "They're making sure the job gets done. Could ambush them and capture or kill the royalty, but we'd have to do it now. Even then, it would be a slaughter. On both sides."

I nodded. "And that wouldn't stop the East from potentially

denotating a bunch of explosives while we're ambushing them. It will be a massacre. No matter what we do."

Not if I used magic, said the new voice within me. *I don't even need the Orb to call lightning from the sky. Just like Elder Erskina, I can summon it at will and direct it at my fearsome enemies. How many lightning strikes will it take to remove the entirety of the East?*

If my people were being threatened, didn't that count as *absolutely necessary?*

Antony was speaking again. "The ink's barely dried on the accord with the South, so it'll be a while before we can harvest the fruits of that endeavour. Our one advantage? If they're *not* going to invade us directly, we only have to spend time and people going through the city, finding the explosives and dismantling them. We can put everyone we have on that. If we slow their trapping of the city and the castle, we stand a chance. More of a chance once the South arrives with help. If we don't starve to death while we're at it."

"Spare as many as you can to do so. I'll help," I said. "We should also evacuate everyone into the castle. And the cathedral, as there won't be enough room up here. This will be the hardest place for them to plant explosives. If they hadn't already."

Bidelia looked uncomfortable. "That may be dangerous, as it would make a single explosion more effective at taking out our people."

"We should offer them shelter, at least. I feel they're going to be confused and frightened, and I don't want them fleeing the city into the wilderness, into the arms of the East," I said.

"Evacuation is a safer option," Bidelia replied. "Even to the underground or to the surrounding bailes, if the small lords can handle it. We may want to evacuate *you* and Your Grace out of the city completely, now."

I was stunned into silence. "No. No! I'm not going anywhere. I promised I'd stay."

Everyone regarded me with surprise and confusion.

"I mean, I'm not leaving. I'm the High Queen, and I have to stay. Otherwise it's a sign of weakness."

"No one believes you're weak, Kiera," Bidelia said in a low tone, laced with warning. Then, louder, "If you wish to stay, that is your call, but we will begin to move people quickly and quietly into the castle and the cathedral, if it makes them feel safer, and I will send word again to the surrounding lords to see how many people they can handle. If we aren't careful about how we approach this, it will only cause chaos—and the East may use that to escalate their plan."

"Speaking of the young Holy One," Antony said cautiously, "he's been spotted. With you. Seems like he hasn't been kidnapped or…indisposed. I take it he's…well?"

I pursed my lips. He was trying to be cordial. "He's fine. He's on a private mission to soothe the people's consciences." It was too easy to lie.

"They're calling him the Crimson Prince," Antony said carefully. "Too fanciful and romantic for my liking. But that's what the people want. They don't seem to mind having him down there. They're not even questioning his strange appearance. To them, he's an entertaining novelty. For now. But I'm wondering what the use of it is, especially given our present…circumstances. If I may, Violet Fox. Is his charade really necessary?"

Antony knew Keegan's memory hadn't returned. Besides himself, only Bidelia and I carried that secret in this room, though no doubt Gobany had discerned it as well, if he had that power.

I had to tread carefully. I couldn't have them losing confidence in my husband, not when he was at his most vulnerable. If they knew I'd alienated him with my magic, that he couldn't accept this new power within me…

"I will speak with him again," I said.

He nodded curtly, but he was no Captain Murdock, the former

head of the castle guard. He was not bound by an inner sense of duty to be here. We had an agreement. He would serve *me*—but I also had to live up to my own promise. If I was withholding valuable information from him, he would see that as a slight. He was a Roamer, not a soldier or a scribe or an advisor.

It wasn't their business anyway. Keegan was *my* husband. Yes, he was their monarch, too. But Keegan was going down a path that only I could follow. And when I caught him…

What? What could I do? Lock him away, as I had been locked away?

He had run from me—just like any Freetor would run from the oppressive nobility.

"Violet Fox?" Antony was saying.

I cleared my throat. I hadn't heard a word he'd said.

"I will discuss this further with Her Highness," Bidelia said tactfully. "Our rightful king may be on a mission, but that does not mean he doesn't need some extra support. Keep an eye out in the streets. Discreetly, while we evacuate and sweep the city. Do not bring him in—Her Highness and I will handle his safe return to the castle. And *then* we'll evaluate what's best for the nobility, and the commoners."

"Yes. We will," I echoed Bidelia. The words felt heavy. They didn't belong to me, but some other queen, who was colder and more distant.

Dominique. Keegan. Conal Driscoll. The enemies—or husband wrongfully turned against me—were cornering me. How could I stop them all? Alone? I couldn't—not all at once.

They were staring at me for answers. I couldn't fail them now. I was their queen.

"As for Dominique and Boris Frostfire," I said. "You're right. If we ambush them, we won't stand a chance. Not in their fortified camp. That's why we have to bring them here. Into the city. Once they're here, *we* control the battlefield and we will be able to defeat them, forever."

"We just spent men and resources driving them out," Antony argued. "Why would you want to invite the tigers back into the cave? Especially one they are rigging to explode? They're too clever to show their faces in a future graveyard."

"We have Leon and Sylvia Frostfire in our custody. They would make a valuable trade," Bidelia said.

"I agree they should be part of the deal…" I remembered Leon's words. If we traded them, they would die. I wasn't sure how I felt about that. Leon deserved to suffer for his crimes, and Sylvia deserved to learn the crimes she committed, so she could feel real suffering. None of that would happen if we offered them to the East. A plan bloomed in my mind, and for a pure moment, I felt elated. "I know how to get Boris and Dominique here. I will dangle something else tempting before them. Something they will not be able to resist."

"And what might that be?" Bidelia asked dubiously.

The high of magic swirled within me as it teamed with my love of a good scheme. "We are going to offer an armistice and surrender to the East."

Shock and uproar overtook the room. Antony leapt form his chair. "You can't be serious."

"It will be. To them," I said. "And while we discuss and eventually dismiss the terms, we will hopefully buy enough time to dismantle the explosives."

Antony slumped back into his chair and the rest of the room began to dissect the plan: how it would work, what was required to convince Boris Frostfire that this was not a trap, and my mind began turning over the *real* scheme.

The East was the real problem. Leszek Frostfire had ordered the execution of thousands of Freetors and Freetor sympathizers when the East occupied the city. Now, he was dead and gone. Boris was the result of generations of hate, had stood by and condoned horrible atrocities; what did he do, the moment he came into his power?

Order the creation of explosives to kill everyone in the capital.

Yet this whole idea reeked of Dominique's ruthlessness. She had travelled to the edge of the world to watch everything I loved crumble. She didn't have to be there—she had wanted to see me dead with her own eyes, so she could return to the North knowing one more Freetor had been downed by her doing.

I was going to return the favour—for me, and for every person she had ever harmed.

I was going to kill Dominique Castillo.

THE NEXT MORNING, I sent Gobany, Bidelia, and three Roamers to the Eastern camp in the mountains to relay the message: the West wanted an armistice to discuss a complete surrender to the East.

The ultimate location of the peace talks was significant. Normally, such a discussion would take place on neutral ground, such as outside the city or within Feenagh Forest, or in a neighbouring province. But as the cold winds in the mountains worsened and a frosty, numbing chill settled over the Western province, a suitable and close-by interior location was required. I didn't want everyone to freeze before the inevitable battle would begin. That would make winning far too easy. I wanted Boris and Dominique to come to me, ideally to the castle, where I had the advantage. In fact, it was one of my demands. Being within the castle grounds wasn't necessary for my secret plan to succeed, but drawing out the initial back-and-forth by making an unreasonable request would buy us some time to uncover potential explosives, evacuate or relocate my people to safety, search for my hidden father, and return Keegan to my side.

I wanted to accompany Bidelia and the others to the Eastern camp to size up Dominique, but Bidelia wouldn't hear of it. "I am your Advisor. Let me do my duty so you can do yours. Besides, if they see you are willing to go to them, they will never agree to come to you. Best you stay safe, here in the castle."

Nowhere was really safe, especially when our enemies had lined the city with explosives, and venturing outside meant seeing your breath and tasting the intense winter to come with little more than the clothes on your back. If Boris thought to detonate his explosives before the peace talks could begin in earnest, Bidelia would make clear that we had Sylvia and Leon in our custody. Even if Boris wanted to kill them to ensure the safety of their singular dynasty, I was betting they didn't want to leave their deaths to an explosion. In matters of both succession and marriage, proof was everything to the surface-born.

Sighing, I reluctantly saw her off in the bailey and spent the day surrounded by servants, Roamers, and apprentices. Everyone had a responsibility and sought my opinion:

"How much broth should we serve each person tonight in the cathedral?"

"Will you sign this letter to the Gareth family, requesting permission for the seventh time to send our citizens there in an emergency?" (I doubted very much they would read anything with my name inscribed, so I signed as Bidelia instead).

"Will you sign eight other letters, requesting asylum for our people?"

"Your Highness, some commoners were spotted clearing trees on royal land, should they be punished?"

"We have moved fifty elderly citizens into the cathedral and stoked the fires. Should we burn the pews if we run out of wood?"

"Should we water down the soup again today?"

I problem-solved my way through the hours. I signed what was put before me, as most of it was a request for aid from the neighbouring bailes. This was the minutiae Bidelia navigated each day—this was the onslaught she saved me and Keegan from. I went from relishing the control and attention in the morning, to extreme annoyance at every minor conversation during the afternoon, to a deep sadness by sundown. Each face seemed more stressed than the last. No one wanted to make the wrong decision. It was better to ask the High Queen, for I would be to blame if something went awry, especially as I was not a true-blooded royal.

We were already stretching our meager rations. They could go no further, so I refused to water down the broth. The South was due to send food and soldiers, providing the relief could make it through the blockade, *and* Omju hadn't been caught forging the High King's authorization *and* no one questioned Kamal's 'decision' to remain here in Marlenia City. I refused to punish anyone who went into the forest to cut wood for their hearths—I would not be cruel. Nor could I afford to be seen as such, after the terror I had wrought. I obsessed over what to tell my people that evening, for I refused to keep them in the dark.

Bidelia, Gobany, and the Roamers didn't return by nightfall, so I oversaw the rationing while Antony coordinated with the Roamers to keep order. This wasn't as necessary as I'd thought, for many refused to enter the cathedral when they saw I would be ladling their broth with the castle servants. Still, hunger was a powerful motivator, and many more grabbed what was rightfully theirs quickly and quietly, retreating to the far back corners of the cathedral to eat in silence and despair.

There was not much to ration now that our fruit was gone. Scraps, tea, and broth comprised the meals, leaving everyone irritable and exhausted, including me. I searched every face for Keegan and disappointed myself at every turn. He had chosen to forsake the warm fires of his chamber and the comfort of his bed. If he wasn't here, what was he eating? Where was he sleeping? What was he dreaming—and was it of me?

Bidelia wasn't there to advise me, so I did what I thought was best as I stood before my people on that first night of negotiations. "We have begun armistice talks with the East." Although it was a ruse to buy time, I couldn't very well say so. Anyone present could be a spy or informant for the enemy.

As I expected, the murmurs became an uproar. "We're

surrendering? We can't do that!" one person shouted. "The Crimson Prince said—"

"What did he say?" I demanded, my voice cutting through the chaos.

Now my people looked worried. I dug my fingernails into my palms. I shouldn't have spent today traipsing around the castle, tending to the minor details of monarchy. I should have been on the streets, finding Keegan, informing him about the explosives and my secret plan to end Dominique, once and for all. I couldn't have everyone thinking that his absence from the castle wasn't part of some grander scheme, if he hadn't already ruined that illusion himself.

"We are negotiating with the East, yes. We have to explore all options to keep us all safe. I know you're scared." I held up the Spear and closed my eyes briefly, feeling its power, and the collective sighs of those admiring the artefact. "Don't forget that we have the Daughter of the East in our custody. And Lord Leon Frostfire, her brother. As long as we have them, the East wouldn't dare touch us." That was the hope, anyway.

"They should burn for their crimes!" someone in the back of the cathedral shouted. Their cry echoed over everyone's heads, stirring similar calls for justice.

"Don't trade them to the High King, we want them dead!"

"We have to protect the Crimson Prince from the East's next attack!"

I gritted my teeth. I'd done my fair share of speeches in my day, but usually Keegan was by my side, or I had donned the Violet Fox's mask and cape. I had to maintain my composure. I couldn't let my anger or magic get out of control. I had to maintain order— for Keegan's sake. "My husband and I and Advisor Mullen are doing everything we can do get more food and ensure your safety. I'll give you more information tomorrow, when I have it." I struck the floor with the butt of the Spear, intending to punctuate the end of my speech, but the sound blasted through the echoing fortress, making my statement more of a thunderous decree.

Before I could make more of a fool of myself, I stepped off the dais and hurried toward the exit. I was High Queen. I wanted my people to be safe. And yet I felt weak, scooping broth into cups and talking about surrender and evacuation instead of ambush and action.

Soon, Dominique will be dead, I thought. *Maybe Boris too. And then the East won't be a problem anymore, and I can focus on what really matters.*

I kept my head down as I navigated the crowd. They parted for me and didn't impede my desire for a swift exit, though snippets of conversation latched onto my ears. Keegan had not shown his face, but his new name was on everyone's lips.

"Why doesn't the Crimson Prince return to the castle and pass judgement on the Daughter of the East?"

"If the Crimson Prince is with us, has the Violet Fox stolen his throne?"

"Why didn't he tell us about the negotiations?"

I yearned to add my questions to theirs: "Where is Keegan?" and "How can he possibly stop my magic from becoming more powerful?"

By the time that evening's rationing had finished and I had escaped back to my chamber in the castle, Bidelia was waiting for me. Her cheeks and fingertips were flush from the day's bitter-cold journey.

"How did this evening fair?" she asked, raising an eyebrow. "You look distraught."

I shook my head. "Did the East agree to talk?"

Bidelia scoffed. "By the time we arrived at their camp and convinced them that three people they clearly saw coming weren't an ambush, it was nearly sundown. They kept us waiting under guard for hours. I thought we might have to run for it and risk an arrow in the back. Then, an important-looking solider told us to return tomorrow, and perhaps they'd listen to our demands. It's all a game to them."

When would it end? How could I keep my people safe when no one would listen? "So, will you?"

"Return? If we haven't found all the explosives, then yes, I advise we return. Seems like you kept the city from falling apart in my absence, so if you don't mind me leaving again tomorrow..."

I looked away. I *did* mind. Keegan was gallivanting in the streets, Bidelia was negotiating for my people's lives, Laoise and Monju were *somewhere* with my love's salvation...where did that leave me? Here. In the castle. Alone.

Not if I went out and convinced Keegan to help me disable the explosives. Without somehow alarming my people of the threat and causing chaos.

If I could show Keegan—the Crimson Prince—just how dedicated I was to helping our people, that I wasn't a monster, maybe he'd return.

Maybe, he'd *remember*.

"Return to the Eastern camp," I told Bidelia, with some confidence. "Go every day, with whoever we can spare, to show the East we're serious. I'll handle the sweep and try to convince everyone to evacuate."

Bidelia smiled. "Yes, Your Highness."

On the second day, Bidelia once again left the castle with a squad of apprentices and Roamers. The search for Keegan distracted me from the gnawing hunger clutching my gut. Focus on the mission and the belly will stop complaining. An old Freetor trick. I gathered my own team of Roamers, left Antony to deal with the day-to-day minutiae, and we scattered into the cold streets of Marlenia City. While the Roamers quietly swept the abandoned homes and dark corners of the city for potential explosives, I focussed on the many public bonfires in the alleys that attracted shivering people from all walks of Marlenian life.

My breath clouded as it escaped my lips and my fingers burned with the cold as I approached each gathering, hope gleaming in my heart. I considered hiding my face, disguising my voice—but there was no point. They knew me now. Their expressions ranged from disinterest to disgust as they laid eyes upon me, surveying the Silver Spear with interest and my magical hands with distrust. But everyone gave me the same answer, afraid of what I would do if I went away with nothing.

"The Crimson Prince doesn't want to be disturbed," said one man, around one such fire. "Unless you're here to hand out the food you're keeping from us, or cure the plague with your magic, go back to your castle."

My hands clenched. "Just tell him to be at the cathedral this evening."

"Whatever food you share with him, he'll just share with us," said another defiantly.

"Good, I hope he does," I replied dismissively, and continued down the alleyway.

But Keegan didn't show at the cathedral that evening and on the third day I grew antsy. Not just because Boris and Dominique had refused my demand once again to meet in the castle, and Keegan was rebuffing me, his wife. Our Roamers had only found two explosive devices so far, and according to the scholars who inspected them, they were powerful enough to crumble a building—but the East would need a large arsenal of these to bring down the entire city and destroy the mountain castle.

"We should attack them," I told Bidelia on the third day in the bailey, before she ventured into the mountains yet again. "I'm coming with you."

"No." She glanced around at the Roamers waiting for her at a distance, knowing she was disrespecting me as High Queen, and then lowered her voice. "I think we're getting somewhere. The

East is getting frustrated that we return to the relative warmth of a castle each night, while they have to huddle together in tents at night to stay alive."

The thought of Dominique sleeping in the frigid cold with her soldiers and servants brought a sarcastic smile to my lips. Good. She deserved to suffer.

But if she deserved to suffer—did she deserve to be killed?

"They know we met with the South and that we...have...their support," Bidelia continued tentatively. "The explosives are proof they intend to blow us high into the sky...but they will want proof that Sylvia and Leon are alive before doing anything rash. They are wearing themselves thin in the mountain. They will come here, even into a nest of explosives, to get warm and see that Sylvia and Leon are still alive." She paused. "What do you intend to do, when they are here?"

I had told no one of my intentions. I couldn't risk anyone hearing that I was planning a murder, even of my sworn enemy, not after what I had done with my magic. I didn't relish in the task before me—but if it helped restore the faith of my people, if it ensured their safety, then I would thrust the knife into her gut and face whatever consequences came after.

"Whether or not Keegan returns to the castle, we will have a real negotiation with Boris and Dominique. We'll try to retrieve as many explosive devices before and during the meeting."

Bidelia narrowed her gaze, searching for deceit. "And what if we fail to find the rest of the explosives before they detonate?"

I blew out a frustrated sigh. "I'll focus on convincing people to evacuate the city today."

"Do it quietly and quickly," she said.

If Keegan refused to meet me in the cathedral or in the castle, then I had to make a bold gesture. Anything to draw him out, so I could win him back—and help my people endure.

That evening at the rationing, I surveyed the hungry faces lining the cathedral, searching for the face of my love, and finding only angry disdain. They knew I was keeping secrets from them. They saw Bidelia and her collection of apprentices and Roamers leave the castle every day for the mountains. They looked at me serving broth and saw only betrayal.

It was time to tell the truth. They might riot. But they would all die if I didn't get them out of the city—and maybe a little pandemonium was exactly what we needed to make that happen.

Keegan couldn't hide among our people if they all decided to leave.

Unless he left with them…

"I have something to say," I said to the packed cathedral, tapping the Spear on the floor as delicately as possible to command their attention. The din silenced.

I studied every person. Gaunt children, struggling to pay attention in the front pews. Their parents and families, attempting to wrangle them. Women clustered, sharing their broth. Men in rags and worn velvet, huddling together to fight the cold. The Roamers along every wall, appearing more brutish each day as they layered themselves with additional armour to keep warm. The children who seemed to only have each other, who weaved in and around the adults like shadows, hoping to be unseen while they pickpocketed away the hours before sleep would overtake them. The handful of apprentices who hadn't gone with Bidelia, their wide eyes taking in the crowd like feral cats. Two stood by the cathedral doors protectively. Two others, Katell and Binna, flanked me. Katell carried a burlap sack gingerly and looked up at me expectantly, waiting for my cue.

"I made a promise I didn't keep," I began. "When I returned to Marlenia City, I didn't know how bad things had gotten. And when I learned just how terrible they were…I thought that I had to keep the worst of it to myself, to protect you. But I'm not going to do that now. You deserve to know the truth. And as the relief from the South likely won't arrive in the next few days because of the—"

"Show us our food! We know you're hoarding it!" someone shouted from the back of the cathedral.

The crowd roared up with the dissenter, but I thrust my Spear up at the ceiling, in the direction of the mountain castle. "You want to go up there and see how empty the pantries are? Go on, then. Go up into the empty shell of Marlenian royalty. I assure you it's just as cold and dark and dusty as it is here. But I sit up there because I made a promise to someone I love. And I stand up here today to keep you safe.

"The East has lined our city with explosives!"

Katell stepped forward and unveiled the object within the burlap sack: one of the two explosives found the previous day.

At first, this didn't have the intended shock and awe I'd expected—because I realized, as I swept the sea of faces, most people didn't know what an explosive *looked* like. If you did and you weren't actively involved in creating them, well, you probably didn't retain the knowledge for long. Thus, our trouble with uncovering them. This particular construction was a small metal chest. With my nod, Katell unhinged the opening, revealing a coiled mess of coloured string around a broken time piece.

"This is an explosive we recovered from the merchant district yesterday, disabled by the Roamers and our remaining scholars," I said, after a moment of confused silence.

The news rippled throughout the cathedral. They may not have known what explosives looked like, but everyone was familiar with the destruction they caused.

"We have it on good authority that the East has placed such devices all over the city," I continued. "They may look like this, or they may not, so we must be on our guard. The ones we have recovered so far have to be manually triggered. They are constructed to have a delay when they are activated."

"It's a Freetor lie!" another dissenter erupted with a deep

booming voice, close to the back once more. "We know you have more food! Give it to us!"

"It's not the work of the East, it's Freetor Extremists!" yelled an elderly man.

"If this was the work of Extremists, the explosives would have already gone off, and all of us would be dead." Of that, I was fairly certain. I also believed they wouldn't kill a Freetor Queen on the off chance I began granting land to my fellows on the surface. We were a far cry from that now. "We had a confession from Leon Frostfire—"

The dissenters grew louder. "Liar! Murderer!"

"Yes. He is," I agreed firmly and loudly, tapping the Spear for order against the floor. "And I doubted him too. But here we are, with proof that the East wants us all dead."

"Attack them in the mountains!" shouted a woman.

"What if the East is here among us, ready to blow us to the sky?" yelled another woman.

"I don't want to die!" a child screamed.

"I don't want any of you to die!" I said, thrusting my Spear in the air again. "So that is why we are negotiating with the East. Whether or not something comes of that, it has bought us time to uproot these devices. If you have seen something similar, tell the apprentices. Tell the Roamers. We will remove it. Otherwise...we don't know where they are. Or how many. That is why I am telling you—you have to leave. It is no longer safe in this cathedral, or the castle, or the Undercity, or anywhere in Marlenia City."

"What about the frozen?" came a young voice from the front.

I pursed my lips as my insides twisted uncontrollably. "I promised you I would fix everything. In my heart, I was talking about a cure for the frozen plague. I know some of you have families who willingly submitted to it, to avoid starvation. That's why we have to work together to identify—"

The stream of dissenters began again in earnest. "She's not

going to save them with her Freetor magic. She's going to let them die!"

Bidelia wasn't here to quiet them. Gobany wasn't here to remind them of the destruction just outside the cathedral. I had only myself and the weaker apprentices and the Roamers. I signalled them and they dove into the crowd threateningly, which only stirred my people into more of a panic.

My fingernails dug so deep into my palms that they broke skin.

"Enough!" I roared, holding up the Spear. "There is a cure and I *do* have it, if you would just *shut up for a minute.*" My knees buckled as the magic swirled within.

No. I had to keep *control.*

"There is a cure for the plague," I said, because if I didn't say something, I would lose everyone and myself. "It requires two artefacts. The Emerald Cloth to revive the body, and the Midnight Tablet to revive the mind. The Emerald Cloth, I found, with the help of my friends. They have taken the Cloth and hidden it under my orders, for I feared the East would take it and use it against us, or destroy it completely. On its own, it can cure your loved ones. But they will not come back the same person. For that, we need the Midnight Tablet. The last of the four artefacts of Dashiell.

"Going out to find a potentially mythical object of extraordinary power is foolish in this climate. I...know that." I swallowed my true feelings. "But if finding the Midnight Tablet to restore your loved ones is more of a motivation to leave the city than the hidden devices rigged to explode around us, then go. Find it. I would be out there myself if...if it wasn't more important for me to remain here, to protect you." I gestured to Katell again, and she carefully placed the explosive in its burlap sack.

When my attention returned to the crowd, I saw him.

He held my gaze with his unusual yellow-green eyes. He wore no disguise. The men and women surrounding him in the aisle pressed against his body as if he were nothing more than a commoner. His face, filthy. His clothes, stained with grime and blood.

His expression, rapt. On edge.

My heart thumped so violently against my ribcage I thought it would burst from my chest. The rest of my speech stalled in my throat. I swallowed my words and tried again. "I'm offering a reward for anyone who can find..."

A young woman standing in front of Keegan took advantage of my moment of weakness. "The Holy One was frozen. The Daughter of the East paraded him through the streets when they took the city."

From the moment I'd returned to Marlenia City, I'd told myself and everyone around me not to discuss Keegan's missing memories. If the people found out their rightful ruler couldn't remember his birthright, there would be chaos. False claims to the throne. Criminals slithering out of the woodwork to lure Keegan into schemes meant to rob and discredit him.

Sylvia had paraded Keegan through the streets. But I hadn't been here then. I didn't know what they believed to be true, what they had actually seen, and what had been embellished after the fact.

Keegan's gaze held mine. His expression was unchanged.

He'd wanted me to tell the truth about what I'd done.

I'd refused. He left.

My non-answer was answer enough. The murmurs swelled. I blinked. Keegan had disappeared. Only the people remained.

"He doesn't remember who he is."

"Explosives...my home..."

"The Violet Fox has stolen his throne."

"She's tricked him..."

"I am asking you, imploring you, to leave this city," I said finally, above the noise. "If you care about your Crimson Prince, *my husband,* if you care about your loved ones—leave this city. If you do, I swear I will do whatever is in my power to protect it from crumbling completely—to save those who are still frozen."

My people shuffled, squirmed, and argued. The cathedral doors swung open and a mass exodus occurred. I gripped the Spear tightly and watched hungrily as they spilled out, chattering about gathering what little they had to venture into the tunnels, or try and slip past the blockades and find a new life in the South, or with family in a neighbouring baile.

I had done it. They were leaving. They would be safe.

But the doors closed with a deafening rumble, giving rise to a flurry of shouting and panic—all directed at me.

Half the crowd had remained within the cathedral walls. The rabble advanced on me, and although Katell, Binna, and the Roamers tried to stop them, they were grains of sand in the avalanche of stones rolling towards me.

"Don't!" My voice carried over them, echoing, dark, and frighteningly powerful. It stopped them in their tracks, allowing the Roamers to get in front and hold the people at bay. Blue tendrils of lightning caressed my fingers, weaving around the arm that held the Spear.

It was revolting. And rapturous.

I searched for Keegan among the abated crowd. He had gone. Perhaps he had never been there in the first place. Or those who truly cared about him had carried him to safety...away from me.

Now it was just me and the unfeeling horde. "If you hurt Keegan—there will be consequences."

I meant they'd face a fair trial. Maybe I'd throw them in the dungeon. That was what the castle guard would have done to me, if not put me to death, if they'd have caught me back when I sliced Keegan's lips open, when I was just the Violet Fox. But the magic coursing through my fingers sent a very different message—one I would have sickeningly delivered if it meant saving his life. Again.

"No one wants to harm the Crimson Prince," said a burly man near the front of the crowd. "He is the true ruler of our land. Regardless of what he remembers."

The statement was a threat though it brought a measure of relief. They accepted him as he was. As I did not.

I squeezed my eyes shut. "This is over. Unless you are sleeping here for warmth, the rest of you, out."

"She's afraid!" one woman shouted victoriously, eliciting a round of jeers.

I stepped deeper into the crowd, tapping my Spear threateningly as I walked up the aisle. Cautiously, everyone drew back, creating a wide gulf between me and them as I ventured for the cathedral doors. Katell and Binna followed at a distance in my wake.

"I'm not afraid of anything," I spat. "I am the Violet Fox. And I am the High Queen. I order you to leave this city, and if you don't, at least find the explosives so we can save what little we have left."

Their faces were the same to me. Men. Women. Old. Young. All of them dirty, smelly. I used to be like them. I used to stand up to authority behind the safety of a mask and cape. But couldn't they see now was not the time?

They blocked the aisle, so I navigated around them. I refused to hide my face or the pain there. The Roamers watched me carefully and I felt the eyes of the apprentices especially as I struggled to keep my anger and fear under control.

In the Grand Square, I climbed into a carriage I hoped was mine and it took off, winding up and around the mountain, yet I could have been travelling anywhere at any speed and I wouldn't have known. I gathered my dress and screamed into it over the crunch of the carriage wheels.

They hated me.

They weren't worth saving.

Weren't they?

My whole life I'd been taught that my people came first. My responsibility was to feed them, protect them, steal for them, and free them from our oppressors.

Now they spat at the very mention of my name.

They didn't want me as their ruler.

Keegan didn't want me.

Keegan—or the idea of him—had turned our people against me. I was a murderer. A liar. A thief. A Freetor apprentice in all but title. Keegan was a prince. A High King. A thoughtful, just person. He was their rightful ruler, not me. If our people didn't evacuate, if we disabled the explosives, if Keegan didn't return to me, it was only a matter of time before I would be deposed.

If the people didn't want me to help—if I didn't deserve to help them—what was I even doing here?

The carriage stopped. I didn't want to get out. The exhaustion of the last three days weighed upon my lids, begging me to crawl back to my chamber to sleep, and yet I just sat there, gripping the Spear. The dissenters were in my head now, whispering their hate, and I was alone with it.

Gingerly, the carriage door opened, startling me. Bidelia recoiled from the door—and from the pointed Spear.

"Sorry," I said, retracting it, burying my face in my hands. "Tell me the bad news. I'm ready."

Bidelia's face was obscured in the darkness, though I could make out her patience-worn-thin expression well enough. "It took some doing. But the East has agreed to come here, in two days, at sundown. They want to discuss an exchange. They do want Sylvia and Leon. We should tell them we want at least a temporary truce, until spring. If not something more permanent."

I barely registered her. I had been primed for the worst.

"Kiera. Did you hear me?" Bidelia asked again.

"Y-yes." She helped me out of the carriage and we strode across the dirt-filled bailey towards the castle doors.

"There seems to be a lot of activity in the Square," she remarked.

"People are evacuating." I felt like it wasn't me talking again. It was some other me.

The lines on her face softened with relief. "Good. That's good, Kiera."

Far-off footsteps caught my attention. I glanced around wildly. The carriage wheeled away to the back of the castle. Only Bidelia and I stood in the bailey. Yet I couldn't shake the feeling I was being watched.

Conal. He was still in the castle. He had to be.

Bidelia hadn't heard the sound. Her hand found my shoulder. "Let's get inside. You look exhausted. Get some sleep, and tell me everything tomorrow."

I nodded just to end the conversation as invisible hands shredded my insides. Somehow, I made it back to my chamber, undressed from my constraining gown and put on a clean white shift, and crawled into the soft sheets of my royal bed.

My father was in the castle somewhere. I had allowed him to roam free with his piece of the Midnight Tablet because I thought that managing the realm was more important. More...responsible.

He had offered to teach me to control my magic. I had refused his help in the dungeons. But now, I needed it more than ever.

I tried to get some sleep. When my mind wouldn't stop whirling, I marched the cold corridors in my shift with the Spear, waving it in the darkest corners, searching for my father. I ventured down into the dungeon, much to the surprise of the single castle guard who denied having seen anyone resembling Conal Driscoll—or felt anything unexplainable. I walked the entire grounds of the castle, including the stables and the hedge maze.

I blinked. The sun rose. There I was, still in my shift, my toes digging into the stiff mud of the garden beneath the balcony.

I ran back to my chamber.

There was no time to sleep. Servants entered at daybreak, noticed my frazzled, dirty form, and wordlessly arranged a bath. Bidelia updated me on the previous day's adventure at the Eastern camp as the servants shoved me into a blue gown, once again, fitted to my thin form. I filled her in on the events of the rationing, editing out the display of magic, though I suspected from her wary expression that she'd already heard the Roamers' version of the evening.

The Roamers, with the help of dozens of citizens, uncovered ten more explosives from the city. People came forward with all sorts of contraptions, most of which were trash. A waste of my followers' time. Others were staggering out of the city, carrying what little possessions they had. Most headed south, by way of Feenagh Forest, hopeful for warmer climates. I heard reports from Antony of surface-born Marlenians attempting to hijack tunnels in the Undercity, hoping they lead to oases deep underground.

As I gave the servants specific instructions for the set-up of the throne room during Boris and Dominique's visit and debated with Bidelia about the best way to move or preserve known frozen bodies throughout the city, I ordered every Roamer to report to me personally if they discovered people whispering about their precious Crimson Prince. Word would spread to the East about Keegan's lost memories—but given the climate, perhaps it wouldn't. In any case, I wouldn't have any surprise mobs bursting into the castle, not if I could help it, not when I had to deal with Dominique.

Of Keegan's movements, I heard nothing. Or, Antony and the Roamers were holding out on me.

I didn't attend that evening's rationing. For the best, Bidelia said forcefully, as she escorted me to my chamber, wearing her favourite long coat with the silver buttons. Remain in the castle. Get some sleep. Those were her *orders*.

I took orders from no one.

As soon as she left for the cathedral, I was back in the dungeons, obsessively traversing deeper into the depths. I justified this initially as searching for explosives, but I couldn't lie to myself as well as I could the guards and the servants. I whispered all of my father's names into the shadows. He was here, somewhere, and I would find him and make him help me.

We were deep into the night when I emerged from the dungeon with the Silver Spear, filthy and exhausted, yet determined to find Conal Driscoll before the sun rose again. I would have settled for finding my husband, too. Perhaps he had snuck back into the castle and was taunting me: *someone* was running from me, in the corner of my eye. I heard their footsteps. I saw a face that looked like him, and yet, it clearly wasn't. They eluded me at every turn. The castle guard responsible for keeping people in and out of the dungeons gave me a strange look as I emerged, smelling like dirt and grime, muttering under my breath.

I stumbled through the castle and out the postern with the Spear as my walking stick in the bitter night. Its power cradled my body, shielding me from the worst of the cold, filling my head with promises of power—so long as I held it close.

Was that not his face in that bush? In that patch of dirt? I felt outside myself as I raced through the dark hedge maze, poking every corner, every strange protruding branch, and every shadow that crossed my path. I dared not call his name, for my desperate breath might have destroyed the fragile hold I had on him—and myself.

Every time I thought I would collapse into a heap, I planted the Spear in the stiff ground and leaned hard. It was truly beautiful and several times, I nearly tore away the fabric that protected my people from its destructive power. Instead, I climbed to my feet, and exhausted, my mind reeling with everything I had done— everything I *would do* come the next sundown—I stumbled back to my chamber.

The door banged against the wall as I threw it open. I gasped and recoiled.

I had expected my father. It wouldn't have been the first time.

Yet it was Gobany, Katell, Binna, Ruchaan, and every other apprentice living in the castle. They stood like pillars in my chamber. Watching.

Judging.

As they had been busy escorting Bidelia back and forth from the Eastern camp, aiding the Roamers with their search for explosives, and helping my people evacuate, Gobany and the rest of the apprentices hadn't turned their discerning eyes on my activities—past or present. Now, as they gathered solemnly in my chamber, their hands clasped in front of them reverently, their gaunt, drawn faces judged me with the severity of the Elders.

I closed the door gently behind me, bewildered as they guided me deeper into the room. Most of the apprentices encircled me, while others stood a stone-throw away. All of them stared at me, unblinking.

Gobany emerged from the group. His burnt face seemed more irritated than usual, and all I felt when I looked upon him was, *is this my future, if I fail to control my magic?*

"We know what you plan to do," Gobany said. "Plotting a murder is the hallmark of a tyrant."

My stomach turned. I had told no one of my plan to end Dominique's life—but now it was written all over my face. "They both have participated in a massacre. Probably more than one, in their respective homelands, with the stories I've heard of how they've treated Freetors," I told them. "I have to prevent all future massacres—and their plot to devastate this city. This province. Our world."

"And to do so, you will sacrifice your life. It will push you too far."

"I am in control," I assured them. "I have…rules for myself. I only call upon my power when it's absolutely necessary."

Gobany sneered and shook his head. The other apprentices echoed his actions eerily. "That's how it starts. That's what the voice says to convince you. By the time you're convinced the voice is right…that is when you are lost."

"Then how do you do it? Call upon magic, like it's nothing?"

I asked. "You've had years and I've had days. Tell me so I don't destroy everyone I love."

He convened silently with the other apprentices. In turn, they exchanged glances, whispered to themselves, and joined hands around me. Their hands glowed a rich blue to the barest of pale silver.

"It's always a choice you make," Gobany said simply. "You learn to distinguish which voice is yours—and which voice is right."

The voices. The pit in my stomach deepened. *My instinct.*

The one thing I had relied upon to stay alive on the streets, in the woods, and here in the castle.

If I couldn't rely on my instinct—how was I supposed to trust myself?

How could I trust *anyone?*

The apprentices didn't berate me for calling lightning from the sky to kill the mercenaries. They didn't comfort me, or offer guidance for the extreme highs and lows that followed my misuse of Freetor magic. I held their gaze for some time, as one by one, they left the circle, until it was just Gobany and I. Normally, I wouldn't have been able to stand such a ridiculous ceremony or charade, and yet, I was held in place by their sheer will. Gobany's pupils were wide saucers, and in them, there were terrible secrets. I blinked, resisting the gut feeling that screamed for me to frolic through them.

At the edge of my awareness, I heard footsteps in the hallway and something scurrying under my bed. People—apprentices?— moved around me and blurred out of existence. Gobany too, after a time, broke from me and left me in the darkness of my chamber. I didn't remember climbing into bed, and yet, I found myself under the blankets. My mind, once a runaway carriage, seemed calmer. The need to patrol the castle grounds for intruders and threats—gone. The desire to find my father seemed distant, like I had dreamed it and not acted upon it.

Then: rustling from the dark corner of the room, by the vanity.

I shot upward, my heart racing, and the Spear was suddenly in my hand. It glowed dimly.

"Conal?" I whispered into the darkness. "Is that you?"

I waited. Just the wind outside, blowing through the room. How I wanted it to be my father. If there was anyone who could help me destroy Dominique…

No. I shook my head. If my instinct was to find my father, that instinct was wrong, because the magic had befuddled my senses.

"Keegan?" I tried again. If he had returned to the castle to be with me…

Outside, the wind died. There was no one else here.

Because of course there wasn't. I was alone.

Slowly lowering back into the soft mattress, I sunk into a deep sleep. Too-real dreams punctuated the morning, when sunlight invaded the room. Servants came and left with a bowl of broth and a slice of old bread, though that may have been a dream, for Laoise was there, and she ate it greedily in the corner. I didn't mind. She was somewhere outside the city, likely scavenging for her breakfast. I desperately wanted her and Monju to return; I missed them deeply.

The room grew darker, colder, and after running from an enemy in a distant land, my dreams relaxed once more. I felt my arms, legs, torso slowly fall back into the mattress again—and then another body, sitting on the edge of the bed. I lifted my arm to reach for him, yet it was too heavy. I was still dreaming.

Keegan would not face me: he gazed out the window, his hands behind his back, his shirt dirty and nearly rotted away. He had only been gone for—how long? Weeks? As I thought about it, the vision of him wavered. His dark curls had matted and fell messily around him, further obscuring his face.

"Why won't you come back to me?" I whispered. My lips felt heavy. Although this was a dream, I was muttering the words as they floated out of my mind. "Help me help our people."

"How can I help them if I don't know how to help myself?" he replied.

"Then let me help you remember."

He shook his mess of curls and moved away from the window, seemingly floating across the room. "Don't kill Dominique," he said as he reached the door. "You're no murderer."

"I am. I have to."

"Why?"

"To protect you. Everyone."

He finally turned to me, his yellowy eyes blazing. His face dripped red. Blood. "I'm going to stop you."

"No!" I called the Spear to my hand, all-too aware of the texture of the cloth binding its real power—

—and heard the pounding on the door. "Kiera? Kiera!"

I gulped air as if I were drowning as the door gave way. Bidelia burst into my chamber and slammed the door shut, alarmed. She was dressed in her finest. She appraised the sweat sliding down my forehead and the blankets ensnaring my legs. "A nightmare?"

My head whipped back and forth as I searched the room. No Keegan. No blood on the floor. The Spear had fallen off the edge of the bed.

"The servants said you haven't left your room all day. That can't be true, is it?" she said.

The sun was low in the sky. But surely it was *rising*, not setting? Groaning, I buried my face in my knees. The apprentices had granted me the rest my body craved—in exchange for the day.

For that evening, Boris and Dominique would grace us with their presence in the throne room. And then, when they were least expecting it, I'd end this, once and for all.

I would become a murderer, again, to save my people.

"At least you managed to down some supper." Bidelia gestured to the tray on the vanity. The bowl was empty and dusted with breadcrumbs. My lips were dry and my stomach was no longer complaining—when had I eaten? I couldn't remember.

Bidelia remained by the door. "You need to be strong for the armistice talks."

Even the word lanced me. "You shouldn't worry about me," I muttered. "It'll be—"

"But I am worried," she interrupted grimly. "You aren't yourself."

"What if this *is* me now?" I replied.

She sighed and gripped the doorknob. "Stop punishing yourself. Go to the kitchens. You deserve food and rest. The servants know you're wandering around at night, talking to yourself."

"I was trying to find Conal."

"As your Advisor, I'm terrified for you. I don't want you to have another...*episode*. We cannot afford for this talk to go wrong."

Episode. Like killing those mercenaries was a rage-induced mistake—and not a desperate attempt to rescue the man I loved.

"It won't," I said, with finality.

She didn't like my tone. But the fate of our people hung in the balance and she likely had better things to do than console me. She opened the door.

"If you see Keegan at the rationing, tell him...tell him to come home," I said.

Bidelia nodded. "I promise I will."

With sundown fast approaching, I threw off the constricting blankets and prepared for the East's arrival.

I had done what I could for my people, yet it was not enough to stop the threats looming above us all. To save them, I would embrace a darker path—because as the High Queen, that was my duty.

"You're not actually going to trade us to Boris, are you?"

I said nothing as I tightened the rope securing Leon's wrists. The bonds were already sound. Antony and the Roamers had ensured that. I was busying my hands in the minutes before Boris and Dominique stormed into the castle—perhaps for the last time. Leon didn't budge; the chains around his ankles were secured to his sister's. Sylvia regarded me and the castle hallways drearily and fidgeted, less in an effort to escape, and more out of frustration.

Two castle guards flanked the side entrance of the throne room. Once I entered, I would end the war with the East, once and for all. Antony was further down the corridor, giving last minute instructions to two Roamers. No doubt Dominique and Boris would use their trip to our castle as an opportunity to plant more explosives. Some Roamers had been assigned to watch any accompanying Eastern soldiers or shadow killers, to ensure they didn't stray deeper into the castle on their journey from the entrance to the throne room. If they tried to detonate an explosive inside the castle, we wouldn't have notice or time before the chaos broke all chain of command.

If the East managed to leave the castle alive, I had no doubt they would give the order to raze the city immediately.

We had to prepare for everything and that made me nervous. I was better at improvising than planning.

"Where did Keegan run off to?" Sylvia asked me instead.

I didn't want to think about him, all alone, accidently tripping an explosive. Or leaving the province for a better life, without me. "He's on a mission."

"He doesn't remember you. Does he?" she said plainly.

It was difficult to hide my reaction. I retracted my twitchy fingers. "No."

"Because of what you did…with the Cloth?"

"Yes." She had been there. There was no point in lying to her—not now. Not when I'd already told my people the truth. All that mattered now was finishing the war as quickly as possible, so I could deal with my husband's missing memories.

Leon frowned. "You mean, Keegan is running around in the streets, with no knowledge that he is the High King of the West and Holy One of Marlenia—and you've taken his throne for yourself?"

"No," I said darkly. The magic rose within me, ready to pulverize him, too. "It is mine because I am married to him and I will hold it for him until we get his memories back."

"And…how were you going to do that?" Leon asked sceptically.

"Magic," I replied. Until Laoise and Monju returned safely with the Tablet, whether it be whole or partial, I had to focus on making amends, with my people and with Keegan—the Crimson Prince. I couldn't abandon them now. Not after I'd wronged them so egregiously. Those who remained within the city hated me and I couldn't have that. No matter the cost, I would prove I was worthy to sit on the throne—with or without my husband.

Sylvia looked concerned. "Well. I don't want to go back to Cogold. Or up to Ninyanas. I want to stay here."

"How many times do I have to tell you? You can't marry Keegan," I said flatly.

"I didn't say…!" She huffed in frustration. "I just don't want to be traded like chattel."

"Neither do I. Grant us an asylum, Violet Fox," Leon said.

"Untie us and we will help you get rid of our brother."

Sylvia's eyes widened. "She won't do that. She *can't* grant that. Only Keegan can grant us asylum." She beamed. "I read that in a tome once, you know."

"I'm the High Queen. I can do whatever Keegan can." And more. "Would he really kill you?"

Sylvia looked uncertain, but Leon bobbed his head. "I would, in his position."

"Reassuring."

"Just…let us go," Sylvia pleaded. "And don't turn us into pulp."

I glared at her. I didn't need reminding of the horrors I had committed—that I was *about* to commit.

Antony limped towards me with a grim, pouty expression. "Roamers are in position, Violet Fox. Are these two suitably secured?"

"Yes. Their bonds are fine," I said. "Wait for my signal, then bring them in."

"What's the signal?" Sylvia asked obtusely as I retrieved the Silver Spear, leaning against the wall. Picking up, I felt its weight and power, reassuring me for the difficult task ahead.

I inclined my head to Antony and the two castle guards with respect. The guards opened the side entrance for me, and I strode through with the Spear.

The throne room, like the rest of the Western castle, had once been a grand place where people would gather to hear the Holy One's justice, where nobles would enjoy each other's company and scheme their way into more favourable positions within the castle, and at times, where grand meetings and celebrations would take place. I had not spent much time here since I'd returned.

Giant Western banners, torn and tattered from hasty negligent storage, hung from the high ceilings and covered the damage inflicted from the many battles the castle had seen in recent months. There were no tables. No chairs, aside from the three thrones on the dais. Eight castle guards—the majority of their troop left—had been stationed around the room. Two of them stood casually by the large doors facing me. The servants had run a long, red carpet from the double doors up to the dais. It too looked in desperate need of a clean. Darker splotches acted as loud beacons for where unsuccessful cleaning attempts had been made.

Bidelia arrived from the side entrance with the news: Boris and Dominique's carriage had ascended the mountain road and arrived in the bailey. The armistice talks could finally begin.

I stepped up onto the dais and surveyed the room. The tight silver circlet dug into my forehead, but I refused to adjust it. It was a reminder of my duty. The Spear anchored me and I took a long, deep breath. Possible, because my dress had no restrictive bodice, as well as no ornate train, no frills, and no sleeves. Full range of movement, for when things turned sour. Given the weather, it wasn't the warmest outfit, yet a cape or hood would have been too ostentatious. A simple black belt with silver buckle ordained my waist, accenting the muted purples and blues of the dress. I had even let the servants paint my face; the blush added colour to my sallow cheeks, the rouge deepened my lips, and the black liner defined my blue eyes. I'd hoped it would add another layer of protection, so Dominique would not notice the fear I saw plainly every time I glimpsed myself in the looking glass.

"Everyone is ready," Bidelia said, folding her hands together neatly and taking her place by the side entrance.

I gestured for her to stand by my side, up on the dais, but she shook her head.

"Are you sure, Advisor Mullen?" I asked.

She smiled ruefully. "Yes, Your Highness."

Sitting on the thrones would send the wrong message. I was the High Queen, I had a right to rule, but I would not take the burden easily. I wished Keegan were beside me—yet if he were, he would have tried to stop me.

My magic itched to be released. But I would hold it, until absolutely necessary.

"Let them in," I said to the castle guards.

They pulled open the double doors. My breath caught. The East marched in perfect order into the throne room. A stalky, sour man who appeared older than his twenty-odd years, Boris Frostfire strode heavily down the red carpet. Boris's stark red coat was decorated with gold buttons and gleaming, golden pauldrons on each shoulder, fashionably brand new. He looked like someone who wanted to be anywhere but here, dealing with me.

Dominique Castillo's presence suggested otherwise. Dressed in black fur from head to toe—no doubt concealing a weapon or two—she bore a sly smile as she drew deeper into the room. I kept a neutral expression, though my heart was racing. If she was here, someone, somewhere else was doing her bidding. I hoped Antony's Roamers had enough time to find and dismantle the rest of the explosives—and whatever else Dominique had planned for me and those who remained within the city walls. Her gaze was unblinking and unyielding: she would do whatever it took to ensure I didn't leave this room alive.

The two royals hadn't come alone. Their military attachés marched in uniform lines on either side of the dirty red carpet: Eastern soldiers, outfitted in full shinning plate armor on Boris's right, and Northern shadow killers, dressed head to toe in black on Dominique's left.

My lip curled in distaste. Because of these two, my people were cold and hungry. Because of them, Keegan had forgotten himself and me. My free hand curled into a fist. No more.

Boris stopped unceremoniously two stone-throws away from the dais, looking up at me with his expressionless, statuesque face. "Violet Fox."

That was as formal a greeting as I was going to get out of the new High King of the East. We hadn't formally been introduced—most of my time around him had consisted of pretending to be a servant for Laoise, who had also been undercover.

"I am High Queen Kiera Driscoll," I said to them. My voice echoed in the near-empty throne room. "That is my name. If you refer to me by my street name, know it doesn't insult me in the slightest, nor does it demean my authority in this room."

Dominique sniffed flippantly. "Where y'is Keegan Tramore?"

"The Holy One is tending to our starving people," I replied, doing my best to keep my voice even.

The two of them exchanged suspicious glances. Something was afoot. Had word reached them about Keegan's memories?

"You presume to speak for the West?" Boris demanded.

I'd made that clear already. He was just playing games with me. "I am, yes."

"By Eastern law, you are not a real High Queen," Boris said flatly.

"Good thing we're not in the East." My fingernails dug into the Spear. This was going to take every drop of patience in my body to endure. Soon though—soon it would be all over. "Though I can see how you would be mistaken. Your defeat in this castle must have left you shaken. So I'll be very clear. You're dealing with me this evening. Unless you want to prolong this negotiation?"

"No," Dominique said, before Boris could object. "She y'is no'tin', and dis is a pointless formality."

"Speaking of formalities," I said, gesturing to their troop of soldiers and shadows, "our agreement was no more than ten fighters per party."

"The East has ten. The North has ten," Boris replied blandly, as if I couldn't count.

Dominique wasn't the current ruler of the North. Her father was. She represented Northern interests in the war, as the Pauper King himself was notoriously secretive and a shut-in. He was quite possibly dead, for all we knew. She was the Daughter of the North—the eldest princess, or daughter of the ruling lord. Whether or not her father condoned or had officially joined the war, we would never know. Dominique had the power to do as she pleased and was more than happy to go to war, especially against me, her primary nemesis. But by law, she was High Queen of the East—Boris's wife. She should not have brought this many soldiers into this room and it had immediately broken the carefully negotiated terms of the talk. I exchanged glances with Bidelia and she shook her head. I had eight guards in the room, plus Bidelia, and Antony just outside in the hallway. Boris and Dominique outnumbered us two to one.

I decided not to belabour the point. I enjoyed a challenge. "No matter," I said coolly. I imagined my father, who had stood upon this dais many a time, aiding the previous Holy One as he made decisions that affected our people for good and ill—mostly for ill. Embodying his breezy manner was comforting and deliciously easy. I wondered how many days it took of pretending to be a confident man in the castle to become the most arrogant. I inclined my head graciously. "We can dispense with the formal introductions and move straight to the discussion of terms."

Dominique was visibly annoyed by my theatrics. "Dis had better not take y'all night, Fox."

"It won't," I replied.

"Where are my siblings?" Boris demanded.

I nodded to Bidelia. I hadn't expected for him to ask for them this quickly, but the East was efficient. She opened the side door. Antony escorted Sylvia and Leon in roughly, throwing them to their knees in front of him. Sylvia nearly fell over but Leon, despite his bonded wrists, kept her upright.

"You don't have to be so rude," Sylvia muttered to Antony. She took in her brother, the multitude of Eastern soldiers and Northern shadows, and of course, Dominique. Sylvia pouted. "It took you long enough to come for us. Gabian is here too, in case you're wondering."

"I wasn't," Dominique replied.

Boris narrowed his gaze in silent evaluation of his siblings. "Are you in good health?"

Leon shrugged. He was noticeably scruffy and dirty. He looked down at his ruined clothes in disgust. "Just hungry."

With a stiff nod, Boris returned his attention to me. "State your desired terms for the armistice."

I took a deep breath. Not too fast, and not too slow, so as to allay suspicion. I had to give the apprentices and the Roamers sweeping the city and the castle enough *time* to complete their mission—while I completed mine. "Here are the terms. We, the West, offer Lord Leon and Lady Sylvia Frostfire, in exchange for a permanent armistice between our provinces—the West, the East, and the North." I looked to Boris and Dominique in turn. "It's time we ended this war."

Dominique laughed bitterly. "Dem? Dat is it?"

"What do you mean, is that it?" Sylvia demanded loftily.

Boris was intrigued, as much as he ever was. Dominique received her husband's reaction with confusion. "J'ou y'are jokin'. J'ou want dem?"

"We would also want official Western surrender," Boris said. "The Holy One title would be absolved, as it should have been generations ago. The West, as a province, would be absorbed. I will be Emperor Boris, first of his name, over all of Marlenia." He cleared his throat. "I believe that was also mentioned in the initial negotiations."

My stomach tightened. That wasn't something I could just *give* them. Not without Keegan present and sound of mind. True, my own instincts were in question, but the thought of giving Boris my home sickened me deeply. "It was mentioned. That will require more...discussion."

"No more discussion!" Dominique snarled. "J'ou will esurrender. Tonight."

I stepped off the dais. The Eastern guard closest to Boris unsheathed his longsword and the shadow nearest Dominique adopted a defensive pose, ready to strike. Trying to take this in stride, I turned toward Bidelia.

Bidelia, eying our guests warily, withdrew a scroll from her coat and ventured forward. She searched my face and seemed to find my secret plan, laid bare. She touched my hand as she offered the scroll. A warning. But I had to do this. She almost didn't let go. I slid the rolled-up scroll from her hands, and moved slowly, deliberately towards Boris, Dominique, and their company of protectors.

I had seconds to act—to get it right. Would Boris immediately order my death? Yes. They might even succeed in harming me. But he would do very little when the castle guards turned their steel in his face. If I didn't succeed in pulverising them all first.

I held out the scroll to Dominique, just out of her reach.

I could choose not to go through with this. Attempt to prolong these armistice talks until Laoise and Monju returned with the Tablet piece, coax Keegan out of the dark alleyways sweetly or by force. I'd already killed. Why not enlarge the stain and rub it in, so as not to soil anything else?

Release your magic. Use the Spear.

Why would I allow my people to suffer, even the horrible rabble, when I could save them all—with the death of a few tyrants?

"This is the full list of terms, as we have discussed them so far," I said. My words felt wooden and not my own.

This was justice.

Dominique's gaze flickered from me to the scroll. She took a cautious step forward and reached for the scroll.

To the untrained eye, the Spear was still completely wrapped—except for the place where the head joined with the wooden staff. The wood and the old, sturdy bindings shone through. I wouldn't even have to stab her. I could just tap her shoulder, or her face, and down she would go.

"Give me de escroll," she said.

I wiggled it in my grip. "Take it."

Dominique moved her hand—and missed nothing.

The Spear slid towards her exposed neck just as she drew her short knife and slashed wildly at me. I recoiled, dropping the false agreement on the red carpet.

"J'ou y'are predictable," she said, grinning.

"And you are dead," I said and prepared to attack again.

But she held her place and her smile. "J'ou wouldn't kill a pregnant woman, would j'ou?"

I caught the Spear just before it could touch her.

"You're pregnant?" Boris looked as surprised as everyone else.

She levelled him with a threatening stare. "J'ou will not espeak again." Her commanding voice blanketed the throne room.

My fingernails dug into the Spear. Dominique was right—the Violet Fox wouldn't kill a pregnant woman. Was she telling the truth? I had no way to know for sure. She didn't *appear* pregnant, though that meant little.

To murder a High Queen was one thing. To murder a pregnant one would be far, far worse. My own people already feared me for my magic and the nobles were wary because I had killed High King Leszek.

But that was not why the Spear shook in my grip. Lie or not, I couldn't risk the death of Dominique's child. Too many had suffered under my reign already. Perhaps this child would not be like Dominique or Boris. Even my enemy's child deserved a chance.

As I shrank back to the dais with the Spear, her amusement grew. Dominique was ready to row with me, pregnant or not. I felt smaller than ever. My face heated. I had been so sure of what I'd wanted and the power within me had enabled my darkest desires.

Or, I really was a tyrant.

The double doors had remained open to assure the East we didn't intend to trap them within the throne room or anywhere else. Most of the Roamers and the apprentices were searching the streets for explosives—leaving the rest of the castle largely vulnerable. This served to show Boris and Dominique just how "weak" we were. When the Roamers had finished making their sweep of the city, a servant was supposed to run in with an urgent message for Antony. Then, we would wrap up the encounter and try to evacuate the city as quickly as possible. So, when a gaggle of commoners waltzed into our armistice talks, at first, I thought nothing of it—until Antony's face lit up with concern.

Keegan was the Crimson Prince. He didn't need to sneak around. Taking off his homemade mask was enough to open any door in the city. And that was what he had done. He led four armed commoners into the throne room as if he'd marched in with four thousand. He said he'd return to stop me when he was strong enough—and I'd believed him. Yet despite my encounter with the hateful rabble in the cathedral, his faithful followers had dwindled. His slip-up with Sylvia and his subsequent, seemingly civil conversation with me, along with my confession about his memories must have plummeted his popularity. Or, our people had heeded my words, and evacuated.

"This meeting is over," Keegan said, taking most of the room by surprise. His voice was hoarse and unpolished. His white tunic had been stained brown and the red blood and muddied further. "Everyone, out of this room. For your own safety."

The Eastern and Northern forces looked to Boris and Dominique for guidance. They scrutinized Keegan's shoddy appearance and my heart sank. He should not have come.

"High King Keegan Tramore," Boris said. "At last. You show yourself."

The title landed on Keegan uneasily. Glancing from Boris to Dominique awkwardly, he tried to evaluate their identities. "Your...Highnesses," he said slowly. Far too slowly. "I'm glad that you're safe."

"Are you?" I blurted out. I had told him the stories of what they had done.

He gave up quickly on pleasantries and he refocussed his concern on me. "Right now, your Roamers are running the streets. People are fleeing for their lives. Ransacking businesses, homes, the cathedral. Some of them are even breaking into the Undercity—"

"Keegan, shut up," I interrupted. "The Roamers are operating under *our* orders. You shouldn't be here, not now."

"Is that how you always speak to me?" he demanded. "What do you mean, *our* orders?"

How could he not know? Had he not been in the cathedral, when I'd shown everyone the explosives? Surely, he would have heard...

I'd tried to find him. He'd refused to come and listen. Had I imagined his presence in the cathedral, as I had today, in my dream?

Had the people turned him against me?

Boris's face glimmered with righteousness. Keegan was feeding into their fears and stereotypes.

I shook my head desperately at Keegan. "You should really *talk* to me or the Roamers *first* before you—"

Keegan pointed at Boris and Dominique. "I heard you plotting. You were luring them here to murder them."

I'd dismissed everything I'd heard or saw when the apprentices had confronted me as an illusion or a dream, caused by my unstable, magical mind. But there had been someone else in my chamber last night other than the apprentices, when they'd held me in their circle.

The dream with Keegan by the window...had that been real?

I'd been so distracted, so tied up in myself. Gobany was right. My instincts had failed me.

"So. You admit this is all a plot," Boris said flatly.

"Obviously," Dominique said deliciously.

"I...I stopped myself..." It was a feeble excuse. I collapsed into the middle throne. There was nowhere to run. Nowhere to hide. They knew I was a murderer, through and through. I curled my free hand around the armrest.

Boris let out a nasal sigh. "This is madness. Seize them both."

As the Eastern soldiers turned their sights on Keegan and his small band, I leapt from the throne. "No!"

My hands danced with lightning. The Spear pulsed violently, heating my palm. Trembling with power, I held Boris's gaze. "Don't touch him."

"She y'is creatin' madness in his mind," Dominique said.

Sylvia, who had been quiet with rapt attention with her brother, finally spoke up from her kneeled position on the floor. "She used an artefact on Keegan in Sallingaire. Then he woke up...and had no memories."

Keegan's confidence faltered. "No, no. I'm fine. This is a misunderstanding. She *is* the queen, and I'm supposed to be the Holy One, but—"

"It's all right, Your Grace, we can see what's happening. We can discuss this later, when the Freetor abomination has been contained," Boris said slowly. He redirected his men's attention to me. "Your tyranny is over, Violet Fox."

"I am not...!" As I clenched my fist and swung, the dancing lightning flew inadvertently at one of the Eastern soldiers and struck him in the chest. He flailed as it snaked around his torso and he eventually collapsed. Sharing the horrified looks of everyone in the room, I leapt out of the throne to explain myself—but my hands glowed brighter, pulsing rapidly with my heartbeat.

Shadow killers and Eastern soldiers alike slithered up to the dais, and I waved the Spear to ward them away. I closed my eyes. I wanted so badly for this to be an illusion. Bidelia's voice cut through the chaos ("Kiera, control yourself!"), Sylvia and Leon protested ("Won't someone just unchain us already?"), Antony commanded the castle forces ("Keep them away from the Violet

Fox!"), and Dominique and Boris shuffled further away from me ("Per'aps killin' her will be more difficult dan I t'ought…")

I blinked. Nearly half the Eastern soldiers had fallen to the floor in front of the raised platform. Many were still breathing. Others weren't. None of them had frozen—this was not the Spear's doing. Beyond them, the castle guards had surrounded Boris, Dominique, and the remaining Eastern soldiers and Northern shadows. We were more evenly matched now, but barely. Keegan's four armed commoners ran from the throne room. So much for his influence. By the side door, Antony had clamped down on Sylvia and Leon Frostfire, in case they thought to escape in the chaos, and Bidelia had one foot planted in the hallway, as if looking for reinforcements.

Keegan knelt on the floor, clutching the dais. "Kiera. Stop. I won't let you abuse your power this way."

The surge of power quieted within me as I took one step after another. The Spear held me upright, the power of it coursing through me, feeding and strengthening the magic within.

If he can't accept you, said the Spear, *then he can't love you.*

No, no it couldn't be true. And yet he looked at me with such fear.

"I'm sorry," I said, though my voice was barely a whisper. I tried again, tears streaming down my face. "I'm…I'm sorry, I didn't want to…"

I was met with obtuse, thick silence. I fell to my knees and the Spear clattered beside me as I let out a long wail. I had tried to be queen and do right. Assassination wasn't right. Destruction. Murder. I'd only wanted to help my people. Somehow, it had all come out so very wrong. This wasn't who I was. It wasn't who I wanted to *be*.

My left hand cackled with lightning. The more I stared at it in fascination and fear, the brighter it glowed.

"I don't know if you can stop me," I whispered to him and myself.

His look was sympathetic. "This can't be who you are."

"And yet, it is."

Conal Driscoll appeared at the threshold of the throne room. His shockingly white hair was flattened and stringy from outdoor travel, and beads of moisture had settled on his long, flowing coat. He tugged on a long rope and flung two attached, squirming bodies to the floor.

Laoise and Monju lay before him, conscious but shivering uncontrollably. Their arms and legs were bound behind them. A soft layer of frost covered their clothing and their faces were red from exposure. They had been outside for some time.

"I told you that I would not let you stop me," Conal said. "That extends to them and their poor reconnaissance."

"A-a-ambushed," Monju managed to say, his teeth chattering.

Bidelia tried to move toward her daughter, but the jumpy, remaining Eastern soldiers in her path raised their weapons at her, fearing further tricks and deceit.

"I have also come to negotiate with the High Queen of Marlenia," he said grandly, bowing. He held up a sceptre, headed by the Orb of Dashiell. "Your piece of the Midnight Tablet—for your friends' lives."

MY FATHER SAILED through the room, past the High King and Queen of the East and their troop as if they didn't exist. He kept his watchful gaze on me, abandoning his grip on my friends' constraints completely. Laoise and Monju squirmed on the floor near the throne room doors. The castle guards moved to help them—and my father pointed the pulsing sceptre menacingly. It swirled with pale blue and navy light. "Touch them, and you all die."

"What is this?" Boris demanded, whirling to face my father. His arm moved to protect Dominique and she brushed it away.

"None of your concern. You can return to your negotiations once I'm done," Conal said darkly, strolling by the disrupted line of soldiers in disgust. He had about as much love for the East as I did. His Tablet piece twirled gently from the fabric tie at his waist.

Keegan climbed up on the dais beside me. "Is that...?"

I nodded. "My father. Conal Driscoll."

I clenched my teeth and leaned on the Spear for strength. I didn't want him to see me this way. So enslaved to the magic within and unable to wield it as beautifully as him.

Because he left you.

"Kill him, before he kills us!" Dominique shouted to her shadows.

My father lifted the sceptre. Cackling lightning shot down from the high ceiling, touching the Orb and filling the air with the thick scent of rain and the muggy outdoors. The Spear pulsed in response, nearly burning my hand, desperately wanting to join in the fun.

The soldiers—and even the shadows—hesitated.

Conal grinned. "As I said, Lady Dominique, you will wait your turn. Kiera. Laoise and Monju's lives are worth a piece of the most powerful artefact. Aren't they?"

"You have to believe me. I don't have it. Just like I didn't have it *before*." Did he not realize that Laoise and Monju had the second piece? He would have taken it from them, if that were the case.

Laoise saw the question in my face. Her lips were nearly purple. "F-f-f-ake."

My stomach dropped as I realized I'd been played. "Laoise and Monju didn't write the letter." I glanced at Conal. "You did."

"I didn't want you to worry," he said sincerely. "Though I didn't realize it would make you remain within the castle. I thought for sure it would raise your suspicion, to send the letter and then hear nothing else. I thought you'd mount a search for them. Lure you to me. Force you to trade. Have I underestimated their value to you?"

I pursed my lips. "I don't have the other piece. You said yourself it was probably underground. Why don't you try there and leave my friends out of it?"

"Because I *know* you're lying to me. Just as High King Kamal was lying." His hand rested over the Tablet half, hanging listlessly from the fabric tether on his belt. He shot a glance at Boris. "She will inflict the plague on you too, once she has extracted this false peace she craves."

Everything was spinning out of control. This wasn't how this was supposed to go at all. "Your Highness, Boris, I really do just want this to be over, though I'm not willing to surrender the West. If you would—"

"She has the High King of the South in her dungeon," Conal continued in admiration. "Isn't that true, Lord Leon?"

Leon perked up, intrigued and unsure of Conal's allegiance or identity. He shot a look at me and then slowly nodded. "I...heard that was true."

Anger flashed across Boris's bland face. "That was your plan? To lure us here, capture us, so you can take our land?"

"No. I want peace so my people no longer have to suffer!" I slammed the Spear upon the platform. Keegan recoiled in surprise. A crack appeared in the dais and slid down to the floor like a black, spindly worm. I pointed the artefact at my father. "Listen to me very carefully. You don't have a leg to stand on here. You were right. I do have magic. And I will use it, trained or not, against you, if you hurt my subjects or my friends."

He smiled, like he had won. "Then prove to me how strong you've become."

I closed my eyes—because his voice was my inner voice, and he spoke truth. I desperately wished it wasn't. I had thought I could murder in cold blood, yet every time before, I'd acted to save someone I cared about. To kill again, a roomful of people...

"It will destroy me," I whispered.

"It won't," Conal replied. "You are stronger than the magic."

I stared at the crack I'd made with the Spear in the dais, just as I had stared into Gobany's eyes in my chamber last night. Focusing on its shallow depth seemed to bring some clarity, as one moment stretched into the next.

"We can discuss this later," I said shakily. I nodded to Antony. "Let's take Boris and Dominique to the dungeons, where they will await proper justice." I fixed a warning glare on the East and their troops. "If you resist, there will be consequences."

Dominique was about to say something biting, and as the castle guards closed in on them, my father stepped closer to the dais. "You would put the needs of your countrymen above your friends, who lay dying?"

Monju had stopped shivering; he had passed out. Laoise didn't break her stare. In the Undercity, we worked together, but on the surface, it was every person for themselves. If you were caught, you said nothing, all in the name of protecting your fellows. It was one of the first lessons we learned when we joined the Fighters.

Even so, my lips trembled. I didn't want my friends to die at my father's hand.

"I've already made myself clear," I said firmly. I nodded again to Antony and the castle guards.

The hand holding the Spear shook violently, and it took every piece of strength I possessed to keep the magic within from lashing out. Beside me, Keegan lifted an encouraging hand, and I pulled away. I feared if he touched me, I would lose every bit of self-control I possessed.

"The crown weighs heavily upon you," Conal said, unimpressed and bitter. "You should leave justice to Keegan. But I understand. I have been where you are, after all. You want them to respect you. Allow me to relieve you of this burden—as a show of good faith."

The throne room blurred, as did foresight from reality. Conal grabbed Boris with unnatural strength and speed. Boris was a large, stalky man, and my father a tall beanpole twice the Eastern King's age. Yet he snapped Boris's neck with no emotion and tossed him to the floor like a discarded doll.

The dead thump of yet another High King of the East sucked all sound from the room. No one dared to speak, lest they attract Conal's attention—or my uncontrollable wrath.

Dominique regarded my father with stunned dread. Her horror became a rippling laugh as tears clouded her vision.

"All hail High King Leon Frostfire," Leon said as he rattled his chains.

Beside him, Sylvia burst into tears, and sought sympathy from her equally imprisoned brother, who offered her nothing but a smile on his scruffy, gaunt face.

There was a moment before everything fell apart, when I noticed Bidelia was no longer at the side entrance. I caught her movement:

Bidelia had snuck around the perimeter of room, towards Laoise and Monju, with a singular, fearless purpose. She worked with deft fingers at the ropes binding them.

The Northern shadows surrounded Dominique, concerned, but she burst from their protective circle, steel glinting between her fingers. The five remaining Eastern soldiers didn't need an order. They drew their longswords.

My father didn't stand a chance.

He didn't *deserve* a chance. I saw it in Laoise's gaze: *We're all next.*

Beside me, Keegan extended his sword awkwardly, for whatever training he'd once had was now gone. Although he looked to be more of a peasant pretending to be king, he spoke like his clothes didn't matter. "General Antony—arrest them all."

Antony looked genuinely overwhelmed by the order—and unwilling to leave Sylvia and Leon's sides to engage with the notoriously deadly shadow killers.

As the North threatened to swallow him whole, Conal caught and held my gaze. He seemed unconcerned about his impending doom as he raised the sceptre. "Now you're free of him."

It was my hopeful glance at Bidelia that tipped Conal off. She had managed to remove Monju's bonds and was working diligently on her daughter's. He turned his head to her, and Bidelia, exposed, stiffened under his attention.

She knew my father far better than I did; they'd grown up together in the Undercity. They had worked in the castle. She had *known* his identity for years and had said nothing to anyone.

Conal realized she was freeing his hostages—and he didn't hesitate. He acted as though there was no history between them, no previous camaraderie. He let loose the magic from the sceptre at Bidelia and my two closest friends.

"NO!"

The primal scream erupted from the back of my throat. My hands stopped shaking as I released everything I'd held back.

Everything happened at once: my left hand called lightning to evil's lie as it surged towards my father. The *thump* of my Spear as it pounded the dais.

Keegan, ready to charge into the fray.

The crack in the platform widened like a monster's maw and ripped across the throne room. Bidelia, Laoise, and Monju—barely conscious again—narrowly scurried away from the quake towards the nearest wall, Bidelia pulling at Laoise and her still-bonded hands. Her shoes scraped against the dirt and rock as the gap expanded towards them. The lightning from the Orb of Dashiell narrowly missed their heads, landing instead on the open double doors. A loud *snap* filled the air as the wood blackened.

With a rumbling roar, the room split and isolated Conal on an island surrounded by the expanding, dark fissure. My lightning struck him in the chest and he dropped to his knees. His grip on the sceptre faltered. Both of us gasped and held our breath as it flew into the air—and we sighed in tandem relief as he snatched it, before it could disappear into the abyss. The Tablet half dangled precariously on the fabric tie over the side; he hurried to secure it further.

The red carpet slid down, and with it, three shadows tumbled into the unforgiving darkness. Eastern soldiers met similar fates, though a few who didn't fall far managed the climb. Dominique teetered on the edge and slipped backwards, skidding deftly away from the widening crevice towards the wall. She crawled towards the side entrance, regardless of who she tossed out of her way, towards Antony, Sylvia, and Leon, who scrambled backward to the door as well as the crack grew ever wider.

I was safe on the dais. I felt outside myself, aware that I was channeling something deeper and bigger to do my bidding, yet simultaneously, able to flex a finger and wiggle my toes.

The walls buckled. The ceiling creaked. Banners collapsed. Beneath me, the dais wobbled. With very little support, it would collapse soon. Friends and enemies alike screamed for me to *stop*.

But nothing could stop me now. *This* was control.

"Keegan," I whispered. "I've got this. Look—"

Keegan was no longer by my side.

Conal waved the sceptre at me and pointed it down at the gap. He was mouthing something. I followed it with my gaze.

Keegan struggled for purchase on the side of the abyss. His weapon was gone. He tried to climb up and out, but the further back the gap moved, the more he wrestled to keep from tumbling to his death.

He looked helplessly up at me and what I had done.

My confidence wilted. I shook my head, wishing it wasn't so, and eventually, the rumbling staggered to a standstill. The silence was strange and welcomed, followed by the uproar of concern, people fighting to move, the scraping of weapons and swords, but all I could see was Keegan.

I jumped off the left side of the dais and deftly scrambled along the ruined floor. I set the Spear down and lay on my stomach, reaching for Keegan with both hands.

He didn't accept my help. Instead, he grunted with effort as he clambered up the side to safety. I slid back to give him room, remaining there on my knees. My heart was pounding and for the first time, I noticed I was drenched in sweat.

Keegan, now on solid floor, scurried backward from me, his face pure fear.

I whispered his name. "Are you all right?"

He swallowed, attempted to reply, and couldn't find the words.

I caught Conal's gaze. He was still trapped on the island of floor in the middle of the room. With a sickening dread, I saw what he saw: Elder Erskina in the Grand Square, when she had attempted to assassinate the Holy One. She too had wrought destruction with powerful magic, creating even more fear and distrust of Freetors.

I had saved my friends, but I had also gone too far. Worse, I had enjoyed it. A smile spread across Conal's face. I wasn't the only one.

My apprentices were right. I was a tyrant. We both were.

I removed the silver circlet and tossed it at Keegan's feet as he stood. The people in the cathedral had been right to distrust me. They had spoken with their hate and fear and because of it I didn't listen. I didn't deserve to be High Queen.

"Wait!" Keegan called after me.

"Just...stay away..." I feared the worst if he came near me.

I grabbed the Spear and returned to the dais, carefully crossing it to take care of the escaping Northern shadows and Eastern soldiers. They scrambled out the side entrance, past a bewildered Sylvia and Leon. The fluttering of black fur, whipping out after them. Dominique.

She wouldn't get away from me. Not this time. Whether I killed her or not, I would ensure she never walked free again. No more negotiations. No more false pretenses. Only me, and her, and one final fight.

Antony and the castle guards had disappeared. Bidelia and my friends, too. Keegan...I couldn't look back at him. Too painful.

The sound of boots scraping on wood—a loud thump—and then a heavy hand clamping down on my shoulder. The dais creaked with our combined weight.

"That was very well done," Conal said gently in my ear.

For a moment, it felt right. I had what I'd always wanted. I turned toward him, unable to move. My hands shook with power. The Orb and the Spear shone brilliantly in greeting, and I felt their need to collaborate, to be one and conquer everything. It flowed through me like pure rage. I clawed at my face, wishing to dig it out, but I couldn't, because it was my birthright.

He embraced me, pinning me in place in a powerful grip. "We could work together now."

The Tablet half dangled at his waist. It was *right there.* Its secrets could be mine.

And then, my grasp on him turned to rage, and I pushed him away. He'd made me chase these artefacts. I had listened to him. Trusted him. Wanted him to be by my side. He'd turned Keegan from me. He would never look at me the same again. Neither would my friends. I leapt from the dais and flew for the side entrance.

Someone, possibly Antony, had freed Sylvia and Leon. They attempted to block my path into the corridor. Leon tried to grab my arm. "Violet Fox, as the—"

"Take it up with Keegan. You've gotten what you wanted," I said bitterly, and breezed past him into the corridor.

I wasn't the only one furiously navigating the madness. Servants, commoners, and soldiers alike mixed into one as they all desperately sought the same thing: escape from the city. The rumours flew as fast as the people around me. The East had planted explosives here, some were saying, and they'd gone off in the throne room. The West had lured the East here to kill the High King. The Holy One was in danger. Advisor Ivor Ferguson had returned, and he had attacked Advisor Mullen because he wanted his position back. The Freetor Queen—*Look, there she is, where is she going? Should we stop her?*—attacked the Holy One.

As I ignored their accusations and falsehoods, I attempted to follow Dominique's tail, though I'd already thoroughly lost her. With Boris dead, would she destroy the city, as she'd burned the cathedral in Sallingaire? Or would she crawl back to the North with her unborn child?

I wanted her to face me. We both deserved to be ended.

I turned one corner and bumped straight into Gobany, Ruchaan, Binna, and Katell—followed swiftly by every other apprentice residing in the castle.

"There you are," I said nervously to Gobany and his friends. "Did you finish sweeping the castle? And...the city? What about the Undercity? Did you find any more explosives? Have the rest of the people...?"

The apprentices glared at me, smelling my misdeeds.

"I had to," I said. "I was defending my friends. Dominique is still alive. Conal—I mean, Ivor Ferguson—" The explanation died in my mouth. "I don't have to explain myself to you. If you were in my position, you would have done the same."

"No," Gobany said definitively. "If you were in *our* position, you would know why we guard the secrets of magic so fiercely." The other apprentices nodded in agreement. "We trusted you. Which was a mistake."

"It wasn't," I said desperately. "Apprentice Gobany...my enemies are powerful. I don't know how else to defeat them. All I want is to destroy magic, to prevent Conal from ruining our lives. I know it doesn't seem that way—"

"You're right, it doesn't seem that way at all," he said. "The Marlenians were right two centuries ago, to send us underground. They saw what would eventually become of us. So it was with Elder Erskina, and so it will be with you. We are going deep, deep into the underground to be spared your tyranny—and we're not the only ones. If you had any sense, you'd isolate yourself, to spare your allies what you will become."

"But I gave up the crown! It can't be...with everyone..."

"Crown or not, Violet Fox, you've always had a place of power among us. All it took was one little nudge." He flicked his finger to make a point; a tiny spark flashed between his thumb and his fingernail.

"That's why I have to find the rest of the Tablet! To destroy magic once and for all!"

"Destroying magic would be destroying life," Gobany said. "It can't be done. Nothing can destroy the seat of power. There will always be another willing to sit in its place. And there is nothing you could trade with the Tablet to make it otherwise." Gobany inclined his head. "Goodbye, Violet Fox."

"Goodbye," each apprentice echoed eerily as they brushed past me like herd animals, eager to escape the chaos of the castle.

Their warnings washed over me as I remained in place, paralyzed with realization. *The seat of power.* It clicked perfectly. So that was where the second half of the Table resided.

I glanced over my shoulder, seeing shadows of faces run by and away from me. The moment I chased after the second Tablet piece, my father would appear over my shoulder and snatch it from my magical, cursed fingers. Best to keep the knowledge hidden—to protect us all.

I retreated backwards. The apprentices were right. I had nothing to trade that would destroy magic—because I had nothing. No Keegan. No friends.

Only the alluring pull of magic.

Let Keegan rule the mob, if he was willing. Let him parlay with the imprisoned and the evacuated and the freshly crowned. Those were surface matters now.

I did what I did best.

I ran.

* * *

It would be a while before anyone thought to look in the deepest, darkest part of the dungeons for their runaway, former High Queen. I closed the windowless door on the cell. Solid, thick walls surrounded me. I couldn't lock myself in, but I didn't need that. Here was where I would stay, even if explosives did me in. I was a Freetor tyrant, and if I didn't sequester myself underground, I would hurt more and more people, including those I loved. I had not been better than my father or the Elders—but I *would* be better, starting now.

I lay in my cell for some time, quietly sobbing, sleeping, and punishing myself. Footsteps rumbled above. Water dripped onto stone nearby. There was no light in this section of the dungeon and it was furiously cold. I curled up on the rocky dirt floor, staring at the Spear next to me, glowing softly. Perhaps, by staring at it long enough, I would figure out a way to destroy it, and the magic, swirling within.

How long I stayed there, I couldn't say. Each moment stretched into another. I dreamed in the darkness, and there were times when I woke, believing the nightmares were real. Rordan spoke to me, *"It's all right, Sis. You can fight it."* But then his body melted in a rush of flames, and I scurried across the floor. Conal loomed over me, his voice a constant loud rumble, shaking my organs from the inside out. *"Your mother would have been proud of you."*

When the cell door opened, I flinched, but it was another dream. A trick the magic played to lure me into escape, so I could wreck more havoc. *Run.* But I couldn't. My inner voice could no longer be trusted.

The warmth and dim light of a lantern filled my vision. I squinted and averted my gaze, tightening my grip on my curled body. The shadowy figure set the light down, and seeing my discomfort, closed the open door gently behind him.

"There you are," Keegan said softly.

I couldn't even look at him. I was so ashamed. He was not real, anyway. I scraped my finger across the floor, counting the seconds until he exploded, died, or became horribly maimed. The seconds dragged on.

"You shouldn't be here," I said finally. My mouth was dry and my voice, raspy.

"I'm the Holy One. As it turns out, I can go where I want, with little consequence. Or big consequences, if I make a fool of myself."

Water sloshed in a skin. He held it to my lips and my aching body grasped it. Sitting up against the jagged wall, I drank heartily. It ran down my chin and dripped on the floor. This was real. Keegan was really here. He had found me.

"Why?" I asked, when I'd had my fill. Hope flickered in me. Could he have remembered?

He knelt before me. I passed him the skin shakily and he took a swig. I caught the whiff of his freshly washed body and tunic, and the gleam of my circlet, resting proudly on his forehead. "I've come to apologize."

"It's hard to apologize for ignorance," I muttered. "You only did what you thought was right. You have little to apologize for. Unlike me."

He accepted that one grimly. "I shouldn't have left you that night. You needed my help, and I...I should have...believed. I should have listened or...asked you more questions about your magic. But I was afraid. I continued to be afraid. I'm...sorry. If I hadn't left, then maybe...things would have been different."

"Maybe they wouldn't have been different. You always had trouble believing when it comes to magic," I said. "I've had to believe for the both of us before."

"That doesn't seem right."

I shrugged. Rocks skidded down the side of the cell as the walls trembled. Above us, movement. "You grew up believing magic was wrong, or just a story, or something you'd never have to understand."

"I don't remember that," he whispered. "I just...felt...like I wanted to save you. It frightened me. I don't know how to fight, though at some point I feel I did know."

I wrapped my arms around my legs, and rested my chin on my knees. "I don't know if I deserve to be saved."

"Yes, you do," Keegan said firmly. "How could you say that? After everything you've done?"

"Exactly. *Everything* I've done. Everything I've told you I've done, because you don't remember *any* of it!" I sucked back a sob. "*I'm* the one who has to apologize. Keegan...I...murdered people. Right before your eyes, to protect you. And it was *so easy*. I almost killed the High King Kamal too, and his protector. You were right. I wasn't in control. Even when I was." I patted the walls with a resolute hand. "That's why I have to stay here. Forever. It's the only way to atone for what I've done. For what I *will* do."

"Do you think you will kill again? Or lose control?"

"Magic always corrupts those in power. Elder Erskina. My father. The apprentices. Magic has defined the Freetor struggle. I thought I was different—that I could control it, to help my people be better. To rid us of our enemies. But the cost is…so high. I don't even know if I'm myself anymore."

"I know," he said, moving closer.

I shook my head. "You don't. You can't."

"When your father killed, he didn't flinch. Maybe you would have went through with your plot. But you didn't. That has to mean something. Your father would have killed again—and you stopped him."

"And everyone nearly died!" I covered my face with my hands. "He's had magic far longer. He's further gone…"

"There is hope for you. Because you *know* the cost. I don't like this power and I see what it does. But we can get through it and stop Conal Driscoll before he finds the Tablet. That was what you told me, when I woke. So that is what we must do."

If he found the other half, he would truly be unstoppable. He would trade anything to remake the world in his image.

I should've pushed him off the dais to his doom. Yet, I hadn't. "You don't know him like you used to. I wish…I wish you would remember. Then you would understand why I can't stop him."

"You can't stop him *alone*." He settled beside me, huddling against me. His hands felt rough, and he ran his thumb over my cloth ring, and I, over the place where his forefinger ended. "Just like the Crimson Prince couldn't solve everyone's problems, running around in a mask, in the filth."

My grip on his hand tightened. "I know."

"I really thought I could help them. Just by being there. Maybe I did. But I think I made it worse for some." He pursed his scarred lips. "It wasn't real. None of it was. I wanted to believe I was making a difference, that I knew what their lives were really like. But how could I? I didn't even know what my life was like, so I tried to take theirs, and fit it into some kind of...mould..." He clenched his hands, trying to make a shape, but couldn't finish the thought. "Even under a mask, I was still a royal to them. It didn't matter what or who I felt I was. I certainly didn't *feel* royal, even though I had this inherent sway. Was I...?"

"You were very royal," I assured him.

"But not...entitled?"

"Not as entitled as some."

He thought about that for a while. "I just wanted to hide and... figure out who I was. But they took me putting on a mask as some kind of symbol. They wanted to follow me. So I just kept...pretending I knew what I was fighting for. Then they started asking questions I couldn't answer. About my father, about the Freetors, about the South and the East. It...scared me that I didn't know. They wanted me to sneak into the castle and get food for them. I said, of course I wasn't going to do that. I didn't have to sneak, anyway. Which was why they hung around, even when they started to suspect something was wrong with me. Though most were too afraid to contradict the Holy One.

"So when I heard about the evacuation, that you'd told everyone I couldn't remember, and the rumours you were running around the castle, muttering about plotting a murder—"

"Don't." I squeezed my eyes shut. That time was a jumble in my mind, even though it was mere days ago.

"They wanted me to do something about it more than they wanted to know if it was true. I had to do something, because I'm—"

"I know," I said quietly. "If you hadn't, they would have turned against you to."

"No. Well, yes. And some did, though most of them were too afraid of the Eastern explosives to remain. But...what I'm trying to say, rather long-windedly, is...the people made for a poor mirror. I needn't have looked so far. Or for so long."

My throat tightened. "Keegan...are you saying...you want your memories back?"

He waved my question away. "They asked me to tell them how we fell in love. They sang a song. They wanted me to sing it, too."

"Monju wrote it for us." I leaned my head against him. "'The Violet Fox on Mountain High.'"

"And I didn't know a single word. I know you said you didn't want to...burden me...with this marriage. I didn't realize what you went through to be with me."

"You went through plenty, too."

This quieted him. His fingertips danced across my cheeks. "Kiera...you asked me, before, if I had feelings—"

The door swung open. The Spear pulsed in recognition. Startled, I pulled away from Keegan and reached for the artefact as my father appeared in the threshold. How long had he been there, listening?

"Leave me be," I said threateningly.

He stepped cautiously into the cell, holding up a hand in surrender. The Tablet half shone brilliantly, still hanging from his belt. The sceptre woke, and the Orb swirled a range of blues and whites. I would not let my guard down. Not after what he made me do.

"Stay away," I said again, clutching the Spear and pointing it up at his chest.

Conal smiled. "I'm not here to hurt the boy. Or you. I would never. Not again."

"I don't trust you." I wasn't sure I trusted myself anymore.

"Good," he said nonchalantly. "I just wanted to ensure you were all right."

I wasn't and he knew it. I wanted to hate him. He had abandoned me, betrayed me, lied to me—and yet, he was the only one who could understand what I felt.

"Don't you have a Tablet to find?" I asked him bitterly. "You're wasting your time here. I don't have the other piece, nor do I know where it is." A lie, just to get him to leave.

"That is why I am here to propose a truce, so that we may find the last half together," he said softly.

The spearhead before me wavered. "You know what I want to do with it, which isn't what you want. Why would I cooperate with you?"

Carefully, to show he meant no harm, he held up the Tablet piece hanging at his waist and examined it thoughtfully. The thin blue aura surrounding the runes and the jagged edges pulsed intensely at his touch. "The same reason you want to cooperate with me, Kiera. I will never willingly give you this piece. Just as you would never give me yours, if you had one. I want to give you the opportunity to have everything you want. I should think I've made it obvious, but despite how it may seem to you, I want you to be happy."

He regarded Keegan pointedly; he was talking about my husband's memories. He also had a fondness for him. He had saved his life, and he'd been around during Keegan's formative years. Keegan had had him while I had not. All of those memories, gone—unless we retrieved the Midnight Tablet, and Keegan agreed to take back his past.

Conal continued, thinking me unconvinced, "The Tablet is the source of all magic. This isn't just about curing a magical plague. This is about providing for your people. Long-term. They are a mob. Children you must take care of."

"Not that you'd know anything about that."

He ignored my jab with a glare. "You are the Violet Fox. High Queen of the West—of all of Marlenia. The people fear you."

"I have given up the crown."

"But you have not given up your marriage, have you?" He glanced between the two of us, intrigued. "With the power of the artefacts—with the absolute control of the Midnight Tablet—you could provide for all worthy Marlenians, forever. And reign over them, forever, if that is your wish. Or keep them from trouble in the shadows as you never age a day. This is the power of the Tablet."

"The apprentices said the Tablet requires a trade," I warned. "It's not a slab of stone you make a wish on."

"After dedicating my life to research and study of magical curio, I am sure enough of its power," he said, with a tone of finality. "I haven't been wrong about the artefacts before, have I?"

Not wrong—but never completely informed. Research wasn't a substitute for the real thing.

"One we have assembled the Tablet, we can decide the future," he said. "I can teach you how to manage your magic. You don't have to wallow, every time you let it free. I have much to impart." His hand hovered around mine. Another sterile, familial gesture that left me wanting.

I closed my eyes. Everything within me wanted to say yes. I wanted to control the magic that had defined my people for generations.

You don't have to destroy it. You could control it, as Conal does. You did it before.

My fingernails dug half-moons into my palms.

"So," he said, "do I have your word?"

Keegan rose to his feet. "I think the question is—how good is your word?"

Conal chuckled lowly. "Once you remember who I am, you'll know."

My husband looked uncertain, but I didn't need a reminder of the risks. "All right. You have a deal. Cooperation. Until the Tablet is assembled."

"And hopefully, beyond," he said. "Now. I have eliminated

much of this dungeon as a location, having spent some time down here recently. The Undercity is vast, though there are a few places I've been recently—"

"I know where it is," I said flatly. I raised a hand before he could protest. "No, I'm not telling you. If you force it from me, I will...do something drastic." I swallowed, not wanting to think about what I'd have to do to keep the knowledge from him. "I will take us there."

"I knew you knew," he said proudly.

He had no idea I'd been telling the truth, before and now. I looked away under his beaming gaze. This is how it could have been—if he'd never left me and Rordan.

Somewhere in the distance, the shouts of men penetrated the sounds of the underground dungeon. A low roar resounded through the ground. Dust rattled down the walls.

"What's going on up there?" I asked Keegan.

Keegan looked uncomfortable. He didn't want to burden me. I held out my hand and he squeezed it, urging him on.

"Leon is High King of the East now. Or so he says. It seems strange, just like that, he is a king. Because of that...he can't control his men. Some of them have run off with Dominique. They've disappeared into the city. Advisor Mullen and General Antony evacuated everyone they could into the cathedral, and some have made their way into the castle as well, but the people were getting antsy. Even when I stood there, holding the mask I'd worn for days while I lived among them, trying to reassure them that we had the situation under control...all they had were questions for me. Why was the East here? Why we were negotiating an armistice? I knew far less than they did." He looked sheepish. "They see the Eastern soldiers, and they think we're being invaded. They think the occupation is happening again, and I couldn't answer their questions. They think we've abandoned them. No matter what I do...it's like it's not enough."

"It never will be," Conal said. "The commoners will be fine. You can assure them once you have the Tablet."

I was about to make a comment on his flippant disregard for the very people we protected when Laoise's voice shot through the darkness. "Kiera? Keegan?"

"Here!" Keegan called.

Two sets of hurried footsteps became Laoise and Monju. Laoise glared at my father, and he side-stepped politely so she and Monju could open the cell door wider. She threw her arms around me and squeezed, hard. She felt a little cold, except in her trousers, where the Cloth burned hot. She still had it—even after her ordeal with Conal. Monju bowed quickly and then gripped Laoise in concern, ready to tear her from this place if necessary.

"Dominique and her men are setting off the explosives," Laoise said.

<h1 style="text-align:center">Fourteen</h1>

Frustration steeled my grip on the Spear. "Let's get out of here."

"Her men have dispersed, all over the city. Some in the castle, too. The Roamers are attempting to track them, though their numbers are greater." Monju said. He gave Conal a passing look of deliberate, cold disinterest. His face showed the beginnings of a beard, and though his time on the road and as a captive had left him thin and disheveled, the sincerity and strength in his gaze lent me the reassurance I hadn't felt since their departure.

As Laoise and Monju led the way towards the stairs, Conal grabbed my underarm and held me in place. He spoke lowly in my ear. "Will you keep your word?"

I wrenched away. "Do you want to see the city razed?"

"You have an army at your disposal. Use them."

This was my chance to stop my father, once and for all. As Keegan grabbed the lantern, I called after Laoise and Monju. "Wait." Laoise hesitated as I ran towards her, stealing a suspicious glance at my father. I lowered my voice. "You have to follow me. Get a message your mother and Antony to tell—"

"The Lady has found the Tablet piece," Monju said solemnly.

My dearest friend blanched. She smoothed out her dusty hair. "We've heard enough about the Midnight Tablet. Believe us." She eyed Conal with great disdain over my shoulder. "Are you cooperating with him now? After what he did?"

"Not *forever*," I whispered. "Just until—"

"You know, my hearing is impeccable," Conal said from several stone-throws behind us. "I suggest you conspire against me somewhere else." The dungeon walls shook and bits of dust and dirt fell on us like sudden rain. He coughed. "Especially not here, if Lady Dominique continues her assault."

I gritted my teeth, annoyed. Keegan joined us. "Has High King Leon Frostfire rallied enough men to help the Roamers?"

I hated hearing that title with his name. "I'm not even sure he's to be trusted."

"None of these men are," Laoise replied. "Mother and General Antony are down in the Grand Square. They're organizing the rest of the evacuation. Some of the Roamers are trying to find the explosives. We can go to the Square. Assuming it's on our way to the Tablet."

"Has our route been settled?" Conal asked, from down the hallway. "May I join you now?"

Laoise pointed a stern finger at him; she looked very much like her mother. "Let's be clear. You are not *with* us. You never will be."

Conal raised his eyebrows in amusement as he strolled towards her. "I can follow you in secret, or I can follow you in plain sight. Your choice."

"Stay in front," Monju said.

Conal inclined his head. "As you wish."

My father led the way carefully up the dark, winding stairwell with Monju on his tail, hand on the hilt of his belted weapon. Laoise lingered beside me and Keegan, furious.

"He almost killed me and Monju and my mother," Laoise whispered. "Oh wait. You were there. So *why* would you deign to think this is a good idea?"

"I'm sorry," I said to her. "But I need his—"

"He *tortured* us, Kiera," she warned me. She blew out a sigh.

"And he won't hesitate to do it again. To us, or you. So I hope you know what you're doing."

I paled as she breezed up the dungeon stairs. The walls around us shook again, this time more vigorously. Keegan took my hand and lifted the lantern, leading me up and out of the dungeon.

* * *

The sun was rising over the Western Province as Monju secured an abandoned Eastern carriage in the bailey. We reluctantly and solemnly huddled in the coach as we rode down the mountain.

The Grand Square was a flurry of military activity, even at this early hour. The men loyal to Leon turned out to be far fewer in number than I'd anticipated. They had hastily torn and tied strips of cloth around their forearms, and more enterprising fighters had found dye—likely from one of the now-closed merchant shops— and smeared a large, red "L" on the front of the armor. A few Roamers circled the Square as well, though most darted in and out of the streets, chasing unseen foes and checking each building thoroughly for explosives. Their breath came quickly from their lips; the air still attacked any exposed skin aggressively.

Atop an old horse was Leon Frostfire. In the last several hours, he'd managed to shave, find a fresh shirt, and don shining armour. A tattered red cape rested on his shoulders, held in place by golden pauldrons—the very same Boris had been wearing in the throne room. A sheathed longsword hung next to the saddle, though he didn't look in a hurry to jump into battle. In fact, he appeared at ease with his new command. Far too at ease.

Before I could scrutinize him further, an explosion rocked the castle above. Chunks of stone and rock catapulted from the west wing. Distant screams from the bailey rattled in my ears. Commoners burst from the cathedral to frantically uncover the source of the sound. Then, a second explosion: this time, from deep within the city. Black smoke billowed up somewhere from the southeastern quadrant. More screams. More shouts.

As more people piled out of the cathedral and into the Square to find out if their loved ones were safe, they spotted Keegan and swarmed him. They thoroughly, disdainfully pushed me away from him with their bodies, while I lifted the Spear, just to keep it away from any exposed, surface-born skin. The questions flew at him like arrows:

"Where are the explosives? Are they in the cathedral, too?"

"I don't feel safe—how can we leave the city? Where will we go?"

"When can we return to our homes?"

"Can we still call you the Crimson Prince?"

I tried to call out to Keegan, but he was lost in the sea of commoners. Laoise and Monju steered me clear of the mob and their fearful gazes as my friends regulated me to a safe distance. Conal navigated the waters as well, though more as a feather, floating where the stream would take him—towards us, within earshot, of course.

"They truly hate me now," I said, more to myself than to my friends.

"They just don't know if they can trust you anymore," Laoise replied.

"They know Keegan doesn't have his memories," I said. "They still love him."

Laoise looked sympathetic. "Don't you?"

He had managed to abate the people and deal with their questions civilly. They formed a protective circle around him.

I had sacrificed so much to be with him. How could we be together, after we'd changed so much? Even if I did manage to give him his memories, he wouldn't take them now. He was a new person. He had new stories, new scars.

I tore my gaze away. "He should leave the city. Between Dominique and…"

Antony trudged into the Grand Square from the cathedral and

spotted me. He waved his hand, navigated around Leon's men and the desperate crowd, and stormed towards the four of us. He caught me by the shoulder roughly.

"Where are you going?" Antony demanded harshly.

I answered his question with a question. "How many explosives have you recovered, and how many do you think are left?"

"Plenty, as you can hear. That Lady Dominique suspected we'd be up to something, and sent her shadows into the city. Some of them got underground, we've heard. I've already lost twenty of my best people just trying to retrieve and dismantle the things, and fight off the deadly killers defending them." He studied me grimly. "Don't know what you think you're doing, but you can't run off now. Not unless it's to retrieve explosives or hunt down Lady Dominique and the men acting in her name."

I stared down at my own hands. I didn't have my father's control. I'd probably end up detonating explosives and killing innocents if I tried anything rash.

Conal's words echoed in my mind. If he wanted, he could run around the city, essentially undetected, and disassemble explosives. Fighting the shadows would be another matter, though the magic would take care of that.

He shook his head slightly. He would not help me. That was not our arrangement.

Laoise noted our exchange sourly. "You are risking all of our lives for a piece of old stone."

"Then run along and help the Roamer General," Conal said condescendingly. "Perhaps you will succeed where he has failed in this...endeavour."

"You know, if you helped us, this *endeavour* of saving the city you once cared about would be over a lot quicker," I said coldly to my father.

"Why would I save something I intend to remake?" he said, with sly smile and a shrug.

"Are you heeding the words of this...rogue Elder?" Antony asked me carefully, glancing between the two of us.

I steeled myself. No doubt after our encounter in the throne room, he had pieced together Conal Driscoll's identity. To the Roamers, blood relation was less important than friendship and romantic bonds. "We have a temporary arrangement."

"More important than the one between you and I, Violet Fox?"

"No, General, believe me. I'm very aware of our arrangement," I replied. Keegan was still being hounded by questions, though some people had retreated back into the cathedral. I looked over to Leon, who hadn't stopped staring at me since I'd arrived in the Grand Square. "Excuse me for a moment. Let me see if I can't grant you some more assistance."

He saw my interest in Leon and sneered. "The Frostfires are not to be trusted, Violet Fox. Take it from someone who knows it firsthand."

"Hold on," I said to Laoise, Monju, but in particular Conal, who was becoming more impatient by the moment.

The curious crowd had thinned by now; most had returned to the cathedral, helped by Bidelia, who I couldn't immediately see but her voice was overwhelmingly present in the Square. I spotted Keegan's dark hair and the glinting silver of the circlet as he fielded the concerns of two distraught citizens carrying an upset baby. Other people had foolishly run off into the city or trudged up the mountain road on foot to get a better look at the damage. I shivered. Moving did take one's mind off the cold.

Leon lazily navigated his horse towards me, maneuvering him with grace and skill. "Violet Fox. I wasn't sure where you'd gone, but I'm glad I waited around long enough to see you before we headed out."

"Headed *out*?" Leon's men had gathered at one end of the Square, waiting for his signal. "Headed out where? What about your sister?"

"Sylvia has opted to stay another few days. Apparently her favourite manservant is not well. They're still up in the castle. Or what's left of it." He shot a glance up the mountain, as if it would fall on him at any moment. "As for *where* I'm going? I'm leading us back to Cogold, of course."

"You gave your word you would aid me."

"I *believe* I said that if you made me the High King—which *you* didn't, by the way, your dangerous friend delivered the killing blow—I wouldn't harm the Freetors. Western Freetors, that is. I don't know if I can keep my promises in the East. There are other interests there to contend with. And you literally can't stop me in Cogold, anyway. Unless you were planning on making the trip?" His brief grin became more serious. "I didn't say I'd help you sort out this…mess. Oh, don't look at me that way. I will assure you won't suffer any more official Eastern attacks, as soon as I wrangle my dead brother's—and my dead father's—troops under my command. I'll send an official armistice agreement in the coming weeks. I've grown tired of the West." His horse harrumphed in agreement.

I glared at him. "You're making a big mistake. You don't even know if there will be a capital city to send an agreement to! Much less people here to receive it!"

"If not this one, send a runner to tell me which other hovel you've crowned anew. As the East withdraws, this is now *your* problem. If I see Dominique, I'll point her in the direction of your Spear." He turned his horse away from me, casting me a smug, satisfied grin. "Goodbye, Violet Fox. But not forever, I hope."

He squeezed the horse gently with his legs and he moved forward, away from me and towards the outer edge of the Square, where his men had gathered. I muttered a distasteful word under my breath at him.

The urge to use magic rose again. *Make him stay. He could do your bidding.*

Yet another explosion, somewhere in the merchant district, rocked everyone. I gasped and steadied myself with the Spear. Leon's horse reared and the young king fought to remain mounted. His men struggled to aid him and not be trampled. This time, barely anyone emerged from the cathedral—they had tied their fates to that of the city, and had accepted whatever may befall it.

I heard Keegan call my name, and suddenly he was there at my side, enveloping me in the safety of his arms. I threw the Spear to the ground, terrified of catching his skin, and clutched him as if he were lifeless once more. His hands sifted through my matted hair, and my fingernails dug into his shirt, unrelenting. All I could think of was him, slipping down into an abyss, and me, tumbling in after him. Because if I had to, I would.

When I pulled away from Keegan, I touched his lips with shaking fingers.

Then, movement. Laoise quietly joined us, and Keegan broke away, his face reddening as he stared at the abandoned Spear. I picked it up as we eyed Leon's hasty canter down the street, towards the gates, with his men barely keeping up.

"He's not going to help, is he," Laoise said.

"No." I tried to not let the worry leak through my words. With the apprentices and Leon gone, we had fewer and fewer allies to call upon.

"We don't have the manpower to dismantle the threat and corner Dominique before the entire capital is destroyed," Laoise hissed. "We could try and find Dominique, but who knows where she is in a city—"

Another explosion. This time, somewhere deep underground. Laoise, Keegan, and I gripped each other for purchase and Conal shot me a warning glare as he gripped his artefacts preciously. He believed the Tablet could fix this—if the piece was where I believed it to be. I had to be prepared to trade everything to safeguard my people's lives.

"You still have…right?" I asked Laoise, raising my eyebrows.

"I've always had it." She patted her trouser pockets. "He never took it from me."

My father's new obsession had blinded him. Likely, he believed that he could retrieve the healing artefact when he needed it, which was all the more frightening.

Antony took my errant glance in my father's direction as permission to approach. My stomach sank. Monju looked as though he was trying to reason with the Roamer as he tailed him, unable to hide his concern. Conal stayed away, surveying the city with crossed arms and an unreadable expression.

"Well?" Antony said, raising his eyebrow at Leon's contingent as they rode further away from the Square.

"You were right," I said bitterly to Antony. "But we're not out of options yet."

His expression suggested that he was out of patience. "I am recalling my men. And calling in my debt."

I hesitated. I had been expecting this moment for days now and he couldn't have picked a worse time. "This can't wait until later?"

"Once the debt is called due, the Lady must repay it immediately," Monju said helpfully.

"That's right," Antony confirmed. His tone was firm though not unsympathetic. This was a business arrangement, regardless of what he felt about me. If I didn't offer him what he had requested—or the best that I *could* give—he would exact some form of Roamer justice. I glanced at Keegan and thought of Keegan and his scarred, whipped back. I didn't want to go through that again.

"Fine. You can have that." I pointed to the massive radius of burnt, destroyed wasteland that Gobany had created beside the Grand Square. "You asked for land and silver, and magic if I could spare it. Which I think we can both agree, is a bad idea, given the circumstances. I suspect many people have already migrated out of the city for good, and no one is going to want to settle or re-settle there, not after our magical interference. The crown will pay for the rebuilding of that district and lend a hand with the labour. You can build whatever you choose there, providing it doesn't block access to any of the established streets. We will rename it something suitably rewarding."

At first, Antony looked startled. He regarded the piles of rubble, collapsed house, and grey pallor of the devastated streets. He knitted his eyebrows.

I blew out a sigh. "I know. You know what? You're right. It's the worst piece of land I could offer you, and I didn't mean any disrespect. If it's not—"

He clasped me heavily on the shoulder and I gasped in surprise. He let out a hearty, booming laugh. "Roamers? Living in the capital city? That's...well. A first. Prime location as well. We accept your terms. Reclaiming part of the land as green space next to the Grand Square would be suitable, no?"

So many Freetors had no land, or claims to land their families supposedly held hundreds of years ago, now held by wealthy surface-born small lords. By granting Antony and his pledged surviving Roamers that area, I was potentially edging out another family or stepping on their claim. That was not a problem I could solve today—or alone.

Conal cleared his throat, stroking his beard thoughtfully. In different circumstances, I would have asked for his opinion. Now... we had to keep moving.

"Green space is a good choice," I said. "But if you're not going to do that now, I would appreciate your help with finding the rest of the explosives. So that we can all live peacefully in a city that still stands tomorrow."

His enthusiasm tempered. "We will do what we can, but our numbers are dwindling, Fox."

"Perhaps Monju can aid in taking out the shadow killers?" he said, raising an eyebrow.

"Your help would be appreciated, old friend, if you're up to the task," Antony replied.

Laoise grew worried and Monju found each of her hands to assure her. He was a skilled fighter with shadow killer training—but as an assassin, he had a particular code. He did not kill often, if at all, when it could be helped. I appreciated the seriousness of his offer. If there was anyone that could track them down, it was Monju Farin.

Still, my unease grew as Antony gave us the rundown. Those who had refused to leave the city had been evacuated to the castle and the cathedral. They estimated there were closer to twenty or thirty shadows in Marlenia City. That, combined with Boris's men, made for an estimated count of fifty enemies. Antony's original one hundred Roamers were down to thirty, plus the castle guards, which numbered around ten. It was a game of cat and mouse, and while the mouse had intimate knowledge of every nook and cranny, the cat was inherently faster, larger, and knew where all the explosives had been hidden. The apprentices had managed to find and dismantle over a dozen during their sweep while we'd entertained Boris and Dominique, though they had focussed on the cathedral, the area around the Grand Square, and the nearest entrances to the Undercity.

His orders clear, Monju set out down the main stretch. Laoise followed, and as it was on our way, I took Keegan unapologetically by the hand and lead him after my friends. He didn't mind, though his grim expression spoke for both of us.

"How will we enter the Undercity?" Conal demanded, striding after us.

"You'll see," I muttered, hating that he was getting ahead of me.

Monju walked with his unsheathed sword. Under his breath, he hummed an unfamiliar tune, perhaps in an effort to hide our conversation. His sharp eyes kept a close look out, though much of his attention was on Laoise. She glanced over her shoulder at Conal every five seconds.

"This is a mistake," she said.

"Then make it my mistake and don't follow me. Go with Monju." They were right to mistrust my judgement. But keeping Conal in my sights was better than letting him run wild. I would give him nothing until he needed it, and even then, I would never let him have the Tablet. He followed several stone-throws behind us, but he could no doubt intuit our conversation.

Another explosion behind us—this time, deep in the mountains.

"They are uncoordinated, at least," Monju said. "Which makes tracking difficult. Even if the explosives are in close proximity, they may have orders to delay their release."

"Not to mention, they have to run and hide every time they're triggered." Assuming they weren't sacrificing themselves each time, which would be foolish for the number of people in Dominique's new, loyal band. With every alleyway we passed, I expected her to jump out at me and Keegan with her poison knife.

Monju cast me a worried glance. "This may take a long time. Much of the city will be destroyed. The people—demoralized. They will want to know why the Violet Fox and her prince were so slow to act, regardless of the actual speed. They may not want to stay in the capital, even if it is saved."

That was the true victory of the North and the East—turning our people against us. Or specifically, me.

But the people still trusted Keegan. He had gone to them in their time of need, listened to them, and lived among them. Even as he was now, they trusted him. I had grown up with them and knew their plight intimately. But that was before the magic within alienated me from them. They wanted to follow someone who wasn't going to explode them into bits. I searched Keegan's face. "I need you to ask for everyone's help."

"The Lady wants innocent civilians to search buildings? The castle? For explosives?" Monju asked, surprised.

"Only volunteers. It's the only way we'll be able to cover the most ground. We can pair them with Roamers who know how to dismantle the explosives—and perhaps, there may be someone with that expertise within the cathedral. I know it's risky. But we don't have a lot of options." Until we found the Tablet—*if* we found the Tablet, if my hunch was correct.

Keegan looked uncertain. "They won't listen to me."

"They will," I said.

"I don't know—"

"Laoise will help," I said, sliding my gaze to her. "And Bidelia, too."

My friend held my gaze for a long moment. I was giving her a way out of helping me. Conal crossed his arms suspiciously, likely suspecting fowl play. Let him suspect I was up to something, I thought. I would not let him harm them again.

Eventually, she nodded. "Should I...join you, when we've finished?"

"If you want to," I said carefully.

"As will I," Keegan promised.

"Monju is at the Lady's service—once the shadows have been cleared," Monju said, bowing.

My heart warmed at that. Laoise, smiling at Monju's gallantry, leaned in. In her ear, I whispered the suspected location of the Tablet.

Conal interceded. "No, no. I see what you're doing here, Kiera. You really believe I'd let Laoise go off to retrieve the other half for you?" He waved a menacing finger at all of us. "Stick together. That is the plan."

"The *plan* is to save our people," I retorted. "You have many powers, but I doubt you can be three places at once. You can follow me or you can follow her and Keegan. Or if you can, keep up with Monju and try not to get killed. Regardless, I am going underground. Which is your surest bet."

My father evaluated me carefully. He saw me, because once, he was me. "Then let's not waste any more time."

He made no threats. He didn't have to. Out of courtesy, he turned away, but I caught him glimpsing at us over his shoulder. Something passed over his expression, almost a greed or a longing, as Laoise and I embraced, Monju bowed, and Keegan touched my face—hopefully not for the last time. None of us needed words. They had their duties—and I had mine.

"Follow me," I said to my father, pointing to the alley that would lead us down to the place of our birth.

THE FIRST TIME I'D ventured to the Central Cavern, Rordan had escorted me to receive the mission that would change my life: infiltrate the castle, become Lady Dominique Castillo, and recover a priceless Freetor artefact. The Fighters had unlocked the grand wooden doors, possibly the only set in the Undercity. I had been enchanted.

The last time I was here, the three apprentices leading the other survivors of Elder Erskina's murderous rampage had summoned me, requesting I find the Spear at the end of the world to rally the Freetors in the war against the East.

Now, I returned to the place I once held sacred—and despaired.

The wooden doors guarding the entrance were cracked and permanently ajar. The keyhole had been blackened. Someone, long ago, had forced their way in here. Conal loomed over me and I tried to ignore his presence, but I felt his excitement building as I pressed forward, into the dimly glowing cavern.

I had always felt a reverence for this sacred place and now, gooseflesh prickled my arms as the magic intensified around me. The walls were impossibly smooth. The violet-and-white patterned floor tiles had long since cracked and grit had scattered across the room like seeds. Before us, the seven stone chairs lay in ruins, silent and dusty, once representing the Council of Elders. The base of the chairs crumpled under their weight; they had once been suspended by magic, but no more.

Each chair had an animal looming over the back, carved delicately in stone: the worm, the crouching badger, the rabbit, the spider, the oversized ant, the fox, and the groundhog. Once, they had been grand pieces of art, representing our revered Elders. Between my last visit and now, they'd been desecrated. Elder Erskina had done great harm to the apprentices and murdered the other former Elders, so it was no surprise to see the spider's legs particularly brutalized.

The seats of power lay before me—and one of them contained the *real* seat of power. The Spear ran hot in my hand beneath its wrapping and the Orb, secured at Conal's belt, swirled intensely. Even if the other Tablet half wasn't in the room, the room itself was a kind of artefact, which wouldn't make our search easier. None of the chairs pulsed the intense, bright blue in response to the other artefacts we wielded.

I worried someone may have pilfered the Tablet half already. I tried not to let my concern show as I roamed deeper into the cavern. I didn't want to make it obvious to Conal that the chairs were my main source of interest, though aside from the two rounded archways on either side of the cavern, there was little else to examine.

Unable to hide the fascination from his face, Conal pressed a hand against the polished walls and closed his eyes reverently— and then realized a thin layer of dust covered everything. He wiped his palm on his trousers in distaste.

"How did you come to know the Tablet was here?" Conal asked me finally.

"The apprentices said as much." I wondered just how deep underground they had gone to escape my tyranny.

"Did they tell you with certainty? How do you know they didn't bring you here to mislead you?"

"I suppose we'll find out if that's the case." The thought hadn't crossed my mind. I had broken their trust; this could be a trap.

Yet I heard nothing of note or concern: just the far-off sounds of Freetors rustling in their home caverns, and the occasional, distant thundering of an explosive. I thought of my friends and hoped they stayed far, far away from my father until I could figure out a way to destroy the Tablet.

After I'd gotten what I wanted from it.

"Apprentices," Conal muttered distastefully. His boots kicked up grit as he suspiciously eyed the entrances for the apprentices' tell-tale tattered blue robes and quirky behaviours. "Handselected by the elderly, for no reason other than complacency, and groomed to know the selected secrets, passed down from Alastar Allayway's time."

"Seems you're still sore from when the Elders rejected you."

He looked surprised. "Who told you that?"

"Bidelia."

He considered me thoughtfully, and upon seeing my contempt, said nothing else about his childhood friend. Examining the Tablet piece attached to his belt, he thumbed the runes and changed the subject. "I have searched part of the Undercity for the Tablet half already. It isn't in the Temple of the Elders, or the Great Cavern, that I could see. It is...difficult to get a feel for the Central Cavern, with its inherent magical interference."

I remembered Gobany's comment about the origin of High King Kamal's bracelet being stolen from the Temple of the Elders. "But you didn't bother to come here, to this cavern, while you were *searching* the Undercity?"

He wandered to the seven chairs, inspecting each one thoroughly, stopping at Erskina's de-legged arachnid. He placed a reverent hand upon it. "I couldn't."

"Why not?"

"The place was crawling with apprentices. They would...know me. Their power is unpredictable, and they would see me as an Elder. I wouldn't have that, not yet."

A chill went through me. My father had leaked snippets of his desired future to me before, which included destroying our enemies and using magic as a tool to shape a desirable world, where Keegan and I would be free to rule—presumably, under Conal's guidance. I hadn't considered how the apprentices would fit into a world where one man possessed the four godly artefacts. Likely, they wouldn't. Gobany had been right to escape with his remaining fellows. Perhaps if I had been smart, I'd have gone with them.

"But you're here now, with me," I said slowly.

A ghost of a smile crossed his features. "Yes, I am." He rounded the chair, without removing his hand. "I remember standing there, as a young man," Conal said wistfully. He pointed to the middle of the cavern, where I myself had once stood and was judged by the Elders. "The Elders believed they knew everything. I wonder..." He carefully lowered himself into Erskina's chair. Finding it suitably stable, he leaned back, folding his hands. "So. This is what it was like."

"When they brought me here, the chairs floated."

"A parlour trick to impress lesser minds."

Unable to plausibly stay away from the chairs any longer, I sauntered towards them. The seats were cracked from earlier abuse, and upon closer inspection, each stone seat glittered. Not because of some inherent magical property, but it appeared the material was not stone, as I'd first assumed. I splayed my hand upon the worm chair seat and applied some pressure; there was some give there. Erskina's chair seemed to hold my father's weight just fine, however. Even the barest touch produced grit that I wiped away on my dress.

Conal looked contemplative in his newly acquired throne. After a few false starts, he said, "Once, I remember Rordan went—"

"No," I interrupted, taking a second look at the gritty slab. "You don't get to do that anymore."

"Tell you a story about your brother?"

"That's right."

"Then you tell me one of him. I'm sure you have many, as you are so quick to point out, from all the years I missed. Come. The stories make the time pass easier."

I set the Spear on the floor. Taking a chance, I slammed a fist down on the seat, startling us both. Chunks and grit flew in my face and I staggered back, coughing. "I'm all right," I said, clearing the air. The seat was not real stone after all, but some thin collection of waxy, ground rocks. Peering beneath the seat, my suspicion was confirmed. The interior of the worm chair was hollow.

Conal stood and turned in one swift movement, taking in the arachnid chair with interest. He brought his fist down hard—and the sickening crack of bone resounded through the cavern.

"Aghhrrghh—" He recoiled from the chairs, clutching his right hand to his chest, trying to hold in the pain.

I hesitated, rising to my full height, but not willing to close the distance between us. "Are you...?"

Turning from me self-consciously, he steadied his breathing. "Just a moment."

A brilliant flash of blue haloed him as he suppressed a grunt. The sceptre and the Tablet piece at his waist synced and pulsed eerily fast; my father's heartbeat. I laid a hand on my stomach. He had retrieved me from the end of the world and brought me back from the brink of death with his healing magic.

He flicked his right wrist and twiddled his fingers. Good as new. Rubbing them absently, he returned his focus to the seven chairs. "Very interesting," he said.

Together, we peered inside the worm-backed chair. Nothing glowed so obviously, but several large chunks of rock had piled within the cavity.

I glanced at my father, and slowly, I dropped my hand inside and grasped a large, oblong lump. Conal inspected it with interest at first, as I drew it out, and then settled again on Erskina's chair. "Are they all like that?"

"Seems that way," I said, unconvinced.

He rested uneasily in the chair, possibly fearing what I'd do if I happened to pull out the other Tablet half. After throwing several non-candidates over my shoulder, he was already bored of the exercise, even antsy, and began inspecting the other seats, and in particular, the fox-backed chair. He considered punching it, flexed his healed fingers, and thought better of it.

"I'm waiting," he said.

"You want me to—?" I asked.

He sighed. "No, finish clearing that one."

All of the rocks had a similar consistency—not real stone, but a kind of waxy, gritty rock. If I squeezed hard enough, I could crush them in my hands. "What is it?" I asked him.

"Not sure, every seat seems to be the same. Even this one." He gripped the remainder of Erskina's spider and gave it a wiggle, and then pressed his fingers into the adjacent seats, testing their give. "What I meant was, I was waiting for you to tell me about Rordan."

I clenched my teeth, hard. "All right," I said coolly, throwing another hard lump over my shoulder. "Once there was a young man with Extremist ideals, who, when approached by his father, became radicalized. Then, he was sentenced to die, and his father and sister stood and watched it happen, like entertainment. The end."

"I meant a new story. And I was trying to help him, as you might recall, but he wouldn't listen. You're still angry with—"

I grasped another chunk of not-stone and it crumpled in my hands. I didn't even care that I was now covered in grit and dust. "A different story then. Once there was a man who kidnapped his daughter's friends and threatened to kill them if she didn't give him a piece of a powerful artefact."

"Those kinds of games are beneath you now, and had I known

you had progressed so far..." He trailed off apologetically. "They were never in any real danger in the throne room, not with the power you wield. Except of course, when you opened up the floor. That could have swallowed them whole, as it did many others."

I pulled out the last rock. Flat—but just a rock. I tossed it and sighed. I moved on to the next chair: the crouching badger. "I did what needed to be done. To protect them."

He leaned forward, his gaze intensely curious. "Tell me how you feel, Kiera."

I made a face as the seat of the badger gave way beneath my fist. I didn't flinch as dust and grit billowed up. "I'm tired. Hungry." I waved my wrist. "Kind of in pain, I guess."

I was being deliberately obtuse and he knew it. I excavated the badger chair, with similar disappointing results.

"No one told me I could achieve greatness through magic. I seized it, but it took me...a long time. It doesn't have to be that way with you. You are managing the madness well."

Managing the madness. The highs and lows of magic. "I don't want greatness. Or the madness. I want to find the rest of the Tablet, so I can be done with this. I was doing fine without you. And I will continue to be fine when you are gone."

"I'm afraid it will be a very long time before we are done, with any of *this*."

Next chair: the rabbit. *Phomp*. Grit up the nose. I coughed and wiped my face on my sleeveless arm, which helped nothing. I glared at him. "If that's the case, then here's the truth. You shouldn't have told me any of it—about the magic inside me, the artefacts, or even the idea that you're my *father*." I said the word with absolute disdain. "I was fine without the knowledge."

"Perhaps," he said coldly. "But one day, you would have woken up with the strange sensation that your life was incomplete. Like someone had hidden the truth about the world from you as a cruel joke. You would have continued your life in the castle with Keegan, and the war would have dragged on. Keegan would have grown wiser, more distant, and less understanding of your drive to venture beyond the four walls binding you to a city that doesn't care whether you live or die. Perhaps he would have eventually chosen Sylvia over you, for political convenience and expediency. You would have run off, seeking adventure elsewhere, finding solace with other lost ones searching for the missing piece of themselves. Then that strange moment would come, when the magic would force itself upon you. By then, you would no longer have the strength of youth. Only the bitter memories of attempting to fit into a useless mould.

"You would have been fine, Kiera—but you would have wondered, and regretted."

I steadied my hands and dug deeper into the hollow chair. More nothing. Slowly, I stood. "I'm not you."

He smiled a little. We both knew that was no longer true.

To Conal's left was the oversized ant chair. Half of its legs had broken off and the chair itself had taken a beating. I shoved my whole arm in this time, unexpectedly, as this seat was weaker than the others.

This chair had been empty when I'd met with the Elders, so long ago. It had seated Elder Raibeart, who had been murdered by surface-dwellers in an unguarded tunnel—or so Erskina had us believe.

Elder Raibeart would say…it contains the source of our magic, Gobany had said.

What had the Elder known, before his life had been taken? What had he told Elder Erskina? Had Elder Erskina used the Midnight as inspiration for the fictional Alastar's Tome? We would never know now.

As I waved away the dust, a glint of blue shone out at me from beneath the crumpling rocks.

Conal saw my hesitation as I knelt. He immediately leapt

from his chair to hover over me. The dangling Tablet at his waist bloomed in response to its half-hidden mate. I couldn't stall. I reached in and clasped it.

"Step back," I said to him.

He obliged, giving me room as I retrieved the artefact half. I blew off the extra grit that had settled between the gently pulsing runes. It was remarkably similar to its twin: the strange writing running on both sides of its face, the broken edge on one side, the size, and the weight.

"You hold the final piece of the future in your hands." He untethered his matching piece and held it up, admiringly. "You have come so far, in such a short time, without any guidance."

Someone, long ago, had went to great trouble to tear these two apart. I hugged mine to my chest, suddenly afraid. The runes pulsed with me, and I heard a faint suggestion at the back of my mind, though when I tried to focus on it, it faded like a dream.

Serious now, he was the first to hold out his half of the Tablet. "You take one side and I'll take the other."

Reluctantly, I nodded. It was only fair. When we'd pieced together the Emerald Cloth, the scraps had knitted together, as if recognizing its fellow siblings. Likely, this would work similarly.

But before I could offer my side to the whole, Conal and I reacted defensively as echoing footsteps approached the Central Cavern. I froze, pressing the Tablet half against my chest in feverish attempt to hide it from the world.

Voices joined the footfalls as Laoise and Keegan slipped through the broken wooden doorway. Relief washed over Keegan's face. He looked exhausted as he trudged towards me, unconcerned that I was about to make history with the most powerful artefact in the world.

Laoise kept her distance as she retrieved the Spear from the floor and eyed my Tablet piece. "You found it."

I nodded. "We were just about to put it together."

She drew a short breath, understanding.

Keegan gently touched my arm in greeting, allowing his fingers to loiter on my bare skin. "I spoke to them. They…listened. We had thirty-seven volunteers. And some more trickled out, after they left."

"I hope they succeed," I said, bobbing my head, though in the back of my mind, I wondered if we had condemned innocents to die at Dominique's hands. If they did nothing, they would die anyway. Perhaps Keegan had made them see that.

"I hope they all succeed. There've been three more explosions, all on the surface. One caved in some of the Undercity entrances on the northeast side. We might become trapped down here," Laoise replied. She gave us a wide berth as she roamed the room with the Spear. She didn't take her eyes off the Tablet halves, waiting to be reunited. "Do you know what they say?"

I attempted to read the glowing inscription on my half. Freetor runes had been created by our ancestors as a secret code to prevent the surface from interpreting our communications. Over time, many Freetors didn't bother to learn how to read, as much of our culture was oral—and none of us wanted our secrets falling into the hands of the surface-dwellers. If something had to be written down, it could be intercepted, whether it was in Freetor code or not.

"I don't know," I admitted, though I felt like I *did* know. Some runes were close to our present-day words, but the closer I peered, the more the meaning seemed to shift. I blinked and looked away, my eyes and mind aching from the effort.

"Maybe it can help us after all," Laoise said, trying to be cheerful.

"I hope so," I said—knowing what I had to do, if this reunification was successful.

Conal looked at me expectantly, ready to proceed. Keegan remained at my side. I glanced at him, but he didn't move away. He clutched my arm tighter. He wasn't going anywhere.

Emboldened, I nodded at my father. I extended my half, and he pushed his forward, and carefully the jagged edges slid into place.

A deafening crack shook the cavern. Keegan held me tighter, searching the ceiling for evidence of a quake or explosion. The two pieces of the Tablet fused together to become a near-seamless whole, and spewed a bright, blue light. I squinted against it, but neither of us released our grip on the artefact.

When the glow stabilized, my father cursed under his breath. The Tablet shone more fiercely now, as did the other artefacts in our possession. Yet while the Tablet halves *did* fit together, they revealed that they had not been halves at all. At the centre of the Midnight Tablet was a missing sliver in the shape of a triangle, imperfect and rough as the other edges.

Keegan's hopeful grip released me as he stepped backward. "That's not...how it's supposed to look, is it?"

"I don't think so," I said.

My father pressed his fingers into the narrow space, and moved them around the surface, as if to smoosh the two halves with will alone. "Must have chipped," he muttered. He peered around me, into Elder Raibeart's destroyed chair. "Is there another piece down there?"

I too ran my fingers over the runes. They glowed dimly at our touch. Keegan attempted to look where my father instructed, not knowing he didn't have the ability to help.

My father and I maneuvered to peer into the remains. Neither were willing to give the other full control of the Tablet, so as Conal obsessively poked around the lumps and rocks in the chair, with Keegan unhelpfully making comments, I glanced over at Laoise, who had fallen silent.

She had seen it first, as she had the most perspective of all of us in the room. She couldn't take her eyes from the Tablet. Her training served her well, for if she had looked to me, my father would have sensed something was amiss.

The Silver Spear had been encased in magical ice at the end of the world when Keegan, Monju, and I had found it. It was enormous, perhaps too tall for me or anyone to wield with efficiency. Everything about the Spear glowed, as it was in the presence of its sibling artefacts.

The orb. The slab. The cloth. The walking stick.

The *walking stick.*

Reluctantly, I released my death grip on the artefact. That, my father did notice. He stopped poking around in the chair and scrutinized me mercilessly. "What?"

"Could the other piece be in the tunnels somewhere?" Keegan asked. "Or on the floor...?" He lifted his feet, fearing he had accidently destroyed the indestructible.

I left them to wonder by the chairs and sauntered towards Laoise. She looked terrified. "You can't, can you? I mean, could it be...?"

Together, we peeled away the wrappings from the Spear. The wooden shaft was covered in Freetor runes, glowing in alternating, pulsing patterns. I ran my finger along the silver spearhead carefully. I had assumed it was steel, or something close to it, yet as I scratched my fingernail against the smooth surface vigorously, I caught a glimpse of a darker material underneath.

Alastar was said to have found the Silver Spear and cursed it, to ward the surface-born from touching the beloved Freetor symbol. Yet if he also had access to the Tablet, and had wanted to prevent its secrets from falling into the hands of tyrants—why not hide the key to the most powerful artefact in one the Marlenians would never be able to touch?

When I had seen my father's piece of the Tablet, as large as it was, I had assumed it was half of a whole. Yet I recalled Kamal in his chamber, talking about the Tablet piece in his vault. He'd never said it was a half. He had gambled in coming to the palace, because he wanted to add the Silver Spear to his collection.

You are blind, Violet Fox. The most valuable of collectible pieces, in your grasp.

He'd suspected it, and yes, I had been blind to what I'd carried with me, this whole time.

I pursed my lips, suppressing a laugh. Conal regarded Laoise and I suspiciously. "Care to explain yourself?"

Laoise handed me the Spear. "If you're sure you want to do this."

I wasn't. But my fingers worked anyway, against instinct. The spearhead had been wedged into the shaft, and upon closer inspection, tied with a thin, unyielding rope. Laoise offered her knife, and as I held the artefact, she picked at black bindings nimbly with her blade tip.

Conal approached now with interest. "Are you desecrating Alastar's weapon?"

"Yes," I replied. It didn't take much. The tiny, taunt bonds snapped free. Gingerly, I plucked the head from the wooden shaft of the Spear. Likely Alastar suspected his descendants wouldn't pry apart their trusted weapon, if they retrieved it from its resting place at all. The edge was deadly sharp, though the missing sliver in the Tablet looked wider.

"It doesn't look like a fit," he said, knitting his eyebrows curiously.

There was only one way to find out. I guarded the spearhead in my fist. "Hold up the Tablet."

"I'm not sure about this," Conal said disparagingly. "You shouldn't tamper with—"

I shoved the spearhead into the Tablet.

The force of the impact took us all by surprise. A blinding light filled the Central Cavern, blasting my eyelids. Conal released the artefact and I only heard the Spear—now the Staff—clatter to the gritty floor. I staggered back and crouched, tucking my head between my knees to soothe my eyes in relative darkness.

It was several minutes before my vision recovered. Conal and Laoise had also been adversely affected—we were Freetors by birth, and as such, our eyesight had been moulded for dim caves and the veil of night. Keegan squinted ahead, less bothered. As shadowy light blocks danced in my vision, I rose unsteadily to my feet.

The Midnight Tablet shone fiercely as it floated in mid-air. The silver spearhead retained its colour and had melded in place; hidden symbols filtered through the metal overlay. The runes illuminated in a wave from left to right, as if silently reading aloud its secrets. I heard them at the edge of my mind: the whispers, calling to me.

Make Keegan whole again, as you did me.

Everything else seemed less important in that moment. Conal breathed audibly deep, and in his long face, I saw he heard the call, too. Our gazes met.

And then I ran for it.

My father was quick, but I was faster. I snatched the large artefact from mid-air. In the split second it was in my hands, the whispers crawled up the base of my spine. If I just said the word, I would have access to a secret knowledge. For a price.

Every fleeting, impossible wish bubbled to the surface. *Father, never leaving. Rordan, here with me, never seduced by the Extremists. Keegan, never picking up the Spear and losing everything. Me, never hurting him.*

The Tablet could change it all. It told me so.

Just on the edge of perception, I saw how things could have been. I heard Rordan's voice from somewhere beyond. I could bring him back from the ashes. Away from the sunlight of the afterlife. I had done nothing to spare him his fate—but now, I could.

Keegan was there, kneeling before me, for I had sunk to the floor in rapture. He was not a dream. He was real. His grip on me and the artefact was firm and grounding. He said nothing. He was only there to remind me that I had a choice: pay the price the Tablet demanded, or don't, and change nothing.

"Kiera...now Kiera..." My father was there too, his voice cutting between the whispers and the real. He stepped closer, guardedly. "You have a valuable opportunity here..."

His voice disappeared into the back of my mind as I held Keegan's yellow-green gaze. The impossible wishes of the past blew away like smoke. Everything I had wanted was before me, and now, like the Tablet, he could be made whole once more.

Yet how could I force a lifetime of memories upon the man I loved?

Hurried footfalls echoed through the caves. I felt for the Spear, remembering too late it was a Spear no more and not within my grasp, when Bidelia entered the Central Cavern. Bidelia's long coat was singed black and her face, filthy. Monju trailed in after her, his weapon dripping with blood.

The two of them stopped short as they eyed the Tablet resting in mine and Keegan's grasp. Glancing about the cavern, she grasped the gist of the events—and then Bidelia recoiled.

"Kiera—Conal!"

And then, Conal was upon us. Without thinking, I shoved the Tablet into Keegan's chest and tackled my father, pinning him to the ground.

I'd thought Keegan would know what to do. It was obvious: run. Take Monju and Bidelia and run for the surface with the Tablet, and either use it to defeat the remaining shadows, disable the explosives— or retrieve the memories he so desperately didn't want.

He did none of those things. As I pinned Conal's arms to the floor and he brewed some magic torrent to throw me off, Keegan rose to his full height, caressing the Tablet with intense curiosity. Bidelia and Monju encircled him, equally concerned.

"There are...voices," he said, mesmerized by the pulsing runes.

Panic fueled me. "Keegan, don't." I wouldn't allow him to become corrupted, as I had. He had little to trade, except his life, and that I couldn't abide.

"But I could have…whatever I want," Keegan said distantly. He blinked, shaking his head, trying to find himself. He tried to use the fabric of his shirt to hold the Tablet, as it ran hot in the presence of its fellow artefacts.

Conal and I were of one mind—but of different body. As I released my father to approach my love in an attempt to reason the Tablet away from his virtuous mind, Conal tripped me and barrelled towards Keegan, his fingers lighting with nefarious intent.

Bidelia ran from Conal's line of fire and joined her daughter, while Monju gave my father a wide berth, his dripping weapon ready to strike at my command.

Keegan recoiled—but not soon enough.

The warning flew from my lips. "No, Keegan!"

He hugged the Tablet to his chest and the blue glow intensified. Conal thrust his hand at the young ruler and curled his menacing long fingers. Seemingly of its own volition, the Tablet shook in Keegan's grasp. With his other hand, Conal shot lightning over Keegan's shoulder.

I assumed he meant to miss. He thought of Keegan like a son. He'd saved his life in the streets—that had set him on the path to where he was now. But Keegan, frightened by the magic and Conal's looming attack, leaned into the lightning instead of away. It struck him in the right shoulder, and then the left. It crawled all over his limbs, burying into his skin like a shining snake. He tumbled to the floor, hitting his head with a worrying *crack*.

Conal gasped, horrified. The Tablet stopped struggling in Keegan's fallen grasp.

"What have you done?" I screamed at Conal.

He stepped back, speechless.

I ran to Keegan's side. My hands darted all over. His skin was ripped. Raw. I smelled his burnt flesh. He was still conscious, though his eyes glazed over. He coughed, and then groaned, and his breath wheezed as his chest rose and fell.

Conal kept his distance on the other side of the cavern, pacing and muttering to himself. I gritted my teeth. The edges of my vision darkened. I felt the magic boiling inside of me, ready to fry him. He deserved it. Laoise had warned me. I hadn't listened.

I could end him now.

"What have you done?" Bidelia demanded. She advanced on Conal, weaponless, and struck him across the face. Stunned, he took the blow in stride, and didn't resist as she grabbed him by the lapels. "You never listened to me, only to your endless greed. Now our children suffer. *I* suffer."

Unable to meet her gaze, he gently took her wrists, and plucked himself from her desperate grip. "I never meant for you to be involved."

"You don't get to decide that," she retorted.

There was nothing he could say to redeem himself, and so he stopped trying.

"Kiera..."

Keegan's voice, weak and sad, brought me back to the present. My tears fell onto his chest. He struggled to hold my gaze.

I couldn't let him die like this. Not at my father's hand. Not by magic.

"I'm going to heal you," I said.

I placed my hands on the burns and reached deep inside myself. I thought of every time I'd sewn Rordan's wounds and how he'd tended mine. I remembered my father rescuing me from the end of the world, how he'd mended my stomach with magic alone. I conjured the smell of medicine, and every other image and sensation I could think of to feed the magic within.

But it wasn't enough.

I wasn't a healer. I had known magic for days, not months or years as Conal had. Sheepishly, I looked to my father. He was paralyzed by fear—except for the shake of his head.

"He's too far gone," he said.

"No. No, he's not!" How desperately I wanted to force him to do my bidding. But Keegan's hand lay heavy on mine, keeping me by his side as he slipped away. I turned my back on my father, my friends, and I cupped my love's face. His eyelids lifted heavily, trying to see me.

"S'all right," he said sluggishly. His hand shook as he placed it on the Tablet. In his eyes, I saw what he wanted. Now that he had arrived at the end, he was ready to know his beginning.

I nodded. The runes brightened as I traced them with my fingertip. No one had used the Tablet in hundreds, perhaps thousands of years—yet as the whispering entered my mind, I was ready to pay the high price for his request. "Return Keegan Tramore's stolen memories."

I inhaled sharply as I felt the very magical essence pulled from within me. I gulped air but it wasn't enough. Blue, silky smoke flew from my fingertips into the Tablet, and the runes blinded me, though I dared not look away or remove my hand.

As I struggled to breathe, Keegan sucked in air readily. His eyeballs darted from side to side, his expression deepening as he took his life back into himself with incredible speed.

His scarred lips parted as he gazed upon me with fresh, renewed eyes.

"Kiera…I…" His words failed him, though we both knew. He needn't say anything more. Keegan had returned to me, whole, and I knew he was not the old or the new Keegan. Just as I was not the old Kiera anymore.

"What happened?" Conal asked. "Kiera, tell me what it did to you."

I wouldn't dignify him with a look. I felt my hands, my face, my body. I *seemed* all right.

Laoise had joined Monju near the broken doors. At my inquisitive glance, she touched her hair and pursed her lips.

I lifted my once-black locks, discovering they had paled to silver. And then a wave of exhaustion hit me, as if I had just run through the entire city without stopping. I felt so…cold. Naked.

Weak.

I slumped onto Keegan. He groaned. Laoise and Monju's

footsteps on the tiled floor were urgent. Laoise and her strong arms helped me sit up. I leaned against her, unable to support my own weight. Monju knelt by my side, keeping one hand on the hilt of his weapon and an eye on my father. Conal wrung his hands, keeping his distance, though no less worried than Bidelia and my friends.

Pebbles trickled down the walls. The far-off shouts of battle were just on the edge of my perception. Vaguely, I was aware of the fighting above us, between the shadows and the Roamers. The thought of joining them, as I'd promised, made me exhausted. I wasn't sure if I'd ever regain my strength, not now.

"Killed some shadows," Monju said absently, also looking sky-ward. "Some still run through the city."

"We will get them soon," I said wearily.

How was I supposed to be of use, if I didn't have the will to do what I did best? The Tablet had exacted a price. My magic—for Keegan's memories. And magic, as Gobany had said, was life. Perhaps the very thing that defined me as a Freetor.

I had nothing else to offer the artefact, except for the rest of my life.

With his memories intact, Keegan would make a far greater ruler than I could ever be. He would make a formal peace with Leon, and Kamal in the South, and bring new prosperity to the province. Dominique would return to the mountains and leave him alone, because he wasn't me. He would mourn me, but he would find another, and Laoise, Monju, and Bidelia would be there to guide him.

I leaned over Keegan, with Laoise's help. "I can save you."

He groaned. "Sacrifice…too big."

"Kiera, you'll die if you use it again," Laoise said worriedly.

Cautiously, Conal stepped closer. "I will do it."

I shot him a glare. "No. You've done enough. You won't fool me again."

To my surprise, he capitulated, though he didn't back away.

"Maybe you should let him," Laoise whispered. "His life for Keegan's."

I shook my head with great effort. How could I say it? "I can't lose either of them."

"All of us, together then," Conal said, glancing at Bidelia as well. "You said there must be a trade?"

I nodded—and then shook my head again. But they weren't paying attention to me. Keegan wheezed violently; Conal and Bidelia approached Keegan's struggling form. Bidelia settled against her daughter, and Conal guiltily crouched by Keegan's feet. He withered under my angry, weakened stare.

He would get what was coming, I thought, for everything he had done. He soon would have no recourse, just as I no longer had the power to stop him. My fingertips graced the runes of the Tablet—and then Laoise's joined mine. Monju's as well. Then Bidelia—and finally, reluctantly, my father. His fingertips touched mine, and I endured it. For now.

Keegan took us all in, overwhelmed, and placed his hand atop of mine. "You honour me."

The five of us split the surrender to the Tablet. I closed my eyes and leaned in towards Keegan, finding his lips and kissing him. I couldn't let him die. I made this selfish wish—*Keegan Tramore, do not die*—and as I felt a portion of my own life drain away, I regretted nothing. I would die sooner, but that was to be expected for the Violet Fox.

Conal inhaled desperately, far more distressed than us three, so much so he nearly pulled away. The price the Tablet extracted from him was far more dear. Yet he did not let go. For Keegan's sake.

Keegan's skin mended. All of his scrapes and bruises from the events of the past day cleared. He even smelled different. Somehow new. As the blue light from the Tablet faded once more, and we were released from our duty, Keegan sat up with tears in his eyes, clutching the Tablet to his heart.

I embraced him, feeling dreadful, and Laoise and Monju fell over me as we piled on Keegan, holding on to that one moment. We were exhausted—but free to be with each other. Bidelia rested her face on her daughter and kissed her on the back of the head.

I was no longer alone.

"I...I don't know how to repay you," Keegan said, muffled from our hug.

Only my father did not celebrate our sacrifice. Conal leapt back, clenching his hands into fists. He retreated to the seven chairs, staring longingly at his fingertips. I expected at least one moment of empathy for Keegan—but no. His gaze settled on me, furious. He had underestimated the cost, and I had swindled the very thing he had worked his entire life to cultivate and loathe to part with. Now Conal Driscoll knew the exquisite payment the Tablet had reaped: his magic.

Bidelia eyed Conal with suspicion, gathered her skirts and coat, and stood. She'd gone far greyer, and the lines on her face had deepened, but her eyes were as sharp as ever. "We are in desperate need. We underestimated Dominique's shadows. They are making quick work of the merchant district. The people are crying out for their rulers. More explosives are being set off every moment. The Roamers are trying, and the volunteers are valiant, but we are still outnumbered. We can't hold them much longer."

She wasn't just talking to me. She also looked to my father. But he was no longer interested in helping. He couldn't take his unforgiving gaze from me.

"There's always a trade," I told him bitterly.

"Evidently," he replied, with equal measure. He clenched his hands into fists and dimly, they emitted some light—but no more than the walls of the Central Cavern. He had been reduced to a useless Freetor curio. He shoved his hands in his trousers. "Do you really want your people to continue suffering, Kiera, when you could have done something to stop them?"

"You also had a chance to stop them," Keegan said, rising with the Tablet clutched securely. "Yet as I recall, you were eager to come here, to retrieve the Tablet."

"From which you benefited greatly. You're welcome, Your Grace," he said, inclining his head sarcastically. He held out his hand. "Now. The Tablet, if you please, so we can get on with this."

I saw his plan a thousand stone-throws away. What was traded away could be re-obtained. I had given it the magic within, and made the Tablet more powerful. Part of us lived on within it, accessible to anyone willing to give up a little bit of themselves—or their most prized possessions. He could easily trade half of his remaining life for power of equal measure, and destroy us all. The more he obtained, the more he could trade, and the more power he would amass.

I slid my arm under Keegan's and felt the runes of the Tablet—and the head of the Spear. I traced the edges. It was firmly in place, but perhaps...

Feed the Tablet, make it stronger.

There was no mortal way to destroy an artefact, my father had warned me.

"Obviously, we're not just going to just give you the Tablet," I said. "If you wanted it badly enough, sure. You could take it from Keegan right now. But first, we have a few things we need to shore up."

This didn't sit well with Conal. "And what would you ask the most powerful artefact in the world to solve for you now?"

Keegan pulled down his sleeves to hold the Tablet more carefully, examining the spearhead within. "We can use it against the Northern shadows. Or we can take this to the dungeons with the Emerald Cloth. Start healing the—"

I shook my head. "No."

"No?" Laoise echoed. Her face was the picture of concern.

My hands trembled as I realized what had to be done. "Not yet.

The first plan is…establishing our sovereignty. Rebuilding the city, to make the people feel safe."

"That's…right," Conal said slowly. "When you heal and release your imprisoned Southern king, they will see firsthand you are not to be trifled with. If you decide to release him at all. You must shape their perception of you."

"High King Kamal attacked me, you know," I told my father, as I coolly walked across the room to retrieve the Staff. It seemed so trivial now. A plain walking stick—and yet, as I held it, I felt renewed. How could I not have realized its effect on me before? It would not give me back the magic inherent within my blood and bones, but if needs be, I could channel its power. I hoped. Without the spearhead, I suspected the curse was broken—though I couldn't be sure, as Freetor runes still donned the wooden shaft. I dug my fingernails into my palms. I had to stay focussed.

Laoise's eyes widened. "He did?"

"Should have been there," Monju said regretfully.

I supposed Bidelia hadn't the time to fill in my friends. Perhaps it was better this way. Though I shot Laoise and Monju a quick glance. I needed their trust, and their help.

My father tried his best to hide his concern, though I saw the intrigue in his eyes. "I assumed he had done you some wrong," Conal said offhandedly.

The corners of my lips turned upwards. He couldn't resist a good story, even if it was painful for me to recount. Tucking the Staff under my right armpit, I sauntered back to Keegan. "Yes. His attack on me is an act of war, making the agreement he and Keegan signed void. Which is…a shame. Our people needed that food and military aid."

Keegan's eyes met mine. He knew very well the High King of the South had signed nothing.

I held out my hand to him and slowly, reluctantly, he passed me the heavy Tablet. The power of holding it shot through me, and the whispers began again—

No. Focus.

Conal evaluated me silently. Jealously. "Perhaps we shouldn't..."

I took a deep breath. I only had so many hands. The only reason he didn't snatch the Tablet from me right now was his fear of me using it against him. Again. "Look. I know you have a plan for the Tablet, and probably these other artefacts, too. But you also said you wanted to see me happy. You can remake the world all you want—but if I don't fix the mistakes I've caused, I...I don't know if I will be able to live with myself." Pressing the Tablet against my chest, I angled my palm towards Laoise. "The Cloth?"

Laoise met my gaze. We had known each other a long time and I had done plenty to shake her trust. I held two of the four most powerful artefacts in the known world. I could use them to wreck havoc or destroy us all.

She reached into her trouser pocket and pulled out the patch-work green fabric gingerly, holding the glowing fabric by stray threads. It drew Conal's eye, and he watched it greedily as she brought it to me, draping it reverently over my fingers.

Conal took a step closer. Cautious, but sincere. "If you restore my power, I can help you right your wrongs."

It took everything within me not to step back. I pressed the Cloth gently against the Tablet. I glanced at the grit on the floor, as if considering Conal's offer, and thought, *Take the power of the Emerald Cloth as an offering, and revive and restore those who have been afflicted with Alastar's sleeping curse.*

The runes glowed and for a long moment, my hand was glued in place. I was expecting some grand shift in the cave walls, or shouts from above, but none of those things happened. Just the usual trickling of water somewhere far off. I betrayed nothing on my face as I glanced up at my father. "And how do I know you won't run off, once you have your magic back?"

His eyebrows lifted. "If you asked me to stay, I would."

I nodded, glancing at Keegan, and then Bidelia.

"Don't give him anything," Bidelia warned me.

"But what if he's right?" I said quietly, over my shoulder. Sweat poured down my forehead and my chest from holding this many artefacts in close proximity. "I was useless with my magic. But my father could use it to…heal. We have a lot of people that are probably dying on the surface right now. Thirty-seven volunteers who said yes to Keegan, to find and dismantle explosives. Who knows if they're even still alive, or how much success they've had?"

He nodded. "Your concern for your people is admirable, if misplaced."

"Then prove me your goodwill," I said. "Give me the Orb."

Conal ran his hands over the sceptre and, considering me carefully, he tucked it under his arm. "Why don't you allow me to hold some of that for you? You must be roasting." He held out his hand.

I moved my left finger. I was no longer stuck. I bunched the Cloth in my palm—its glow had dimmed considerably. The Tablet pulsed blue with my heartbeat, made stronger by the Cloth's power and the Staff's proximity.

I pretended to give it some thought. "Do you think," I asked him, "that everyone could live under the sun peacefully, with magic?"

"We can ensure it," he promised. "With the four artefacts, and my restored power, we can remake the world. To suit us both."

It was tempting. I nodded. "Then take the Tablet."

Laoise clutched Monju tightly. Keegan took a cautious step forward. "Kiera, don't—"

"We have to remake the world," I said softly and held out the Midnight Tablet—and grinned. "Catch."

I tossed the Tablet and the Cloth into the air.

Conal scrambled to catch it—until he saw me coming at him with the Staff.

He thrust forward with the sceptre. A loud snapping sound filled the air as lightning surrounded his arms. The Staff collided with the Orb of Dashiell.

Artefacts couldn't be destroyed by mortal means, so I had to get creative. The Orb smashed into thousands of pieces, as it had before. Flying shards went everywhere. I closed my eyes and turned my head as the end of the Staff splintered and split, peeling away at one end. The Tablet landed with a smash on the floor, though it remained intact. The spearhead wiggled in place.

Keegan rushed for me, while my friends went for the Tablet. Laoise snatched it away from Conal's reach, and huddled between Bidelia and Monju for protection. Monju pointed his sword at Conal. Keegan withdrew a knife as well, ready to jump into the fray. Both young men looked to me. They were waiting for permission to rush my father, and end his life.

But I couldn't do that. I leapt backward with the Staff as Conal staggered among the shards. They still reflected and glowed on the cavern floor, but desperate, he knelt, his fingers bloodied he pressed them among the shards.

I brandished the Staff and pressed forward. "Step away."

My command startled him, and for a moment, I saw the old man within. Regretful. Wondering. "What do you think you're doing?" he demanded. His eyes flamed. He had spent countless hours piecing the Orb back together after it had smashed before.

"Back," I said again.

He took one small step away, and then another, barely enough to clear the Orb shards.

I gestured to Laoise. "Put it on top of the shards."

She hesitated, but as I pushed forward, keeping the Staff level with my father's throat, hoping he wasn't stupid enough to try something. Laoise came forward, and did as I asked.

"Stay back," I muttered to her.

Fearing my plan, she said nothing, and retreated to Monju and her mother. Keegan moved forward cautiously, but I shook my head at him, too. This was between me and Conal.

He narrowed his gaze. "Your actions here are futile."

"I don't think so." Feigning a kind of dance, I stepped on the Tablet, hearing the crunch of the Orb shards beneath me, and thought, *Take the remaining power of the Orb, and strike down those aligned with Lady Dominique and dismantle the explosives threatening our city.* I jumped away as the remaining power drained from the Orb shards. "I'm going to destroy it, so you are never tempted again."

I rose the non-splintered end of the Staff just as Conal dove for the heavy Tablet, scooped it up in his arms and scuttled backward, wincing. I lunged for him and missed. Monju and Keegan pressed their attack, but faltered as Conal's grip on the Tablet tightened.

"Wait," I said to them. My heart pounded. I tried to remain calm. I had been so close.

"Release it," Keegan said, worried.

Conal hugged the Tablet to his chest. "You can no longer enforce your will. Sacrifice has its own price."

"Yes, it does," I said sadly. "That's why I can't let you run free."

He scoffed. "You cannot keep me here." A smile slid across his face, so maniacal and cold, as he slowly closed the distance between us. "You and I never have to sacrifice again. That is why magic exists. To redefine the rules."

I trembled—but only for a moment. "Perhaps," I said, gripping the Staff tightly, "you woke up one day realizing your life was incomplete. Like someone had taken something away from you or denied you what was rightfully yours. And you spent years fighting to retrieve it, under a different name. You sacrificed everything. The love of your life. Your friends. Your family." I looked to each of my friends in turn, and finally squared him with a glare. "I'll always wonder and I'll always have regrets. But I'm strong enough to accept the price of protecting what I've fought for. Which means, in that way, I'm not like you at all.

"I promised I'd save you from magic, Conal. You're going to be just fine. Because I will make the trade."

He bristled at my use of his first name—and his face despaired as he feared the worst.

Keegan rose his knife. "No, Kiera..."

With one swift motion, I pressed the good end of the Staff against the Tablet, still in his arms—and held it in place. "Take the remaining power in this artefact, and create a prison powerful enough to hold Conal Driscoll."

He lunged for me, splaying his hands. Blue light auraed his fingers and swirled around his palms. A magnificent light show in the middle of the underground. He reached for my throat and I leapt back as ice sprung from the gritty floor and ensnared his feet. Much like the block of ice that had held the Silver Spear, the magical frost grew in a rectangular block from the floor up, swirling around Conal's legs.

The Staff, drained of its power, had a final use. I gave the Staff a final shove, and punched out the spearhead piece from the middle of the Tablet. It clinked to the floor, bounced, and tumbled beside Conal. He nearly fell over as he reached for the spearhead, but ice shot upward in all directions, forming an icy layer of glass between him, us, and the one piece of the Tablet that would make the arte-fact functional. He pressed his hands against the ice walls, and then pounded them, but the magical ice would not break, for this prison had been specially made for him alone.

I felt ill.

A humourless laugh escaped his throat as he regarded me from head to toe, pressing the now-useless Tablet to his chest. "If you think by destroying the artefacts you are ending magic, you are mistaken. I could entertain you with the stories of a thousand magical items, each one with a curious history, hidden around the world. Waiting to be found."

"Don't bother."

He smiled slyly, though his confidence wavered as the ice rose around him. "You won't be able to hold me. Not forever."

"I'll hold you for as long as I live. That is forever enough." I threw the now useless Staff to the floor. "As long as there's magic, there will be someone who covets it. That's how the inequality continues. But if I destroy all knowledge of magic, and another like you is born without acceptance or the ability to control their power, then we're only going to find ourselves here again."

"So what are you going to do?" Conal asked.

I pursed my lips and thought about it. "I'll have to live with myself and what I've done. Just as you will."

He couldn't move. The ice rapidly formed a rectangular, solid cage around him, growing in a beautiful floral design. Large frosty leaves and flowers bloomed around his feet, his chest, and his neck. He struggled, though he was in no pain. I could grant him that mercy, at least.

"Will you ever forgive me?" he asked.

I swallowed, hard. But I forced myself to meet his gaze. This was not the first time he had asked. It didn't matter that I was crying, that my hand was shaking uncontrollably. I would not back down.

"Whether I do or not," I said, "you will never know. For you will never leave these caves again."

"Then I will be here. When you need me." He pressed his hand against the icy glass as it swallowed the rest of him whole.

I CRUMPLED—BUT Keegan was there to catch me. I sobbed into him. "You did it. You did it," he whispered, and he held me.

"We did it," I said.

The Tablet had taken my magic, my strength, and my father. I wasn't sure if my legs would hold, but Keegan lifted me up, and steadied me. Conal Driscoll would be forever preserved in ice, locked by the magic he so coveted, unable to escape. Laoise and Monju breathed a sigh of relief and with Bidelia, they examined the ice block, as if it would crack at any moment.

"I couldn't let him die," I said. "Am I weak to keep him like this?"

"It's not weakness," Keegan said, touching the small of my back. "It's love."

About that, I wasn't certain. I took the spearhead from the remains of the artefacts and clenched it in my fist. This sole reminder, I would keep; it would be my burden to bear.

I smashed the rest of the shards until my arms grew weary. Splintered, cracked, and drained of magic, I couldn't quite allow myself to let go of the Staff. It felt like I had destroyed an old friend. I examined each stray twig on the stone floor for what felt like hours—until Keegan coaxed me away.

Bidelia had already departed. Laoise and Monju lingered by the doors, talking in subdued whispers, stealing occasional glances at me and Keegan. I smiled at my friends warily. I was ready.

"Now what?" I asked, staring at the brokenness around us.

He touched my cheeks, my face, my lips. "Now, we live."

Hand in hand with Keegan, I left the Central Cavern—hopefully, for good.

* * *

I didn't expect to be forgiven for the pain and suffering I'd caused. As I breached the surface, my people cast weary looks at Keegan and I and scuttled away. To them, this was just another day of barely surviving an onslaught. Unless Monju composed a ballad about it, they would never really know what had happened in the Central Cavern. Not that they were ready to bestow their gratitude anyway. Yes, I had used the power of the artefacts to reverse the sleeping curse, curtail the power of placed explosives, and contain my father's greed. But to my people, I'd mismanaged their city, destroyed their castle, and allowed two foreign provinces to nearly blow the capital into the sky. The Violet Fox had a lot to learn about being a ruler. I breathed in their fear of me, their disgust, and knew I'd have to learn how to wade through this remade world.

I didn't need a cheering crowd to validate my victory over my father and the temptation of magic. Just walking through the streets with Keegan, both of us whole and present, was enough. He smiled at me, and the corners of my lips tilted upward. We had a long way to go, and a lot of work to repair the hurt we had wrought. To each other, and our people.

The faint rumbling of carriages from down the street captured our attention. Flags and banners bearing pale yellows, blues, and pinks fluttered in the morning air. The South had come. Omju poked his head out of one of the carriage windows, and when he saw me and Keegan, he waved. Carriages, wagons, and carts passed us, filled to the brim with baked goods, fruits, crops, and bags of ingredients. Hopefully it would last until the blockades cleared up, and real trade could resume.

There was no room for the people to gather or pilfer from the carts, though some tried. Keegan gestured for Omju to continue on to the Grand Square. Our people deserved something good, after so much bad.

"We're going to have to deal with the South," I said, staring at my boots.

Keegan let out a slow breath. "Didn't you say the High King was a Race addict? It would be very unfortunate news were his family and his people to discover that a drug-addicted royal attacked the High Queen of Marlenia."

I raised an eyebrow. "Blackmail, Your Grace? I seem to recall that being distasteful when I brought it up."

"These are desperate times, Your Highness," he replied.

And then, from behind us: "J'es, dey are."

Dominique Castillo hooked my love from behind and dragged him backward, pinning him against her chest, her knife gleaming at his throat. He stopped struggling.

"J'ou will pay pour what j'ou have done," she said.

Slowly, I edged closer to her. "I know that you think you're owed a death, because of Boris. But killing Keegan like this won't give you satisfaction."

Tightening her grip on Keegan, she dragged him backward. "Dis knife y'is poison."

"Then kill me," Keegan said bitterly, and then elbowed her in the chest. He wormed his way out of her grasp and stumbled backward onto the ground.

A crowd, hiding in their homes and in the alleyways from the shadow killers and the explosives, formed a circle around me and Dominique. Our reputations had proceeded us. I had no more Spear to defend myself and my love, but the memory of the destruction in the throne room was fresh on her face, and she eyed me warily.

Keegan drew the knife at his belt and looked ready to charge, but upon seeing the determination on my face, we shared a moment—and he tossed me his weapon. This was between me and her.

"You have no men left, and those who have sworn to you have died, just to destroy Marlenia City," I said to her. "You have no alliance with the East. No man will recognize your unborn child as a contender for the Eastern throne now that Boris is gone, though you will try, I have no doubt. My people will find the remnants of the explosives, if any remain, and they will be destroyed. The war is over. You're the Daughter of the North again."

"De war is *never* over!" she retorted, her eyes a burning flame. "I do not need Boris." Her gaze drifted away from me, as if she relieved his death in that moment. Her voice was calm, although she worked hard to keep it that way. "I y'only need pour j'ou to be dead."

"I'll fight you, Dominique. But I'm not going to kill a pregnant woman. Even if she's a murderer and a terrible person."

"J'ou wronged me first," she reminded me.

"You're right. I didn't kidnap you, though I accept that by taking your name and your position, I changed your life forever. But I'm not the one who continued to exact revenge, time after time. I did one wrong against you, and you've done many. How many times do we have to go around until we are even and done?"

Her smile didn't reach her eyes. "Y'until one y'of us dies."

The crowd stirred. "Kill her!" someone shouted.

"And what about your child?" Keegan said. His voice quieted the dissenters around us. "Is that the kind of life you want to give them? A mother who is obsessed with revenge?"

"De child will learn right from wrong," she said cryptically.

"The child will grow up in a world very different than ours," I added. "We both know what it is to grow up out of step with the capital. When I was you, the ladies called your father the Pauper King. Do you really want to isolate your child and feed them hate?"

"Dey will be queen of de Nort' and d'East," she replied.

There was no getting through to her. The Elders must have known when they chose Dominique, how similar we were. We were both stubborn and nearly impossible to reason with.

Still, I had to try. I let out a long breath. "Here's what I propose. We call a truce."

The crowd murmured. Dominique fumed with them. "De Nort' does not recognize—"

"Not between the North and the West. Between me and you. Call it a pact between two women of power. I won't hurt you today, for your unborn child's sake. And you won't hurt me today, because I will incinerate you with my fingertips." She didn't know I'd sacrificed my magic—likely, no one would believe me if I told them the truth, not after what I'd done. "There will come a day when one of us lets down our guard. That might be after you give birth. It might be when I'm on a diplomatic mission to the North, or even the East, if you succeed there. Or maybe, I'll be dying, wounded in a forest from some battle. Whatever the circumstance, I expect you to be there. Just as I will be for you. Then, and only then, will we finish this. Regardless of circumstance or bodily affliction."

"Dat is nonsense." She lunged for me.

I dodged her desperate jabs and tried to get in a few of my own. Duck. Spin. Lunge. Her heavy fur coat weighed her down and slowed her movements, but my exposed arms could be the landing site for her poison—again. I doubted Monju had another cure, and my father was no longer here to heal me. My fingers trembled at her every swing.

I wouldn't have another dead person on my conscience, not even Dominique. As she cried and charged, I ducked and kicked her backward, onto the street. Her knife went flying into the crowd, and my people parted way or dodged, afraid of her infamous poison blades.

I pointed my knife at her, though I didn't advance. She had no weapon. She was on the ground. Beaten. Yet she rose. Slowly, defiantly. She made her hands into fists, and I thought she was going to risk it all against me. For a long moment, we regarded each other. I mirrored haughty posture. Her hair, dark like mine used to be, whipped around her face, unable to hide a hatred that would never dim, never die.

"Run, Dominique," I said, smiling.

Her gaze narrowed—and the crowd gave way for her. Without looking back, she set off down the street, away from the mountains.

Keegan trudged forward, kneeling to pick up Dominique's poison knife as the Daughter of the North became smaller in our sights. A few people chased her and Keegan called them off.

"Let her be," he said. "The Daughter of the North leaves Marlenia City in peace. For today." The surrounding crowd muttered. They had not gotten justice from their Crimson Prince, but they recognized the renewed tone of authority in his voice. He was the High King again, and he knew it.

"That was...very noble of you," he said.

I set my lips in a firm line. Noble would have been placing her in a carriage and delivering her to the North—just to persuade the Pauper King, or whoever was alive up there, that the West wanted peace.

"We should ensure the guards mark her departure," Keegan said. "Otherwise, she might remain here and pretend to be you."

I frowned. "We certainly can't have any more masked fighters wandering around the streets."

Raising an eyebrow, he ran his maimed hand through his disheveled hair. I expected more of our people to linger around or request a formal address, yet Omju's Southern caravan had stolen their attentions. The Southern Freetor was handing out packages, bags, and baskets left and right to anyone greedy enough to reach for them. I spotted Bidelia speaking with the caravan drivers to get an accurate count of the goods Omju had secured. It was unlikely the supplies came all the way from Xii—perhaps he had gathered support from closer border towns sympathetic to our plight. Laoise organized the families with children into one line, while Monju worked with Antony and the remaining Roamers to bring order to the burgeoning crowd.

"We should take care of that, before it turns into another riot," I said grimly.

"Agreed," Keegan said.

Though neither of us moved. My face fell as I stared up at the mountain castle. It looked ready to fall apart. Again. The streets were abandoned, and I couldn't see it from here, but I knew other streets had been blown sky-high. People had no homes. Freetors had no land. The apprentices had fled. The artefacts lay in a heap in the Central Cavern.

"Kiera?" he said, seeing my despair. "Tell me what you're thinking."

My heart sank as I traced the scars on his lips. "I...I think I have to go."

New lines creased the skin between his eyebrows as he frowned. "Why? No. I just came back."

"I have to hide the remains of the artefacts, so this never happens again." Or if it did, it would take someone far longer than we did to assemble them. By then, I hoped to be ash and dust. I would travel to the remote corners of the world and bury them in obscurity—and tell no one of the journey.

I took his hands in mine and kissed them, stroking his bandaged forefinger.

"How long will you be gone for?" he asked.

"I don't know. Long enough, so when I come back...you'll be in love with me again."

"I never said I didn't love you, Kiera," he said tenderly. He caressed my jawline. "Stay, and allow me to give you a ring that isn't made of cloth."

My heart swelled as my eyes blurred with tears. I felt people watching from the alley, but I didn't care. They needed to see us together, as one. "I don't think I can be High Queen. Not after what I've done."

"You can be whatever you wish at my side, crown or no crown."

I nodded, relieved. Grateful. "Then I'll find the greatest forge, and return with rings fit for the ruler of the land."

He touched my cloth ring, and leaning in, said, "Stay for this night, at least."

Our lips met and we kissed as if I was leaving right then.

We would rebuild the city and our lives without Elders, without magic, and without tyrants. Peace would not come easily for my people, and there was much to be done before I could earn it myself.

Because I was the Violet Fox, and this was not the end of my story. Together with my love, however long I had with him, I would work each day so that our people could live free, under the sun.

THE VIOLET FOX'S ADVENTURES ARE NOT OVER.

KIERA DRISCOLL WILL RETURN.

Acknowledgements

This was a really challenging book to write! I'd always thought that book four of this series would really end it... but...maybe not? Thank you for reading it, I hope you liked it enough to want a fifth.

Many thanks to Mum, Dad, Marie, Joe, and Aunt Kerry for their continuing support, to Jessie for all her help and ingenuity. Thank you to Sam, who keeps me going when things get tough.

And of course, many loves and thanks to Dave, who loads the car, drives me places, hangs my banners, distracts the kitties, buys me ice cream and popcorn, and contributes his good taste and constructive criticism.

- THE AUTHOR -

Clare C. Marshall grew up in rural Nova Scotia with very little television and dial-up internet, and yet she turned out okay. She is the founder and author-publisher behind Faery Ink Press, where she publishes young adult science fiction, fantasy, and horror novels. Her fantasy novel, *The Violet Fox* was given an honorable mention in the 2016 Whistler Independent Book Awards and its sequel, *The Emerald Cloth*, was nominated for Best YA Novel in the 2019 Prix Aurora Awards. When she's not writing or fiddling up a storm, she enjoys computer games and making silly noises at her two cats, Pinecone and Pavlova.

If you enjoyed this book, you can find more from the author:
Website: FaeryInkPress.com
Facebook: Facebook.com/faeryinkpress
Twitter: @ClareMarshall13
Instagram: @FaeryInkPress